Renée Harrell

Aly's Luck

Hunting monsters press

Aly's Luck

Hunting Monsters Press

First Printed in Paperback / March 2012

Cover illustration by 1 Rat Studio Graphics
contact: 1RatStudio@gmail.com

ISBN: 978-0-9829221-5-6

Printed in the United States of America

10 9 8 7 6 5 4 3 2 1

This book is dedicated to
Matthew and Rachel,
T'ing's first visitors.

Before the Beginning

Aly shifted in the chair, feeling it react to the movement and remold its surface to her body. Artificial sunlight sparkled down on her and she caught the scent of a mountain fir in the re-circulated air swimming around her. All at once, the building's silver walls seemed to press upon her, a metal coffin threatening to seal her life away.

Stay in your seat and get this done, she told herself. *You fill in some forms, you pay a lot of money, and you take a vacation. Everyone takes vacations.*

Even you.

So why was the skinny man with the weirdly-translucent skin arguing with her?

In front of her, the name plate on the desk proclaimed the argumentative man was HEBER BLAUVELT. Beneath his name were the words, Travel Agent. The man said, "Please call me, 'Heber'."

"Must I?"

Heber Blauvelt blinked at her, his mouth forming an uncertain half-circle.

Aly said, "Travel's no longer prohibited. Not for years now. Tourists *do* go to T'ing."

"Not the intelligent ones," he said. "At least, not if they're sane. Have you even glanced at Fenckens? You must have."

"I've seen the travel brochures."

"Not nearly the same thing." Pressing a skeletal finger against his desk, Heber transformed the face of his desk from cherry wood into simglass.

Letters appeared almost instantly:

Fenckens Guide to Intergalactic Travel

Your Destination: *T'ing (the Bugworld)*
Preferred Carrier: *Boorian Spaceways*
Language: *Y'togish/T'ingese*
Currency: *Dibblestick*
Suggested Travel Dates: *N/A*
Holiday Calendar: *N/A*
Recommended Accommodations: *N/A*
That Romantic Getaway: *N/A*

Fenckens Tips for Travelers: Following the Great Slaughter (Bugworld vs the Universe), severe restrictions were placed upon the import of advanced technology into T'ing. Initially, all weapons were banned while devices of limited technological value were allowed for import. Seven years later, following the Rain of Blood (Reign of Blood/ Bugworld vs the Universe II), further restrictions were imposed.

Since that date, T'ing has made little progress. Seemingly bereft of scientists or researchers, the planet remains technologically backward. An inhospitable environment, T'ing provides few leisure opportunities for anyone, including the native-born.

The Council of Worlds Recommends: *Dangerous, unsafe for the foreseeable future. Not suitable for travel.*

Heber tapped the desk again and its surface rippled briefly before adopting its wooden face. "There are other options. I can show you images that'll make your head spin. With your budget, you can go almost everywhere."

"I've been there."

His brow wrinkled. "Been...?"

"Almost everywhere."

"The rings of Trimurti –"

"Two years ago."

He said, "Maybe a different galaxy. Once you've stood on the rim of the Hanzuo Crater –"

"Last year."

"The plains of Radegast?"

"Six weeks ago."

"Radegast. Really." The agent studied her. "You must have an adventuresome spirit."

"Those trips were work-related. I need a vacation. I'm a transporter."

"Oh," Heber said without inflection. "How interesting." He made no effort to sound interested at all.

Mustn't blame him for that, Aly decided. *He's probably spent his whole life as a Dome drone, riding the tube from home to work and back again.*

Never feeling the kiss of a summer breeze or the bite of an arctic wind. Never tasting fresh rainwater. Never inhaling the scent of freshly-spilled blood.

Such a sad, wasted life.

"The customer is always right," he told her. "Even when she's wrong." He tapped on the desk, then tapped again more rapidly. "Consider it done. You've just bought a round-trip ticket to the Bugworld."

"Thank you."

"It's your funeral." He laughed. "Who knows? You're a transporter. You might survive. You might even come back."

"I'm lucky that way," Aly said.

* * *

Deep inside the fortress of Dr. Ketu, the shape-changer was in a bad mood.

Syr said, "This is not my idea of a holiday."

"I never used the word, 'holiday'."

"You asked if I wanted to have some fun. Feasting and whoring and lying on the beach."

"Okay, I admit, I made a mistake," Dobbins said. "I assumed, if a place is surrounded by water, it has beaches."

"You also assumed this island would have plentiful females and stocks of food."

"I did." Dobbins grunted as his shoulder popped. He rotated his left arm, pulling it free from the red-streaked manacle. He grinned. "See? We're as good as out of here."

The changer frowned. "It can't be good for you, the thing you do with your shoulder."

"I don't do it often."

"You did it six months ago."

With one arm free, the rest of the manacles were quickly unlocked. Dobbins dropped to the floor.

Finding the Dungeon Master's whipping stand, he dragged it over to the shape-changer.

"Once we're free," Syr said, "I want some time to do something pleasurable. Travel somewhere we can just enjoy ourselves."

"Sure," Dobbins said easily, climbing onto the stand. He reached for the restraints binding his friend. "We get back to Zirmunqdir, we'll set something up."

"There's a passenger ship at the spaceport. It departs in three days."

Whistling lightly, Dobbins worked on the ties holding the changer. These bands were bigger and stronger than the pieces that had held him to the wall but their mechanical workings were just as basic. He said, "You'd think a mad scientist would understand the value of a good lock."

Freed from his ties, the changer fell to the ground. Rolling to his feet, he stood and brushed himself off. He asked Dobbins, "Can we get there in time?"

"Depends."

"On?"

"How many guards are out there."

Solemnly, they contemplated the dungeon's only door. Lifting his muscular purple leg, Syr kicked at the wooden bar holding the rectangle closed. The bar splintered into two and the door flew open.

A single, startled guard jumped away from the opening. At the sight of the changer, he dropped his weapon and ran down the corridor, screaming.

"Zirmunqdir, here we come," Dobbins said happily.

Chapter One

Cygxz was worried.

Oh, he wasn't afraid. Not of a chund, anyway. True, this one was female and, in his experience, the females of a species were always the meanest and nastiest of their kind. But she was also a softbody.

A softbodied chund posed little threat to a Bug. Even when the chund was armed.

This one carried a large-knobbed stick and a tiny knife with a shiny, serrated blade. The stick would bounce harmlessly against his hard pincers; his hooked beak could easily snap it in half. The knife, as small as it was, wouldn't so much as scratch his shell.

Nonetheless, he worried.

It was largely agreed that all chund were crazy and this one, this Aly Krebbs, was the craziest he'd ever met. She refused to eat the good meats and dead things he offered her (and at a substantial discount from the township retail rates), preferring to subsist on the leaves, nuts and berries she found.

She acted as if she enjoyed the outdoors and pretended to like walking. The two of them hiked until Cygxz was certain his legs were going to fall off - and one of them did, its budding brown replacement still too short to provide him with a comfortable sense of balance.

And, really, to what end? Now they were in the middle of nowhere, with nothing to show for it.

Cygxz' own food supply was growing dangerously low. Still, this Krebbs refused to be dissuaded.

"You promised to find the Crystal Cave," she said. "Your word is your bond."

What nonsense. She acted as if a promise was something that needed to be honored.

He should have insisted on payment in advance.

With each day's passing, he found himself growing more despondent. Finally, on their sixth night out, he scurried beside her to offer a confession. While she gnawed at a twig or a stick or some brown-colored thing, he managed to catch her attention. He told her the 'Crystal Cave' she sought was given a different name by the explorers of his world.

"We call it, the Cave of Doom," he said, his voice breaking in just the right spot. "It contains terrors. Night things. Monsters, some call them."

Krebbs smiled at him, crunching down the last of her brown whatever-it-was. She rolled out her sleepsak.

Cygxz looked at her with large, worried eyes. "I'm not certain I can protect you."

Shrugging a jacket from her shoulders, the chund folded it neatly. She unbuttoned her blouse. "I can protect myself."

He goggled. Had Krebbs never seen a mirror? Had she somehow failed to realize she was covered in pink flesh, carrying no more armor than a mewing pupa?

Truly, she was mad.

"Perhaps you've been told of the jewels lining the walls of the cave," Cygxz continued doggedly, if a little less certainly. "Gemstones. Beautiful, pulsing

11

crystals of such beauty they seem to sing to all who see them."

The chund yawned.

"Naturally enough, you want to find the cave and strip it of its treasures," Cygxz said. "Ruin its beauty for generations to come while enriching yourself, however temporarily. Such greed is understandable. Commendable, even."

Krebbs touched the buttons at the side of the 'sak. With a sigh, the bag unfurled.

"The cave's riches are only a myth," the guide told her. "A bit of whimsy to amuse our off-world visitors. I've walked these trails for many years. I know this. But I know something more.

"The Cave of Doom holds a dark power inside its bowels. A wicked magic so enticing it draws the innocent inside. My cousin, young Styxz, went exploring inside the cave. He never returned." A yellow tear rolled down the side of Cygxz' beak. "No one who enters the cave ever returns."

He dabbed at his eyes, as if overcome by his memories. It was, he felt, one of his finest performances. No tourist was immune to the horrors of his 'Cave of Doom' presentation. Inevitably, they pleaded with him to be returned to their chundhuts.

Naturally, he always agreed. Usually after negotiating an additional fee.

He checked for his customer's reaction.

Aly Krebbs was buried inside her sleepsak. He was watching her when she began to snore.

Loudly.

In the days that followed, the situation worsened. Krebbs kept pace with him, no matter how quickly he moved. His sense of self-preservation kept them alive while her uncanny sense of direction drove them on. Within an hour, maybe less, they'd be within sight of their destination.

Cygxz was aghast.

Delivering a client to her preferred destination was an amateur's mistake. To do so without extracting additional monies? Such a thing simply wasn't done. The other guides would be furious.

No matter what the payment, he had no intention of entering the accursed cave. Something inside that black hole had gobbled up Styxz. If there was a creature lurking in there capable of ending that ill-tempered horror, it would make short work of anyone else.

Clearly, he was in a predicament. If he refused to follow the chund, he would lose the balance of the fee owed him. Yet he'd given too much time to this project to leave without full payment.

Sourly, Cygxz examined his customer. The Krebbs-chund was perched atop a boulder, her tanned legs tucked beneath her. Catching his glance, she waved at him.

He drew back, stiffening his antennae haughtily. She returned to assembling the boneless mush of her mid-day meal.

If only something would eat her, he mused.

Once considered, the thought teased at him. Such a tragedy wasn't beyond the realm of possibility. Everyone knew accidents happened. Hardly a season passed without one or more softbodied tourists wandering into the jungle, never to be seen again.

Still, this softbody had employed a guide. There would be little demand for a guide who lost his clients in the brush. Even less for one who allowed those clients to be eaten.

Nonetheless, Cygxz felt the idea deserved further consideration. If Krebbs were to disappear, he'd collect his fee in total (and a hefty bonus on top of it, judging from the size of the sackett tied to her belt). It would be the first time he'd ever lost a customer - well, almost - and his reputation would likely survive.

It wasn't as if there were other chund with her, ready to spread the news of her disappearance. She would just... vanish. As deranged as she was, it might even be a good thing.

A kind of public service, come to think of it.

It wouldn't happen without a spot of nastiness, though. Krebbs was surprisingly resourceful for a chund. Not that it would matter in the end; he was hard-shelled and she was not. 'Resourcefulness' only went so far.

Any evidence of foul play would soon disappear. When the smell of a dead thing wafted into the air, something always came along to eat it.

He felt a bit peckish himself.

"We're almost there," Krebbs said, waking Cygxz from his reverie. "The cave, I mean. I can feel it."

He blinked up at her. "You're right. It's over the next rise."

The words came out clumsily, his tongue growing thick with excitement. He could feel his twin hearts racing beneath his shell. The two blue spots on his thorax grew warmer, an indication they would soon turn purple.

Krebbs wiped a food crumb from the corner of her mouth. "What is it?"

"Your sackett." His tongue snaked along the exterior of his beak, reaching up nervously to groom an antenna.

"Your fee, you mean." She slid down from the boulder. "Your fee is earned once we've found the cave. You'll get what you're owed when I've returned to the township."

"Of course." He dipped his head in an obsequious manner. Doing so, he scuttled closer.

The chund appeared unconcerned by his approach. She wore a bemused expression, scratching lightly at her chin as he planted himself in her path.

"Don't be stupid," she said.

Whatever *that* was supposed to mean.

Cygxz was short for a Bug, barely reaching Krebb's shoulders, but he had width, accented by the thick plate of his shell, and he had power. He lifted his two sets of arms away from his body and raised his pincers in attack position. The end of each barbed pincer was colored in a brilliant green.

"Stupid it is, then," Krebbs said. Her little pointed nose twitched.

Clacking his pincers, Cygxz charged.

She waited for him, her eyes bright. He swung his primary claw and she stepped beneath it. From behind her back, her knobbed walking stick appeared in her right hand. Sweeping the stick at her foe's feet, she upended him.

Cygxz crashed backward. In a sudden, hard whoosh of sound, the air escaped from his lungs. His head smashed against hard ground. Unable to stop himself, he bounced forward before falling onto his side, his antennae wiggling wildly.

Krebbs walked past him, rapping the knob of the walking stick against his beak. The blow sent the sky swimming before Cygxz' eyes. When his vision cleared, he rocked back and forth then staggered to his feet.

The chund was gone.

"Tourists," he muttered heavily.

Krebbs' brown tunic was dark against the yellow sky as she topped the hill in front of him. Somehow, she was already well ahead of him.

He'd have to hurry or she'd find the cave. If she found the cave's opening, she'd enter it - she was *exactly* the type of person who would do such a thing - and be eaten. Whatever ate her would likely steal her sackett as well.

Where was his profit in that? He sighed. He simply had no choice.

Cygxz skittered after her.

Krebbs glanced up as he drew closer. Still holding her knobbed stick, she was almost exactly at the center of the mound. Thin whispers of whip grass waved beneath her feet. These were nothing like the thick, reed-like stalks growing at the center of the jungle. Healthy vegetation shrank away from the mound, daring only to grow along its perimeter.

Perhaps the soil here was too thin to nourish plant life. Perhaps there were other reasons.

Cygxz crept toward his client. His antennae bobbed in a submissive manner.

"An apology?" Krebbs asked.

"It is not an apology," he said, bristling at her. "I am sorrowful for our misunderstanding."

"I understand you perfectly. I understand you're a liar, a cheat, and a lousy guide."

"I'm an excellent guide! The best in the township."

"You couldn't find the cave."

"Anyone can find the cave. Even you. You're standing on top of it."

The chund studied the ground beneath her feet.

"There's no trick in finding the cave," Cygxz told her. "The challenge is finding the entrance. There's a single hole, only one. Find it once, you'll have to try twice as hard to find it again."

"Why?"

"It moves."

"Holes can't move." She dropped to her hands and knees. Crawling forward, she wet the fingers of one hand. Extending the hand, she skimmed her fingertips above the ground.

Holes can't move, she said. Cygxz shook his head disapprovingly. Softbodies thought they knew everything.

"It isn't safe," he said.

Suddenly, her hand froze in mid-air. Her interest sharpened as she moved to her left. She brought her fingers to her mouth again, lapping her tongue against their tips.

Disgusting.

He strolled casually toward her. The female was squatting and that limited her mobility. Her damnable walking stick had disappeared, vanishing when she knelt to explore the mound. Most importantly of all, her neck was exposed.

Cygxz knew the rule: Take a beast by the neck and it was at your mercy. Hold the neck and you own the spine. Control the spine and the skull is your toy. Open the skull and, well - there wouldn't be any further arguments about collecting his fee.

It wouldn't be an enjoyable kill, he knew. Her snippy attitude ruined any possibility of that. Even if he waited to eat, he'd be lucky to have any appetite at all.

He was almost within killing distance. As his pincers extended, Krebbs looked up sharply.

Cygxz swung a pincer westward. "There it is! The entrance!"

Her head followed his gesture and Cygxz lunged at her. One of his feet stumbled over the walking stick - *So that's where it went* - and he pitched forward. He slammed into the ground, his beak digging into the dirt.

Krebbs reached for her walking stick. Spraying grass from his mouth, Cygxz cried, "It was an accident!"

She rapped the knob of the walking stick against his beak. Tears flooded his eyes. Shaking them away, he saw Krebbs creeping along one side of the mound, her fingers fluttering lightly above its grassy surface.

Cygxz lurched upright. "We need to come to an understanding."

Ignoring him, she inched forward.

"The hole used to be at the side of that boulder. The red one."

Krebbs' eyes went to the large, colored stone jutting from the surface of the mound. When she stood to her full height, dirt and grass fell from her knees.

"There's no reason to look there now," Cygxz said. The dismissive expression on her face irritated him. "I told you, the entrance moves. It isn't just an opening to the cave. It's a trap. The ones below, they're clever. They cover the old entrance as they build a new one. Explorers – explorers who think they know so much - stumble into the new holes while looking for the old ones. And then they're eaten up!"

"Oh, I get it." Krebbs crossed her arms. "You're the only one who can help me."

"Exactly right."

"So, this is the part where I'm supposed to get scared."

A whisper of hope sprang alive in Cygxz' chest. Could it be? Was the chund frightened? At last? The tone in her voice seemed oddly flat for a frightened softbody. But she was not the usual tourist.

She started toward him. "This is the part where I say, - 'Oh, please, dear Cygxz, I've made a terrible mistake'."

Well, yes, she was correct about that, too. "You want me to take you back?"

"This is where I offer you anything you want, if only you'll return me to the township in safety." She tugged the sackett from her waist, widening the bag's mouth. "Is this enough?"

Dibblesticks and gemstones filled the small bag. It wasn't quite the rich bounty he'd imagined, but it would certainly do.

This was turning out to be a good day, after all.

"It's *nearly* enough," he said. "It's not easy, the way back. A bit more dangerous. Other expenses will almost certainly arise. But, for now -" He reached for the sackett.

Aly Krebbs yanked it from his grasp. "You'll get nothing."

Cygxz' beak dropped open. "What?"

"Not a dibblestick, not a gemstone." She cinched the sackett closed. "When I return to the township, I'm reporting you to the authorities. Corrupt as they are, there must be some rules they follow."

"But –" His mind reeled. "This is the part where you're frightened! The part where you give me riches! You said so yourself!"

"This is the part where you leave."

"I'm your guide!"

Her hand curled around the walking stick. "Go."

"It isn't fair," he told her. "Not fair at all."

The walking stick rose up in the air. Cygxz sped up, backpedaling quickly. "Because of our bond, our friendship, I've decided to leave for now. Perhaps when you get back -"

Before he could finish his statement, a cloud of grass at his feet weakened, separated, and Cygxz spilled into the earth.

Chapter Two

Dropping the walking stick, Aly bent to the spot where the Bug had disappeared. She tore the grass away from the opening. With bright sunlight behind her, she peered into the opening.

"Cygxz?" From the blackness below, there was only silence. "Cygxz!"

Finally, his voice floated up to her. "Am I lucky."

"Are you hurt?"

"I found the entrance."

"I know."

"Other guides, they never would have taken you here," he continued. "Other guides would have tried to scare you off, lead you back to the township. Surely I deserve some sort of bonus for this."

Aly dropped the carrypak from her shoulders. Loosening the straps, she spilled its contents onto the ground.

"It's dark down here. Too dark for someone with only two eyes. There's some light from the crystals in the cave walls. I think... yes, some of the bigger crystals have gemstones in them." Cygxz paused. "Why, look over there, a big stone, violet-hue. A Jayll stone, I'm almost positive."

Another pause from below. Then, "A Jayll stone, they're rare. A few hundred dibblesticks in any marketplace. If I wasn't multi-lensed, I'd never have seen it. How fortunate for you that we're working together." His voice grew smaller. "We are still working together, aren't we?"

Aly picked through the carryall's contents. Taking a tiny bottle, she dropped it into her tunic's top pocket. She shook free a coil of rope, wishing it were longer.

From below the hole, she heard a whimper. "Are you hurt?"

"A scratch, that's all. A twisted arm, a broken leg or two. No cause for complaint."

She remembered how Cygxz had sulked for two days after chipping one of his minor claws. "Can you walk?"

There was no answer from inside the cave.

Aly searched for an anchor to secure her rope. The whip grass waved under a light breeze, free from any visible obstruction. Bracing her arms about the opening, she dipped her head into the darkness.

Slowly, the world below came into view. Tendrils rose from the floor of the cave, waving helplessly.

"You're on your back," Aly said softly.

No Bug would willingly take such a position. On its back, a Bug was nearly helpless.

"I am *not*," Cygxz protested in a quavering voice. "I am resting - on my side - while I consider whether to share these treasures with you." He swallowed audibly. "Pull me up and I'll bring the Jayll stone with me."

"A Jayll stone. A desert jewel. Yet here we are, in the jungle."

"That… that makes it all the rarer, don't you see?"

She saw the situation all too well. There wasn't a Jayll stone in the cavern below. She doubted if the cave entrance held anything valuable; if it did, Cygxz would never have revealed it. He'd have enticed her with a different lie.

She also knew, if the situation was reversed, or if her guide found it profitable or expedient, she would certainly have been left to die. Sometimes there were advantages to being a Bug.

Lifting up from the opening, she commanded, "Talk to me."

Cygxz' respirations sounded a little loud, a little fast. Running her hands along the curve of the hole, she felt the sharp edge of a root scrape against her palm. Pinching it between her forefinger and thumb, she gave a tug.

Sandy loam jumped upward, spraying a few small pebbles. The brown shoot lifted from the ground. The root was a little longer than her hand and not as thick as her smallest finger.

"Did you hear something?" Cygxz called.

Aly caught her breath. Having studied the caves of T'ing, she knew they rarely contained treasure. She also knew they were seldom left empty.

Urgently, she dug through the thin soil. Finding the smooth contour of the root, her fingers curled around it, and she yanked at it. It ripped through the grass, growing longer as it came into the sunlight.

It was almost the length of her arm now. Still barely thicker than her little finger. Not nearly stout enough.

"The sound is getting louder," Cygxz said. He moaned softly.

"Scared, Bug?" Aly asked. "You want to be scared of something, be scared of me. You'd better be carrying a Jayll stone when you come to the surface." She tugged at the root. "We split ninety-ten. You're the ten."

"Ninety percent for you!" Cygxz cried. "I found the entrance!" His tone made it clear: Regardless of his situation, he wasn't about to accept the lesser portion of his imaginary findings.

"Anyone can fall through a hole."

"But I fell through it first," he said. "Sixty-forty. You're the forty."

The tips of Aly's fingers were beaded with blood. "Eighty-twenty, then. Twenty percent for you, but only if you carry the gemstones back to the township."

"Seventy-thirty," Cygxz countered. "You're the thirty. Because you're a chund and I pity you."

She looped a coil of rope around her palm. Forcing the loop under a bent section of root, she knotted it. The root wasn't thick enough but it would have to do.

"The sound is here again," Cygxz said. "It's not as loud anymore, but it's closer. Don't you hear it?"

"I'm coming in."

"I don't see anything." His voice trembled. "I don't see it but I can smell it. I can *hear* it."

Kneeling over the opening, she heard it, too. It was the sound of a great beast, a low rumble in its throat. Over the rumble, she could hear its tamped breathing. It was a wet, wheezing sound, masking a shriek behind every exhalation.

24

The creature's odor wafted up to her and she almost gagged. The smell of dust and rot. The smell of disease and death.

It was the smell of a Zneeth.

"Every cave has its noises," Aly said. She tightened the line around her waist. "Every cave has its smells. A good guide would know that."

"I'm scared."

The rope held firm in the bend of the root. She braced her feet inside the circle of the hole. In the few seconds it had taken her to get ready, the scent of disease had grown stronger.

From somewhere inside the pit, there was a cracking sound as if something had pressed its weight upon a fragile surface. The sharp snap echoed through the cavern, so loud and unexpected that it gave her pause.

"I'm scared," Cygxz said. "I'm scared, *I'm so scared*, I'M SO SCARED!"

"No!" Aly shouted. "Don't be frightened, don't you dare be frightened!"

Cygxz' scream answered her. It was high-pitched and horrible, wailing and wailing, terrified –

Then gone.

She sagged against the rope, closing her eyes. Knowing better, she cupped her hands over her ears.

But the Zneeth is silent when it feeds.

Chapter Three

"You came to me," the Bug said.

"So?"

"I'd hoped you might be reasonable," the mudhut's proprietor said. "A few days ago, I sold a sleepsak to a female chund. A Terran, like you, but not as irritating. She had a little pointed nose."

Dobbins raised an eyebrow. "And?"

"She paid my asking price without complaint. Every stick of it."

Dobbins considered the offerings he'd brought to the mudhut. There were a handful of coins, some semi-precious gemstones, and three thick towels bearing the legend, *Mel's Travelrama.*

On the opposite side of the counter, the mudhut's proprietor had placed a grappling hook with rope, a nightblack stocking, and a pair of gloves. The grappling hook was three-pronged, with a hook on the end of each barb. The nightblack stocking was too large for a man but could be made to fit. The gloves were an amazing find. They each sported five fingers and might actually fit Dobbins' hands. They were exactly what he needed.

All in all, it was more than he ever expected to find on a world like this.

"Look at how little you offer me," Dobbins told the Bug. "A sleepsak for a Terran, sure, an item like that is something special. No wonder the female paid your price. But I've brought you treasures and you insult me with this – this junk."

The shop owner's eyes narrowed. He responded in his own tongue, a chattering string of sing-song syllables.

"I don't speak Bug," Dobbins said. "I've told you twice now. Basic. Use Basic."

The Bug pointed at his pile of goods. Smiling, he chattered at him again.

Dobbins turned to his companion. "Syr, speak to him. Tell him, if he wants to complete our trade, I have to understand him. He has to talk in Basic."

The Bug chittered away. Syr raised a large purple hand and the shopkeeper's monologue faltered. The tall hominoid spoke to him and the Bug's expression turned sour.

"Basic," the shopkeeper grumped.

"As a kindness," Syr told him.

"I dislike Basic."

"This way, we can talk to one another," Dobbins said. "We can get to know one another."

"I already know you," the Bug pointed out. "I dislike you."

"Y'togish is a difficult language to master," Syr said, "and my friend is still learning its intricacies. He's missed so many of your novel suggestions. I, for one, never realized the metal hook was intended to fit inside a body orifice. But I've not travelled as widely as Dobbins."

"The softbody is your friend?"

"He's seen more worlds than I. Dealt with more traders than I."

"And yet he survives?"

"Hey," Dobbins said.

The Bug slapped the countertop sharply. "Junk?" He pointed an accusing claw in the human's direction. "You begged to see five-fingered gloves. Now, you say they're garbage? You pleaded to examine the hook. Now, it's worthless?"

"I expressed a general interest in those items," Dobbins said. "I didn't plead."

"It's hard to tell with a chund." The shopkeeper sniffed. "Stay on T'ing for long and you'll almost certainly end up begging for something."

"I don't think so."

"Your ignorance reveals itself once more," the Bug said. "I've given you my terms. You want the trade or not?"

"Not."

"Hah!"

Who knew Bugs could smirk? Gripping Syr by one well-muscled arm, Dobbins guided his friend to the back of the shop. "I need the emergency fund."

"No."

"It's our money, it's for emergencies, this is an emergency. Give it to me."

"You told me we were shopping for essentials. These things aren't essential."

"You thought I meant food."

Syr glowered at him. "What use would an honest citizen have for these items? After the incident on the ship, you swore there'd be no more chicanery."

"You ate this morning."

"That has nothing to do with it! Although," he acknowledged, "it *has* been hours since we last fed."

"No sticks then?"

"Not one."

28

"So be it." Dobbins returned to the front counter. Unfolding a towel, he returned his belongings in its center. "No deal."

"Don't be foolish," the Bug said.

Knotting the cloth, he tucked it under his arm. "Let's go."

The Bug reached out, catching the human's sleeve. "No one else will trade with you. I'll make certain of it."

"Small concern," Dobbins said. "It hardly matters now. After all, what is a man without honor?"

"A chund."

Syr crossed his arms. "You said it was time to go. Why do you continue to linger inside the doorway?"

Dobbins asked the Bug, "Do you know the Mound Lord?"

"Mound Lord Tzzle?"

"Yes, Tzzle," Dobbins spat the unfamiliar name. "Tell him, with my regrets, that I won't be at the estate tonight."

"I know *of* the Mound Lord," the merchant said. "I've seen him pass by my hut. I've never actually met him."

"Beg his forgiveness for my absence," Dobbins continued. "Offer my apologies. Tell him my friend is hungry. Tell him the demands of my friend's stomach are more important than my sworn promise. Perhaps the Mound Lord will understand."

"Mound Lords are not known for their understanding," said the shopkeeper.

"Who is this 'Tzzle'?" Syr asked.

"Mound Lord of this township," the Bug said. "Very rich. Very powerful."

29

"He's an acquaintance," Dobbins said. "A close associate."

"We made planet fall only days ago," Syr said. "How is it you made such a friend so quickly?"

"I've a gift for making friends. While you ate, I canvassed this area's pathways. While you ate, I shook hands and claws and talons. I've made quite an impression on those in power – while you ate."

"I don't recall you missing any meals," Syr said tartly. "Perhaps one of your new friends can lend you the
currency you need."

Dobbins dropped his head. "Is there to be no end to my disgrace?" he asked quietly. "Is this how you wish to see me, imploring strangers for the nub of a dibblestick?"

"That's not what I meant." Reluctantly, Syr reached into the pouch at his waist. His fingers caressed the intricate carvings on the face of the dibblesticks. "These things on the counter. Why do you need them?"

"For the bork hunt tonight. The Mound Lord invited me." Plucking the sticks from Syr's hand, Dobbins placed them on the counter. "There's quite a competition to get the first bork of the season. If I do well, Mound Lord Tzzle will certainly view us with favor. It can only improve our situation."

The Bug studied Dobbins. "I've never heard of a bork."

"Not much of a hunter, eh?"

"I've done my share."

"Wonderful." Dobbins smiled icily. "I'll request the Mound Lord invite you on his next hunt."

"Me?" Behind his shell, the Bug somehow appeared to grow paler.

Dobbins patted his chest, as if seeking a writing instrument. "What was your name again?"

"Ah, ah, ah. Borks! Yes. Now I remember."

"Are these creatures dangerous?" Syr asked.

The Bug watched Dobbins for guidance.

"There's some danger," he admitted. The Bug nodded eagerly.

Dobbins continued, "The ridges on their backs are deadly, of course, tipped with a corrosive poison. The gloves should help protect my skin. It wouldn't do to spook the beasts; I'll wear the body stocking as camouflage. The grappling hook, well, that's standard equipment."

"In a hunt."

"To climb. One has to be able to chase one's prey. Few beasts are as agile as a bork."

Syr said, "Why no weapon for so dangerous a foe?"

"Exactly!" Dobbins directed his gaze toward the shopkeeper. "These sticks should cover what I need." He beamed back at Syr. "A weapon for the borks."

The Bug's claw locked onto his offering. "You need a weapon, too?"

"The Mound Lord will hear of your generosity."

The shopkeeper snapped his beak shut, stifling an unhappy retort. He counted the four dibblesticks twice, as if willing them to somehow multiply themselves.

"You don't look like much," he finally said, bringing his doubts into words. "Small even for a

31

softbody, nearly hairless, too thin in the arms and legs to be good eating. Worst of all, you have no money."

Dobbins gestured grandly at the dibblesticks. "What do you call this?"

"No money." A tone of defeat crept into the shopkeeper's words. "Still, you're clearly dishonest. Mound Lords admire that trait above all others."

"What I want, what I need, is a spitzpistol."

"A spitzpistol!" The Bug steadied himself by locking a central leg onto the counter's edge. "Even on the black market, such a weapon is a rare find. A discharged pistol goes for ten times what you've offered."

"Won't do me much good if it's discharged, will it?"

"Besides," the merchant said, "it's illegal to sell such things on T'ing. Especially to an off-worlder."

"A blade, then."

"A good blade costs twice what you offer."

"Mound Lord Tzzle -"

"It's not a blade you want, anyway," the Bug interrupted. Struck by sudden inspiration, he rummaged behind the counter. "Blades aren't any good on a bork hunt. What you want is gas."

"Gas?"

He lifted a dusty cylinder into the light. "Read it for yourself."

Dobbins squinted blindly at the faded lettering on the label. Years of neglect had left the can dented and scraped. Even if he'd understood the Bug's language, he wouldn't have been able to read this.

"What's it say?" he asked Syr.

"Who knows?"

"Bork gas," the shopkeeper told them. "Plainly labeled."

Dobbins took the can in his hand. It felt sticky.

"It's preferred on social occasions," the Bug said. "Occasions such as your hunt tonight. It's considered more sporting."

Prying the protective lid from the cylinder's top, Dobbins asked, "Is it poisonous?"

"Poisonous to borks. Harmless to Bugs and lower creatures like yourself."

"Good." Dobbins pressed the nozzle and a cloud of mist sprayed into the merchant's face.

He screeched, covering his eyes as he stumbled backward. Wiping his face, he glared at his customer with reddening eyes.

"You've got a deal," Dobbins said happily.

* * *

Syr waited as Dobbins collected his purchases. Clearly, the devilry ahead demanded something more potent than something found in the nozzle of a long-forgotten spray can. Just as clearly, his friend couldn't admit as much without losing face.

"Grab the carrypak," Dobbins said. Opening a small satchel, he dropped the gloves inside.

Syr slung the carrypak over his shoulder.

Just like that, the last of their capital was gone. They hadn't eaten since daybreak and the desk clerk at *Mel's Travelrama* was making thinly-veiled threats about the monies owed on their room.

Syr hoped the bork hunt proved profitable.

Chapter Four

Lost in thought, the guard undulated forward, his bodyshells slapping softly against one another in a rippling motion. Crossing toward the front wall, he puzzled over the problem of slime.

Like all Twills, the guard inherently left a glistening trail of mucus behind him wherever he travelled. The mucus – slime, really – was transparent-yellow in color and carried a lingering sour odor.

Because of this, no Twill had ever been given Mound duty. Unfair as it was, the guard could expect to remain in the outside yard forever, genetically condemned to patrol the interior wall surrounding the estate.

Personally, he thought, *I like slime.*

Clink! At the sound, the Twill's head swiveled.

A grappling hook dangled over the top of the wall. A thin line extended from the base of the hook, leading over the wall and back into the hands of its sender.

The would-be intruder had excellent timing; the street patrol had passed the area only minutes earlier. The grappling hook slid away, seeking a hold as it moved over the surface of the inner wall. It was a hopeless effort. While the exterior had a face of rough stone, its opposite side was smooth and seamless. The barbs of the grappling hook had nothing to grip.

A moment later, the grappling hook bumped over the top of the wall and disappeared.

Taking out a notebook, the Twill noted the time and location of the incident. He would file his report but no one would care. The intruder had acted after the street patrol was gone.

Hmmm. The guard brought his eraser down on the notebook. Using tiny, cramped lettering, he copied over the old notation.

Perfect. By changing the time of the event, it appeared as if the trespasser had attempted entry during the middle of a scheduled patrol. Admiring his handiwork, the Twill reflected, *How can the others possibly explain this?*

They couldn't. Dereliction of duty carried a substantial penalty. The members of the patrol would face demotions. There would be pain.

The Twill enjoyed pain, if he wasn't the one experiencing it.

When questioned about his note, the Twill knew exactly what he'd say. "I'm sure the street patrol *meant* to make their rounds," he'd offer. "Something must have happened. Perhaps they stopped to get a drink, or feed, or rut. I'm just a bellyfoot. Who can tell what legged creatures do?"

The word would spread quickly. The two guards on street patrol would be punished. The Twill might even be allowed to watch.

It was so much fun when members of the street patrol were punished.

Clink! The grappling hook bounced against the inner wall again. For a moment, it lay motionless against the seamless surface.

Frowning, the guard examined the hook as it was pulled, ever so slowly, backward. Each leg of the hook had a wicked barb molded onto its end. The burglar must have studied the estate, learned of the interior wall, and planned to circumvent it with the aid of these barbs.

Imbecile.

The grappling hook bounced away, disappearing over the top of the wall. The Twill opened his notebook. Two attempts! The street patrol was *definitely* in trouble this time.

Clink! The grappling hook reappeared. It dangled in front of the guard.

The Twill frowned again. If this damnable fool remained outside the wall all night, throwing his hook back and forth, he'd almost certainly be caught. Even the street patrol wasn't blind. If nothing else, the *clinking* noise would alert them.

If such a thing happened, the burglar would be captured. The street patrol would be praised. There would be commendations. They might even be awarded ribbons.

The Twill often dreamt of receiving a ribbon.

He grabbed the grappling hook at its base. Feeling a tug in response, his grip tightened.

Might he arrest the burglar himself? No, he dare not. Someone would certainly question how the intruder had gained access onto the grounds. Better to hold the rope, he reasoned, let the thief climb almost to the top of the barrier…and then let go.

The Twill could imagine the sound of leg after leg after leg breaking, fragile shell and bone meeting the unyielding surface of the ground's hard rock.

A chund's head appeared over the edge of the wall. He gave the guard a cheery nod.

"Softbody," the Twill said, disappointed. "I so hoped you'd be a Quoxelpede. Something with a lot of legs."

Bracing his feet against the side of the wall, the chund pulled his upper body into full view. "Mating season, is it?"

"No!" The Twill's antennae wiggled in disgust. Rocking his arm slowly, he pulled the hook from side to side. The softbody weaved with each movement of the rope. "Would you fall and squish if I let go?"

The invader looked over his shoulder and at the ground below. "I don't think I'd *squish*." He shifted his feet against the tugging motion of the rope. "Would you stop that?"

"Dizzy?" The Twill swung his claw more broadly. Slithering sideways, he found more room to pull on the hook. The chund shuffled back and forth over the outer surface of the wall, refusing to release his hold.

Now, *this* was entertainment. "What is your name, chund?"

The softbody danced across the barrier, following the action of the rope. Scowling, he didn't answer.

"If you don't tell me, I'll let you drop."

"I'm Dob - uh, Dobernack."

"Ho." The Twill stopped swinging the hook. The sudden loss of motion caused the burglar to slip, banging his knee against the rough rock before he stood upright again. "Ho. Dob Dobernack. Chund have such foolish names."

37

"What's it to you, slime-slinger?"

The guard stiffened. "What did you say?"

"What's the matter? Slime in your ears?"

The Twill brought the grappling hook as far to his side as possible. The taut rope rubbed against his body. "Say goodbye, Dob Dobernack-chund."

Straightening his legs, the thief twisted his body, yanking at the rope. The hook tore from the Twill's claw. It shot forward, one of its barbs striking a shell and splintering it. The metal arm dug into the muscle underneath.

The guard called out, in shock and alarm. Having dropped from sight when the line went loose, Dobernack climbed back into view. "Stings, doesn't it?"

It stung fiercely. "Let go of the rope so I can remove the barb."

"I'd fall."

"Not if you stand on top of the wall."

The chund's forehead wrinkled in concern. "I'd make a pretty easy target from up there."

The Twill released his spitzpistol from its holster. Elongating as little as possible, he set it on the ground, away from the mucus pooling at the base of his body. "You're safe."

Dobernack nodded in acceptance. He pulled at the rope, bringing himself closer to the top.

The guard cringed with each tug of the rope but his antennae wiggled in anticipation. The top of the wall was covered with an innocuous-looking blue mold, a parasitic growth that ate into living flesh almost instantly. By skittering along the outside of the wall, the chund had avoided the mold. Once he stood in it, his bare ankles would make an inviting treat. He would be in agony.

Releasing the cord, the softbody bent his legs and sprang forward. His hands slapped against the top of the wall and he somersaulted over it. The incredulous Twill watched as he crashed down onto him.

The crawler's elongated body spasmed at the blow. He lurched backward, fighting to maintaining his balance as the man spilled to the ground.

"Arrr!" The Twill tore the grappling hook from his body. Pieces of shell rained on the ground and a bubble of clouded pus rose from the wound. Wincing, the guard snatched at his spitzpistol.

He leveled it at the intruder. "Why aren't you screaming?"

Dobernack held his hands out, palms first. His gloves dripped with wall mold.

"Clever," the guard conceded. He adjusted the control on his weapon. "I don't mind telling you, this is more than a little inconvenient. How am I going to explain it? Pieces of chund everywhere -"

Moving with the speed of an accomplished thief, Dob Dobernack stabbed his hand forward. Two goopy fingers slid past the Twill's broken shell to find exposed flesh.

Too late, the guard jerked back. "That hurts."

The Twill wiggled about, trying to relieve the burning sensation. It didn't help. His long body shook inside his shell. Hissing in pain, he fired his spitzpistol at the chund. The errant shot sizzled away the largest branch of a nearby tree.

39

A second shot sent a blinding flash against the interior wall as a thin, white line dug into the surface. In the distance, a voice called out.

Clawing at his shell, the Twill didn't notice as the burglar retrieved his grappling hook and crept into the shadows.

* * *

Dropping from a ledge high above the surface, a Mound guard glided downward, her translucent wings spread wide. Three foot guards raced from the base of the Mound, drawing spitzpistols as they ran. They formed a half-circle at the front of the Twill.

The Twill weaved blindly, firing his gun. The weapon's dangerous spray lit up the night sky.

"Dob!" the Twill screamed. "Dob Dobernack!"

"He's gone mad," the first foot guard said.

"That's the way it is with bellyfoots," the second foot guard said. "They snap."

"To the ready!" said the Mound guard, touching to the earth. At her command, the foot guards braced their dominant arms into firing position.

"Set your mode!"

"Which setting?" the second foot guard asked. "Stun or splatter?"

Confronted by an armed Twill, one driven insane by his proximity to slime, there shouldn't have been any question of which mode to choose. But the crawler's spitzpistol was nearly discharged. Even as the Mound guard watched, a weakened blast burped from its nozzle, burning the grass along the edge of

40

the inner wall. With another touch of the trigger, the gun would be harmless.

She told the others, "Your choice."

"I used to work street patrol," the first foot guard said flatly.

"We all did," the second foot guard said.

Each of them locked their weapons. They waited for a signal from the Mound guard.

"Fire," she said.

Chapter Five

Dusk approached when Aly returned to the hole. She dropped her carrypak on the ground.

There was work to be done.

The root remained exposed and undisturbed. Digging at its base, she found a stronger anchor for her rope. Securing it, she dropped through the opening as the cord fed through her fingers. With the sky above her growing smaller, she concentrated on her breathing.

Full and easy breaths. Calming breaths.

Her feet touched the ground. Removing a vial from her tunic's top pocket, Aly thumbed its lid open. A swarm of microscopic flies came alive, streaming from the bottle. They gathered around her, basking in her body heat. In return, they lit the cavern ahead of her.

Cygxz' body was almost at her feet, wedged between a crooked brown stalagmite and the cavern wall. On his back, frozen in position, he appeared untouched. His beak was open, his eyes wide with terror.

She brushed his head softly. She jerked back as it crumbled away, the empty husk of his skull collapsing.

Suddenly, her legs felt weak.

Control yourself. You've seen worse.

Past her fallen guide, the walls held no wonders. There were no gemstones to have teased poor Cygxz, no crystals to color and brighten the cavern. But the walkway before her held a sight that would have horrified any Bug.

The floor ahead was dotted with Bugshells of all sizes and hues. The majority of the body casings led into the earth, their owners having survived entry into the cave with better luck than her guide.

There was a chance Cygxz hadn't seen the abandoned body armor. Trapped against a wall, barely able to move, he couldn't have seen much.

She hoped so, anyway, for his sake.

Aly approached the nearest complete shell. The casing was colored a mottled orange, the type of covering commonly carried by a member of the servant class. Being careful not to press upon it, she studied it.

Its owner had been taller than Cygxz but not as stout. A neat, smooth-edged hole was drilled into its forehead. The unfortunate creature was probably screaming as it had been sucked up, its soft essence liquefied and drawn through the hole.

From her waistband, she removed a thin, wickedly sharp dagger. *What's it going to be, tourist?*

She could be out of the cavern and gone from the plateau in a half-hour's time. After all, this was supposed to be her holiday. An adventure was all well and good but she hadn't come to T'ing to be eaten.

You came here for a bit of fun, she told herself. *That's what you promised yourself, anyway.*

Don't you want to see a monster?

Well, did she?

It was different when it all seemed like a game. Different when she thought the Zneeth, if there

were a Zneeth to be found at all, would reveal itself
only from a distance, snorting with impotent rage.

What if there are gemstones? The thought
came unbidden but she couldn't ignore it. *Not a Jayll
stone, no, but what of a Quizert ruby? Not very
valuable, as rubies go, but rare. Its heart so red it
seems to bleed.*

Quizert rubies were found only on T'ing. And
only in its jungle caves.

It didn't seem possible that this pit held any
such wonders. Still, when she first arrived at the
township, every creature she approached knew of the
Crystal Cave. Everyone agreed the cave existed and
most said it could be found, vaguely, in the region
where Cygxz promised to lead her.

None of her contacts had spoken of treasure.
Only one of them mentioned a Zneeth.

She knew her guide had seen her as just
another softbody. Tall for a female chund, auburn-
haired, a creature whose hazel eyes turned to green
when angered. He hadn't cared she was a transporter.
It was one thing for someone to carry documents for
the rich and powerful. It was another thing altogether
for that person to hike for days through treacherous
terrain.

Will a Zneeth feed on a Terran?
Did she really intend to find out?

Averting her eyes from Cygxz' abandoned
shell, she considered the rope dangling from the
opening. Chastising herself, she turned from the
entrance.

The truth was, she didn't want to leave. It
wasn't about finding rare stones. In her profession,

she'd had countless opportunities for illicit wealth. For her, money was never important.

"Adventure's afoot," she murmured softly.

Really, it would be foolish to leave now. She'd spent most of her savings and traveled half a galaxy to find this cave. She would never again get the chance to explore its secrets.

Besides, she was far from helpless. She'd go into the cavern, a little further at least. If things changed, if she became uncomfortable with the situation, she'd leave.

As simple as that.

With the lighting flies illuminating her direction, Aly picked her way along the path of broken and emptied shells. Moving deeper into the cavern, she noticed how some of the coverings bore signs of a different kind of struggle. There was no neat hole to mark the demise of these spelunkers. Where they'd fallen, the surrounding walls were marked by the dried stain of splattered blood.

A Zneeth didn't kill like this. There was another killer hidden in these catacombs.

Her source of light splintered as the lighting flies darted around her erratically. Listening, Aly didn't hear anything unusual. Inhaling deeply, she caught a fresh scent. The hint of a blood-smell teased at her nostrils.

Ahead of her, a shadow separated from the darkness. Pausing briefly, it began a slow advance. Behind the flickering light of the flies, another shadow drew closer. Then another.

Her trackers were the size of large Terran dogs. Stalking her, they moved in near silence. Many-legged, they carried their bulbous bodies with improbable grace.

Kildebeests.

The Bugs detested them. They used every opportunity to root out and slaughter them. Forced out of the cities, the surviving kildebeests had learned to hide away from populated areas.

They liked holes and dark places where they could prey upon the lost or unwary. They preferred to eat Bug above all else, but, in a pinch, Aly imagined a softbody would suffice.

They were loathsome things. Pivoting on the heel of her foot, she saw it was too late to retreat.

More kildebeests had entered behind her. They'd slinked through the side tunnels, tunnels she'd ignored because of their low ceilings. There were several of the creatures; at least eight by her count. They moved toward her with careless disregard, their bobbing bodies suggesting boredom with so easy a kill.

Turning back, Aly walked quickly. She wanted to run but didn't dare outpace the lighting flies. If left in darkness, she'd die.

Her feet crunched over bits of abandoned shells. Rounding a corner, she came to an abrupt stop. The pathway divided, its two forks leading in opposite directions. Each disappeared into blackness.

Suddenly, the lighting flies scattered. Aly swiveled, her dagger held high. A brown-bulbed kildebeest leapt at her and she dodged away, slicing her blade across the creature's belly.

Screeching, the kildebeest reared back in pain. Blood spraying from its wound, it fell to the ground.

Forcing her forearm below its jaw, she drew her knife across its throat.

A line of blood curled along the side of her hand. Pushing with her boot, she thrust the monster's body from the knife.

Grouped behind her, the remaining kildebeests stood in stunned silence. As if of one mind, they retreated to a safer distance. Gathering together, they formed a circle, each occasionally glancing in her direction.

Aly wiped her hand as the lighting flies hovered around her. Knowing they sought her physical warmth, she remained curiously comforted by their disdain for the cold-blooded kildebeests.

From somewhere inside the circle of killers, a kildebeest's words rang out. "It got Jojo!"

The beast's chittering tongue was a fair approximation of the Bug's own language. She understood it easily.

The kildebeests viewed Jojo's body solemnly. One after the other, they studied Aly.

"It has tiny fangs," said one.

"Useless," agreed another.

"It has a blade." They considered her dagger, wet with blood. They seemed amused by the size of the weapon.

"It carries no shell to protect it."

"It has no talons," one said, giggling.

"No claws," agreed another, who giggled as well.

"*It got Jojo!*" a yellow-scarred kildebeest said, roaring with laughter. Soon, the cave echoed with the sound of the kildebeests' merriment.

Aly withdrew to the edge of the fork, knowing her only escape to the outside world was somewhere behind her enemies. Some of the lighting flies flew away, their remaining glow fading.

"It has no shell," announced an older, faded kildebeest as the laughter faded. "No talons, no claws. Yet it killed a member of our pack."

"Luck," stated the kildebeest beside him. There was a murmur of general agreement.

The old kildebeest stamped a leg impatiently. "Jojo was a fierce warrior."

"He was a bully," said a tiny-bulbed, younger member, "because he was big."

"One of the biggest." The words drifted from the center of the group, the speaker unseen. "One of the biggest... and the juiciest..."

The kildebeests looked at one another with a new comprehension. "Jojo was always among the first to feed," said the yellow-scarred kildebeest.

In unison, they fell upon Jojo's remains.

His bulb burst open and they ate greedily, making loud, slurping noises. Blood flew through the air, splashing the walls and splattering Aly's tunic.

She watched with a horrified fascination. The tiny-bulbed kildebeest slipped, falling under the legs of its larger brothers, and became part of the meal itself. Within seconds, there was nothing left of it or Jojo.

"I'm still hungry," a kildebeest complained.

Aly bolted, lurching onto the left leg of the fork before her. After a few steps, the path dropped sharply, spilling her to the ground. She fell, rolling end-over-end until the ground leveled out. Her head spinning, she lay in the darkness.

48

"Which way did it go?" came a kildebeest' voice from the hollow above.

"*That* way."

"Ohhh, that's a mistake."

"A bad mistake."

"There won't be anything left of it," a voice grumped.

"What's left won't be worth eating," another complained.

"Anything left is always worth eating," said a third voice. The kildebeests guffawed again, enjoying their wit.

Feeling along her waistband, Aly discovered she'd lost her dagger in the fall. On her knees, she swept her hand in front of her, groping for it. As her fingers touched its hilt, she realized the lighting flies hadn't followed her. They should be flitting around her, bathing her in light.

Instead, the blackness surrounding her was complete. She could feel her heart pounding.

There was something wrong down here, something bad, and the kildebeests knew it. They could easily pick their way down the path after her, but they didn't dare.

A kildebeest doesn't miss an easy meal without good reason.

She'd chosen the wrong route. Although, maybe, it wouldn't have mattered which way she'd gone. Maybe she'd made her fatal mistake the day she booked passage to the Bugworld.

"It's called the Cave of Doom," Cygxz had told her.

The Cave of Doom. What part of that had sounded like fun?

Well, honestly - all of it.

Above her, the kildebeests cried out in alarm. Shrieking, their voices disappeared as they ran.

Too late now.

Her fingers tightened around the dagger's hilt. Behind her, a grating noise scraped the cavern wall. Climbing upright, she turned toward the sound.

The lighting flies were back, dancing in front of her. Scattered in a large arc, their bodies only offered pinpoints of light. Aly couldn't see anything of the creature they surrounded but she knew it by name and reputation.

It was a Zneeth and it had come for her.

The monster reveled in the terror it could inspire in others; it lived for it. It wanted to frighten her, fill her mind to the breaking point, and send her screaming. When she panicked, it would track her down and destroy her.

Discarded below the surface, her lifeless frame would never be found. Just another vanished tourist, lost to jungles of T'ing.

Closing her eyes, she willed her heart to calm its beating. Her breathing deepened and slowed. The first wave of fear subsided.

"I'M SO SCARED -" Cygxz screamed.

Aly's eyes opened. The lighting flies were closer now. From inside their midst, Cygxz cried out again. It sounded as real as if it were happening for the first time.

The scream choked off abruptly, echoing the guide's death. A thin, reedy sob bubbled from the Zneeth as it mimicked a different victim's death wail.

"No!" she shouted, the word escaping without thought. She twisted, her legs pumping as she leapt up the sharply-angled path. Her fingers tearing at the packed dirt, she forced herself upward. Scraped and bleeding, she dragged herself to the cavern level where the kildebeests had stalked her.

Aly staggered forward as something wrapped itself around her ankle. Tripping, she fell.

Rolling onto her back, she kicked at an unseen cord. The fleshy rope slid up her leg, tightening its grasp. Even as she clawed at the ground, she felt herself sliding downward.

Lighting flies flickered around her as a heavy weight settled upon her lower torso. From the glow of the flies, Aly could see -

There's nothing there.

The Zneeth leaned closer, its fetid breath washing over her. "No!" it cried, using her own voice to mock her.

Aly shot her right arm forward, driving her dagger into the emptiness before her. The weapon struck home and the monster roared, its cry of rage shaking the cavern.

Loosening its hold, the Zneeth shed its invisibility. It appeared in front of Aly, the bobbing lighting flies reflected in the black pupils staring down at her.

In training, she'd seen holographic representations of a Zneeth. They were wildly inadequate.

The creature rocked back on two of its six legs, its large and heavy limbs stranded with muscle. Each of its feet was tipped with massive talons. The Zneeth's thick body was encrusted with scales of an almost-luminescent red. A tentacle stretched from a flap in its throat, slapping at the scales as it worked to free the dagger from its lip.

A dozen eyes pitted its forehead, riding above two protruding lips as moist and discolored as Xzzertian slugs. Curling in and out of its mouth, a pink trunk glistened under the pinpricks of white light. Inside the trunk, rows of tiny sharp teeth revolved with each rumbling inhalation.

Rolling over, Aly squirmed between the monster's thigh and its underbelly. Forcing herself to her feet, she hobbled away, her ankle throbbing, as the glow of the flies disappeared into darkness.

Unable to see her surroundings, she slowed her pace. Behind her, there was the sound of metal falling onto rock. The Zneeth snorted triumphantly. In her mind's eye, she could see its massive head sweeping back and forth, looking for her.

She slid her hands along the wall. The surface felt dry and cool, the stone wall curving as it guided her forward. Surprisingly, a yellow glow taunted her from somewhere around the bend.

Beneath her, the floor vibrated as the monster shifted in the pathway. The cave shook as the creature slammed into the cavern walls, impatiently turning itself around in too small a space.

Aly peered around the corner. The corridor ended there, a solid wall of rock behind it. Despite the promise of the yellow glimmer, there weren't any lighting flies to welcome her. There was no gleam of moonlight to offer some faint hope of escape.

Nowhere to go, after all.

On the back wall, a bit of moss clung to the face of the rock. Small and misshapen, stretching only a few centimeters in diameter, its strands were infused with a weak light. Its illumination was so soft, the glow would vanish under sunlight. In the darkness of the cave, however, the light almost seemed bright.

Aly reached out. Bending under the pressure of her fingertips, the moss brightened as she touched it. She hesitated, surprised, as it lifted from the wall. Now golden in color, it wrapped itself softly around her hand.

"Alive, are you?" she asked. "Silly thing. You've picked the wrong host."

Behind her, she heard the sound of scales scratching across stone. Musk filled the corridor, reeking of dust and age and death.

The Zneeth had arrived and was waiting for her.

"Go," she told the fungus, moving her hand toward the wall. The moss clung to her, a gentle heat infusing the back of her hand. Using the fingers of her free hand, she lifted it free. Its glowing strands released her reluctantly.

She placed it on the wall. Almost instantly, the moss flowed back onto her wrist.

Behind her, the ghost of Cygxz screamed.

What's the matter with me? Aly wondered.

Something felt wrong. Or, rather, she knew something was wrong because – she felt good. Her ankle no longer hurt. Her scrapes and cuts didn't sting.

She wasn't afraid.

You've got no chance, transporter. A Terran can't fight a Zneeth.

Did she have any choice?

Aly faced the monster. "Come on, ugly. Do your worst."

53

The Zneeth's form flickered in front of her, as if debating the merits of its invisibility. Finally, the creature solidified.

Its eyes fixed on her with a new look. This wasn't the gaze of a hunter playing with its prey. All of its eyes glowered at her with hatred.

Slowly, the Zneeth's trunk uncurled from its mouth. The trunk's opening flared as the sound of a dying kildebeest filled the passage. Within seconds, a new cry filled the air, a second kildebeest in its death throes. Then a Bug begged for mercy, his voice stumbling over his words, his mind frozen by the horror in front of him.

Aly knew, then, she'd been mistaken. She *was* afraid, the terror drumming quietly inside her chest, but it was different now. Her mind remained clear and unaffected.

Stepping forward, she struck at the rip in the creature's mouth. Dumfounded, the Zneeth's death-noise dribbled into nothingness.

"That was for Cygxz," she said.

A teardrop of blood splashed to the ground as the Zneeth snarled. Hunching its shoulders, it retreated from her. When Aly raised her hand to strike again at the animal's wound, it flinched.

A Zneeth frightened of a softbody? Frightened of anyone?

It didn't make sense. Then she realized the Zneeth's eyes weren't looking at her any longer. They were fixed on the glow encircling her wrist.

"Is this what you want?" She plucked at the moss. Its strands released and it dangled in the air above her arm. "Did this belong to you?"

A gasp of sound escaped from the Zneeth.

54

The moss stirred under her grasp. Stretching out for her, it quickly wove itself back around her hand.

"It's mine now," she told the monster. "You can't have it. It doesn't want you, anymore."

Aly leapt at the Zneeth, her fist slashing at the wounded lip. The great beast bellowed in fear. Its thick legs backpedaled desperately, pulling its body out of the passageway.

Turning, it ran from her, its anguished sobs echoing behind it.

* * *

Overhead, the sky was black. The stars were bright.

Lifting herself from the cave's opening, Aly crawled onto the thin grass of the mound. Coiling her rope, she placed it in her bag. Standing, she placed the carrypak onto her shoulders.

There was a long journey before her. Even without Cygxz to distract her, she wouldn't reach the township for days. Her water was almost gone. She could do without food.

The night air had never smelled so sweet.

Not much of a treasure, she thought, looking at the moss gripping her wrist. Its golden light was so soft she could barely see it.

No treasure but one hell of an adventure.

Brushing the hair from her eyes, she began walking.

In its lair beneath the surface, the Zneeth wailed.

Chapter Six

The nightblack stocking pulled over his head,
Dobbins ran to the base of the Mound. Pushing
through the fronds of a large, waxy plant, he stepped
out of the moonlight and into shadow. The leaves
enfolded him, hiding him from view.

Behind him, Bugs barked foul-tempered
babble and, seconds later, spitzpistols fired. The
sounds remained distant.

He was safe for now; as safe, anyway, as most
chunds who arrived on T'ing. He examined the
mountain of hard mud, rock and sticks rising above
him.

This isn't going to be easy.

The Mound was framed against the night sky,
its upper entrances annoyingly far from him. Lesser
guards patrolled the surface, paying little attention to
the holes leading into the bottom chamber. He knew
the ground level access wouldn't present a challenge.
But why should he bother? The poor, humped-over
creatures scurrying through these openings were of
the servant class. At most, he'd find the galley or,
possibly, the birthing chambers.

The second and third levels appeared equally
worthless. If a level lacked a guard, it lacked
valuables. He wasn't risking his life for a sip from a
stewpot.

Overhead, a pair of Mound guards floated
across the sky. They drifted lower, their bodies

gliding toward the inner wall. Peeking through the fronds, Dobbins saw something smoldering on the ground. It was the Twill's crumpled body.

What remained of it, anyway. A number of Bugs lingered by the corpse, drawn to the smell of burning flesh.

Even the Mound Guards were drawn to the scent.

The Mound Guards circled lower in the night air. The fliers were the elite members of the Mound Lord's cadre and the only ones considered for command. It wasn't enough to be born with wings. It took power or status to retain flight.

The walkers, crawlers and sliders didn't care about such things but Dobbins had seen more than one grounded Bug carrying its wings like a burden of birth. Those fliers had been clipped; some had never flown. The government liked to control who floated in its skies.

There was a rebel force, the Sktzers, fighting the authorities over this very issue. Dobbins had never seen a Sktzer. Until this night, he'd never seen a Mound guard, either.

All of them appeared to be of the same order, carrying bright green shells with orange markings. Except for their larger size and coloring, they looked like most Bugs. Every one of them was an armor-plated malcontent with deadly pincers, pointed beaks, and compound eyes seemingly able to see everywhere at once.

Silhouetted against the dark sky, the Mound Guards cut through the air with the grace of ill-tempered angels. Aloft, they were majestic and powerful. They appeared more than capable of protecting the Mound Lord and his fortune.

To find those riches, Dobbins was going to have to climb. He'd have to do it without his gloves, though. Wall mold still dripped from both palms and he couldn't risk coming in contact with the acid. Dropping the hand coverings, he kicked them to the base of the flowering plant.

For the next few hours, the grappling hook and its metal barbs would be of no use, either. Their wicked tips would rip through the hive's surface of dried mud and twig. He buried the hook and the gloves under a pile of leaves. When it came time to leave, he'd want to know exactly where to find his tools.

He took a deep breath in, considering the job ahead of him. He enjoyed heights and climbing, and the packed earth of the Mound would make this ascent especially easy. It offered ready-made handholds for anyone with flexible fingers and an opposable thumb.

He was encouraged, too, by the behavior of the guards. Too rarely challenged, many of them were gathered at the interior wall. Feasting on their fallen companion, they ate without the slightest suspicion that there was an intruder in their midst. If all went well, he'd be inside one of the uppermost chambers before they even returned to their posts. Unobserved, he could pilfer to his heart's content.

Getting off of the grounds, *that* might present a challenge. He could hardly count on a succession of ill-tempered Twills available to act as a distracting late night snack. But something would work out. It always did.

Well … not always. Not on *TIAN'S GATE*. But most of the time.

The bright light of the moons spilled from behind the structure, leaving him in shade. Covered by the stocking and hugging the Mound's surface, he started the climb.

At the entrance to the second level, he scrambled onto a ledge. As expected, an unimpressive room greeted him, its shelves filled with drinking bottles and small earthen jugs. There was nothing of real value here. No reason to linger any longer.

Flexing his arms, he could feel his biceps tighten. Too many weeks aboard a space cruiser had softened him. He supposed he should have spent more time exercising and less time throwing dice and dealing cards.

Dobbins grinned. At the time, dealing cards had been more profitable. More fun, too.

The next level would come easily. Two openings higher and he'd be at mid-point. At mid-point, if not before, he'd really start to feel the climb. By the time he reached the very top level - and how could he not go to the highest entrance? - he'd be exhausted. But it was only there that he'd find the Mound Lord's chambers.

It was there, too, where the guards would round most frequently. The uppermost level held the greatest danger. It also held the promise of richest reward.

He couldn't wait to explore its secrets.

A rustling noise came from the ledge above him. *Wings?*

Possibly. Even if ignored by the Mound's guards, these landings provided an easy resting place for a flyer.

Best to stay away from the ledges, he thought.

It would make for a longer climb but it was safer. As long as his arms held out.

* * *

Passing the fourth level of the Mound, Dobbins found fewer handholds. This high above the ground, the once-prominent ridges of the hive were smooth with age. The packed earth felt as hard as stone.

His progress slowed to a crawl.

Not yet in sight of the Mound Lord's chamber, he needed to rest. His fingers were cramping, his arms were numb, and his legs ached for relief. Topping things off, a cold wind had begun to blow. It knifed through his protective stocking.

Shuffling sideways, he heard two voices speaking loudly. Flattening his body against the face of the Mound, he spread his legs wide to keep himself from sliding lower. His fingers dug into the dirt, seeking a hold.

Above me. Bugs, two or more.

They were directly overhead, using the chittering noises that passed as their form of verbal communication. He'd been to a lot of worlds, heard more than a hundred different tongues, and this was the only one that made his ears hurt. Every sentence was filled with a series of hisses, growls and barks, each sound clattering against the next in the most unpleasant way possible.

Only the Bugs would develop a mean *language*. It was one more reason to get off-planet as soon as possible.

Dobbins' body trembled. He wasn't going to be able to cling onto this spot much longer.

No choice, then.

He threw his arms over the top of the upper ledge. Straining, he dragged his body atop the hardened dirt slab.

A pair of startled guards stared down at him. They remained frozen as Dobbins sat up, letting his legs dangle over the edge of the platform.

"Sktzers," he said, the word wheezing from him.

The two guards exchanged a glance. Babbling forcefully, the bigger guard thrust his spear in Dobbins' direction. He ignored it.

It felt marvelous to be sitting again. He was fairly certain nothing had ever felt so good in his entire life.

The guard's spear poked closer toward him. Dobbins said, "Sorry. Can't understand a word you're shrieking."

The big guard considered that. "How'd you get here?" he asked in Basic.

Adapting the same tongue, his partner said, "It's a chund."

"I know."

"But how did he get here?"

An expression of long-suffering crossed the bigger Bug's face. "I've just asked him."

"What does it matter, how I got here?" Dobbins waved a hand dismissively. "Here's what matters: Sktzers have invaded the township!"

"Sktzers? In the township? Ridiculous."

The little guard frowned. "That's bad, Brizz."

61

"He's lying." Brizz knocked the shaft of his spear against his partner's head. "Wake up. Sktzers are forest-dwellers. They stay away from the township."

"There are hundreds of them," Dobbins told the smaller guard. "They're screaming for justice. They demand no wing be clipped, that every flying Bug be allowed to soar." He gestured for the guard to lean closer. "They want the Mound Lord's head."

"No!"

Dobbins nodded grimly. "The streets are wet with blood."

The little guard reeled in shock. "What should we do?"

"Escape while you can! Fly! Fly for your lives!"

Brizz laid a heavy claw on his partner's shoulder. "Before you desert your post," he told the first guard, "before the Mound Lord issues a warrant for your capture, before you get chopped and stewed for the eating enjoyment of everyone you've ever irritated – think about this."

The smaller guard blinked up at him.

"Do you see any Sktzers? Are the skies filled with rebel hordes?"

"But the streets are wet with blood!"

Brizz lowered his spear until its pointed tip pressed against Dobbins' stomach. "Be truthful, chund. Your stupid story is confusing him."

Dobbins jerked as the spear poked him. A small tear appeared at the center of the body stocking, a tiny circle of red blossoming beneath it.

"Maybe I haven't been exactly factual," he admitted, "but the rebels are a problem, aren't they?

Wasn't there an instant, a tiny fraction of time, when you wondered if what I said was true?"

"No."

"And if a Sktzer invasion is even a faint possibility," Dobbins persisted, "aren't you woefully unprepared?"

"It was never a possibility."

"Hey. *Hey!*" The small guard's antennae grew rigid with anger. "There aren't any Sktzers. The chund lied to me!"

Brizz held up a claw. "Wait. I want to know what his game is."

"I don't like to wait." The small guard's tongue licked hungrily at the tip of his beak.

Standing, Dobbins said, "Luckily for you, I have the answer to the Sktzer dilemma."

He slipped his hand into a slit in the body stocking. When he did, Brizz's spear moved upward sharply.

Carefully withdrawing his hand, Dobbins displayed a canister to the Bugs. "This is for you. Your salvation."

"What is it?"

"Gas."

"Gas," Brizz said stonily.

"Absolutely."

"For Sktzers."

"Nothing better." He tilted the can toward the shorter guard. "Sktzer gas, plainly labeled. I assume you'll want to read the small print."

"Ummm." The smaller guard squinted at the can. "Yes."

"If the rebels were to attack the township," Brizz said, "which is even less likely than you surviving our discussion this night, I'd rather have a spitzpistol. Or a mace."

"I like blades," his partner said.

Brizz held the tip of his spear to Dobbins' throat. "So, as you can see, your gas is useless."

Dobbins shook the can. "But it stings fiercely."

"So?"

He pressed the nozzle and a wet fog jetted into the big guard's eyes.

"YYYyyaaaarrr!" Brizz bellowed.

Dobbins spun away from the spear's tip. Before he could run, a jointed arm encircled his throat from behind. The small guard let his own spear clatter to the ground as he secured his hold on the human.

"Got him," the little guard said. "Want me to snap his neck?"

Wiping at his face, Brizz chattered nastily in his own tongue. His partner grunted agreeably. He forced Dobbins around, until he was facing the other Bug.

"What'd he say?" Dobbins asked.

"You really want to know?" The guard's pincers straightened Dobbins' shoulders while his claws retained their hold on the prisoner. "Brizz has plans for you."

"Ah."

"He's going to run you through with his spear, then slice you with his dagger, then club you with his mace, then shoot you with his spitzpistol. And then –" Here the small Bug paused, allowing a chuckle to escape. "Then he's going to spray you with your very own gas."

"I've come up with an even better idea," Dobbins told the pair.

The little guard's pincers smacked him on the top of the head. Dobbins' teeth slapped together, cutting off the rest of his conversation.

"After Brizz is done, I get to kill you," the little guard said.

The Bug lifted Dobbins' arms, exposing his chest. "He's in front of you," his captor said to Brizz.

Tears dripping down his beak, Brizz kept his eyes tightly closed. Gripping the shaft of his spear, he prodded forward gingerly until he found Dobbins' stomach. He cocked the arms holding the spear. Smiling, he savored the moment.

"One little problem," Dobbins whispered to the smaller guard.

"Yeah?"

"If he runs me through with the spear, what's to stop its head when it exits?"

"That's why I'm here," the guard replied. His beak dropped open. "Hold on...."

Leaning into the guard's arms, Dobbins kicked off the ground and thrust his heels backward. His feet bounced against the shelled cup between the Bug's legs.

"Uumph!" the smaller guard gasped. Jarred by the blow, his upper arms weakened and Dobbins fell. Brizz shot his spear forward. The lance whistled over Dobbins' head as it struck, splintering the little guard's shell. The head of the spear buried itself beneath the broken barrier.

The stricken Bug clutched at the spear's handle, fighting to keep it from slicing further into his body. Gasping, he tried to speak. A thin, reedy whistle of air escaped from his mouth.

"Not so clever now, eh, chund?" Brizz twisted the spear's handle with a flourish. "What's the matter? Kildebeest got your tongue?"

Dobbins crawled out from between them. Behind him, the small guard's head sagged, his beak dropping almost to his chest. His arms fell uselessly to the sides of his body.

Climbing to his feet, Dobbins said, "Have mercy."

"Mercy?" Chortling with delight, Brizz threw his weight against the spear. Forced backward, the limp body of the second guard teetered at the lip of the outer ledge before slipping from its surface.

The abrupt change in balance yanked Brizz forward. His claws locked onto the spear's handle, he skidded forward.

"Help me, Trygll!" he commanded blindly, straining against the load dragging him to the edge of the earthen slab.

Picking up the remaining spear, Dobbins walked over to Brizz. He said, "This is gonna look bad on your record."

Blinking back tears, the big guard forced open his eyes. "Chund?"

"Surprise." Dobbins bumped the sentry with the butt of his spear. Brizz's wings flared out as he fought to keep his footing. Soundlessly, he tumbled off of the ledge and into space.

Dobbins paused, listening for the outcry to follow. He heard a soft *whump!* as something hit the ground.

Silence followed the fall. He waited.

Still nothing. It was as if the pair of guards had plummeted to the earth, unseen by the other sentries.

"Guess my luck is changing," he told the spear. Holding the weapon, he crossed the ledge. This wasn't the uppermost level but there were guards at the entrance. There must be something valuable here.

Small and easily portable items would fit neatly into the pockets he'd sewn into the body stocking. Gemstones and dibblesticks would do nicely.

Large, wide-mouthed ceramic pots filled the inner chamber. Each pot was plugged by a circular lid and each lid carried a metal ring at its center. The pots were carefully arranged to allow a path to the exit.

Dobbins squatted beside the nearest container. Too heavy for him to move, the pot was half-again the size of a man and etched with a revoltingly realistic depiction of Bug carnality. In an effort to underscore his lack of good taste, the potter had colored the work in varying shades of dung and vomit. It was the kind of handiwork only a Bug could appreciate.

"To each his own," Dobbins said agreeably.

This pot seemed to be exactly the type of thing a Mound Lord would use to store valuables. Resting the spear at his feet, the Terran gripped the metal ring with both hands. He pulled. When the ring didn't turn, he pulled again, harder.

The lid sat atop its container, unmoving.

He wiped his hands on his bodysuit. Taking several deep breaths, he gave the lid a tremendous yank.

His fingers slipped free. He fell to the ground.

The stopper remained securely in place.

Wearily, Dobbins used the spear's shaft to stand upright. "The harder the struggle," he reminded himself, "the sweeter the spoils."

Gripping the spear's shaft, he tried to wedge the point of its metal head between the pot and the lid. It didn't so much as chip the impenetrable seal.

This is taking too much time.

Luck only held for so long. Any minute now, the fallen guards would be found and a search started.

Flipping the weapon over, he smacked its wooden end against the top. When wood met ceramic, a shock ran up his arms. He nearly dropped the spear.

The lid itself remained undamaged.

He shook his head. What was supposed to be a nice break-and-enter had somehow turned into a smash-and-grab. He hated smash-and-grabs. They were always messy.

Besides, they lacked style.

"Not that you give me a choice," he told the lid pointedly. He slammed the spear's butt against it. Lifting the spear high over his head, he brought it down again.

Again. *Again.* With the last blow, the spear's flat end splintered.

"You think this is funny?" Exasperated, Dobbins took the spear by the end of its handle and swung it in a vicious circle. The head of the weapon crashed against the side of the pot and the container burst open.

Thick sauce erupted into the room, its spray escaping in a pungent, brown arc. Chunks of decaying meat and splintered bone were carried along with the sauce, decorating the floor and most of the nearby containers. A nauseating stench filled the air.

Food pot.

The gray tongue of a jungle wombat bobbed gently in a puddle of gravy. A multi-jointed kildebeest leg glided along the curve of the nearest pot before falling, wetly, to the floor. Sticking to Dobbins' body stocking was the brown, fat finger... of a soft-bodied chund....

Suddenly, he felt a desperate need for fresh air. Bent over, he stumbled for the outer ledge.

Perched on the entrance's lip, Brizz grinned at Dobbins. Two other guards fluttered their wings from behind him, hovering outside of the doorway.

"Something smells good," Brizz said.

The guards shied back as Dobbins' spear flew past them. Wheeling around, he leapt over the remnants of the shattered pot. Grabbing at the room's rear door, he threw it open.

A windowless hallway faced him, its nearest occupants at the far end of the corridor. Slamming the door shut, he went in the opposite direction. Sprinting along the tunnel, his soft-soled shoes padded over the dirt.

Options, Dobbins demanded of his suddenly uncooperative brain. *What are my options?*

His were limited.

He could stay in the hallway, battle with the guards - and be killed and eaten.

He could lie to his captors, somehow fabricating a logical explanation for his behavior tonight - and be killed and eaten.

He could plead for mercy, while offering to put his not-inconsiderable skills at the Mound Lord's disposal - and be killed and eaten.

Or he could run and trust to prayer. He could pray the corridors were too narrow to allow the guards to spread their wings. Pray their aim with a spear was inaccurate. Pray he found a place to hide before they reached him.

His chances? Optimistically, maybe one in a million.

Behind him, he could hear someone opening the tunnel door.

Dobbins ran.

Chapter Seven

"Deadbeat."

That single ringing word stopped Syr before he could climb the stairs.

"Deadbeat." Again, the same unpleasant word. This time, spoken in Basic.

The desk clerk wore a happy sneer on his face. Abandoning the stairway, Syr approached the front desk. "Fine evening to you, good Bug."

"Eighteen dibblesticks, chund," the desk clerk replied. "Past due. Payable now."

Not for the first time, Syr wondered why anyone would choose to stay at *Mel's Travelrama*. It wasn't as if it were an authentic Mound. Rising only two stories above the ground, it lacked both history and charm. Yet, even at a price of three sticks daily, there were always a few tourists lingering in its lobby or digging into their pockets to rent one of its rooms. Unlike Syr, the tourists were impressed by the structure's mud and twig walls. They delighted in the pervading gloom darkening every corner and found joy in the moisture leaking up from its bottom floor.

He'd heard one couple whisper about experiencing the 'real' Bugworld. The same couple would have squirmed with delight at the desk clerk's nastiness.

Syr lacked their particular level of appreciation. "Payment is forthcoming. My friend, Dobbins, is arranging for it."

"Your friend Dobbins has a honeyed tongue." The Bug stopped short, stricken by the delicious imagery of his words. He said, "However, he has no more money than you."

"He has made new friends. As we speak, he is meeting with Mound Lord Tzzle."

"He is not," the Bug said flatly. "I was in the Mound Lord's service. Only if your friend was stewed and offered as an appetizer would the Mound Lord give him a moment's attention."

Syr sighed. "Let me collect our things."

"These?" The Bug lifted their two satchels and carrypak to the front desk. He dropped them with a thud. "These remain the property of the chundhut."

"Under whose authority?"

The Bug tapped at the sticker clinging to his chest. *Hi!*, it read. *I'm Mel!*

Every employee of the chundhut wore a similar sticker. Each of them answered only to the name of 'Mel'.

It was another reason Syr had tired of this shelter. Giving a last glance at his belongings, he turned to discover two large rust-colored Bugs standing before him.

"One other thing," Mel said.

"What?"

"Three towels are missing from your room. I'll need them back."

"I don't have them." Syr stepped to one side. The rust-colored Bugs shifted along with him, their barrier intact.

"Restitution has to be made. The District Manager demands it. Missing items must be replaced or paid for. No exceptions."

"I can't replace what I don't have."

"Oh, dear," Mel said, with a snicker. "Whatever shall we do?"

One of the rust-colored Bugs said, uneasily, "I don't like this."

"You'll do as you're told."

"Look at him," the Bug said. "Violet skin, violet eyes. The purple mane of hair. You didn't say anything about a changer."

"Frightened?" the desk clerk asked.

"Not of you, crawler," the Bug said. "Why the District Manager keeps this place, I don't know, but we'll collect his payment one way or another. If we don't take this one, we'll take someone else."

Syr noticed that the other guests had left the reception area. For the first time, he realized the rust-colored Bugs weren't wearing the hotel's identification stickers.

Slavers. He wished he weren't so hungry.

"Idiot," Mel said. "Have you seen his stomach? It's flat. You can see the ridges of muscle beneath it. Have you ever seen a changer that wasn't swollen with fat?"

The pair of Bugs studied Syr.

"He's tall," the first rust-colored Bug said.

"Changers tend toward height," the second pointed out.

"Wide of shoulder, broad of back."

"Muscular arms and legs. Strong."

"But," Mel pointed out, "not fat."

The slavers stayed with Syr. This time, when he shifted to move past them, it was Mel who hurried around the desk to block his path.

"He has the coloring," the clerk said, pressing a hand against Syr's chest. "I'll give you that much. He may even be a changer. Does it matter? He doesn't change."

"Never?"

"Maybe he lacks new options. Maybe he hasn't fed enough. Or, my guess, he's chund-lucky. He only looks like a changer."

"In other words," the second rust-colored Bug said, hooking an arm under one of Syr's biceps, "he goes to auction." To his partner, he said, "Let's go, Stynx."

"You don't want to do this," Syr said.

"I *don't* want to do this." Stynx agreed, taking Syr's free arm. "But the DM checks the books every week. He expects to get paid."

"The clerk doesn't know me," Syr said, not moving. "He hasn't been with me every hour of every day. He hasn't seen what I do when I'm not here."

"Enough talk." The second slaver pressed his claw in deeper.

Beads of sweat appeared on Syr's forehead. "I won't go."

His body trembled and the Bugs shook with it, pulled from the floor by the strength of its spasm. The cords of muscle on Syr's neck swelled, growing thicker as his neck elongated. His temples pulsated. His head grew larger and changed color, orange scales tearing their way from beneath his skin. The scales fled down his neck, covering it, but stopped at his shoulder blades as if prevented from going further.

The Bugs shrieked in alarm as Syr's bloated head bubbled and expanded in front of them. His nose widened and the ridge between his nostrils disappeared, creating a snout that stretched toward them.

Syr's eyes grew large and slanted, glowing with a crimson fury. Fangs sprouted inside his mouth. Liquid dripped from their wicked points, burning into the floor as the surface was seared with acid.

Below the neck, his body appeared unchanged. If anything, his frame had grown thinner, leaving the tunic to drape over it more loosely. His legs shook as he struggled to remain upright while balancing his oversized head.

"*Release me*," this new Syr demanded in a silky voice of dark malevolence. A whisper of smoke drifted lazily from his snout.

The Bugs remained rooted in place, the slavers' arms linked with Syr.

"I'll feed on you." Syr's head dipped lower. Feeding sounded good. It had been too long since he had fed.

Mel was the first to break and run. "Take *them*!" he cried, scrambling for the stairway. The sticker fell from his chest as he ran away.

This burst of action freed the second slaver from his reverie. Releasing his hold on the captive, he skittered after the panicked Mel. Only Stynx remained. He jerked at his unwilling arm but the frozen joint refused to bend.

He had his chance. Time to feed.

"No," Syr told himself, the word growling from his lips. "Not now."

His body swayed as he willed his creation to fade. His head wavered and shrunk, dissolving, reforming, until the frightened slaver again looked into Syr's tired eyes.

"Let me go," Syr said without force.

Weariness weighed upon him. He'd done a Stingen Fire Beast; the upper part of one, anyway. If the fates had been kind, he'd have saved the transformation for another time. If he'd been fat and ready, he could have reveled in this new creation. It would have been a glory to become so magnificent a creature.

Lost forever now.

At last, the slaver dropped his arm.

"May I leave?" Syr asked.

"Yes," the Bug croaked. "Yes. We don't want your kind."

Syr walked past the bags on the front desk. He'd have liked to take a change of clothing; he doubted the slaver would dare object. But the room's rent was owed. Until the debt was paid, their belongings would stay here.

He paused at the front of the chundhut. "What about the District Manager's payment?"

"No worries, changer." The slaver lifted the *Hi! I'm Mel!* name tag from the floor. "We'll find something to bring to auction."

Chapter Eight

Brizz led the way as the guards hobbled into the corridor. Dobbins watched them pause at the far end of the hallway, talking heatedly. Their argument settled, they scrabbled forward.

Despite their bulky bodies, they were moving almost as fast as he was. At a second glance, he corrected himself.

They weren't almost as fast as he was.

They were faster.

A side tunnel appeared and he took it. Within a few footsteps, the tunnel branched into two more and he ran to his right. The corridor was dark, its lighting globes either absent or broken. Either way, he welcomed the gloom.

Dark spaces had always been kind to him. Protected by a lack of visibility, he could get lost in this maze of interconnecting pathways. Experience told him, his hunters would soon tire of the chase. They'd give up.

Dobbins felt good. He felt lucky. *This is more like it*, he thought.

He ran into a wall.

Rubbing his nose, he stepped back. No one, not even a Bug, would build a tunnel that ended without reason. It made no sense.

He ran his hands over the wall, seeking an explanation. His fingers found a handle and he smiled.

The door was locked.

Behind him, the guards filled the opening of the corridor. The narrow passageway prevented them from entering side-by-side.

Advantage, Dobbins.

With the guards entering one after the other, he'd be able to fight them, one by one. While even the smallest of his enemies was more powerful than he was, the guards were Bug-witted. In a battle, he'd have the full resources of his mind. They were limited to size and strength....

And spears and claws and pincers and beaks.

Desperately, he threw his body against the locked door. Uttering an unhappy creak, it held firm.

Brizz started forward but a second guard restrained him. Once more, the Bugs argued among themselves. They weren't speaking Basic but, to Dobbins, the meaning of their words was clear.

They each wanted the fun of killing him.

Bracing his back on the opposite wall, he kicked his feet at the door. It creaked shrilly. He kicked it a third time. The door bulged forward and the lock released with an audible pop.

The guards exchanged worried glances. Bumping into one another, they forced themselves into the tunnel.

Dobbins threw the door open, shielding his eyes from the interior light. Entering the room, he wedged the door closed with his body.

The room around him was huge. Its walls were the color of old earth but its smell was surprisingly sweet, as if freshly scented. Curled in the middle of the room was a giant gastropod.

The gastropod cocked its head, observing Dobbins with a bemused expression. It gibbered to him in its alien tongue, its voice high and tinkling.

He'd never seen anything like this creature. It was easily fifteen-foot long, a rolling mountain of white flesh. Thick pink bulbs protruded from its body at irregular intervals; lightly-veined cords dangled from the alabaster skin of its underbelly. The gastropod held two tiny arms from its chest, with two useless claws dangling limply from their ends.

While he watched, one of the thing's pink bulbs erupted. It sent bits of pink flesh scattering across the room, leaving a faint and aromatic odor behind.

The door bounced behind Dobbins' back.

The gastropod continued gibbering at him. When he stared back blankly, it shook its head at his lack of comprehension.

"Reach above your head," it said to him in Basic. "You'll find a bolt. If you slide the bolt into its guide on the wall, it will hold the door shut."

Dobbins felt his mouth sag open in surprise. The door bounced into his back more forcefully.

"Use the bolt, sweets." The gastropod smiled reassuringly, the huge crease in its mouth lifting upward.

Reaching up, he found the bolt and slid it into place. When the guards slammed into the door again, it held firmly.

He faced the gastropod. "Why?"

"The outer lock is unreliable. Almost anyone can open it. *You* should know that."

79

The guards rammed against the door. In the corridor, they screeched unhappily among themselves.

"Why did you tell me how to bar the door? I broke into your room. Aren't you frightened of me?"

"Should I be frightened, precious?" The creature laughed lightly. "No one would hurt me. This is my home. I was birthed here and I have birthed here. I have always been here. I have grown as the Mound has grown. I am among the biggest of the Bugs. I am the most desirable. I am Mother Slug."

The slug paused, waiting for Dobbins to make an appropriate comment.

"You're certainly... corpulent," he said.

"Corpulent," said Mother Slug. Her face wrinkled happily. "Corpulent, yes. But too rarely entertained, anymore."

A tapping sounded at the door. Softly, Brizz raised a question from the outer hallway.

Mother Slug chittered back at him.

"In Basic?" Brizz asked, confused.

"As a whim." To Dobbins' astonishment, she winked at him. "Now, what is it?"

"We're searching for a chund."

"There is certainly no challenge in that. They seem to be everywhere."

"This is a particular chund," Brizz persisted. "We think he's in your room. He's dangerous."

"A softbody?" Mother Slug asked. "Weak and tiny with a patch of black fur on its head?"

"Yes."

"Dangerous?"

"Yes," Brizz said.

The slug quivered with amusement, the rolls on its body shaking in happy unison. "Go," she said. "There are no dangerous chunds here."

"But we saw him enter your room!"

Mother Slug undulated across the room, bringing her head down to the closed door. "Do you doubt me?"

An uncomfortable pause lingered outside.

"No, Mother," Brizz said, finally. A new voice rose in protest only to be silenced by a loud slap. Mumbling among themselves, the guards stomped off.

Mother Slug considered Dobbins. "Are you dangerous?"

"Me?"

"I thought not." She beamed at him. "I know why you're here."

"You do?"

"You've heard about me. My followers in the Mound, my admirers in the township, they can't help themselves. They know better than to talk about me but, still, their tongues wag."

Speechlessly, Dobbins nodded.

"You've heard so many delicious rumors, haven't you? You had to see for yourself, no matter the danger." She regarded him with kind eyes. "You're wicked, sweets. Softbodies aren't permitted in the Mound."

"I know."

"Now that you've seen me, what are you going to do with me?" A mischievous thought crinkled the folds of her face. "Mate?" Her body vibrated with laughter.

From the outside corridor, new footsteps were heard. The door's handle twisted sharply, before the door struck the inner bolt. Denied entry, an angry voice spoke from behind the barrier.

Mother Slug frowned. "It's *him*," she whispered, "and he's in a snit. Hide in the back room."

Dobbins hurried to the tiny room at the rear of the chamber. Cluttered with pots, it appeared to be a storage space. Squeezing past the first few containers, he closed the closet's door.

A small vent on the far wall offered fresh air and a glimmer of light. The vent was too small to allow access for man or Bug. The room had only the one door and no windows.

Trapped, he thought.

From the outer room, the bolt squeaked as it was freed. Alien voices grew in volume as the door was opened.

He couldn't understand a word being said. Sinking onto the lid of the nearest pot, he waited to be found.

* * *

The three guards waited in a half-circle behind their master. "Where is it?" the Mound Lord demanded.

"Where is what?" asked Mother Slug, unperturbed.

It was the only first move in a delicate game, she knew, but Mother Slug had played these games before.

The Mound Lord held power, it was true, but the Mound survived and flourished through the machinations of Mother Slug. Her supplicants were vast in number and no one - no Mound Lord, no District Manager, not even Father Lygt himself - would want such an army to rise against them.

It would do no good for her to remind anyone of this. To maintain order among his troops, the Mound Lord needed to show he was in control. Mother Slug understood the politics behind his behavior. So she let him fuss and fume and stomp about. Where was the harm in it, as long as it came to naught?

Besides, she liked this latest Mound Lord. His replacement was bound to be worse.

"The trespasser," he said.

"I don't know what you're talking about," she said.

"Don't toy with me."

Mother Slug cocked her head in his direction. "Sometimes you like it when I toy with you," she said, coquettishly.

"It was a chund!" said one of the guards abruptly.

Brizz and the other guard looked aghast. Averting their eyes, they stepped back from their companion.

The Mound Lord's glistening black head moved slowly in the outspoken guard's direction. "What did you say?"

"I..." The guard's hooked beak rose before falling shut. "Nothing, my Lord."

The Mound Lord nodded.

"But I heard him speak," Mother Slug said pleasantly. "He must have said *something*."

The guard turned to his comrades for support. Their eyes remained focused on the floor.

"A chund entered the room," the guard said. "We all saw it."

"Nonsense," said Mother Slug. "If a chund was here, you'd smell it."

Even as she spoke, one of her pink bulbs burst. It sprayed the room with bits of flesh and its own sweet odor.

"Your scent -"

"You were hallucinating," Mother Slug pronounced.

"What?"

"Whip grass makes an unpleasant cud," she continued, "but its addicts can't seem to help themselves. They say it allows them to see such marvelous things while they sleep. After a time, they don't need to sleep at all. I've heard they have visions all of the time." She gazed down at the guard. "Is this true?"

"No. I mean, I wouldn't know." Nervously, he tightened his grip on the spear. "I swear to you, Mound Lord."

"I know, Kqrrt," the Mound Lord said. "You mustn't think I'll judge you by Mother's words. She may have forgotten how highly I value my guards. She may not know you once saved my life."

Kqrrt let the spear's tip drop. "Thank you."

The Mound Lord's arm came up, a spitzpistol in his claw. "Dereliction of duty," he said, pulling the trigger.

The upper portion of Kqrrt's head exploded. Released from the claw holding it, the sentry's spear fell to the ground. Its owner followed almost as quickly.

"What of you two?" the Mound Lord asked the remaining guards. "Did either of you see a chund?"

"Chund?" asked Brizz.

"It was Kqrrt," the second guard added. "He was the only one."

The Mound Lord waggled his spitzpistol at the corpse. "To the stewpots with this one. No snacking along the way."

The guards dragged the body from the room. When they entered the outside passageway, the Mound Lord closed the door behind them.

"Did Kqrrt really save your life?" Mother Slug asked.

The Mound Lord nodded. "But what were the odds of it happening again?" He slid the door's bolt into place. "Now show me where you've hidden the chund."

"Must we have this conversation again?"

"I want the truth this time."

"There was no chund here," Mother Slug said. "Only a creature of fine sensibilities." She stretched her body proudly. "It came to gaze upon me. It was enraptured with me."

"It killed one of my guards."

Mother Slug's eyes lit up. "It did? Its love is strong." A new thought occurred to her. "You killed one of the guards."

"So? I've killed dozens of them. It's different with a chund. Chund are, well - chund."

85

"The chund is gone."

"How could he have left?" The Mound Lord's eyes searched the room. "There's only the one exit and it was blocked. Nothing could have escaped from this room" His gaze settled on the back room. "Why is the door shut?"

Mother Slug rolled in front of him. "I closed it. It will be days before I feast again."

"Why is that?"

"The chund wanted to be as one with me. I favored it."

"You ate it?" The Mound Lord viewed the floor. It was littered with bits of dropped food, shreds of pink flesh, and pieces of meat and shell.

"Every morsel," Mother Slug said. She poised her thick body before him.

The Mound Lord regarded her with fresh interest. "Was there blood?"

"There is always blood."

"Did he cry out?" he asked huskily.

"I've never heard a softbody scream in such terror."

The Mound Lord rubbed at his thorax. "Your concern for the chund stirs me."

Mother Slug smiled at him. "We spoke in Basic."

"I know Basic."

"Tell me I'm corpulent," she said.

Chapter Nine

In the end, it was the sucking noise that drove Dobbins to open the closet door.

The words had been bad enough. At first, he'd been surprised to hear a conversation he could understand. He listened with amazement, feeling heat rise up his neck as his face flushed scarlet. Feeling like the filthiest of voyeurs, he forced himself to pay attention. If the lovers' steamy words turned into a discussion of edible off-worlders sitting in a nearby closet, he needed to be ready to act.

The conversation had never taken that particular turn. The voices had softened and disappeared. Shortly thereafter, the sucking noise began.

Waiting inside the closet, the outer room seemed to throb with a wet and sloppy reverberation. The picture it brought to mind was absolutely disgusting. Dobbins decided he had to open the door. Reality couldn't be as ripe as the tableau painted by his imagination.

The cubicle's door opened, showing Mother Slug resting in the center of the room. Curled into a tight ball, her sides swelled and depressed with a rhythmic consistency, creating the noise he'd heard. From the center of the ball, hidden among her folds of fat, he heard a lost, enraptured moaning.

Except for Mother Slug, the area appeared to be empty.

"Sweets." She raised her head. "Stay out of the corridor. The guards are still there, waiting for you."

"I've nowhere else to go." A wave of flesh rippled along the gastropod's body, riding down the curls and onto whatever she held in her grip. The moaning grew louder.

Dobbins knew he shouldn't stare. He couldn't stop himself.

Mother Slug followed his eyes. "This is not for you, little one. You have no bodyshell to protect yourself. When I squeezed, your body would burst." She fluttered her eyes at him. "Or would you like that?"

"No!" Dobbins said sharply.

The ridge in Mother Slug's mouth dipped downward. A thousand tiny teeth sparkled in the room's light. For the first time since he'd met her, she looked angry.

"It's too soon," he added hastily. "I've not yet had time to offer a proper courtship. I must win your favor before daring to ask for more."

The ridge lifted, covering her teeth. "You would bring me gifts?" Mother Slug asked. "Deadmeats and decayed things?" A furrow wrinkled her brow. "Others are not so considerate."

Her sides stiffened as she tensed her lower body. A muffled scream sounded from inside the ball.

A moment later, she loosened her body and the rhythmic throbbing sound returned. "I am too generous," she confessed.

"Is there another way out?" Dobbins asked.

"There's the secret passage in the room where you hid," Mother Slug told him. "You have to reach into the pot at the back." She shook her head. "You had time to find it. You're not very clever, dear heart."

He considered the little room doubtfully.

"It isn't for me," Mother Slug said. "It's for my paramours."

He returned to the closet. It seemed to exist only as a receptacle for food pots. There were two large containers against the back wall. "Which one?"

There wasn't an answer. Mother Slug dipped her head into one of the folds of her curled body. The sucking noise faded.

Dobbins squeezed his way to the back of the room. He hadn't forgotten his difficulty in removing a pot lid earlier. But Mother Slug fed from these containers. If her small arms were able to work the tops, then it wasn't strength that opened them.

He tested each pot in turn. Each was as heavy as the other and both made a sloshing noise when he nudged them.

These two pots were marked with a different design than their smaller brothers. Kneeling, he examined the first pot more closely. It was carved with multiple images of Mother Slug.

He used his thumb and forefinger to prod into various indentations and along the carving. The dried remains of spilled food pressed beneath his fingernails.

Dobbins hated having dirty hands. He hated dirty fingernails even more.

He forced himself to repeat the process with the second pot. Again, nothing happened. The pots remained obstinately sealed.

"What a waste of time." Standing, he batted at the ring in the center of the first pot's lid.

It spun, clockwise.

Grabbing at the ring, Dobbins turned it again. Unscrewing, it lifted free from the container.

Inside, the pot was filled with a dark goo. A thin crust had formed over the surface of the goo and mites danced across this fragile support. He barely had time to register any of it. The putrid stench rising up from the container wiped all thought from his mind.

Don't inhale, he told himself, *don't inhale, do NOT inhale.*

He nearly fell over his own feet as he staggered to the closet's doorway. Standing in its opening, he gasped for fresh air.

I'll breathe through my mouth, he reasoned silently. *I won't use my nose, possibly ever again. I'll be a mouth-breather and it won't smell so bad.*

It can't possibly smell so bad.

His stomach lurched at the thought of Mother Slug eating from those pots.

Pushing the image from his mind, he replaced the first container's lid. Twisting the second pot's ring, it opened as easily as its brother.

Again, a pool of ooze greeted him. The surface was crusted over but, this time, it appeared as if entire colonies of mites were flourishing atop the liquid's skin. A piece of creamy-white tentacle floated just beneath the crust. He sucked in air through his mouth, his eyes watering from the aroma escaping from the canister.

He pulled the nightblack stocking up and over his mouth, then pinched his nostrils closed. The odor from this second cauldron was every bit as strong as the first.

He'd checked the only containers at the closet's back wall. They were food pots, nothing more. Feeling cheated, he peered into the outer room.

Mother Slug uncurled herself. In the center of the relaxed coils, a black-shelled Bug stretched contentedly. His body glistened with dripping mucus.

The Mound Lord. Quietly, Dobbins closed the door between the rooms. *Satiated. Probably growing hungry.*

He considered the containers in front of him. *There* has *to be a way out. If there isn't a way out, I can't escape and if I can't escape, I'm going to be caught. I don't want to be caught so there has to be a way out.*

The second pot remained open, its stench growing more foul by the second. Returning to it, he slid his hand into its pool. Its soggy welcome ran up his arm, saturating the stocking covering it. He pressed in deeper, ignoring the floating objects drifting ever closer to his face. With the liquid lapping toward his upper chest and neck, he finally touched the bottom of the pot.

Its terrain was round and uneven, the base as solid and unyielding as the rest of the container.

Dobbins pulled his arm out. Using his dry hand to press a clean section of stocking against his mouth, he gulped in air. He'd have thought the fetid smell would have grown familiar by now, less overwhelming. He was wrong.

A husky voice chittered from outside the room.

The Mound Lord was at the closet's entrance. With this realization, Dobbins forgot about the awfulness of the stocking clinging to him.

"That delicious smell is food." Mother Slug spoke in Basic. "I opened a container to help it rot."

A claw *tinked* against the metal of the closet door's handle.

"Are you to insult me," Mother Slug wondered aloud, "by feeding at a time like this?"

The handle stopped turning.

"And why is it you never bring me any gifts?" Mother Slug asked.

The husky voice chittered, somewhat uncertainly. The door handle was released. Heavy footsteps strode away from the closet door.

Opening the first container, Dobbins plunged his arm into the horribleness filling it. His hand found the smooth, cool bottom. A metal loop bumped against his fingers.

Not very clever, indeed!

The ring rotated without resistance. On the third turn, it dropped into emptiness. Dobbins felt himself yanked forward, the sleeve of his stocking caught between the ring and its swivel. He stifled a cry as he was sucked into the container and through its base.

His upper body struck hard earth as the contents of the pot splashed to the ground with him. Above him, the plug, the ring and its swivel dangled from the base of the pot.

Coughing, he sat up. Tearing at the stocking, he peeled it from his body.

Fingers of light spilled from the closet overhead. The earthen walls of the tunnel in front of him led into darkness, its ceiling too low for him to stand. A Bug coming through the tunnel would have had to crawl.

Hunched over, Dobbins pushed his hand along the wall and started walking. Judging by the gentle slope of the passage, he suspected the tunnel would curve into a spiral, its length determined by the structure of the Mound itself. If he had to follow the tunnel to ground level, he'd be walking for hours.

Not likely, he reassured himself. *There has to be a side exit around here somewhere.*

* * *

Hours later, Dobbins' entire body ached. His arm and the side of his chest hurt from the fall he'd taken earlier. He was hungry and growing thirstier by the minute.

Following the tunnel, he'd hear voices whenever he went over or beneath or beside an occupied chamber. The words were indistinct, muffled by the dirt walls protecting the speaker. At first, he tried to hear what was being said. But no longer. Now, he only wanted to go home.

"I'm not a slaver."

The bullying tone came to Dobbins from out of nowhere. He fell forward, dropping onto his palms and pushing his stomach to the ground. All sense of tiredness vanished immediately.

"You can say what you like," a second speaker said. "I know better." This voice had a hollow quality to it, each word sounding with its own faint echo.

From a prone position, Dobbins saw dots of light shining up from the floor ahead of him. He inched forward.

"You made a mistake," the hollow voice continued. "You're going to be in trouble."

Dobbins pressed an eye to one of the points of light.

A green-shelled Bug was below him, standing in the center of a small, nearly empty, room. A second Bug, long-limbed and thin, was seated in front of him. The second Bug carried a jointed yellow shell, the type most often seen on night feeders.

"I'm not just visiting," the seated Bug said. "I live here."

"In the Mound?" the standing Bug asked.

"In the township."

"But you don't speak our language." The green-shelled Bug held a thick length of root in one claw. "You speak Basic."

"Basic and Squirach."

"Because you're a Squirch."

"Yes!" Agitated, the Squirch's cheeks swelled out like small balloons. "I'm a trader. Basic is all I need."

"If you're a trader, where are your gemstones?"

"You took them!"

"You don't want to say such things." The thick root smacked against the Squirch's forehead. The skin instantly darkened where it had been struck, puffing larger.

The Squirch rocked with the blow. His beak flattened in anger. "I'll say what I like," he said, his cheeks blossoming like little balloons. "I know the District Manager."

Unimpressed, the green-shelled Bug scratched at the scar below his mouth.

I may be new to this planet, Dobbins thought, *but even I realize that's the wrong thing to say.*

The brute with the scar wasn't in the service of the District Manager; anyone working in the hive belonged to the Mound Lord. A newcomer to the Mound, the Squirch was about to get a lesson on this region's hierarchy of power.

His leg cramped and Dobbins shifted. When he did, it sent a stream of powder falling through one of the viewing holes. He held his breath.

Glaring at his captor, the Squirch didn't notice the line of dirt dropping into the room. But the green-shelled Bug saw it.

He smiled.

"I *do* know the District Manager," the Squirch said, reacting to the smile. "I've attended many of his blood feeds. I'm well aware he wants the slavers to increase their body count. Fine, do it. I may even buy a slave of my own."

The Bug adjusted the root in his claw. "The District Manager has his issues. The Mound Lord has a few of his own, too."

"I must have looked like a tourist to you. In a bawdyhut, all alone. Easy prey."

"The DM needs slaves to sell. The Mound Lord wants food for his pots."

"You're going to be sorry you brought me here. I'm a very important Squirch."

The green-shelled Bug swung from his waist, the leg of the root catching the prisoner under his chin and throwing him into the corner of the room. The Bug said, "There's no such thing as a very important Squirch."

He raised his head in the direction of the spyholes. He nodded at the unseen watcher.

So much for Mother Slug's secret passageway.

Dobbins climbed to his feet. If a low-level thug like this knew about the passageways, was there anyone who did not?

Keeping a hand on the wall beside him, he guided himself forward. He didn't want to be trapped in these corridors if the green-shelled Bug came searching for him.

It was time to find the exit. The gods help him, he missed *Mel's Travelrama.*

Chapter Ten

Aly paused outside the seedy structure, searching for a sign above its door.

This particular building lacked both a sign *and* a door. The smooth-edged opening before her served as the hut's entrance, displaying all of the warmth of a gaping mouth. Unmarked and unwelcoming, this bawdyhut didn't exist to serve tourists. Only a deranged vacationer would schedule a stop on this side of the township.

A large, cracked lighting globe dangled from the ceiling, throwing its fractured glare across the room. Smaller globes, most of them in equal disrepair, hung over the alcoves lining the walls. Each alcove sported its own worn and dirty table. There weren't any chairs.

To one side of the entrance, a pair of Bugs sat in a shadowed recess, talking in whispers. Toward the rear of the hut, a second set of Bugs sat apart from one another. No one stirred as Aly entered the room. In a place like this, it wasn't wise to be too curious about a stranger.

And then there was the bartender.

"Pay attention, friends," he chittered in Y'togish. "We've got ourselves a live one." Ensconced behind a hardmud wall, the bartender smirked at her.

The wall had a circular opening cut into it at eye level, revealing the bartender's moon-shaped head. If trouble broke out, he had the inner wall to protect him. More importantly, the drinks and cash were safely cocooned.

The Bug's dull eyes were pinched closely together over his broad beak, his tan face speckled with flecks of faded blue. "You know what I like best about softbodies?" he chittered to the customers around him. "The smart ones know better than to come here!"

A shrill whistle sprayed from his beak as he enjoyed his own joke. Finally, he bestowed his attention on the Terran. Using Basic, he slurred, "You want somethin'?"

"I do." Aly didn't enjoy speaking Basic. She could have used a host of other languages; even Y'togish was preferable to this simple tongue. Basic was drab and uninventive, a tool to be used only when communicating with the dullest of creatures.

Creatures like this barkeep.

"I'm looking for Captain Mulvaney," she said. "Have you seen him?"

"Mulvaney." He rolled his lumpish head over his shoulders before chittering to the others, "Must be the captain's trollop. He's not known for his taste."

His comment passed without a response from the audience. Pretending to ponder her question, he told Aly, "Can't say I know him. Mulvaney, was it?"

"That's what I said."

"Describe him to me."

"I've never actually met him." She moved closer to the bartender's quarters. Corked bottles filled the shelves. Tankards and cups were jumbled together, each silted with a covering of dirt. On the packed earth floor, there was the outline of a trap door.

"Mulvaney is a softbody," she said. "He's a starship captain so he probably carries an air of authority. I was told he was an intelligent man and not unattractive."

She peered directly into the bartender's eyes. "But I could be wrong," she chittered in Y'togish. "He could be every bit as stupid and ugly as you."

Laughter whistled from the beaks of the patrons.

The bartender scowled. "You want information, you buy a drink."

"Water, then."

"I've got better than that."

"Do you serve something with pieces of entrails floating in it?"

"Most of my drinks are like that."

"Water, thanks."

The bartender uncorked a dusty jug. Finding a mug with a cracked lip, he poured a dribble of clear liquid into it. "Two-bits stick."

Aly removed a dibblestick. Counting down its six indentations, she snapped off the bottom third. "Captain Mulvaney?"

"He comes here." The broken stick dropped into the bartender's pouch. "Fairly frequently."

"Do you expect him today?"

"I've heard talk."

"I'll wait." Keeping her mug, she headed toward an alcove.

"What?" the bartender called out behind her. "No tip?"

Aly placed her drink on an unoccupied table. Tugging an empty crate upright, she sat down.

The space cruiser, *TIAN'S GATE*, was in dock. The ship's arrival resulted in rumors and speculation that had spread three towns over before reaching her. Only two of the rumors seemed to have any credence. She doubted the first and was suspicious about the second. Once she found Captain Mulvaney, she'd learn the truth.

The first and somewhat frightening touch of gossip concerned the captain delivering contraband technology to the planet's despot, Father Lygt. A hundred cycles ago, the Council had issued an edict severely limiting imports into the Bugworld. Advanced weaponry was at the top of the Council's list but almost every type of technological advancement was forbidden in one way or another.

Father Lygt could not be trusted. The Mound Lords and the District Managers could not be trusted. Even the citizens of T'ing were not to be trusted.

In general, Bugs were hated and despised by the rest of the known galaxy. They'd earned their enmity fairly, trying to conquer or destroy almost every planet within their solar system. That was, until the Council and its warships stepped in and returned their world to the Dark Ages.

T'ing now existed as a place of push carts and simple tools. At some terrible time in the future, this would change. Just as small-time smugglers brought in supplies of ogrebots and spitzpistols, the day would come when some avaricious fool would dare go further. He'd fill a space cruiser with terrible weapons of destruction, circumvent the patrol ships, and find his way to this wretched rock's spaceport.

When that black day happened, Father Lygt would welcome the fool warmly, kill him, and have his remains for supper. It was the only reason why no one had tried such an exchange to date. Even the greediest of traders had a sense of self-preservation.

Mulvaney was said to be an honest man, as space captains go, making him an unlikely smuggler. Career officers were rarely so stupid as to strike any bargain with the likes of Father Lygt.

Which left the second rumor as the most plausible reason for the ship's arrival.

Mudhut whispers said Mulvaney had discovered two dangerous passengers aboard his ship. The pair was so dangerous, per the story she was given, he didn't dare place them in the brig. Forced to make an immediate landing, his only option was T'ing's outdated spaceport.

Supposedly, the space cruiser's engines were roaring when *TIAN'S GATE* fell to earth. No one had been notified the ship was coming in; by every account, the authorities were shocked to see its great silver-blue hull drop from the sky.

What followed was even stranger. While the spaceport was in disarray, the captain released his two disreputable passengers into the township. They escaped into the township before the port's security force could take them in for questioning.

'Taken in for questioning' was only a euphemism, as Aly knew. The Bugworld had no prison system. After all, a prisoner in a cell needed to be clothed, sheltered and fed. A prisoner in a stewpot, on the other hand, made few demands.

Once Mulvaney freed his passengers, legal entanglements followed. For a time, it appeared as if the captain himself might be taken in for questioning. More recent scuttlebutt suggested most of the problems were finally resolved, with the appropriate bribes made, strings pulled, and official apologies issued. *TIAN'S GATE* was expected to launch shortly.

If there was an open seat on the cruiser, Aly wanted to be in it. She was ready to end this vacation.

"Are you alone?" A stranger's words broke into her reverie. A rust-colored Bug stood over her, holding a metal tankard in one claw, a mug in the other. He set the mug on the table.

Inside the cup's mouth, there was a purple-colored fluid. The Bug told her, "Stir it and you'll find a surprise."

"I've got a drink."

He settled across from her, his bodyshell separating as he lowered onto his haunches. "It's rare to see a visitor so far from the chundhuts. You must have a bold spirit."

Was he trying to pick her up? A *Bug?* "I'm waiting for someone."

For the first time, she noticed that there was a sticker on the Bug's chest. *Hi!,* it read, *I'm Mel!* The sticker itself was torn and wrinkled, as if it had been wrenched in a fight.

"There are places here most tourists never see," the Bug said. "I can show you wonders."

Aly relaxed. "No more wonders. I just want to go home."

"Safe voyage." The Bug lifted his tankard in salute.

She lifted her cup in return. "Cheers."

"You're going to drink that?"

There were dots of color in the water, tiny and swimming. "I guess not."

"Try the drink I brought you."

There were things in the other mug, as well. "I think I'll pass."

A look of irritation crossed the Bug's face. A noise at the entrance of the bawdyhut caused Aly to brighten.

"Excuse me," she said. "I believe Captain Mulvaney has arrived."

* * *

Dobbins paused in the doorway. His arm and chest were bruised, his body a little sore, but he felt marvelous.

And why not? His luck had finally turned. He'd survived his escapade in the Mound Lord's Comb and how many off-worlders could say such a thing?

Not many, he guessed. Lady Fortune was at his side. It was only a matter of time before she fully embraced him.

He considered his surroundings with a generous eye. The bawdyhut was poorly lit, dark in some areas, almost black in others, but the gloom would work to his advantage. There was a bartender watching over the customers but Dobbins had met his kind before. Drop a few dibblesticks in his claw and he'd remain blind to the activities surrounding him. The hut's clientele might prove to be foul-tempered but they'd be a gullible lot. It stood to reason: No intelligent Bug would spend his evening in a pit like this.

It was the kind of place where a man of certain abilities could make some money.

Syr spoke over his shoulder. "I don't like this place."

"Go back to our room," Dobbins said. "You're tired. You worked all day."

Syr looked at him reproachfully.

"I *would* have worked," Dobbins protested. "I wanted to work. They wouldn't let me. They said I wasn't strong enough."

"There's no food here."

"It's a bawdyhut. No one comes to a bawdyhut for food."

"Still."

"Don't tell me you're hungry. You ate at mid-day with the rest of the Grunts."

"They promised all I could eat," Syr said. "It wasn't all I could eat."

"You eat quite a bit."

"It was brute labor. You need to eat quite a bit."

A deck of cards, Dobbins thought, *that's what I need. Dice would do, or starman's blocks, but a deck of cards would be best.*

"They get mad," Syr said, "if you take all the food you can eat."

"I haven't eaten today. You don't hear me complaining."

104

"When I was digging in the mines," Syr said, "I didn't hear you at all. I didn't see you, either."

"There's something you should understand. If we'd both worked as Grunts today -"

Syr made a dubious coughing noise.

"If we'd both worked as Grunts today," Dobbins tried again, "and if we both continued to work as Grunts for every hour of every day of the rest of our lives, we still wouldn't earn half enough to buy the cheapest seat off this planet."

"What would happen," Syr inquired, "if only I worked as a Grunt for every hour of every day of the rest of our lives while you, armed with excuses, slept?"

"You're missing the point," Dobbins said. "I've got a plan."

"Why do I bother collecting my wages at all?" Syr opened the pouch at his waist. "I should have the Dolegiver present them to you directly."

Taking the two dibblesticks, Dobbins twirled them between his fingers. "Money in the bank."

"You know what happened the last time you gambled."

"Trust me, it won't be gambling." Tucking the sticks inside his waistband, he strutted into the building.

A solitary Bug squatted at the center of the room, her head lolling drunkenly above the scarred surface of a table. A money pouch lay in front of her, its drawstrings loosened. A cream-colored gemstone had spilled from the pouch.

An empty crate was positioned haphazardly across from her. It was an omen.

105

The Bug tilted her beak upward as he approached, her one good eye gazing at him blearily. Where her other eye had been, there was a puckered socket. Spittle had leaked from the corner of her mouth, leaving an ivory crust to mark its path.

"I've been looking for someone like you," Dobbins said cheerily to the creature. "A Bug of high character." Even this close, it was difficult to tell if her cream-colored gemstone was of good quality.

From across the room, he heard a voice: "Captain Mulvaney!"

Mulvaney?

He whirled about, his eyes searching the entrance. No one was there. He pivoted slowly, seeking the captain, but found only the bent heads of the bawdyhut's patrons.

At the rear of the room, a softbody stood in an alcove. A female. She waved at him tentatively.

He waved back. It was a woman, the gods be praised. A Terran woman, too. The first one he'd seen in a long, long time.

"Captain Mulvaney?" she called, more hesitantly.

There was a tug at his trousers. The Bug croaked hoarsely, "I've been looking for someone like you, too."

The Bug's money pouch had vanished, replaced by a multi-colored ball and a worn deck of cards. Just as miraculously, the Bug's drunkenness had vanished as well.

"You like to play two-fingered narlap?" she asked. "Three-fingered's better. Riskier."

"Later."

"I've got dice. I can get blocks."

"*Later.*" Dragging the crate with him, Dobbins crossed the floor. He carried himself in a military manner, his chest swelled out in his best approximation of a starship's captain.

He thrust his hand out toward the woman. "Don't believe we've met," he boomed, coating his words with a Scottish accent.

"Aly Krebbs," the woman replied.

Not bad, he thought. She was attractive, in a stringy kind of way. Too tall and somewhat small-breasted for his taste, but not altogether displeasing.

There was a full sackett knotted at her waist. It bulged nicely.

A dusk-colored Bug rose from the side of the alcove. "The creature that came in with you," he said to Dobbins. "It's a shape-changer."

Dobbins' smile froze on his face. "I'm sure you're mistaken."

"I've seen his kind before," the Bug insisted. "You can't go by his frame. His body might be muscled but he is what he is. Look at his skin, his mane." He gripped Dobbins' shoulder. "I've heard you've had trouble with his sort, Captain. Recently, too. Fair warning."

"Yes. Well." He tugged the claw from his shoulder. "Thank you."

"It ought to be worth something," the Bug said. "Fair warning."

The woman was watching the pair of them. Dobbins pulled a dibblestick from his waistband. Before he could break it, the Bug snatched it up. Skittering around the table, he raced for the door.

"Hey!" His outcry did no good; the Bug was gone. When the woman faced him, Dobbins smiled weakly.

"Have you been in a fight?" she asked.

He realized, then, how his outfit must appear. It was dirty and torn, a wounded survivor of his trip to the Mound.

"Exactly right," he said. "There are those on this world who take a ship's honor too lightly. Although they might have watched their words more closely if I'd been in uniform."

"Where is your uniform?"

"On the *TIAN'S GATE*, naturally," he said easily. "A Captain's life is one of rules and regulations, my dear. As much as I'd prefer it, you'll not see me walking these streets in my dress whites."

An inspired performance, Dobbins thought. He sounded every bit as puffed up and insufferable as the real Captain Mulvaney. "But enough about me," he said, lowering himself onto the crate. "Tell me about yourself."

"I've heard the *GATE* is lifting shortly," Aly said. "True?"

The ship is still here? Dobbins said, "Perhaps."

"I want passage on it."

"Me, too."

"Pardon?"

"I'm eager to leave as soon as possible," he said. "I'd bring you aboard if I could. There isn't room."

"Captain -"

108

"But while the ship is docked," Dobbins rested his hand on top of her fingers, "perhaps we can get to know one another better."

Aly retrieved her hand. "What do your friends call you?"

The unexpected question caught him off-guard. "Dob -" he blurted, "- ernack." Why did everyone want to know his name? "Dobernack Mulvaney."

Her face wrinkled uncertainly.

"It's a family name."

"Dobernack, I'm not seeking a romantic liaison. I need a seat on your ship."

"If only I could."

"There must be an open cabin. You've lost two passengers."

"They aren't lost," Dobbins said darkly. "I know exactly where they are."

"So, it's true."

He narrowed his eyes. "Is that all this is about then? Passage on my ship and nothing more?" He scooted the crate over the floor. "Nice to have met you."

He was starting to leave when her hand caught his wrist. Her fingers were long and delicate, her nails were clean. She smelled... not dirty. Dobbins hadn't smelled anything so good since he'd been marooned on this planet.

"Please," she said. "Please stay."

He sank onto his seat.

"Tell me what happened," she said.

He didn't answer immediately. Then he said, "You want to know the truth? The real truth?"

Aly nodded. Distracted, she picked up the mug in front of her. She sipped at it, her eyes widening when she realized what she'd done. Pursing her lips bravely, she swallowed. "Go on."

Dobbins rested his arms on the table. There wasn't any hurry. Syr was chatting with the bartender and the one-eyed Bug had left the hut. Nobody else in the place was of much interest.

Except for this Aly Krebbs. He considered her with renewed admiration. *Definitely worth an effort.*

Besides, it took somebody special to swallow down the bile served in bawdyhuts. He wondered if she'd eaten the eye that came in those kinds of drink.

It intrigued him. Without a doubt, she was an unusual woman.

Leaning forward, he said, "First, I need to tell you a little bit about the starship."

Chapter Eleven

I hate to admit it, he told her, but the *TIAN'S GATE* is an intergalactic pig of a ship. Originally outfitted as a mining vessel, it was designed to carry ore, not passengers. At least, it was until the fleet's accountants discovered that passengers paid better.

To its credit, the star cruiser is safe. Slow but safe, ugly but safe, cramped, dirty, miserable... but safe. In every advertisement, the cruise line crows about the ship's safety.

It can brag about nothing else.

The passenger list is usually full because tickets are cheap. There's a reason for the discounted fares. The ship's accommodations are laughable. Even the staterooms are barely bigger than the undersized beds they contain.

The lone recreation room offers outdated vids and holos, running the same images in a continuous loop. The kitchen struggles to serve its substandard food and the dining hall always has an odd smell about it. One of the passengers remarked that it was as if something had died within the cafeteria walls, but somehow still managed to have fresh bowel movements each day.

Under such conditions, who can blame the passengers for seeking some form of escape, some fresh entertainment? On this trip, that's exactly what they did.

Whoring was a popular pastime, regardless of sex or species, and fighting had its advocates, but the brightest minds sought out games of chance. Unfortunately, there's one drawback for those who enjoy putting their earnings in play. You see, a starship travels under nautical law and nautical law prohibits all forms of gambling.

In the conflict between the passengers' wishes and a cruise line's unbending rules, tragedy is certain to follow. It's inevitable. The finger of blame is most easily pointed in hindsight and there are those, today, who point it squarely at the Captain of the *TIAN'S GATE*.

*

"They point the finger at you," Aly interrupted. "You're the Captain."

"True."

"And you like to refer to yourself in the third person?"

"While recounting this story," Dobbins said, "yes. Yes, I do."

*

A former military man, it may be the captain found himself most comfortable in the role of an unthinking disciplinarian. If so, he wasn't the first. Still, had he let the dice roll and the cards be shuffled, taking ten percent of each pot, everyone would have benefited. Quoting rules and regulations only served to drive the games below deck, into the ship's hold.

As the days passed, the gaming activity grew ever more popular. For the first time, many of the passengers were enjoying their stay aboard ship. It would be too much to say every person on the *GATE* was happy, but the general mood had lightened. A large part of the reason for this could be attributed to a fellow named Dobbins.

*

Aly asked, "Dobernack?"

"Not Dobernack," he corrected. "Dobbins. Altogether different."

*

Dobbins may not have been conventionally handsome, but he had a rakish air about him that fostered admiration. Still, when he first came aboard, most eyes were drawn to his companion, a shape-changer named Syr. Tall and enormously fat, as shape-changers tend to be, Syr was a quiet fellow. Soon, the changer faded into the background. Meanwhile, Dobbins' popularity continued to grow.

If not for one unfortunate incident, the pair would be on the *TIAN'S GATE* today. It started with a run of luck.

Bad luck for Dobbins.

Good luck for the Lizard.

He wasn't really a Lizard, of course. He was a Txarrian or a Vengling; you know, one of those soft-scaled humanoids that uses a breather whenever they're off-planet. He *looked* like a Lizard, though, and his breather only added to the effect. Its hissing noise made it sound as if he was always sibilating his consonants. Even for a Txarrian - or a Vengling - the Lizard was extremely sensitive about the *sss*sounds he made. Dobbins had been indelicate about the subject and the Lizard was seeking revenge. He thought he'd found it through the magic of a multi-colored ball and a new deck of cards.

"Sit beside me, Dobbins," the Lizard told him. "I want to show you a game. Three-fingered narlap."

Dobbins joined him. "You don't have three fingers."

"That's the name of the game," the Lizard replied crossly. "You don't need three fingers."

Within seconds, the Lizard dealt his cards, the ball bounced, and Dobbins lost a small portion of his wealth.

*

"How do you know this?" Aly asked.

"What?"

"What happened in the ship's hold. What the Lizard felt, how Dobbins reacted. Any of it."

"I have my sources," he said. "You want to hear the rest of the story or not?"

*

The game continued and Dobbins kept losing. The Lizard didn't take every pot, some of the others added a trifle to their winnings, but the major contributor to all was the poor, disadvantaged Terran.

114

The Lizard chortled with every victory, his breather hissing merrily. He took joy in discussing the human's ineptitude, the times he'd fumbled the ball, the shrinking of his assets. What no one seemed to notice was, Dobbins was doing a little better with each hand. He was learning how to play the game.

He bided his time. Twice, he threw in his cards rather than accept a weak pot. The preening Lizard grew overconfident. When he bet too heavily on a questionable hand, Dobbins had him. He manipulated the multi-colored ball in a knuckling move that nearly cleaned the Lizard out. On the very next hand, he dealt himself seconds. It swept away everything the Lizard had left on the table.

"Tough luck, snakeskin."

Which was all Dobbins said. He didn't brag. He didn't gloat. When he dealt the cards again, the Lizard left.

The game continued without him as the Lizard snuck his way upstairs to find a dupe to do his bidding. The next thing anyone knew, a smaller, younger Lizard was asking to join the game.

His name was Dix, and he knew how to handle a deck of cards. Despite his skills, he claimed that three-fingered narlap was new to him. When he called for the ball, Dobbins was pleased to pass it.

Dix flicked out the cards and tossed the ball. Dobbins watched him with amusement. Young Dix was undercutting the deck, and dealing seconds, and doing a terrible job of both. He threw himself a losing hand and Dobbins took the pot.

In his youth, when he was still learning, Dobbins had done the same type of thing himself. He could have called for the ball, as was his right, but he saw no reason to embarrass the new player. The deck was reshuffled and the cards went out. Dix knuckled the ball in a clumsy move, a truly pitiful effort, and a good hand of cards went for naught.

Dobbins won again.

Finding humor in the situation, he looked to the other players. They glared back at him in an angry silence. His pile of winnings had grown to twice the size of anyone else's.

Dobbins took the ball. Dealing, he stacked his hand with red cards. Spinning the ball, he threw it so its yellow surface would peak. It was the very recipe for a losing game. He fed Dix four black cards and a green Emperor. It wasn't a perfect hand, but so close to it that Dix could bet heavily and expect to win.

Dix bet recklessly. Dobbins matched him. The others withdrew, muttering unhappily, and Dobbins felt a twinge at the financial loss he was about to endure.

Instead, Dix folded his cards. The pot went to the Terran.

"He cheats."

It was the voice of the first Lizard, standing at the front of the room. The knife he held had the biggest blade that Dobbins had ever seen.

"The human won five hands in a row," the Lizard told the others. "It can't be done. Not in three-fingered narlap."

A murmur swept through the room. Because of its combination of ball and cards, narlap rarely rewards the same winner more than twice in a row.

"I wasn't the guy cheating," Dobbins protested. "It was the little guy. It was Dix!"

"Dix lost every hand."

"Yeah," Dobbins admitted. "He's lousy at it."

"He is not!" proclaimed a white-faced Gligget at the Lizard's side. "Dix is one of the best narlap mechanics around."

Dobbins knew then how he'd been scammed. He pushed his winnings to the center of the table. "Keep it. I'll get my money back later."

"I don't want your money," the Lizard said. "I want your skin."

"Don't blame you. I've seen yours."

For some reason, the quip inflamed the Lizard. Gripping his knife, he moved closer.

"Dobbins." The deep voice, so seldom heard, caused everyone to stop.

Dobbins' shape-changing friend walked through the crowd. Syr was rarely seen in the hold, preferring to seek the earthier pleasures of the ship's lounge. In his absence, the Lizard had dismissed him as a threat.

But he realized his error now. The Lizard lowered his knife.

"I didn't cheat," Dobbins said to Syr. "Not this time."

"Apologize."

"They set me up."

"An apology costs little."

Dobbins knew as much but it grated on him.

"Hurry it up, Terran," the Lizard demanded, a smirk on his face. "I'm waiting."

Dobbins gave it an extra beat. "*Sssssorry.*"

117

The Lizard's eyes bulged in disbelief. Screeching, he leapt for the human's throat. Syr's strong arm pushed Dobbins to the deck, below the slicing arc of the Lizard's knife.

The human fell beneath the card table. The blade's tip ran along the changer's forearm, breaking the skin.

"Don't look!" Dobbins cried, as a thin line of blood welled to the surface of the muscular purple arm.

"It was an accident," the Lizard pleaded, his knife falling to the floor.

It was too late.

As you may know, a shape-changer's instinctive reaction to danger can sometimes be suppressed but the sight of his own blood will force a transformation. Even as the Lizard called out, Syr's head was devolving. His face crumpled inside itself, his arms and legs withered, and his tunic split apart. The cavity in his chest yawned open, revealing a hungry mouth inside.

It was the sound of screaming that brought the captain and his security force into the hold. They arrived in time to see a bronze-colored Swort bite off one of the Lizard's arms. Before they could act, the Swort swallowed it whole.

The Lizard was in the wrong and everyone in the room knew it. But the Captain wouldn't listen to reason, correcting course for the nearest inhabitable planet. He wanted the Terran and his changer put ashore as soon as possible.

*

"So here we are," Dobbins said.

"We?"

"You and I."

"Why didn't you confine the pair to their quarters? Or the brig, if you were worried about them?"

"That's what I asked."

Aly raised a puzzled eyebrow.

"That's what I asked *myself*," he said. "Then I dug into the five thousand rules regarding space travel and found Section IX, subsection V, paragraphs II, III and IV."

"There's a regulation for something like this?"

"There's a regulation for everything," Dobbins said unhappily. "Section IX, subsection V, paragraphs II, III and IV are about shape-changers. The last paragraph can be adapted for morphs and shifters, too, but the section was written specifically for changers."

He slipped his hand under the table, resting his palm on Aly's knee. "Everybody knows, shape-changers rarely leave their home planet. When they go off-world, it takes special permission to carry one aboard a passenger liner. Every changer has to sign a waiver before they can even board a ship. If there's the least little problem, the tiniest little peccadillo, the changer gets off-loaded like so much bad freight."

"Your first concern is for your passengers and crew," Aly said. "You acted responsibly."

"You're too kind." He gave her knee a squeeze. "I might be able to find room for another

119

passenger on the ship. After all, the Captain's Quarters are really too big for just one man."

Aly's arm dipped downward and it suddenly felt as if Dobbins' fingers were trapped inside a vise.

"But where would the captain sleep?" she asked in a voice of velvet.

The vise squeezed tighter.

"With the Second Mate," Dobbins managed. "At the opposite end of the ship. Far, far away from the Captain's Quarters." He rested his crippled hand in his lap. "You don't look that strong."

"How much is the fare?"

"We'll agree on something reasonable." He pictured the full sackett hanging at her side. "Payable tonight, of course."

"Don't be ridiculous." Swaying slightly, Aly gripped the edges of the table.

"Are you okay?"

"It's...." She looked at the mug on the table. "I drank so little."

"Mr. Dobbins!" The name was spit out from behind him, each word accented with a Scottish brogue.

Twisting his neck, Dobbins found an older man at the center of the hut. The man was dressed in the garb of a spaceship captain.

"Captain Mulvaney?" Dobbins stood, throwing a glance toward Aly. "My cousin," he offered weakly.

Ashen-faced, Mulvaney sprinted for the exit. Dobbins watched him go, marveling at the speed of the white-haired man. Too late, he felt an arm curl around his throat.

"What happened to your Scottish accent?" Aly asked.

* * *

Standing at the bar, Syr took a sip of the free drink the bartender had given him. It had an interesting tang to it, a bitter edge that pleased his tongue. Seeing Captain Mulvaney rush past, he lifted a friendly hand in greeting.

Mulvaney blanched at the gesture. He broke into a run, knocking over an incoming Bug as he escaped into the night air.

The fallen Bug let loose a stream of curses. Syr liked Bugs. He enjoyed their gleaming shells, their multiple limbs, their endless shapes and sizes. He enjoyed their imaginative use of language.

He took another taste of his drink. The barler's sand in it added a certain texture to the liquid. The grit of the sand was subtle, but unmistakable.

It wasn't nearly enough to incapacitate him. He wondered why the bartender would try to drug him.

* * *

Aly threw Dobbins aside, sending him crashing to the floor. "I ought to break you in half," she said.

She couldn't believe how careless she'd been. She braced herself against the table as a new wave of dizziness threatened to overwhelm her.

121

If she hadn't been so cloth-headed, she'd have demanded to see some identification. This Dobernack - this *Dobbins*, she corrected herself - may have been the only Terran male she'd seen on planet, the first reasonable Mulvaney, but that wasn't excuse enough for her carelessness. There had never been a cruise line so desperate as to employ someone like *him* as their captain.

Through dulled eyes, she noticed the bartender's sharp attention to her behavior. He dipped his beak and disappeared into his niche.

When Dobbins rose, she caught him by the arm. "Pray you haven't cost me passage off this world," she said. "You're a liar and probably worse. I could kill you here and now and no one would say a word about it."

"I doubt –"

She released him. "Scat."

He touched her lightly on the shoulder, as if in apology. Aly shrugged his hand off and a jolt of pain ran through her. Fire filled her chest, so hot and terrible it threatened to overwhelm her. It felt as if her heart had been torn from her.

Such a thing couldn't happen, of course. A heart couldn't be stolen....

Closing her eyes, she surrendered to the blackness.

Chapter Twelve

Click, click, click! "Useless, absolutely useless."

Click, click! "No meat on her. Not enough muscle to work the mines."

Click! "No good for rutting."

The Slavemaster's claw hovered over the tabletop, but didn't quite drop. "Nothing wants to breed with this sort. Whatever possessed you to take her, Stynx?"

Stynx winced at the sound of his name. "I told you," he said, smoothing the tattered nametag across his chest, "I prefer to be called 'Mel'."

"Nonsense."

"You have the authority. You could change my name."

"Why would I do such a thing?" the Slavemaster asked. *Click, click, click!* his claw bounced upon the tabletop, clacking its jaws together. "Your name is not Mel. You have a perfectly fine name, given to you at your birthing. I know, I was there."

In a flash of insight, Stynx understood how he'd received his name. As if reliving some distant memory, he saw himself, mewing and helpless, struggling to break free of his gelatinous birthing sac. The hive workers lifted his newborn body free from the viscous foam surrounding the sac. They raised him high above their heads so that everyone could see.

"It's a male!"

"A male! A strong male!"

Excited voices filled the birthing chamber. The sound carried down the long corridor to the Slavemaster's quarters.

"He'll need a name," the Brood Mistress said, "a strong name. A creature's future is shaped by its name."

"Pykkt!" someone suggested.

"Klunn!" another hive worker cried.

"Mel!" Might someone, anyone, have suggested such a miraculous name?

Stranger things have happened.

Click, click! "I've chosen the name for this one." The Slavemaster appeared in the chamber, his rasping voice causing the hive workers to cringe. "A special name. Let me tell it to you."

"Stynx!" the Slavemaster said sharply. "Are you listening?"

Stynx bowed his head.

"I ask you again, how much do you think this new slave will bring?"

With an accounting due at the end of every cycle, this was no idle question. While the District Manager was responsible for the total monies collected, it was the Slavemaster's job to provide the merchandise for sale.

The previous cycle had not been a good one and the Mound Lord had expressed his unhappiness. The current cycle was almost over. If the Mound Lord was dissatisfied again, someone would be punished.

"She must be worth something."

"I would have thought so," the Slavemaster replied. "A visitor rarely comes to our planet without resources."

"I've searched her room. You have everything."

"Clothing, a dagger, a few baubles. An empty carrysak, a used sleepsak? That's all?"

"It is."

The Slavemaster asked casually, "What happened to her money pouch?"

"She didn't have one."

Click! The Slavemaster's claw snicked against the tabletop. The Slavemaster didn't have bulk or strength, but his pincers were extraordinary. Notable for their size, age had given them a certain luster.

Stynx couldn't take his eyes from the wicked curve of the claw in front of him. In the Slavemaster's prime, it had punctured many a bodyshell.

"Why is it you lie so poorly?" the Slavemaster said. "It will only handicap you later in life." He raised his claw up, allowing the light's reflection to play over it. "Assuming, you understand, there *is* a later life."

Why did I ever want to be a slaver? Stynx asked himself. It was the curse of his name, he was certain of it. "The bawdyhut bartender was there. You can ask him."

"Ah, the bartender. He tells me she carried a handsome pouch, full of dibblesticks and gemstones."

"It was gone before I took her."

The Slavemaster viewed him doubtfully.

"She spent the evening talking to another chund," Stynx said. "Maybe the chund took it."

"The bartender says he saw it in your hand. He says you emptied her pouch into your own."

"I never did!"

"I know," the Slavemaster said. "I was *lying*. See how easy it is?"

Walking around the table separating them, the older Bug rested a claw on Stynx's shoulders. "She holds no riches, she's a softbody, she carries little meat upon her frame," he said. "Why did you bring her to me?"

"The District Manager's orders -"

"- never included someone such as this," the Slavemaster finished. "Chund, certainly, but not of this quality. She should have been allowed to remain a tourist. It's all she's good for."

Stynx felt the Slavemaster's claw lift from his shoulders and nudge softly against his unprotected neck. It was too late to tuck his neck under his shell; the insult would be undeniable.

"I made a mistake," Stynx said.

"Was that it?" The edge of the nail rubbed back and forth across Stynx's skin. "Do you think we should let her go?"

"Go?"

"Open the cage, return her belongings. Release her."

"You never let them go."

"There are always the food pots." The Slavemaster returned to his place at the table. "Yes, there's an idea."

"I didn't mean that."

126

"What, then? What are you saying?"

"We have to - I mean, we need to sell her," Stynx volunteered belatedly. "It's what the DM wants."

"Did the District Manager tell you as much?"

"He spoke to my cousin, Jokynn."

"Well, what was said?"

Wallowing in indecision, Stynx didn't reply. Anxiously, he rubbed at the nametag on his chest.

"Let me make this easy for you," the Slavemaster said. "Sales remain slow and the DM is growing desperate. He doesn't care what goes up on the block. If it's worth two-bits stick, he wants it sold."

"That could be so."

"But there's more, isn't there?" the Slavemaster asked. "When this inferior chund goes before the crowd, I'll be hard-pressed to find a bidder. If she goes for naught, the DM will send a report of the sale to Accounting. Accounting will send it to the Mound Lord. The Mound Lord will see it and wonder if my skills have diminished. Not a single bid? He'll question whether he needs a new Slavemaster."

"The Mound Lord would never replace you," Stynx said, without conviction.

"The DM would, and happily. He hates me. He'll claim it was my incompetence that caused the last two cycles to lag. My fault, the sales have slumped."

"I never thought of such a thing," Stynx said, without conviction.

"If such a series of events came to pass, the Mound Lord would have my head."

"All of your slavers would weep, Slavemaster," Stynx said, without conviction.

"Then we mustn't let such a thing happen," said the Slavemaster. "It won't happen if I can find a bidder for the female. A bidder that offers, say, three dibblesticks for her. Three sticks aren't nearly enough to save the DM's cycle but it would save me."

"No one would offer so much. Not for her."

"Someone might if given the proper motivation," the Slavemaster said. "Don't you think so… Mel?"

Chapter Thirteen

Awakening, Aly tasted dirt in her mouth. Sand seemed to have crept under her eyelids and her ears felt as if they'd been stuffed with cotton. Her nostrils rebelled from the stifling odor in the air around her.

At least I'm alive, she thought. It didn't seem like much, but she might come to appreciate it later.

Sprawled across a hard, uneven surface, she feigned unconsciousness. She lay still, alert to the sounds around her.

"You're awake."

Still, she didn't move.

"Remain there if you like." It was a Bug's voice, the words spoken in Basic. "I saw your eyelids flutter. I know you're awake."

Aly at upright, causing her stomach to lurch violently. The cage swirled before her eyes.

The cage? She stared disbelievingly at the framework around her.

She was imprisoned. Her belongings gone, all of them. Even her clothing.

It was that man's fault. That liar's fault.

That *Dobbins'* fault.

"Sleep was sweeter, eh?" The voice came from the box at her side. This second cage, larger than her own, contained a solitary Bug. The Bug's bodyshell was almost iridescent in its play of colors.

"Can't you speak?" the Bug asked.

"Yes."

"You don't seem like much."

"Why am I locked in here?"

"To keep you from escaping." The Bug wore a sour expression, as if wishing she'd been jailed near a more intelligent life form.

Aly gazed across the grounds. There were large boxes and small, each holding a single prisoner. Most of the captives were Bugs of different colors and classes, but there was a sprinkling of other species as well. Regardless of their origins, the creatures behind the bars appeared dazed, drugged or defeated. A few lay without moving on the floor of their cells.

In the center of the yard, a Quoxelpede strolled in her direction. Casually shifting a club from leg to leg, it tapped the wooden shaft from cage to cage.

"I haven't done anything wrong," Aly said.

"We both did something wrong," the Bug told her. "We got caught."

"But why?"

Returning to the corner of her box, the Bug didn't reply.

Aly examined her enclosure. Square in shape, it wasn't much taller than she was. Spreading her arms, she could reach the bars at each side.

The bars themselves were braided from reeds as slender as a child's finger. Interwoven with one another, they formed thick yellow rods half as thick as her wrists. Crisscrossed from corner to corner, they let her gaze into the outside world without providing any opportunity to join it.

The same reeds were woven more tightly to form the mat beneath her feet. The ceiling overhead was identical to the floor below. She could find no door, no latch, and no lock. It was as if the cage had grown up around her while she slept.

She pulled at the bars, her arms straining.

The Bug's beak pointed in Aly's direction. "Wasted effort, chund."

"Chund." She slapped a hand against the cage in frustration. "Don't call me 'chund'. It's insulting."

The Bug watched silently.

"Tourists are told that 'chund' means an off-worlder, a visitor," Aly said. Switching languages, she said in Y'togish, "But that's not what the word means. A chund is a victim, a loser. Someone for your kind to rob or cheat or kill. I'm a person, I have a name. Got that, *Bug*?"

Still on her haunches, the Bug closed her eyes.

Typical, Aly thought.

She studied her prison again. If it had a weak spot, it would be found at the joints. She kicked out at a corner. Her foot bounced harmlessly against the ungiving barrier.

"You speak the tongue," the Bug said from her box.

"Surprising what a chund can do, isn't it?"

"You may as well rest. Your prison is made of Lygt rod."

"So?"

"The first Father planted the fields with its seed. The fields are harvested and its grasses sent in, wet, for the Slavemaster's use. His underlings weave the strings together. Once dried, no claw or pincer can break these bars."

"The Slavemaster built these?"

"We're to be sold at auction. Your cage is tagged for first bidding."

Aly threw up.

She'd felt the urge on awakening but managed to fight it down. The bawdyhut's trickle of poison had run like a razor down her throat, only to hide in her stomach. Finally, it erupted. Blue-tinted bile stained Aly's mouth. It dripped from the bars to the ground below.

"Barler's sand," the Bug said knowingly. "Few creatures want such venom in their belly."

Aly wiped at her chin. The palm of her hand retained a blue tint.

"What's your name, softbody?"

"Aly. Aly Krebbs."

"My name is Hhney," the Bug said.

The inside of Aly's mouth felt as if it were dotted with bits of stone. She spat, unsuccessfully, the grit keeping its hold. "When were you caught, Hhney?"

"Day before last. I left my camp and the slavers were there."

"Did you fight them?"

Hhney smiled. "With enthusiasm."

"I wish I'd had the chance," Aly said. "I'd have broken his neck."

"Whose neck?"

"Dobbins. The Slavemaster's flunky. A short, dark-haired, treacherous, lying Terran!"

"A softbody in league with the slavers?" Hhney said. "I don't think so. What would happen if a dispute arose? The softbody would find itself at auction or worse. Not many welcome those working conditions."

"He was in league with them, I promise you."

"Every slaver I've seen has been a hardshell."

"Not this one." Aly remembered the rust-colored Bug bringing a drink to her. Moments later, Dobbins was pulling a crate to the table and giving the Bug some money.

"You must be special," Hhney said. "The Slavemaster himself has been checking on you. He had my cage pushed back to make certain I didn't bite you." She looked offended. "As if I would."

"Hhney doesn't feel like biting anyone." It was the Quoxelpede, standing between the two cages.

Reaching up with an alabaster leg, the guard tugged at the top of the Bug's enclosure. Three of its other legs stretched to hold the sides of the panel. As the Quoxelpede worked, the front wall toppled over.

Hhney rose from her squat. A green puddle was visible in the corner where she had crouched.

"You're bleeding," Aly said.

"It'll stop," the guard said. The front half of the Quoxelpede's body shackled Hhney's pincers and claws. Keeping two feet on the ground, it used its back legs to loosen the hidden catch on Aly's cage.

The box opened and the legs passed the front panel to the ground. The sentry kept its segmented body curled in front of the pair, blocking any avenue of escape.

133

"What if you're wrong? What if she keeps bleeding?"

A pair of flicking appendages reached in for Aly, pinning her arms and legs together. "More for the stewpot."

She felt herself spinning along, her body carried outside of the cage as she rolled along the soft bristles of her captor's body. Weak and dizzy, she found herself beside Hhney as a pair of shackles snapped over her wrists.

"She has beautiful markings, doesn't she? The flyers always do." The Quoxelpede yanked at their shackles, jerking them forward.

"Oh, wait," it said to Hhney, "I almost forgot. You don't fly anymore, do you?" Its lips curled into an ugly smear of a smile. "You can't. Your wings were clipped."

The smile in place, it turned toward Aly. "One less Sktzer to worry about, I say."

Soundlessly, Hhney drove forward, using her beak to slash at her tormentor. Riffling backward, the Quoxelpede raised its free legs to catch at the angry Sktzer. Pushing a single leg against Aly's torso, it swarmed over the other Bug, knocking her to the ground.

It passed its wooden club from leg to leg until the weapon hung over Hhney's head. It said, "Rebels are trouble. You think Father Lygt cares what I do to the likes of you?"

Hhney squirmed beneath the sea of legs. When the club dipped forward, she stopped struggling.

"Better," the Quoxelpede said. "You'll make a proper slave yet."

Forgotten by her captor, Aly studied the foot holding her. Its wide fore and back pads were thick with callus. The inner ridge between the pads appeared soft, the skin so thin as to be almost transparent.

She bit into the fold, her teeth tearing at the sensitive tissue. With a squeal of pain, the Quoxelpede threw her backward.

She stumbled to the ground. "Run, Hhney!"

The guard's legs pressed against Hhney, keeping her from moving. At the same time, it swiveled around, its segmented body keeping Aly pinned to the earth.

"You hurt me," the guard said in disbelief. It dangled its injured foot in the air. "You *hurt* me!"

It loomed over the woman. "Now it's my turn to hurt you."

Chapter Fourteen

A slave auction, Syr thought. *I hate slave auctions.*

Slave auctions, public executions, bio-termination games: they all suggested a certain disregard for life he found distasteful. He identified more readily with the unwilling participants of such events than he did with the spectators gathered to watch them.

A sigh escaped his lips. Where was Dobbins? His Terran companion insisted they meet here and, two hours later, he still hadn't arrived.

"I'm going to do a little mingling," he'd said, back at *Barney's Hut-O-Fun*. "I'll catch up with you later. Go ahead and enjoy yourself." He dropped a handful of dibblesticks and gemstones into the pocket of Syr's tunic. Before Syr could ask where the riches came from, his friend was gone.

Lately, Dobbins had shown a particular eagerness to mingle. Syr was worried by this fresh enthusiasm.

The Bugworld was no place for optimism.

Brushing his hand over the pocket, he was comforted by the bulge beneath his palm. It was a blessing to have this much cash on hand. Even a changer could eat well with this amount of money.

Still, he'd known better than to fill his stomach in the *Hut-O-Fun*. Despite its name, there was little fun to be found at *Barney's*. Besides Syr, the bawdyhut's entire population this morning had consisted of two drunken Bugs and a single unwary tourist. The tourist had somehow been coerced into buying the bartender and his friend drink after drink.

The tourist was a Scarlet Glovt, a thin little creature with a tan, hairless body. When Syr approached her, she hissed at him.

He didn't know why she didn't like him but, now, he didn't like her, either. Let her overpay for substandard fare.

Seeing a crowd file past, he left the bawdyhut and headed toward the auction yard. Crowds were wonderful. There were so many forms to memorize, so many functions to absorb. There were at least a dozen new changes ahead of him, if he could only concentrate.

Concentration was proving to be difficult. Dobbins should have been back by now.

Standing at the outermost edge of the common area, he searched for his companion. There were hundreds of heads in front of him. Most of the spectators were Bugs, but a number of tourists had flocked to the area as well. Off-worlders were often drawn to such exotic events. Sometimes, they'd buy a slave for a few days, before consigning him or her to the community food pots.

An elevated platform, shaped in a semi-circle, lay several meters to the left. Serious bidders were moving toward the display area, wanting to be recognized when they made an offer. Because all merchandise had to be paid for at the conclusion of the auction, Syr knew the bidders would be carrying their wealth with them.

If Dobbins was mingling here, he'd mingle most profitably.

The first slave was led onto the raised stand. Her guard, a Quoxelpede, chained her shackles to a hook in the center of the stage.

The throng around him shuffled in disappointment. A nearby Bug said, "A softbody."

"A chund. Not much of one, either," said another Bug.

"A Terran. Why waste your bid?"

Syr recognized the Terran. It was the female who spoke with Dobbins the night before; the one who passed out in a stupor. From the way she weaved on the platform, it looked as if she might be drunk again.

Pity, he thought. She had a pleasing face, strong of feature but soft in appearance. If he was being honest with himself, he'd have to admit he liked more than her face. He especially liked her naked form, even with the streak of blue on her chin and the blue dots speckling her chest.

His body flushed with a familiar heat.

"*No*," he told himself.

* * *

"Beware of the shape-changer in the crowd," the Blob said. "He has light fingers."

Why is it, Dobbins thought, *that there's always a Blob around when you don't need one?*

138

He'd been *this close* to taking the swollen money pouch of the Bug in front of him. At the sound of the Blob's voice, the Bug noticed the gelatinous shape drawing closer. Repulsed, he quickly left.

Even a Bug had its standards.

The yellowish fellow beside him was undoubtedly a Mandirat or, maybe, a Vankusian. In any case, it was one of those soft puddings of a species that most resembled a melting ball of wax. This Blob was like all of the others, his greasy skin flopping in folds on top of one other and then dripping downward. If it wasn't for his eyestalks, he'd have looked like something slowly congealing inside a food pot. For this reason alone, Dobbins believed, the Bugs should have loved him.

The Blob said, "The changer lacks skills. He's clumsy. I noticed him right off."

Whenever he tried to emphasize a point, the Blob swung his arms. Each arm made a sucking noise as it peeled away from the torso and a wet, smacking noise when it returned home.

"I wanted to warn you," the Blob said. "I feel a bond with you."

"Great."

"You and I, we have external ears. Those others," a waxy finger pointed vaguely at the multitude around them, "who cares about them? Let the changer empty their pockets."

Dobbins couldn't see any ears on the Blob. *Maybe his ears aren't on his head*, he thought.

"Consider this fair warning." The Blob's tone suggested, *And fair warning ought to be worth something.*

139

Dobbins dug inside his shirt for Aly's sackett. If he didn't give this stranger some kind of reward, he'd rant and carry on and everyone would notice them. This wasn't the time to be noticed.

But it stung, it really did, to pay for false information.

At the bottom of the sackett, he found a chipped gemstone streaked with visible fractures. "Here we go," he said, his spirits lifting. "Fair value."

The Blob's eyestalks swung from the gemstone to Dobbins and back again. Lifting a half-turn of yellow skin, the Blob displayed his own money pouch. He gave the gemstone a distasteful flick, as if afraid its presence would soil the contents of his purse.

"Ears aren't the judge of character they used to be," the Blob said.

Petulantly, he bumped against Dobbins before losing his way into the crowd. Bugs and tourists alike separated, giving the rotund lump a wide berth as he disappeared among their number.

Dobbins wiped at his shirt unhappily. It was wet where the Blob had struck him. Ransomed from the *Travelrama*, this was his best shirt, and now it had a stain on it, right at the waist, right -

- right where his sackett used to be.

He searched under his shirt but the bag was absolutely, irretrievably gone. He'd been played for a sucker. An easy claim of 'fair value' revealed where he hid his valuables and the Blob's bad manners had masked the opportunity to take them. Dobbins could almost admire the ease of it.

On the other hand, the weight of the Blob's own money pouch felt nicely heavy in his hand. *Close enough to call it an even trade.*

There was a stirring inside his upper shirt pocket. Dipping his fingers in, he removed the Tatter-rag.

The creature resembled a tattered rag, that was the thing. He'd never owned a pet, had never felt any need to own a pet, so he certainly didn't go around giving names to every stray what's-it he found. Anthropomorphism had no place in his life.

"I had to call you something," he explained to the Tatter-rag.

After stealing Aly's sackett, he'd been shocked to feel something moving inside her bag. If he'd lifted a money pouch from a Bug, it would have been a different story. Bugs saved all kinds of trifles, leeches, and maggots to nibble on later. Aly Krebbs, though, was a different story. She left much to be desired but she hadn't struck him as a closet maggot-eater.

Krebbs' sackett held a few dibblesticks, some coins, a handful of gemstones, and this torn and ancient rag. Touching it, he felt relaxed. Letting it wrap itself around his wrist, he felt something more. He didn't know exactly what to call it but he felt *ready*: sure of himself, confident, eager to take on the world. His mind had never seemed sharper. His fingers positively ached for the opportunity to lift a stranger's pouch.

Pouches that, even now, swirled around him. Curling and flowering the Tatter-rag, he tucked it into his upper pocket like a poor man's handkerchief.

141

Seeing a Bug with a mottled orange shell directly ahead of him, Dobbins joined her. He said, "Beware of the Blob at the back of the crowd. He has light fingers."

Her attention on the auction platform, the Bug pretended not to hear him.

"I wanted to warn you," Dobbins said. "I feel a bond with you."

The Bug pushed a one-bit stick into his hand. "Be gone."

A one-bit stick? Insulted, he hurled it to the ground.

The gesture was wasted. The Bug kept her back to him, her eyes on the stage in front of her.

Dobbins knelt to retrieve the one-bit stick. Depositing it into his purse, he contemplated the Bug's money pouch dangling directly over him. Fat as an overripe fruit, it hung from its carrybelt by a pair of drawstrings. The drawstrings were double-knotted.

Light fingers wouldn't lift this prize. Those ties required the touch of a dagger's blade.

The crowd groaned when the first slave came into view. Chittering voices rose, filling the air. Dobbins eased his hand downward, feeling for his knife. At the side of his leg, he felt a wet, sticky spot where the dagger's sheath used to be.

The Blob was good. He had to give him that.

Click, click, click! "Opening bid."

The words, spoken in Basic, caught Dobbins' attention. "First offer?"

The Slavemaster's grey beak turned from side-to-side as he sought a response from the crowd. "Asking four sticks."

It was a reasonably low sum for an opening bid. Dobbins stood butt his view was blocked by the Bugs in front of him.

"Asking three."

Once, Dobbins had seen a slave sell for less than one stick. It had been embarrassing. Even the slave had appeared chagrined. Only stew meat went for less.

"Asking two." The Slavemaster's voice took on a new urgency. "Four-bits stick?"

Standing on his toes, Dobbins still couldn't see the auction platform. Bumping past the mottle-shelled Bug, he managed a view of the hopeless creature facing the audience.

A female. A softbody biped, a Terran. Female and naked, fairly scrawny, but somehow familiar. In fact, she looked a lot like –

Aly Krebbs?

Yes, that's exactly who it was. A shame, really, but Krebbs should have known better than to visit that part of the township without escort. A bawdyhut like that was no place for an inexperienced tourist.

"Four-bits stick," a rust-colored Bug called. Powered by the strength of his bid, the crowd parted, allowing the bidder to move toward the auction platform. He appeared out of breath, as if he'd been running.

Dobbins focused on Aly again. She was as small-breasted as he'd imagined and a little wider in the hips than he'd thought. All in all, though, her bits and pieces appeared to be nicely assembled.

He felt an uncomfortable stirring in his loins.

"*No,*" he told himself.

"Asking one," the Slavemaster called out.

"One stick!" It was the voice of the same rust-colored Bug, now standing in a different section of the crowd.

Does he think someone bid against him? For a softbody?

Dobbins' nose wrinkled at the smells surrounding him. Abruptly, he remembered the seductive quality of Aly's smell. It came to him from nowhere, this odor of scented soap and woman. A smell like that, on a world like this, was wonderfully intriguing.

What would it hurt, to make one bid?

"She'd kill me," he reminded himself.

It was true. If he purchased her, the unstable Krebbs would likely express her unhappiness in a violent fashion. If he bought her and she somehow didn't kill him, he'd be obligated to dress and feed her, shelter her, *provide* for her, and pretty soon it would be hard to tell which one of them was the slave and who was the master.

He was pretty sure she'd kill him, though.

"Two sticks!" the rust-colored Bug called out. He was hunched over as if he was trying to hide behind the Bugs around him.

"Taken," the Slavemaster said happily. "Asking three."

"Three sticks," a new bidder called out, in a deep, familiar voice.

144

A bit too familiar, Dobbins realized in horror.

The auctioneer seemed confused by this unexpected offer. He searched the crowd, seeking the bidder. "Three sticks?"

"Four!" the rust-colored Bug offered.

"Four?" The Slavemaster asked, sounding positively befuddled. "Four sticks? For this chund?" Belatedly, he added, "Taken."

"Five sticks," Syr said.

His purple arm was held rigidly skyward. Moving quickly, Dobbins squeezed through the spectators. He was almost at the changer's side when he saw the rust-colored Bug shake his head.

The Bug was done with his bidding.

The Slavemaster nodded. Lifting an unusually large claw, he *clicked!* for attention. He opened his mouth to speak.

"Six sticks," a voice said.

This new bid came from a Bug standing a few steps in front of Syr. This one wasn't rust-colored; his brown shell was streaked with the ivory-colored lines of age.

Syr raised his arm again. Dobbins clutched at him. Straining, he brought the big hand back down.

"What?" the changer asked.

"Six sticks is a high price, don't you think?" Dobbins asked. "A little too rich for us."

Syr lifted his right hand. "Seven sticks."

"Quit bidding on her!"

"Eight sticks," said the brown-shelled Bug.

"She doesn't belong on this world." Syr counted the dibblesticks in his hand. "Nine!"

145

Aly raised her head, searching the crowd. Somehow, she found Dobbins.

"You!" she cried, her voice cutting through the noise surrounding them. She sounded angry.

The Slavemaster smacked her on the buttocks. "Silence."

She stomped down on his foot. When he raised his claw to strike her, she stomped down again.

Limping, the Slavemaster dragged his podium away from her. Positioned at the far side of the platform, he said "All done?"

The brown-shelled Bug's antennae flicked the air in irritation. "Ten sticks."

"This Krebbs is as foul-tempered a woman as I've ever met," Dobbins said to Syr.

"I like her."

"She doesn't like me!"

"Eleven," Syr said.

"Eleven dibblesticks," the Slavemaster said. "Eleven?" He considered Aly in amazement. "Taken."

The brown-shelled Bug turned toward the changer. "Do you want her for mating?"

Syr didn't answer. His body color flushed a deep a deep violet color.

"Oh, please, no," Dobbins said to Syr. "No, no, no."

Syr cleared his throat. "It has been a long time since I've mated."

"Twelve sticks," the Bug said.

"Thirteen."

146

"Stop bidding!" Dobbins said to his friend. "You don't have thirteen dibblesticks. Do you know what happens when you can't make your bid?"

"What happens?"

"I don't know. I'd rather not find out."

"You have more sticks in your pouch."

"We need it for lodging. For food."

Syr held out his hand.

Cursing, Dobbins dropped the Blob's pouch into it. Opening the purse's mouth, Syr did a quick count. "Together, we have twenty-six sticks."

He hadn't spoken softly enough. The Bug shot his claw into the air. "Twenty-seven sticks!"

The crowd burst into voice, chittering noisily. Syr looked crestfallen, his chin dropping to his chest. Brushing at his pants, Dobbins pretended not to notice.

"Did you really think you'd beat me?" the brown-shelled Bug asked. "You never had a chance."

Dobbins pretended not to notice the Bug's attitude, either.

"Chund shouldn't be buying slaves," the Bug said. "Chund should be slaves."

And on and on he went.

Chapter Fifteen

So that's what happens when you can't make your bid, the District Manager thought.

He rarely came to the sales and had never before seen a bidder fail to cover his purchase. If this punishment was standard procedure - and it might not be; the Slavemaster was livid, after all, and may have swung his club with more gusto than was usually seen - but if it was, well, he'd have to come to the auctions more often.

Enjoyable as the sight had been, the DM couldn't ignore the problems it created. Yes, he'd seen his trusted assistant beaten and caged, to be sold in the next day's trading, and a memory that special was worth its weight in gemstones. But, now, it was left to the DM to find the female chund his assistant was supposed to have bought.

It shouldn't have been a challenge, buying a slave at auction. You stick your claw in the air, bid whatever you must, and collect the creature. But Oggry had wildly overbid for the slave (twenty-seven dibblesticks for a softbody? Madness!) before somehow losing the DM's purse in the process.

I work and I plan and this is what happens, the DM thought. *I just can't win.*

His original plan was simple enough: Have his slavers collect a dozen or so inferior specimens, throw them into the auction, and blame the Slavemaster when they sold for two sticks or less. With luck, it would muddy the sales reports enough to buy him some time.

If the Father grew impatient with the monies collected…well, at least the DM would have the satisfaction of knowing the Slavemaster was swimming in the food pots with him. He detested the Slavemaster and his freakishly-big claws. If he never heard him *click, click, click*-ing again, he'd be a happy Bug.

So far, things hadn't worked out as hoped. Too few captives had been collected. Worse, the Slavemaster was keeping careful notes when something weak or useless was offered for sale. *Poor Quality Skirch, 2 ½ sticks* was one such notation and it irritated the DM every time he looked at it.

Then, on the very day of the latest auction, it appeared that salvation might be at hand. The Mound Lord sent word that Father Lygt was seeking a female chund. Specifically, he wanted Aly Krebbs, a Terran. One of the worthless softbodies the slavers had captured in a back alley bawdyhut.

The DM couldn't believe it. What luck! To seize this opportunity, all he had to do was bring this Krebbs to the Mound Lord. The Mound Lord would present her to the Father. If the off-worlder was valuable enough, no one would care about a few bad sales cycles. The Mound Lord would be rewarded and the DM could expect a promotion.

Everyone would be happy. Except Krebbs, of course, but she was a chund. She didn't deserve happiness.

The DM told the Mound Lord he had her and the Mound Lord alerted the Father. After everyone had been advised (except the Slavemaster. Best to keep him in the dark), his assistant had said, "She's first on the block."

"When does the bidding start?"

"Within moments."

"Get her!" commanded the DM. "Pay whatever pittance it takes."

Which is when things fell apart. Acting as if he'd never seen an auction, Oggry offered too much, lost his purse, and another bidder came forward. A pair of bidders, actually. These new buyers had been awarded the slave. Soon, they'd be returning to the auction yard to collect their purchase.

Two off-worlder males, buying the female Krebbs. It must be mating season for chund.

Then he saw them, rounding the fence in front of him. Hurrying over to them, the DM said, "Spare a moment?"

"We're busy," the little chund said.

"So am I."

The little chund spoke again. "We already have one."

"One of what?"

"One of whatever you're selling. We each have one. We have no interest in getting another."

"I'm not selling, I'm buying."

The chund plodded on as if he hadn't spoken. The DM sped up until he was in front of them. Walking backward, he said, "The slave you purchased? I want her."

"She's not for sale."

So, the bigger, purple chund *could* speak. The DM said, "You'll make a profit."

The little one perked up. "Let's hear him out."

"Dobbins," the other warned. Purple-skinned - or was it violet? - he resembled a shape-changer but his body wasn't quite right. Too little fat, too many muscles.

A metamorph, possibly? No, metamorphs are mute.

"She wasn't supposed to go to auction," the DM said. "It was a mistake."

"She's not for sale," the purple one repeated.

It was then the little chund's pocket came to life. A tiny fungus rose out of the sleeve, wriggling at the world.

It was strange to carry such a thing, yes, but chund were strange. As odd as it looked, the fungus reminded the DM of something.

Something he'd been told about or heard in a story. In a story?

Of course!

"The thing in your pocket," he said. "What do you call it?"

"I don't call it anything," the little chund said. "Why would I give it a name?"

"Just asking."

"It's not as if I go around naming things. Either something has a name or it doesn't."

The DM said, "Its threadlike filaments, so unusual. Quite curious." Feigning indifference, he added, "Would you care to sell it?"

"I thought you wanted the slave."

"I do."

"This, too?"

"Why not?" he said pleasantly. *Best to appear casual. It would be a mistake to reveal too much interest.*

The chund scratched at the thin hair on his head. "How much?"

151

"Say, five dibblesticks?"

"Five sticks? No."

"Let me double my offer," the DM said.

"You'll pay ten? Not for the slave, just for this… thing in my pocket."

"Yes."

"Would you offer twenty?"

The chund's audacity was remarkable. The DM said, "Twenty sticks is a lot to pay for a curiosity."

"Let's go, Syr."

"I'll pay it," the DM said. He reached for his money pouch.

The chund said, "Twenty was the old price."

"Naturally." The DM exhaled slowly. "How much is the new price?"

"Forty. Forty dibblesticks."

"I don't carry that much."

Behind the chund, two slavers came into the yard. It was Jokynn and his cousin, Stynx. The DM wiggled his antennae discretely, trying to catch their attention.

"I don't want it for myself, you understand," the DM said. "It's for the Father."

"The Father? You mean, Father Lygt?"

"He likes the oddments of our world," the DM said. "He collects them. I'll tell him about your generosity, let him know the name of his benefactor." He would, too, but only if the Father was displeased with the purchase.

The little chund was clearly impressed. The DM felt he might not need the slavers, after all.

"If it's for the Father," the chund said, "why do I need to deal with you?"

The purple one said, "It's time to collect our purchase."

"What's the hurry? I've promised you a profit on your slave. Besides, I'm still interested in the, um... web in your pocket."

The instant he said it, he wished he could swallow his words. *You shouldn't have called it that,* he berated himself silently. *Why did you call it a web?*

He wiggled his antennae more urgently.

"Why did you call it that?" the little chund asked. "Why did you call a web?"

"I had to call it something." Blessedly, Jokynn noticed the DM's signal. He gestured to his cousin and the two of them drifted closer.

"It doesn't look like a web." The little chund sounded miffed. "It looks like a rag. A tattered old rag."

"Fine."

"If you're going to call it anything, you should call it the Tatter-rag."

"I don't think so." Satisfaction in his voice, the DM said, "Jokynn, Stynx, I'm glad you're here. Grab these two. Take their belongings and throw them in a pen."

The purple chund turned.

When the two slavers saw him, they ran from the yard.

* * *

Closeted within his inner chamber, Father Lygt brooded.

He didn't like these funks, he often killed something just to break such a mood, but here he was, all alone, brooding. He couldn't put his claw on it but something was the matter.

It wasn't anything to do with the inner chamber, of course. The inner chamber was a marvel. His spiritual ancestor, the first Father Lygt, had overseen the raising of its rock walls, the laying of its cobblestone floors. He'd had hundreds of gemstones inset into the ceiling, their colors scattered over his head as if thrown by the hand of some careless giant. If the space had contained even a single window, any source of outside light at all, the jewels would have been dazzling.

The centerpiece of the room was a crystal throne. Built during the time of the Devastating Famine, it cost thousands of dibblesticks. Beautiful beyond description, it was utterly useless; no hard-shelled Bug could sit in it for any length of time. The first Father had dreamed of such a throne and demanded it built, seat and all, in accordance with his fevered nightmare.

Giving only cursory attention to the rest of his massive Comb, the founder's interest had remained concentrated on the inner chamber. It was to be his secret place, known only to Father Lygt, and to the hundreds of Bugs who helped build it and the tens of dozens that, even today, helped repair and clean it. Demanding perfection, he found perfection given to him. Three hundred cycles after his passing, the chamber remained as he first envisioned.

Except for the paintings on its walls. Those were ever changing, weren't they?

The current Father Lygt, his brooding teetering toward depression, focused gloomily on the works of art. The first painting had been hung on the wall facing the useless throne, with each new piece of artwork marching in a line away from it. Fourteen different paintings, fourteen different images. Each done by a different artist. Despite such differences, there was a common theme on each canvas.

It's these damnable paintings, Father Lygt thought. *That's why my mood is so sour.*

The second Father Lygt commissioned the first portrait. Although its garish colors had softened with age, the piece still retained a certain vitality. The subject matter, the beheading of the first Father Lygt, was enough to capture a viewer's interest. If the artist had faltered a little in his rendering of the victim (and the first Father's face did look a little loopy, his eyes wide with surprise), he had recovered nicely in his depiction of the victor. The second Father appeared almost heroic in his wielding of the broadsword. The overall effect would have been even more powerful if he hadn't been shown crouched over, as if sneaking up from behind.

The next masterwork, showing the second Father choking on a piece of poisoned meat, had been commissioned by the third Lygt, the second Father's former chef. And on and on they went.

When he came into power, the fifteenth Father remembered standing beside the crystal throne and laughing at the follies of his predecessors. Squatting here now, he realized the paintings had brought him less enjoyment of late. It was becoming too easy to visualize his own body falling onto a pit of spikes (the fifth Father) or drowning in a ceremonial stewpot (the

155

eighth). Only the most recent piece remained entertaining. He still chuckled at the fourteenth Father's comic look of astonishment as he settled into a bed of corrosive slime.

How long, Father Lygt pondered, *before there's a painting wearing my face? Will my look of astonishment be as comic?*

His dark thoughts grew darker.

He'd already survived numerous attempts on his life. Spitzpistols, the weapon of choice, were banned from the Comb. He'd brought in his own kildebeests to surround and protect him. Guards patrolled the outside entrance and monsters lurked inside the tunnels. No one entered without his permission. No one left without his release.

He'd outlived the previous Father by six cycles. Only the original Lygt had lived longer. None of this mattered. He could feel death at his side.

It wouldn't happen. He wouldn't let it.

He gave his love to no one. His secrets were withheld from all. He asked counsel of only his most trusted Bugs but discounted any advice offered. He had tasters for his food and drink; his staff was rotated constantly; and only the Reader was allowed inside his inner chamber without an escort.

He had the Reader castrated to curb his ambition. The Reader didn't seem to mind.

Despite his many precautions, time was running out.

The Reader told him as much, lifting his head from the Book when he realized the meaning of its words. Forty cycles, he'd said. A Father could span forty cycles but never more.

Father Lygt was entering his thirty-seventh cycle then.

Trembling, the Reader retreated into his tome. He expected to die and rightfully so. Only the most ignorant Bug would presume to tell the Father his demise was at hand and not anticipate a similar fate for himself, if somewhat sooner.

Had Father Lygt not been stunned by the prophecy, he might have finished the Reader then. As it was, his claws flipping pages in a blur, the Reader found the passage that would save him.

His mouth dry, his voice rising in volume, the Reader read, "Let me tell you how a humble Bug became glorious."

With those words, Father Lygt was aggravated into action by the other's stupidity. When the Reader should have been running for his life, he was babbling on about the first Father.

Father Lygt raised his pincer to strike him.

"... and he found the Web," the Reader said, skipping whole sections of text, his words tumbling together, "*and his cycles became without number.*"

Father Lygt's pincer remained in the air. "What?"

"Until he lost the Web," the Reader added from memory. "With the loss of the Web, he was glorious no longer."

Father Lygt considered striking the Reader as a way to lower his pincer with dignity. Instead, he inched the claw lower.

"Tell me again," he said. "Especially the part about the cycles."

No longer faced with imminent death, the Reader backtracked through the book and read the section in its entirety. With the discovery of the Web, the Reader said, the first Father's powers grew tenfold and his enemies fell to the wayside. Had he kept it, he might be Father yet. Instead, the Web was lost forever, abandoned in the Cave of Doom.

"Lost forever? What do you mean, 'forever'?" Father Lygt asked.

"It's a subjective term."

"What I want to know is, does this mean the Web *can't* be found or that it *hasn't* been found?"

The Reader's expression was one of a Bug who knew how to grasp at straws when they were offered. "It's lost forever," he said, "until you find it."

"Good."

Since then, the Father had listened to the story repeatedly. He considered learning to read so he could study the tale himself but why bother, really? A Father had better things to do than read books.

The story captivated him, offering his only hope to extend his reign. But, now, he was entering his thirty-ninth cycle.

Time was running out. He had to find the Web.

A timid tapping at the door broke his concentration. "Who is it?"

"Mox, Father," came the toadying voice of his servant. "The Mound Lord of Xzzert is here."

He opened the door. Mox cowered on the ground, his head bent in abject apology for having disturbed his master.

Truly, Mox was the only Bug he could trust. Too weak to pose a threat, he was the sycophant's sycophant.

"He brought his sales figures, Father," Mox whimpered.

Work, work, work. Deciding even a tyrant had his duty, Father Lygt stepped into the outside corridor. "Is he in the Great Hall, then?"

Striding forth without an answer, knowing Mox would scurry after him, the Father remembered he'd summoned the Mound Lord for a specific reason.

But why? There were so many Mound Lords, so many reasons to cajole or threaten them. Was there a punishment due? A reward?

The answer lurked outside his memory, teasing him.

No matter, he decided. It would either come to him or he'd discipline the Mound Lord for some imagined transgression. Everything would work out in the end.

Waiting in the center of the Hall, fidgeting with his paperwork, the Mound Lord looked guilty of something. He always did, though. It was hardly conclusive evidence.

"How do you explain these sales figures?" Father Lygt bellowed.

The Mound Lord jumped, his paperwork scattering. "Fa-aather," he replied, blurting the name. Bending to the ground, he feverishly gathered the loose sheets.

"Sales are up," whispered Mox.

"You're sure?" It was to be a reward after all. Father Lygt felt a sense of disappointment. "I wish I had a dozen like you," he told the Mound Lord with false good cheer.

"You do," Mox said, his voice low. "Xzzert's sales per population count are among the five worst districts."

"How much are sales up?"

"Three percent."

"*Three* percent?"

Startled, the Mound Lord spilled his paperwork again.

"I'm not rewarding this cretin for a three percent increase," Father Lygt said. Could he punish him for an increase, no matter how small?

Why not?

"The chund," Mox reminded him.

His memory came flooding back. "Ah," Father Lygt said. To the Mound Lord, he said, "The chund. Where is she?"

The Mound Lord clutched his papers to his armor plate. "Chund?"

"You told me you'd found her." The Mound Lord stared mindlessly up at him. "The female softbody. The one searching for the Cave of Doom."

"I've done some research," the Mound Lord said. "The guides tell me most caves are known as the Cave of Doom."

"I know." He'd lost three expeditions in various Caves of Doom. "But this chund hired a guide to explore a cave I haven't seen. She returned without her guide. Upon return, she sought an audience with a starship captain. Those are the things I've learned.

"What I haven't learned is what she saw or where she is at this moment," he summed up. "You were supposed to bring her to me."

"I don't have her."

160

"Bring my club, Mox," Father Lygt said, casually. "The one with the spike protruding from its head."

"I had her!" The Mound Lord's papers shook in front of him, as if he were a tree about to shed its leaves. "The Slavemaster put her up for auction."

"Did she fetch a good price?"

"We made an extraordinary profit."

"That will be a comfort to you," the Father allowed, "as you simmer in the food pots. My club, Mox."

"I can get her back!" swore the Mound Lord. "My District Manager awaits in the anteroom. He is an excellent spy. I swear to you, he'll find her. He'll bring her back to us."

Mox waited for direction. Wiggling an antenna for patience, Father Lygt said, "Once found, will the Slavemaster put the chund up for auction again?"

"He was beaten and thrown in one of his own cages. He'll work the trenches for the rest of his life."

"You consider that a punishment?" He gave the Mound Lord a telling glance. "I wouldn't have been so lenient."

He crossed the passageway, stopping under the arch leading into the Great Hall. "Don't disappoint me again," he said.

Chapter Sixteen

The wagon rolled over a carpet of copper-colored needles, its wheels turning almost soundlessly as it moved through the forest. Sasga trees lined the trail, their rusty branches stretching toward the sky. With the sun directly overhead and shining brightly, the setting was nearly idyllic.

Watching Dobbins as he squatted on his haunches, fighting to control the erratic movements of the beast pulling their cart, Aly ignored the beauty around her. Too many memories, both recent and past, occupied her thoughts.

"Transporters live dangerous lives," she remembered the lecturer saying, almost nine years ago. The Vengling faced a classroom of fifty students. Despite the hiss of her breather, her words captivated the audience.

"When you're entrusted with the documents of the powerful," the Vengling said, "someone equally as powerful will want them from you. They'll want them badly. They'll kill to get them."

Sitting in the classroom, Aly saw her best friend blanch at the mention of death. Since childhood, they'd been inseparable but she knew, then, she'd complete her training alone.

"It's no better when you carry valuables for the wealthy," the Vengling continued. "You'll never rest. Who can be trusted while you hold such riches? Deceit will surround you. Temptation will stretch out

162

its bony hand to touch you. Your worst enemy may be the one you trust most."

Of the fifty students, only eight graduated. Of these, one died during his second run, betrayed by a beloved uncle. To the best of Aly's knowledge, only three of her classmates were still transporters.

If the Vengling thought this job was dangerous, Aly reflected, *she should try taking a vacation on T'ing.*

The travel brochure promised a simple world, one never to be transformed by the black wizard of technology. A world of unspoiled treasures and magnificent caves.

The travel brochure lied to her. The chundhuts were dank and boring; the bawdyhuts were dank, dangerous and boring. With chicanery a national pastime, the Bugs habits soon grew too predictable to be amusing. Only the Crystal Cave - now and forever, remembered as the Cave of Doom - had proven to be interesting. It held no fortune, true, and her guide had died. But she'd survived the kildebeests and fought a Zneeth. She'd gotten her money's worth.

I should have returned to the township, waited for my ride, Aly thought. *Done the regular tourist things. Wasted some money, seen the sights, pretended to have fun.*

Even in hindsight, she knew she couldn't have played that game. The pretense would have been as bad as being drugged, enslaved, and sold at auction.

Well, no, not really. Not that bad.

Privately, she acknowledged that the universe was a place of vast perversions. Within the almost limitless range of desires, there might be some vacationer somewhere who welcomed the opportunity to be stripped of her belongings, given slopwork clothing to wear, and forced to ride in the back of a rickety cart next to a genial shape-changer. However, she wasn't that particular person. Her next vacation, she was going to a civilized world.

No, strike that thought. She was never going on vacation again.

The only good thing to come out of any of it was the Tatter-rag. Dobbins was mortified when the name slipped out. Now he was calling it 'the thing', 'the web', 'the weed'. Anything but what it was.

Aly liked the name. *It might be the one good idea the little man ever had. He ought to take credit for it.*

Caressing the moss on her wrist, she ran a finger along a golden strand. Was the Tatter-rag itself a good thing? Or did it have its sinister side, after all?

She doubted she'd ever forget when Dobbins stole it from her. The sense of loss had been incredible. At first, she blamed the feeling on the spiked drink she'd taken. Now, she didn't know.

Having the Tatter-rag in her possession bolstered her sense of self-assurance. Even with the creature locked at her side in a sackett, she felt calmer, somehow better. More capable.

It was a wonderful feeling. If a transporter's greatest asset was her talent for survival, then the ability to reason under pressure was of paramount importance. Almost magically, the Tatter-rag heightened that ability.

But did it? Did it, really? Or did it offer a fool's promise?

When she last carried it, a slaver drugged her. A thief snatched her purse. She found herself victimized when she'd never been a victim before.

She stroked the Tattter-rag's soft threads. It didn't look evil.

"Evil?" she asked herself.

How silly. It was a harmless little creature enjoying the warmth of her body. That was all.

What does it drink? she wondered. *What does it feed on?*

The thought came to her, unbidden. She remembered how much she craved to hold it again. She remembered how reluctant Dobbins was to part with it. The changer asked him three times before he returned it to her.

Transferring the Tatter-rag, the thief's knees buckled. He would have fallen if Syr hadn't supported him. The next morning, he complained that his fingers felt stiff and wooden. He'd been in a bad mood ever since.

What does the Tatter-rag feed on?

It didn't matter, Aly supposed. It would be gone soon enough. She'd made her bargain with these scoundrels and she'd live by it.

After the auction, when Dobbins and Syr came for her, she was livid. She'd be damned if she was going to be any man's slave. Especially *that* man.

"But I don't want to own you!" Dobbins wailed, sitting on the ground with one hand pressed to his cheek. "I didn't even want to bid on you!"

It had been an unprofessional act, really, attacking him before she'd assessed the situation. There was no excuse for the burst of satisfaction it gave her.

165

Dobbins offered to reimburse her for the sackett he'd stolen. She didn't have anything else; her room at the chundhut had been emptied by the slavers who carried her off. Her ticket off T'ing disappeared with her belongings.

Dobbins didn't have nearly enough money to replace the precious ducat or her travel documents. What he did have was the Tatter-rag – and the moss belonged to Aly. Reaching into her sackett, she let it flow back onto her arm. Sinister or not, it had saved her.

Syr told her the DM had offered to buy the 'rag. "He said it was for Father Lygt," the changer said. "If the Father wants it, it must be valuable."

And, so, a deal was struck. Dobbins would finance their journey to see the Father. Syr would provide their protection. Together, the three of them would sell the Tatter-rag for as much as it would fetch.

Dobbins would collect half the money. Aly would get the other half. She prayed she'd get enough to purchase transport off the Bugworld.

What part Syr played in all of this wasn't exactly clear to her. In all of her travels, she'd never known a shape-changer. He was different than she'd imagined. He was quiet but not shy; apparently honest but in partnership with a crook.

His entire relationship with Dobbins was odd. When they were together, Dobbins pretended not to steal and Syr pretended not to notice when he did. By all rights, the thief should have felt shackled by the changer's disapproval and Syr should have felt trapped inside a moral quandary. Instead, they welcomed one another's company.

The changer's legs hung from the back of the cart as he watched the passing scenery with obvious pleasure. Of the three of them, he was the only one who appeared content with their situation. Given any other choice, Aly knew she wouldn't be here. Dobbins, too, made no secret of his desire to be back in the township.

She smiled to herself. How could she have thought Dobbins wanted her as his slave? He hadn't even wanted to bid on her!

Her brow wrinkled in thought. If Dobbins hadn't wanted to bid on her, why did he buy her?

Unless he didn't.

She considered the shape-changer's handsome profile. So far, he'd only been kind and solicitous toward her.

I get half of the payment. Dobbins gets half. What does Syr get?

Some questions were better left unanswered. Aly slid to the farthest end of the cart.

* * *

The krawler yanked at its harness, leaving the trail and wandering toward the beauty of the sasga trees. Struggling to correct its direction, Dobbins snapped his whip loudly.

Slithering forward, the serpent seemed puzzled by the thong slapping at its head. It faltered only after the bit tugged at its nostrils, reminding it of its original mission. Slowly, its cylindrical body returned to the path.

What was I thinking, buying a krawler?

167

"Krawlers don't have a mean bone in their body," the wrangler had told him. Which couldn't be argued, Dobbins knew, because krawlers didn't have *any* bones in their bodies.

"They're docile and eager to please," the wrangler said. What he somehow forgot to mention was that creatures were impulsive, forgetful, and a great deal less intelligent than most of the rocks they undulated over.

Dobbins decided he shouldn't blame himself. He hadn't wanted a krawler. He wouldn't have bought this one if the Krebbs woman hadn't spoken up.

"Only you," she said, "would consider buying something called a 'crawler' when we're in a hurry."

It was her fault, really, nagging at him. Along with the krawler, he purchased provisions and a wagon. Because the wagon had been built for Bug use, it didn't have a seat. He could have sat on the footboard but that would have relinquished all control of the cart to the krawler's whims. For a Terran to maintain the reins of the harness, he had to squat.

It was uncomfortable, squatting all the time. His legs were cramping.

For a few more dibblesticks, they could have outfitted the wagon with a seat. But, no, Krebbs had insisted on buying some clothing.

"Syr's tunics are too big," she complained. "Everything you have is dirty or useless."

"I've got a new pair of pants."

"Too short," she said, "for me, anyway."

It had taken the last of their money to cover her gangly body. Her yellow undershirt was never meant to accompany the too-tight red shorts clinging to her undersized butt. Covering this ensemble with a short, blue robe had only compounded the problem. A less charitable man might have said she was dressed like a color-blind escapee from an intergalactic circus.

Not that he'd say anything like that. If he did, she'd probably hit him.

Again.

"It's not like I expect to be repaid," Dobbins told the back of the krawler's head. "Not all at once, anyway. It's not that I begrudge helping a fellow Terran, either. But a little gratitude would be nice."

Gratitude? Krebbs had never heard of the word. When she was led from her cage, what did she do? Did she fall, weeping, into Dobbins' arms? She did not. Blushing, did she try to cover her exposed body with hands that were seemingly too small for the task? Not her.

Naked as the Morning Star, she stood right in front of him. "This is your fault," she snarled, as if that made any sense, and then decked him with her bony right hand.

A hard *bony right hand*, he amended. The bruise on his cheek was large, darkening, and tender to the touch.

For some reason, she felt he was responsible for her troubles. It was as if he had demanded she go to a bawdyhut and guzzle the swill placed in front of her. Personally, he knew better than to drink from cups containing eyeballs.

Krebbs was mean and humorless. How could he be expected to spend days and days on the road with such a spiteful woman?

Slaves. They were nothing but trouble.

169

A wilicant, Syr decided.

A wilicant would be just about right. If they were attacked at this very instant, if marauders swarmed them, he could probably transform into a wilicant without risking grave physical harm.

Not that a wilicant provided much defense. Its appearance certainly wasn't prepossessing. Should an enemy come across one, he'd dismiss it as a thin, wooden branch, broken and fallen to the ground. If that same enemy strode over the wilicant, failing to step upon its poison sacs that so closely resembled red berries, nothing would happen.

A wilicant offered little protection but it fit Syr's immediate criteria. It was small, immobile, and potentially dangerous. It wouldn't require much energy to make and maintain such a change.

He had very little energy left. His usual good health had deteriorated to the point where he was actively involved in the Four Stages. No changer took such a challenge lightly.

His body was thrown into the first stage, hunger, when he transformed aboard the *TIAN'S GATE*. In all of the adventures that followed, he found less and less to eat. The layers of fat that fed his changes were depleted. It was embarrassing, how obscenely his muscles bulged. His abdomen was taut and flat. It would require many feedings to bring him to health.

It would take only one ill-considered change to throw him into the second stage, wasting. Then his body would feed upon itself. If this happened, it would require a grand feasting to return his strength.

Without copious amounts of food, he'd fall into the third stage, coma. From there, the fourth and final stage, death, would inevitably follow.

Dobbins didn't know of the Four Stages and Syr had never educated him. What good would it have done? His friend tried his best. Had he known of Syr's condition, he'd refuse to eat. He'd give Syr his own food and that was the last thing they needed now.

Without sustenance, Dobbins would grow weak. If his mind became clouded, they were lost. Because, while Syr admired Aly for her courage and strength, it was going to take more than physical prowess to escape this planet.

Their survival was going to depend upon cunning. Aly was smart but she wasn't clever. Syr had never even learned how to effectively lie.

Dobbins was their only hope.

If I have to change, Syr thought, *then that's what I'll do. I'll become a wilicant. The only problem is, a wilicant is only good against one careless, rather unlucky, foe.*

And there are two Bugs following us.

He spotted the first one before they left the township. Slinking after them, trying to watch as they purchased supplies for their trip, this particular Bug was ill-suited to be a spy. No wonder, since he'd never been trained for the task. It was one of the slavers Syr had seen at the *Travelrama*, the one not named 'Stynx'.

The slaver lacked subtlety. Entering the hut behind them, he appeared flummoxed over what to do next. When they bought their wagon, he bought one, too. When Dobbins purchased the krawler, the slaver bargained for a dalapoke. Had Aly and Dobbins not been sparring with one another, they'd have noticed him, too.

Yesterday, he followed their cart to the edge of the forest. At nightfall, he reined the dalapoke around and turned toward the township. This morning, his wagon returned. Two Bugs rode in the wagon now, their faces indiscernible at this distance.

"Syr," Aly said. There was an edge to her voice.

"I've seen it. Two spies on our trail."

"Not them," she said. "They've been tracking us since dawn. We've got another kind of trouble."

Their wagon began to slow.

"Heads up, everybody!" Dobbins called out.

The krawler lurched to a stop.

In front of them, the forest was filled with Bugs. Some of them rested on the trees' lower branches while others swayed from the upper limbs. Their bodyshells were all of a kind, streaked with rainbow-colored markings.

"Not the usual Bug," Dobbins said.

"Sktzers," Aly told him.

Syr glanced behind them. The dalapoke wheeled away, its driver snapping the reins of its harness.

"What do they want?"

"The same thing every Bug wants. Whatever we're carrying. Whatever we have."

Syr pulled back the canvas sheet covering their provisions. "If they need food, let's share with them."

"They won't care about beans or hardtack," Aly said. "Why should they settle for grain when they've just found a supply of fresh meat?"

"We don't have any meat."

She waited.

"Oh."

Aly gestured at the whip in Dobbins' hand. "You know how to use that thing?"

"A little."

"Let me have it," she said. "If they get any closer, I can put its barb in an eye or two. That ought to slow them."

"We don't need the whip." Dobbins picked up the straps of the krawler's harness and gave it a jiggle. "We have a changer."

When the wagon resumed movement, three of the bigger Sktzers pushed off from the trees. Spreading their wings wide, they circled the wagon from above.

"Give Aly the whip," Syr told Dobbins.

"Why? "

Reaching over, she took it from his hand.

He shrugged. "Fine. Keep it, I don't care, but there's only one thing the Bugs respect. Power. Raw strength."

In the air above, more Sktzers circled above them.

"There are too many of them," Syr said.

"Not too many for a hydravore."

"I've been a hydravore."

"I didn't mean, change into a hydravore. I meant something *like* a hydravore. Something as nasty but with fewer heads."

"There aren't many creatures like a hydravore."

"There's a fire beast."

"I've done a fire beast."

"*Like* a fire beast." Ahead of them, the sasga trees were clear. Every Sktzer was in the air.

Syr said, "I was thinking of doing a wilicant."

"Great! A wilicant is good."

"Really?" he said. "I was worried. A wilicant is so small."

"It's small?"

"I wish it had teeth or claws."

"No teeth?"

"If it could move, that would help."

"It can't *move*?" Dobbins asked Aly, "How good are you with the whip?"

"They're coming," she said.

The Sktzers fell from the sky.

The rebels carrying weapons led the attack, the tips of their spears pointed at the targets below. The Bugs were silent as they fell. The only noise to be heard was the wind rushing past their wings.

"I have to concentrate," Syr said.

"No," Aly said. "We have to run."

"Yah!" Dobbins shouted, snapping the reins of the harness. Started by his urgent command, the krawler gave a jump.

The cart jerked forward. Aly fell against Syr, her momentum carrying them to the edge of the wagon. With the humanoid's big arm wrapped around her protectively, the two of them fell to the rock-studded earth.

* * *

174

Striking the ground, Aly's fall was cushioned by the changer's body. His arm dropped loosely as she rolled to her feet.

"Syr?"

He lay motionless beneath the branches of a tree. Reaching under his head, she felt the rough texture of a large rock. When she pulled her fingers out, they were tipped in red.

She reached for the whip. Before she could grasp it, a clawed foot stepped on its lash.

"I can always use a new whip," a voice said in Basic.

Thin in build, the Sktzer viewed Aly with contempt. More Sktzers lighted beside him, their spears held loosely.

Her voice quivering, Aly said, "I've hurt myself." She balanced on one leg, curling the other behind her protectively.

"Life is pain," said the thin Sktzer. Leaning on a spear, he lifted his leg from the whip. One-legged, he stretched for it.

Aly kicked out with her foot, sweeping the Sktzer's support from under him. Before the others could react, Aly dropped to his side. Gripping the underside of his beak, she pulled his head onto her lap. Holding his spear in her free hand, she pressed its tip to his neck.

His legs thrashing, he fought against her hold. She pushed the spear's blade in deeper, cutting his skin. "Do remember," she said. "Life is pain."

The surrounding Sktzers raised their weapons. "What are your intentions, chund?" a broad-shelled Sktzer asked.

"Depends on my options."

"There aren't any," the broad-shelled Bug said. "Kill him if you'd like. Lywd would tell you the same, if it wasn't Lywd you were holding."

The Sktzer stiffened in her arms. He uttered guttural protests from behind his closed beak.

"If you're going to act, best do it now," the Bug said. "Such an opportunity may not return."

"Tskett," the Bug beside him cautioned. "Let your beak be closed."

"You doubt me?" Aly asked.

"It's not a question of doubt," Tskett replied. "You hold the weapon. It must seem very large against Lywd's throat. With Lywd gone, it will seem very small against the rest of us."

Aly heard the flutter of wings. Well before she saw him, she heard Dobbins' voice.

"*You* don't like the Mound Lord," he cried. "*I* don't like the Mound Lord. We're like – like brothers-in-arms!"

A Sktzer carried him to earth.

"Did the softbody fight well?" Tskett asked.

"He *ran* well," the Sktzer said. "His beast stopped to eat the bark of a tree. The chund was seeking a place to hide when we caught him."

"Why isn't he dead?"

"He speaks of riches. He says they carry a gift for the Father."

Tskett asked, "What kind of gift?"

The Sktzer shoved Dobbins forward. He looked at Aly. "Are you hurt?"

"No."

"What about Syr?"

"All of the members of your party are alive," Tskett snapped. "For the moment. Show me this gift."

"It's hidden."

"Why does this not surprise me?"

"I want to make a deal."

Please don't, Dobbins, Aly thought. *Our situation is bad.*

Don't somehow make it worse.

"Tell me your deal," Tskett said.

Dobbins smoothed his shirt. "This is the way it's going to work, got it?"

The other Sktzers turned their beaks toward Tskett. Even Lywd, the spear pushed against his throat, seemed amazed by the prisoner's display of impudence.

"Go on."

"Fetch our wagon," Dobbins said. "The shape-changer goes in the back. You'll leave your spears beside him. Krebbs and I will ride in the front. We'll be followed by one - only one - Sktzer of your choosing. The others stay here, on the ground. When we feel safe, we'll leave your spears and Father's gift in the center of the trail."

"You've thought this out."

"It's a good plan."

"Yet I've managed to think of a better one," Tskett said.

Dobbins stumbled as the collar of his shirt was yanked from behind. An older Sktzer, his colors fading, clutched at his arms.

"My companions and I will take you to our camp," Tskett said. "We'll torture you at our leisure. You'll give us your treasure. Before we gut and eat you, you'll tell us everything you know about Father

177

Lygt." The Bug paused, reviewing the plan in his mind. "Yes, that should work."

"What about the female chund?" one of the Sktzers asked.

"She comes, too. They all come."

"What of Lywd?"

"Lywd will probably die," Tskett said. "Take her now."

Chapter Seventeen

Kaya had been on vacations before, but never one like this. She couldn't wait to return home and tell everyone how wrong they'd been about the Bugworld.

True, her trip started poorly. At first, there was her stay in the terrible chundhut and its awful food. The Bugs seemed to take enjoyment in snubbing her, walking away whenever she approached. She'd never felt so alone. She spent the first few nights with oily tears seeping from her cheek glands.

"But that was B.R.," she told herself. When she talked about her trip, as she would, her tales would begin with all of the things that happened A.R.

After Rypnn.

"I've been looking for someone like you," he said. She actually checked behind herself, trying to see who he wanted. His eyes remained fixed in her direction.

"I need somebody bold," he said. "Someone with spirit."

He knew her, that's what was so remarkable. He knew her *soul*. Where others dismissed her as another workbody from the rendering mill, he saw into her heart.

"Come with me," he implored. "Let me show you a cave worthy of your beauty. The Crystal Cave."

His voice dropped into an intimate whisper. "It's filled with treasures."

Would her friends believe her when she recounted the many nights they spent together under the stars? Would they whisper among themselves, wondering about the guide and the lady, the Bug and the Blob? Would they wonder if they'd been…intimate?

They might. They just might.

What new magic will happen tonight? she wondered. Rypnn lay nearby, not far from her sleepsak. Pretend as he might, she knew he wasn't sleeping. He had something on his mind.

From out of the darkness, Rypnn said, "Kaya?"

"Yes?"

"I have a confession to make."

Kaya rolled over, thrilled to hear such words. Rypnn, too shy to hold her hand, was about to share his secrets. "Tell me."

"It probably doesn't matter." His words floated to her from across the void. "But there's another name for the Crystal Cave."

"That's all?"

"I wanted you to know."

"The name doesn't matter," she said, a trifle curtly.

"In the township," the Bug said, "I've heard it called the Cave of Doom."

Kaya knew she must have misunderstood him. "Caves tend to be gloomy," she tried.

"*Doom*," Rypnn said. "The Cave of *Doom*."

So. Rypnn, her Rypnn, had deceived her. She could feel her wonderful adventure disappearing.

180

"The Cave contains - terrors," Rypnn said, his voice breaking for a moment. "Beasts who feed on the gray skin of Blobs and newcomers." His voice grew worried. "I'm not certain I can protect you."

Kaya tried to order the facts as she knew them. She was on an alien world; in a sleepsak, exposed, on the plains of Xzzert; in the care of an untrustworthy guide who had taken her a great distance from the nearest township; and, come the dawn, about to explore the Cave of Doom.

With a sinking feeling, she confronted the last, most terrible truth: *I've been so stupid.*

"We can start back in the morning," the Bug said. 'We'll tell everyone you explored the cave. I'll swear to it."

Mildly, Kaya asked, "If I've explored the cave, why didn't I find a gemstone?"

"I carry an uncut stone of good quality. It will look as if you plucked it from the cavern's deepest wall."

The Blob wished she could disappear inside her sleepsak, waking up to find herself at home. "Why did you lie to me?"

Rypnn said, "You can have the stone at wholesale."

A sob escaped her, a gurgling cry of despair. Tears dripped from her cheeks, running along the folds of her body before falling into the padding of her sleepsak.

"Did you hear something?" Rypnn asked suddenly.

She controlled herself. She wouldn't let him have the satisfaction of hearing her cry.

181

"There's something out there. Out in the night."

From the fields, there came a crackling noise. It sounded as if dried whip grass was being trod upon by a large, lumbering foot. The sound repeated itself, growing louder, as the steps came closer.

"Stop it. I've had enough of your games."

"Don't you hear it?" Rypnn asked in a quavering voice. "Don't you smell it?"

Once he said those words, she realized there was a hint of something in the air. Something fetid. It could be her sleepsak, though, or even Rypnn himself.

"I'll want the gemstone appraised before I pay you for it," Kaya said.

Not that she had any hope the appraiser would be any more honest than Rypnn. In the end, she'd buy the stone.

"It came from the Cave of Doom," she'd tell her friends. "I knew it would be dangerous but I insisted we go. Rypnn came along, wanting to prove his love to me. And then - oh, poor Rypnn."

If pressed, she'd squeeze a few tears from her cheeks, refusing to elaborate further. Rough-edged and bearing the rock it was carved from, the gemstone would speak volumes to her impressionable companions.

Plus, she was getting it at wholesale.

The footsteps, if footsteps they were, thudded to a stop.

"It's here," Rypnn cried. "But there's nothing there. There's nothing there...and it's standing over me!"

"I believe you," Kaya said crisply. "I believe there's nothing there."

"Zneeth!" he screamed. "Zneeth, Zneeth, ZNEEEEE –"

His words chopped off sharply.

"Rypnn?"

Did he think he could trick her again? Of course, he did; he thought she was a fool. She was smarter than he knew, though. Every devotee of natural history knew Zneeths were subterranean creatures.

A Zneeth on the surface? Unbelievable.

What could Rypnn hope to gain by this clumsy ploy? She didn't know. But, somehow, it was going to cost her.

The noise of crackling whip grass told her the footsteps had returned.

"I'm not paying a single stick more than wholesale," she said. "Well, maybe a stick. No more than two."

To her surprise, it was a Zneeth after all.

Chapter Eighteen

Tskett's body was silhouetted in the doorway. "We have prisoners."

The Leader raised her beak from the food pot. "Where is Lywd? He knows not to bring back live food."

"Lywd's body feeds the stewpot."

"Did you kill him?"

"No. He died in battle."

The Leader wiped a claw along the bottom of her beak. "Lywd did not want me to return."

"He was alone in that desire."

"He had his supporters," she said. "He was strong, not deformed as I am. He would have challenged for the leadership."

"He would have lost."

"If he had not?"

"I would have fought him," Tskett said.

The Leader considered her mate affectionately. "Lywd knew as much. It's why he didn't challenge sooner." Standing, she fluttered her wounded wings. "Why do we have prisoners?"

"They claim to carry hidden riches to Father Lygt."

"Kill them. We'll find the riches later."

"But if we don't? Can we afford to throw away this opportunity?"

The Leader glared at him.

"The male is soft," Tskett said. "Torture will open his mouth."

"I have no taste for it." She closed her bodyshell, tucking in the wings. "Do as I ask. Finish them."

"You can't be weak and remain our leader. Now, more than ever, you must show your strength."

"Is it a sign of strength to inflict pain on the helpless?"

"Hhney," he said, "you know it is."

She followed him into the compound. Sasga trees surrounded them, enclosing the small clearing that was their home. From the mudhuts formed at the trunks of the largest trees to the tiny Mound at the back of the encampment, everything was the color of needles and dirt. It was all camouflaged to elude the Father's eye.

Walking past the Elder's hut, she wondered if this Mound would remain undetected for another cycle, allowing hatchlings to be raised.

Probably, she thought. *The Father isn't worried about a few dozen Sktzers. He's not worried about my kind at all.*

After too many years of inactivity, rebels warranted nearly as little official attention as chund. They were no longer feared. These days, they were clipped and sold at auction.

A clutch of flyers had gathered at the center of the clearing. Inside their cluster were three prisoners, each tethered to a central stake. The largest of the three lay crumpled to the ground, unmoving.

"Off-worlders? Why would they be journeying to Father Lygt?" Drawing closer, Hhney clutched Tskett by the arm. "You brought a *changer* into camp?"

"He may have value. The softbodied male says he must stay alive."

"Destroy it!"

"Soon," Tskett reassured her. "Look at his body. He can't harm us." The changer's skin was molded to the tight muscles beneath it. "When we attacked, he made no effort to change. He sleeps now because he's hurt and sick."

"Is there disease?"

"The meat should be good."

Hhney said, "I want his wrists secured, his head and neck bound. A guard stays with him at all times."

"Done."

The Sktzers separated, allowing Hhney and Tskett into their circle. Leaping to his feet, the male chund cried, "Ho, brother rebels!"

He spoke in Basic. She hated Basic, hated the very sound of it. Although she knew the tongue, she could barely stand to use it.

She wouldn't use it now, either. Let the chund wonder what was being said.

"My friends call me, Dobbins," the chund said, "and I suspect we're going to be friends."

"Shorten this one's tether."

"When I heard the Leader was coming," Dobbins added, "I never imagined she would be so stunning."

Hhney studied him. "Why is it this kind always lives through battle?" She looked to the Sktzer at her feet. "How goes the paste?"

186

The Sktzer crushed the pestle into the bowl. "The needles aren't dry enough. They grind slowly."

Dobbins opened his hands to Hhney. "Our treasure." He spoke loudly, as if the volume of his voice might coerce his captors into using Basic.

"What is it?"

Tskett lifted the item. "A fungus."

The thing arched its yellow body upward, reaching for him. When it touched him, Tskett dropped it as if he'd been stung.

"What did he say it was?" Hhney asked.

"Their treasure."

"That's what I thought." Forced to accommodate her prisoner's ignorance, Hhney switched to Basic. "Where is your gift for Father Lygt?"

The captive retrieved the fungus from the ground. "We trade you this wonder for our freedom."

"Listen to how he lies," Hhney said in Y'togish.

"Does it have a name?" Tskett asked Dobbins.

"I don't know." He tipped his head toward the female chund. "She calls it the Tatter-rag."

"It looks like a tattered rag."

"There's no value in a fungus," Hhney said.

"The Father desires it," Dobbins said "He wants it desperately."

"He lies with such sincerity," said one of the Sktzers behind her. "He could be a Bug."

"Why would the Father need such a thing?"

"We've wondered that ourselves," Dobbins told the pair.

Tskett said, "The chund responds to every question but somehow avoids giving us any answers."

187

"Torture should help. How could I have been so short-sighted on the subject?" Hhney pointed her pincer at the female chund. "This one may have the answers we need. Take her to my hut."

"I make first claim!" A grating voice cut through the crowd's noise. Bulling her way forward, a tiny Bug pushed two larger Sktzers out of her path.

"Soldyn." In accordance with tradition, Hhney bowed her head. "We carry your sorrow."

"A sorrow shared is a sorrow softened." One after another, the words toppled from Soldyn's beak without real emotion. The ritual complete, she said, "Will you honor my claim?"

"I shall." Hhney prodded the shape-changer with her foot. He didn't move. "I fear he will offer you little satisfaction."

"He is not the one claimed." Soldyn yanked at a different tether. "The female is the one I want."

"What is your name?" Hhney asked.

"Aly. Aly Krebbs."

Tskett said, "The softbody killed her mate."

"He was helpless when she took him," Soldyn said. "It is my right."

"Her claim is just," Tskett said. "Besides, the male will provide the information we need. If not now, then soon."

"Take the female, then."

The widow Soldyn said, "By right, I will address my claim in private."

"As you wish."

Aly's hands were bound behind her back before the tether was freed from its stake. Soldyn took the cord encircling her neck.

"May her death be slow," Hhney said. Like Soldyn before her, she seemed to find no pleasure in speaking the ceremonial words.

"May her death be slow," the other rebels intoned.

"May her death be painful," Hhney said.

"May her death be painful," the rebels repeated.

"May her meat be sweet."

"May her meat be sweet!" The rebels cheered.

Lost amidst the chittering voices, Hhney saw the Dobbins chund turn toward Aly. "You okay?" he asked.

"I've been better," Aly said.

* * *

Four sturdy pegs were driven into the floor of Soldyn's hut. Straps were tied to Aly's wrists and ankles before she was forced to lie, spread-eagled, on the ground. Soldyn knotted each strap to its own peg.

"Leave me," she told the guards.

"We'll remain outside your door," the first guard said.

"You will not!" Soldyn exclaimed. "Where were you when Lywd died? Where were you when my tears fell?" She struggled to regain her composure. "This chund's agony will sweeten the memory of Lywd's death. It's my memory to hold. I won't share it with you."

She waited in the doorway until the guards were out of sight. Returning to Aly's side, she said, "Lywd was a fool."

Using a yellowed nail, she snapped the ties closing the woman's robe. "Killed by a softbody. His very death is a joke." The nail pressed into the undershirt, tearing the thin fabric. "I'd kill him myself if he were here. Let this be a lesson to you. Don't let passion guide you when you mate."

The yellowed nail dropped to Aly's chest. It found her ribs, where the skin was red and scraped. "Recent but not fresh. It will do for a start."

"The paste." Entering the hut, Hhney carried the mortar in her claws. She gave it to the smaller Bug. "Use it sparingly."

"I'll use it as I wish."

"If you put too much on a wound, you'll kill the chund. A thin coating is all you need. With the smallest amount, she'll scream."

"You speak to me as if I've never used it." Soldyn ran a claw through the mixture. "This is too thick. It won't mix into the blood as it should." She stirred the paste with the tip of her nail. "Look at its color. The needles are too young."

"The season is new."

"Older needles can be found!" Soldyn snapped. Her expression changed, as she heard the harshness of her tone. "I'm sorry, my Leader. I meant no offense."

"It's been a trying time for all of us," Hhney said. "I can't express how I felt when I heard Lywd was dead." She paused at the hut's entrance. "Let me leave you, in the hope you'll find solace in this one's misery."

The Leader left. Resting the mortar on the floor, Soldyn crouched beside Aly. She lifted her claw, its nail coated with a cloudy residue. "The paste is most miraculous. It brings no pain to unbroken skin but old wounds grow fresh once more."

She lightly brushed the nail over the softbody's abraded flesh. Aly gasped. Biting her lip, she turned her head.

"Admirable," Soldyn said. "No words, no weeping. But the ache was there, wasn't it?" She rubbed dirt over the torn skin. "You're strong. You may hope to cheat me of my satisfaction. You cannot.

"I touched you with the least of the paste. The pain you felt was nothing to the agony I could have brought. Do you understand me?"

With the side of her face pressed to the ground, Aly said nothing.

"Your silence offends me. I could have screams."

"I understand."

"Good." Soldyn lifted a measure of paste from the bowl. "Understand this, too. The agony I could have brought is nothing to the suffering I *will* bring. Do you want to know why?" Without waiting for an answer, she gave her own. "Your scrape is healing. Nerve cells have died. Your body has had time to work, to begin its repair of the damage."

Swallowing hard, Aly said, "With a fresh cut?"

"The nerve cells will be alive, receptive. New blood will open passages through the pores. Trust me when I tell you, there are worse things than death."

"I believe you."

"There's no need for you to suffer," Soldyn said. "Show me the Father's gift and I'll bring your end quickly."

"I'll take you to it."

"I see." Soldyn slapped the muck on her prisoner's chest, smoothing it over her injured ribs.

Aly screamed.

Soldyn pushed the chund's squirming body flat to the ground. Wiping the mixture off, she brushed cool dirt over the injury. "You don't lie as well as your friend."

Aly whimpered.

"The gift," Soldyn said.

"All we have is the Tatter-rag." Desperation crept into the woman's words. "It's an oddity we found. It must be worth something!"

Soldyn laid her clean claw between Aly's breasts. "A few sticks are meaningless." She bent her nail forward, its tip puncturing the skin. She pulled the nail across the chest, carving a short line. "I need riches."

Blood filled the tear. "Please."

"You've taken my mate. I deserve value in return." Cradling the bowl in her arm, Soldyn leaned over her body. "Lywd was stupid, but he was strong. He was going to challenge the Leader for me. He resisted the idea for the longest time. It was only when she returned to us crippled that he finally listened to me. He would have fought her. I would have tasted her blood. I would have eaten her meat."

Her face soured. "Lywd trusted me. I'd have killed him easily. Then I would have led the sept."

Scooping more paste from the bowl, she wiped it below Aly's laceration. "You see what you've cost me? Killing Hhney without getting caught, that's always been my problem." On the unbroken skin above the cut, she added a circle of

192

green. "Tskett never leaves her side. Best to kill him, too."

Two glops of paste went at perpendicular angles to one another. "An accident would be best. Everyone understands, accidents happen." Soldyn squeezed the gummy glue between her claws. "How would this feel on torn wings?"

"I can tell you," Hhney said from the hut's entrance.

Soldyn sat, frozen. "I didn't know you were here, my Leader."

"When I was taken," Hhney said, "I considered it my ill-fortune. I'd gone to meet you in the hollow. When the slavers' net fell on me, I was pleased you hadn't yet arrived. At least one of us was spared."

"Do you blame me now? I was delayed."

"They sheared the tips of my wings." An undercurrent of loss vibrated in Hhney's words. "It was the first thing they did. They stole my flight, but even that wasn't enough. There were questions to be answered. So, when you ask how the paste feels on torn wings, I can tell you from experience. It burns."

"Give me my mourning. Leave me with the chund."

"This is not a chund," Hhney replied. "This is Aly. This is my friend."

Soldyn felt the tip of a spear nudge at the separation of her bodyshell. Hhney said, "When my lies satisfied them, the slavers put me to auction. Aly was caged beside me. She fought with me. If I hadn't been weak and heavily shackled, I might have escaped."

"We bought your freedom."

"Disguised and at risk, Tskett bid for me. No others were there."

"If you owe the chund a debt, I'll renounce my claim."

"What of your act of betrayal?" The spear's head pushed Soldyn's bodyshell apart. Its sharp point pressed against the tissue of Soldyn's wings.

"What do you mean, my Leader?"

"I was outside your hut. I heard what was said."

"I never...." Soldyn's words faltered. She gave a tiny nod to herself before dipping her claw back into the bowl of paste. "Would you kill me for a few words, loosely uttered?"

"Gladly."

"Then you give me no choice." With a sweep of her claw, she smeared the new paste into the chund's wounds. "Listen to her die."

Aly's wrist came free of its strap. "That hurts," she said, clutching Soldyn's throat.

Hhney drove the spear forward. Tearing through Soldyn's wings, it buried its head inside her back. Held in Aly's grip, the Bug uttered a soft gasp and sprawled onto the floor of the hut.

* * *

Hhney kicked the body aside. "The paste shouldn't have hurt."

"It wasn't the paste." Aly loosened the strap holding her other arm. "Her nail cut me, that's all."

"Did she suspect?"

194

"Never. Thanks to you, I knew how to act. You told me to scream and I did. I wept for her." Sitting up, Aly said, "You saved my life."

"The debt was mine." Hhney placed a foot on Soldyn's shell and yanked the spear from her. "We have too few weapons to leave them in the body of one such as this."

* * *

I'm alive, Soldyn thought. She kept her eyes closed as wetness spread across her back.

"What was in the mortar?" the female chund asked.

"A harmless mixture, ground from tree bark and tinted with juices," Hhney said. "If I'd more time, I could have thinned it properly."

Her head bent under her arm, Soldyn couldn't see either of them. *Leave*, she commanded silently. Her body was in shock and pain would come soon. Once they were gone, she could escape into the forest.

First, the Leader had to leave the hut. Later, Soldyn would seek her revenge; yes, she would.

"What's that?" the chund asked.

"This?" Soldyn felt Hhney settle beside her.

"It looks like more paste."

"Thinner," Hhney corrected, "and with a slightly different hue."

"What's it for?"

Over the beating of her heart, Soldyn heard the scrape of a claw against the stone surface of the mortar.

195

"It kills," Hhney said. She leaned beside Soldyn and whispered, "But first, it burns."

Chapter Nineteen

In time, the screaming stopped. It grew quiet in the mudhut. Stepping outside of the shelter, Aly heard the blare of a horn.

"Trouble," Hhney said. She raced toward the center of the encampment, with Aly running beside her.

The sentry's alarm emptied the mudhuts. Sktzers encircled the clearing where Dobbins and Syr were bound. At spear point, the District Manager was brought before them.

Hhney said, "Vykk, who is this?"

"We've captured a spy," the sentries' commander announced. "Skulking about at the east end of the camp."

"A spy, Vykk?" Hhney asked. "Only one?"

At his commander's nod, a tall Sktzer dragged a body to her. "There were two of them," the sentry said.

"His head eluded us," Vykk explained.

"It was covered with blood," the tall sentry said. "I thought I had a grip on it."

"I understand."

"It was rounder than most heads. It squirted from my claws."

Vykk waved at the sentry to be quiet. "The headless one was a slaver named Jokynn. The one in front of us is the District Manager of Xzzert."

"It's rare to see a DM do his own dirty work."

197

The DM spread his arms. "Brother rebels!"

"Oh," Hhney said distastefully. "One of those."

Aly recognized the DM; at least, she thought she did. Wasn't he the Bug she'd seen at the back of the auction grounds?

Maybe.

"We need to speak," the DM told Hhney, "but not in front of the others." He started toward her when the commander's claw caught him.

"How did you find our camp?" Vykk asked.

"I followed the chund."

"Why would a District Manager follow after chund?" Hhney asked. On her questioning look, Aly gave a puzzled shake of her head.

"That's only one of my secrets."

"Tether the spy. Bind his claws." Ignoring the DM's protests, she passed the empty bowl and mortar to the junior sentry.

"Find some old needles," she said. "I've used the last of the paste."

Tskett reached for Aly, locking his claws onto her upper arms. "Why is the softbody free?"

"Soldyn renounced her claim."

"More for the pot, then."

"Want to try me, Bug?" Aly asked.

Hhney tapped Tskett's beak. "Release her."

"What?"

"Release her or make your challenge."

He faltered. "Hhney?"

"Decide."

"I make no challenge." Opening his claws, he dropped his head. "Forgive me, my Leader."

198

Taking Aly by the arm, Hhney led her to the front of the crowd of Sktzers. "I need you not to speak," she whispered.

Aly nodded.

Hhney called, "Tskett stands at my side. Are there any here who challenge me?" Her loud call silenced even the DM. When no one responded, she said, "Soldyn is dead."

A buzz of speculation greeted the announcement.

"Who's Soldyn?" the DM asked. Vykk cuffed the side of his head, causing his beak to snap shut.

"Doesn't anybody here speak Basic?" Dobbins complained. He ducked when the commander swung at him.

"Soldyn sought to betray us. She brought treachery and deceit into our midst. This one," Hhney raised Aly's hand, "fought beside me to stop her." Giving the others a moment to absorb her statement, she said, *"She is as Sktzer born."*

It shocked the crowd. When the first voice was raised in protest, its speaker hidden in the crowd, the words were spat out. "She's a chund!"

"Never," another voice rose up, gaining strength in its anonymity. "No chund is as Sktzer born!"

Hhney shouted over the voices building around them. "Who stands with me?"

Silence fell.

"I do," Tskett cried in a loud voice.

"I do as well," said Vykk. Beside him, the tall sentry nodded as a few more voices rose in support.

Hhney gazed into her sept. "Who stands against me?"

Heads turned but their owners' beaks remained closed.

Lywd would have spoken up, Aly thought, *if prodded by Soldyn. With the two of them gone, the dissidents have no leader.*

"It's done." Hhney released Aly's hand. When Aly opened her mouth to speak, she pressed a claw softly to her lips.

A thick-waisted Bug came to the front of the circle. "What of their treasure?"

"Bracck." To Aly, Hhney whispered, "Lywd's closest friend. Soldyn's lover." To Bracck and the crowd at large, she said, "What of it?"

"May we not see it?" he asked.

Hhney turned toward Dobbins. "The tattered rag."

He knelt, holding it at arm's length. "Our gift."

Hhney took it from him. Lifting it by its sides, she displayed it to the Bugs around her. Their faces suggested it was no more impressive on a second showing.

"The tattered rag has value," Tskett said. "You can see it in the District Manager's eyes."

The DM tugged against his tether. "There are many things I can share with you but I speak poorly from the inside of a stewpot."

"We shall see," Hhney promised. Releasing one end of the Tatter-rag, she let it curl around her claw. "Bracck, bring the Elder to me. The gray-shell may have the answers we seek."

Reluctantly, Bracck left the clearing. The tattered rag glistened on the Leader's claw, shining with a golden color.

"Hhney," Aly said. "Your wings."

Hhney's bodyshell was parted. She'd spread her cropped wings without realizing it.

The faces in the crowd were horrified.

Hhney shook the Tatter-rag from her claw. "It's wicked," she gasped.

"Yes." Aly picked it up. Instantly, she felt better, stronger, as it looped around her wrist.

Hhney's bodyshell folded closed. "I felt whole. I felt as if I could fly." To Tskett, she said, "You held the Tatter-rag earlier."

Her unspoken question lingered outside of her words.

"I did not hold it for long," he told her.

Bracck returned, a stooped Bug doddering after him.

"Hhney," the Elder said.

"Know your place, ancient one," Tskett reproached him. "This is our Leader. Address her properly."

"I know who she is. I helped build the Mound that held her sack."

"She carries a title."

The Elder's antennae wobbled indignantly. "She held no title when I carried her from her birthing sack. Where was her title when she mewed inside my arms?"

"It's all right, Tskett," Hhney said.

"There was no mention of a title," the Elder said querulously, "when she first begged for food."

"Oldest of fathers, I seek your wisdom," Hhney said.

Her respectful words had a mollifying effect on the Elder. "You were always my favorite."

201

"I know."

"I never felt the urge to drown you."

"I'm grateful." She led him to Aly. "Please show him your tattered rag."

She held it out for the Elder. The Elder brought it toward his face. "What is it?"

"I'd hoped you would know. Father Lygt has displayed an interest in it."

With a squawk, the Elder threw it to the ground. "It moved! It reached for me!"

The District Manager smirked at the Sktzers around him, as if he alone held some marvelous secret. The Elder said, "It's alive."

"Yes," Hhney said wearily, "yes, we noticed."

"Father Lygt?" The Elder remained rooted in his spot. "He wants it?"

"Yes."

The Elder's body tottered forward. He raised the Tatter-rag to his eyes. "Father Lygt," he said, staring at the moss as though he'd never seen such an object.

Irritation twisted Tskett's face.

The Elder's pitted beak bobbed up and down. "I know what this is."

"Tell us."

"There were stories about it." He stroked the Tatter-rag with reverence. "Legends, really."

The expression of smug satisfaction vanished from the DM's face. "Old fool. He remembers nothing."

"A long time ago," the Elder said, "before we recorded time, our tribes were as one. The Sktzers were strong. This was our strength and our symbol."

"Why waste your time, listening to his prattle?" demanded the DM.

"This is the Web," the old Bug said. "The Web of the World."

* * *

The old-timer is certainly chattering on, Dobbins thought. *In Y'togish, naturally.*

Wonder what he's saying?

Whatever the words, he'd captured his audience's attention. In some manner, the Tatter-rag had allowed this antique to seize a moment of glory. Dobbins could tell the old Bug was going to milk this moment for everything it was worth. He clearly intended to share every last bit of his wisdom with the unsuspecting Sktzers around him.

It's all Bug stuff, anyway, Dobbins decided. *Doesn't matter to me.*

The guard watching over Syr was as captivated as any by the Elder's speech. His spear hung loosely over the shape-changer's stomach. To Dobbins' relief, Syr's chest was rising and falling with a comforting regularity.

Dobbins pulled lightly at the collar around his neck, his fingers running over it without finding a catch. Its tether was staked to the ground but the leash was long.

He edged closer to the changer. "Syr, wake up."

His words caused the guard's claw to snap onto the shaft of the spear. He gestured angrily at the prisoner.

Dobbins moved back. It took only a few short steps for the guard to ignore him again. Fascinated by the Elder's speech, he focused on the old gasbag.

Dobbins had to act. Somehow, Syr had to be awakened.

He collected a few rocks from the ground. As bad as their situation was - and it was bad, almost as bad as the fiasco on Tiq Woo - he had a feeling that things were about to get worse.

While it was good to see Aly somehow still alive, he didn't think her survival would help their immediate situation. It didn't even matter that she seemed to have been accepted by the head Bug, the one with the bad wings. No, there was trouble ahead.

There was a thing in the bushes. Red-bodied. Bulbous. Too many legs. Too big a mouth with too many teeth.

A mouth that large was made for one purpose. It was made for eating other creatures. Bugs, probably, but softbodied creatures, without a doubt.

Pretending to stretch, he lobbed a pebble in Syr's direction. The stone skipped under the guard's gaze and across the changer's tunic without effect. Pinching a similar rock between two fingers, he made another try. This time, the oval-shaped pebble bounced off the humanoid's thigh.

Syr slept on.

The creature in the bushes approved of his efforts. Raising a bristled foreleg, it waved at him encouragingly. Dobbins could have sworn the thing was grinning.

From the opposite side of the camp, a second beast scuttled from tree trunk to tree trunk. Its four pairs of legs lent it speed as it bobbed along the outskirts of the clearing.

Then Dobbins saw a second pair of the things, crouched among the trees. Had the sentries remained on alert, one or more of the monsters would almost certainly have been spotted. As things stood, the sentries had abandoned their posts when they'd captured the District Manager. The commander and his immediate subordinate stood with their backs to the new visitors, unaware of their arrival.

The Sktzers were dangerous but the big-mouthed brutes surrounding the camp might be even worse. Dobbins shivered with repugnance. Holding a larger stone between his thumb and forefinger, he threw it forcefully. Shooting over Syr's chest, the rock caught the guard on his lower leg.

The guard jumped. Rubbing the injured area, he glared at Dobbins.

Pretending to be busy, Dobbins drew a stick figure in the dirt. From the corner of an eye, he saw the guard seeking the guilty party. The Sktzer considered Dobbins and, then, the unconscious Syr. Finally, the Bug stared at the District Manager.

The DM smiled at the guard. The smile appeared particularly unctuous.

Favoring his sore leg, the guard walked over to the official. Without saying a word, he shoved him. The DM pitched forward, crying out, his tether trailing the collar as he fell. He gave a little bounce as he struck the earthen floor, spinning about, and his claws came into the guard's view.

The DM's claws were bound securely.

The guard stomped over to Dobbins. "Why aren't your hands bound?"

"My hands are weak," Dobbins said. He'd removed the bindings on his wrists almost as soon as they'd been applied. "My nails are useless. Why would anyone bind me?"

"Protocol should be followed," the guard complained. "How are we to defeat Father Lygt if we don't observe our own rules? Soft and useless as you are, the Father would have had his guards bind you."

"Tie me, then, if you must. I mean, if you're scared."

The guard pushed Dobbins over. Striking the ground, he gave a bounce not unlike that of the DM. Pleased, the sentry returned to his post to listen to the Elder.

Ignored again, Dobbins crawled over to Syr. "Wake up."

In response, his friend rolled onto his side.

Stretching his tether as far as he could, Dobbins worked the knots holding the changer's wrists. Softly, he said, "Time to eat."

Syr's eyes fluttered open. Before he could speak, Dobbins clapped a hand over his mouth. "Hushed words."

Syr nodded in understanding. Once the hand was removed, he said, "I'm hungry."

"We're in trouble."

"How bad is it?"

"It's a lot like the time on Tiq Woo. Only, imagine if the Rat King had been replaced by giant arachnids."

Syr's eyes widened. Sitting up, his hands found the collar around his neck.

"And this time," Dobbins continued, "we don't have some self-proclaimed wizard to help us."

206

"I must feed."

"You could eat the Sktzers if you changed into something really big."

"You know it doesn't work that way."

"You could eat one of the red-bulbed things." A movement in the forest turned his head. "There's one!"

One of the monsters leapt onto the trunk of a tree. It hung onto the bark briefly before climbing toward the upper branches. It moved effortlessly, vanishing among the cluster of needles above it.

"How many are there?"

"I've seen five so far. I'm guessing there's more. Why?"

"When you told me our situation was like the time at the citadel, only worse," Syr said faintly, "I thought you were exaggerating."

"I wasn't?"

The butt of a spear slapped the ground between them.

"You," the guard said, staring down at Syr. "You're awake!" He shouted to the crowd around the Elder, "The changer is awake!"

Hhney signaled for the Elder to stop speaking. Her eyes flicked from the guard to the softbody to the shape-changer.

Smiling, she said, "How wonderful."

* * *

Tskett moved in front of Hhney, blocking the prisoners' view. "Wonderful?"

207

"The shape-changer must be mollified. Have you noticed his hands are free? Have you seen the strength in his arms?"

"A changer with rolls of fat is powerful. This one is hungry."

"Would you risk it? I won't." To Aly, she said, "Does the purple one speak our tongue?"

"Fluently."

"Tell the shape-changer he's safe with us. Use Basic so his little companion understands, as well."

"Are they safe?"

She turned to Tskett. "When they're relaxed, end them. The changer first."

"No!" Aly gripped the spear in the warrior's claw.

Tskett tried to pull away from her. She put a second hand on the weapon, fighting to keep it.

"End them?" Aly asked. "*Kill* them?"

"They'll not feel the spear," Hhney assured her. "No one wields the weapon better than Tskett. It will be a kindness."

"You can't."

"We do what's best for the sept. You're one of us now. Act like it."

"As a Sktzer born."

Tskett released his spear. "Keep it, softbody. I'll find another tool for the job."

Aly blocked Tskett's exit. "If I'm one of you, how can you do this?"

"Don't feel pity for them just because you've traveled at their side," Hhney said. "The changer is not welcomed here. His companion is a hindrance. We'd be best served if they were dead."

"What about the District Manager?"

208

"His time will come. He may yet have a value."

"You'd let the DM live," Aly said. "But you would kill - my - my mate?"

"Your mate?" Tskett froze.

"That's right."

Hhney looked past her and at the captives. "I didn't know."

"You do now."

"Yes," Hhney said. "Of course, we'll spare the life of your partner. With which one are you joined?"

Sighing, Aly said, "Both of them."

Chapter Twenty

Crouched behind the gangan bush, Puff waited for the exactly-right-perfect moment to invade the Sktzers' encampment. Waiting didn't come naturally to her; as one of Father Lygt's Assassins, she much preferred a quick, brutal kill. Today, in an effort to display her leadership abilities, she remained in place.

Waiting, waiting, *waiting*, for the perfect moment to attack.

She could feel the other kildebeests stirring around her. They didn't like to wait, either.

When they went on this mission, Father Lygt's flunky gave them a whole list of instructions. The Assassins were to follow the District Manager, watch out for the raggedy thing, do this, do that, beware of this, watch out for that....

Really, it was a bit much. An Assassin's job was to kill things. Rend their meat and spray their blood.

"Munch them up," Puff said to herself.

Munch them up is what an Assassin did best. It wasn't fair to ask them to do anything more. Besides, how was a kildebeest to remember everything the Father wanted?

The part Puff did remember was Mox standing beside her, saying urgently, "*This next part is vitally important.*" But he looked so solemn when he said it, his tiny Bug face all folded and bent with concern, that Puff wanted to laugh. Now, all she could remember was Mox saying, *"This next part is vitally important"*, all crunched up with worry. Whatever he said next was lost in the mists of memory.

A giggle escaped from her. Well, it couldn't have been *vitally* important, could it?, or she'd still remember whatever it was he told her.

From the bush beside her, she saw her second-in-command, Tink, rise up, wiggle a red foreleg, and then flop down behind the bush.

Tink did it again – *wiggle, wiggle* – before again flattening himself to the ground.

"What are you doing?" Puff asked.

Tink shifted his eyes elsewhere, pretending he hadn't heard.

"Tell me."

"The softbody."

"So?"

"It amuses me." Tink scuffed a rear leg over the dirt, kicking dry needles into the air. "It saw me and its mouth dropped open. Its eyes got big."

"It saw you?"

"It didn't tell anyone."

"Stop waving at it!" Puff surveyed the encampment. Trust a softbody to stay quiet? Softbodies weren't any good at keeping secrets.

An hour earlier, the Sktzers had grouped together, drawn to the old Bug. Now that the Elder had stopped talking, some of them were drifting off. Soon, one of their sentries would enter the forest. An alarm would be sounded and the element of surprise would be lost.

But where was the raggedy thing the softbody carried with him?

Puff had meant to keep an eye on it. It was one of the few instructions she remembered but, at a critical moment, she'd been distracted by a cloud drifting overhead. Blue-tinted and stringy, the cloud shifted shape as she watched. For a brief time, it resembled Father Lygt, eating his own head.

It was such an amusing sight she'd forgotten all about the raggedy thing. When she turned back, the softbody had lost it. She was almost positive one of the Bugs had taken it.

Although the softbody might have eaten it. She wondered if it was in his belly.

There was only one way to find out.

"The raggedy thing," Tink said in a low voice. "There it is!"

Then Puff saw it, too. With the Elder's followers disbanding, there was an open avenue leading from him and into the forest. The Elder stood at the end of this empty column, an appearance of self-satisfaction on his Buggy face. The raggedy thing was in plain view, clinging to his arm.

"Want me to get it?" Tink asked.

"Race you," Puff said.

"Rend their meat."

"Spray their blood."

"Munch them up!" they said together.

Their bulbous bodies shook with suppressed laughter. Puff raised two arms, signaling to the other kildebeests to ready themselves.

"Fun, fun, fun," she said.

* * *

One after the other, the swarm invaded the camp. Skirting the underbrush, bounding past the bushes and trees, they fell onto the unprepared Sktzers.

"Kildebeest!" the Elder shrieked as a red-bulbed beast leapt upon him. With a twist of its fangs, the invader ripped the old Bug's life away.

The District Manager whirled about, watching the Elder's killer run for cover. He saw the Web held in one of its legs.

"About time," he grumbled.

Pandemonium erupted around him. Working in pairs, the kildebeests brought the Sktzers down, slashing at their legs and finding their throats.

The Sktzers' crippled Leader stood back-to-back with the chund she'd welcomed into her rebel band. Wielding spears, they swept their weapons at the kildebeests crouched before them.

"Don't hurt the softbody!" the DM called out to the Father's Assassins. His words disappeared in the uproar around him.

He could only hope the kildebeests remembered what Mox had told them. He'd stood beside the flunky as he went through his instructions.

"This next part is vitally important," Mox said, wrapping things up. "Bring the female chund to the Father."

Puff, the lead Assassin, appeared amused by this command.

"Make certain you bring her back alive." Then Mox said a peculiar thing: "It will be on the District Manager's head if you don't."

Why should it be on my head? the DM worried. *It should be on the Assassins' heads! On Puff's head!*

But, no, nothing would happen to them, no matter how badly they performed. The Father loved his pets. He bred them more for their striking color than for their intelligence. Raised by the Father, trained to obey the Father, they were pampered from birth. He taught them how to behave. They actually followed his commands.

Most of the time.

The DM yanked at his tether, trying to pull it free. No good. Seeking help, he saw a kildebeest feint toward the Leader, withdrawing as the point of her spear nearly caught him.

The kildebeests grinned at one another. When they did, the chund slashed at the nearest one, slicing away its foreleg and sending it to the dirt. Before the beast could bring itself upright, the chund thrust her spear into its body.

It skewered the squealing thing, pinning it to the ground. When the softbody pulled her spear free, the Assassin was dead.

The grin gone from its face, its partner moved out of range.

The Leader gave a bleating cry, one claw pointed upward. Tskett – her second-in-command? Her lover? What? – took to the sky. As if of one mind, the remaining Sktzers unfolded their wings and followed.

Airborne, they met one last defeat. The trees that had sheltered their camp for so long held murderers that leapt from their coppered limbs, flinging themselves into space.

Falling, the kildebeests clutched onto whichever Bug was closest. Tskett avoided embrace but many of his brethren were less lucky. One after another, Bug and 'beest plunged to the forest floor.

The rout was complete. The DM counted the dead bodies surrounding him with no small satisfaction.

The Assassins would feed well this night.

The shape-changer and his companion remained tied to their stakes. The changer's name was Syr, he remembered; Dobbins was the small, useless one. Ignored by the invaders and abandoned by their guard, the two of them struggled mightily with the tethers holding them. Syr's face was beaded with sweat as he strained to break an ungiving tie. Dobbins, having found an abandoned spear, tried to saw through the other cord.

Neither one was working on the strap leading to their own collars. Each was trying to free the other.

Stupid creatures, the DM thought. *Self-preservation is nature's greatest rule. Everyone knows that.*

It was amazing the changer and his friend had survived this long.

Puff bobbed through the camp, followed by a second kildebeest. Each of them carried a section of Bug pinched between their fangs. Swinging by its antenna, the Elder's head dangled from the second kildebeest's mouth.

They stopped in front of him. The DM pulled at the collar around his throat. "Get this off me. I'm in a hurry."

The Elder's head dropped onto the dirt and pine needles. "So?" the second kildebeest countered.

215

Folding her legs, Puff lowered herself to the ground. Letting her meal fall from her mouth, she snapped her teeth over the cord holding the District Manager. It fell apart as cleanly as if sliced by the beam of a spitzpistol.

It was then the DM saw the Web, riding the second kildebeest's left forward leg. "Give me that."

The kildebeest danced away. "Father doesn't trust you."

"Tink is right," Puff said.

"Can't trust a Bug," Tink said.

The DM reasoned, "Father Lygt is a Bug."

"Can't trust Father," Puff said.

"You were sent to help me."

"To follow you," Tink amended. "To make certain you did your job. To bring this -" he lifted his leg teasingly, "- to the Comb."

"How does it taste?" Puff asked.

Tink scrunched his face disagreeably.

"You tasted it?" the DM said in horror.

"One nip, that's all."

"I would have," Puff said.

To be fair, the DM thought, *the Web looks no worse than before.*

The more he considered it, the less likely it appeared that this worn fungus possessed any mystical powers. The chund holding it had been taken prisoner; the old Bug droning on about it was the first to die in the raid; and a kildebeest had even eaten part of it without benefit.

Father Lygt was expecting magic from the Tatter-rag. When miracles didn't happen, someone was going to suffer.

The DM didn't want the someone to be him.

216

"Keep it, then," he said. "You're responsible for it from this point on. But I'll want your help with the female chund. Collect her for me and I'll go."

"What about the others?" Puff asked. She tilted her head toward Dobbins and Syr.

"Do what you'd like."

Tink smiled happily. "I've never eaten changer."

The DM said, "Now that I think about it, neither have I."

Puff jumped to her feet. "Maybe you aren't going to eat changer. Maybe changer is going to eat you."

"What's that supposed to mean?"

"He's loose!"

In unison, the District Manager and Tink whirled toward the captives. Still tethered, Syr had pulled his stake from the ground. He cradled it against his chest.

The changer was pale, his purple skin drained to pink from exertion. He staggered over to his companion, dropping to his knees.

Tink snickered. "Weak changer."

"Fresh meat," a new voice said.

Wuffer, the largest of the Assassins, joined them. A rich crimson in color, she led a handful of followers into the clearing.

The DM checked on the female chund. A lone kildebeest remained to watch the chund and the Sktzer leader. It yawned in boredom then quickly retreated when Aly's spear lashed out at it.

"Fresh meat," Wuffer said again. "*My* meat." She said the words to Puff, her challenge evident in her tone.

Unconcerned, Puff tugged at the broken antenna on the Elder's head. It released with a pop! And she chewed on it contentedly.

Wuffer loped ahead. The changer's body was bent over. He was bathed in sweat, the sheen highlighting his vulnerability.

"Syr!" Dobbins yelled.

Before Syr could react, the kildebeest was on him. The changer brought his forearm up, sacrificing it to Wuffer's fangs to protect his face and neck. She bit into the arm, shaking her entire body in an effort to drive her teeth to the bone. Intent on the kill, she didn't see Dobbins until he'd plunged his spear into her bulb. The wound jetted blood as he repeatedly stabbed the Assassin, again and again.

Interesting, the DM thought. *Not as useless as I imagined.*

Rolling the Elder's antenna in her mouth, Puff continued chewing. She watched without expression as Wuffer reeled, collapsing at the chund's feet.

Dobbins yanked the spear free. Syr's tunic was spotted with blood. His arm was coated with it.

Blood. Changer blood.

The DM tried to retreat. Refusing to move, the crowd of kildebeests blocked his path.

The changer's eyes rolled in his head as Dobbins clutched at him. His embrace muffled the keening wail building from inside Syr's chest.

The kildebeests rose to their feet. Membranous wings spread out from behind the body of the chund.

"Changer." Puff swallowed what remained of her snack. "Changing."

218

The softbody released his friend, providing room for the transformation.

"Bug?" one kildebeest hazarded.

"Sktzer."

A purple rebel appeared, its dry wings stirring the needles on the floor below. Its limbs trembled with infirmity. Its markings were as faded as the Elder's.

"Old Sktzer," a kildebeest pointed out.

"Dying Sktzer," another one said.

It was Tink who offered the favorite definition: "Dead Sktzer!"

Laughter bubbled among the monsters. In unison, they swarmed ahead.

Chopping with his spear, Dobbins cut frantically at the straps leading to the heavy post. The spear's barbed head split the first tie with a desperate blow; the second separated when struck again. With Tink at the front of the pack, Syr grabbed Dobbins. His wings beating desperately, he carried them both beyond the reach of the Assassins.

Emptied of kildebeests, the trees overhead no longer held any danger. The two of them lifted slowly, black silhouettes against the darkening sky.

Tink leapt after them, his mouth closing on empty air. In a playful frenzy, the rest of the kildebeests joined him. Leaping and snarling, they pretended they might catch their prey.

The DM shouted, "They're getting away!"

"Twit," Puff said, in mid-air.

"We know," Tink said.

Both of them settled to the ground, giving the District Manager a reproachful glare.

"Not them," the DM said. He aimed his claw across the forest floor. "*Them!*"

The kildebeest guarding Aly and Hhney was dead, the broken shaft of a spear protruding from its mouth. Left unguarded, its prisoners were running for the forest.

"Catch them!" the DM screamed.

* * *

Why should we catch them? Tink wondered. *When did this become our job?*

Then, *What happens if we* don't *catch them?*

A dark suggestion came to mind, and then a second, and then a third. There were a hundred horrid possibilities that might occur if the chund escaped, and each of them filled Tink's mind with terror.

Puff gave chase. Tink charged ahead even faster, passing the other kildebeest. He ran faster than he'd ever run; much faster than any chund could go.

Ahead of him, the Sktzer's leader broke through an opening in the bushes, the female chund at her back. Tink darted around the growth, mindful that the pair had recently killed two of his brethren.

Springing over a low-lying thicket, he landed atop a carpet of sasga needles. Dirt flew into the air, obscuring his vision. With a sneeze, Tink skidded to a stop. Puff bumped into him before stopping as well.

"Where are they?"

There was nothing to indicate the path they'd taken. Aly's scent lingered among the bushes, but went no further.

"The trees?"

"No time to climb a tree," Puff said. "Above the trees."

Sktzers flew over the forest. The one in front carried their Leader; the second in line held the female chund. Two others flew at the rear of the procession, following the faded changer and his friend. They stayed alongside them, almost as an honor guard.

"Too bad," Puff said.

"Real bad." Tink practically bounced with anxiety. "Father wanted the chund."

"Gone now."

Puff's lack of concern was maddening. "There will be punishment," Tink said. "Father will be mad!"

"Father's been mad before."

"There will be suffering. Limbs will be lost. Eyes will be plucked!"

Puff cocked her head quizzically.

"I like having eyes!"

Puff said, "We didn't promise to bring back the chund."

"The DM did!"

"We're not the DM." Spinning around, Puff headed toward camp.

Tink hurried to catch up with her. "The DM is in very, very bad trouble."

"You want to tell him?"

"I want to tell him."

Together, they began to laugh.

Chapter Twenty-One

"Have the Assassins sent word?"

His head bent so low, his beak almost touched the floor, Mox said, "Not yet, Father."

The fawning pose did him no good. He heard the shake of the starman's blocks, rattling like dry bones inside Father Lygt's claw. The rattling stopped and the blocks fell beside him.

"Six green," Father Lygt said.

His eyes squeezed shut, Mox could barely breathe.

"Moons," Father Lygt finished.

Mox opened his eyes. "I'd never lie to you, Father. You don't need the blocks with me."

Father Lygt didn't respond. Collecting the starman's blocks, he stacked them in a tiny pyramid at his side. In manner and voice, the Father seemed no different to Mox than he'd ever been. He remained ruthless, self-serving and egotistical. If he hadn't gone insane this morning, he'd have remained someone to respect.

At dawn, he summoned Mox to join him. Once his aide-de-camp was present, he pointedly ignored him. Talking to himself, the Father wasted the morning by playing with his starman's blocks. Too frightened to be bored, Mox remained at his side.

Watching the blocks fall, watching them roll. Knowing a bad roll was a terrible thing.

Passing the anteroom, he'd seen a Mound Lord, waiting for the Father's attention. And not just any Mound Lord. This was the Mound Lord of M'cchau!

The Father must have summoned him. At the height of the harvest, he'd left his region, traveling to the Comb. At the time of year when every Mound Lord was busiest, he was called to leave his workers and abandon his fields.

It was madness. Absolute madness.

Mox blamed the Reader. Other Fathers had shown little interest in the accursed Book or its guardian; they might amuse themselves with the retelling of a favorite pornographic passage, but they never used it for anything more. The current Father called for it daily, wanting to hear all of its secrets. The Reader was spending more time in the inner chamber than Mox himself.

Page after page had been read to the Father. Mox decided he'd listened to so many words, so many sentences, so many paragraphs, that it had left him unhinged.

Too much reading, he thought, *will do that to anyone.*

"Bring in the Mound Lord," Father Lygt said to his guards. He completed his pyramid, the benevolent moons turned to the inside, the deadly asteroids facing outward. "I'm ready to see him."

With a Bug at each side, the Mound Lord of M'cchau entered the Great Hall. Every region had its own Mound Lord and Mox knew them all. This one was the best of the lot. Taller and broader than most Bugs, Skirl combined his stunning good looks with a taste for senseless cruelty. It was a rare and winning combination. It marked him as a possible successor to the Father himself.

The Mound Lord lowered his head. "Father."

Father Lygt waved for the guards to step aside. "It's been too long, my friend. I've missed your visits."

"I beg your forgiveness," said the Mound Lord, with the charm of someone who's always forgiven. If he was angry over the Father's untimely summons, there was no sign of it.

"I trust your journey was pleasant."

"It was a welcome respite from my duties." Skirl raised his head. "I've been so busy. The region is growing."

"Your region is my biggest."

"To your glory."

"It is also among the strongest." Before the Mound Lord could speak, Father Lygt added, "To my glory, of course."

"May your cycles be many," his visitor intoned. "Is there a reason I'm here, Father?"

"Squat with me, Skirl." Father Lygt toyed with his pyramid of blocks. "Do you like games?" Lifting the uppermost piece, he tossed it to his visitor.

The Mound Lord caught it, star side up. "I've been known to make a wager."

"Do you win?"

"I have my share of luck."

"Luck is so important, isn't it?" Father Lygt took the blocks, passing them to the Mound Lord.

The Mound Lord grew uneasy. "It's been a while since I've played with the starman's blocks."

"Not as long as you suggest, I think," the Father said. "Not that it matters. Our game will have different rules. New rules."

"New ones?"

"I made them up myself. Mox and I have been playing for hours."

"Might I enjoy the game another time?" The Mound Lord offered a bright smile. "As you know, the crops are ripe. My Overseer always works hardest with my whip to encourage him."

There was no answering smile on Father Lygt's face. "Throw the blocks."

The Mound Lord half-opened his beak, as if he might protest. Seeing the Father's face, he let the blocks tumble from his claw. They hit the floor of the chamber, rolled, and lay still.

"What do we have, Mox?" Father Lygt asked.

It took a moment for Mox to respond. He was mildly surprised to still be in the Great Hall. With the Mound Lord's arrival, he'd expected to be dismissed.

Instead, Father acted as if he was to participate in their meeting. He didn't know whether to feel flattered or frightened. Mox said, "Three brown. Moons are the predominant shape."

"Moons." To Skirl, the Father said, "The blocks say I should trust you."

The Mound Lord's confident manner slipped a notch. "The blocks tell you?"

"You see, my childhood companion, I've begun to worry. My spies tell me you're frequenting the bawdyhuts. Spending more than you earn. Winning the small bets while losing the large ones."

"It isn't true."

"It's a concern. Gamblers don't tithe as they should. They feel they have other commitments. Suddenly, a quarter of a region's wealth begins to seem like too much."

"I would never cheat you."

"The carts you send are as full as ever." Gathering the blocks, Father Lygt put them in the other's claw. "I examined a recent wagon load myself. It was a cart full of dalapoke dung."

"I don't remember each particular shipment," Skirl said. "You realize, I can't supervise every load I send."

"The top layer was as rich and fragrant as anyone might have hoped. Below that, the dung was cheapened by sand and rock. The sand and rock gave bulk to your offering. But, had I spread it in my fields, what could I have grown there?"

"I knew nothing of this!" At the tone of his voice, the two guards drew closer.

"Throw the blocks."

"On my return, I'll send another wagon load. Two."

"The blocks."

The Mound Lord's tongue wet his beak. "You'll not find my honesty reflected on the face of these stones."

"Throw them, Skirl."

Shaking them, he released them to the floor.

"What do you see, Mox?" Father Lygt asked.

"Two green. Stars."

"Stars, is it? Only two, and green, but acceptable. Not as good as moons but good enough." Sweeping with his foot, the Father pushed the squares toward his visitor. "Throw them again."

"But I had stars," the Mound Lord said in an anxious, whining voice. Hearing himself, he scowled. Angrily, he picked the blocks up. He let them fall without being shaken.

"Moons," the Mound Lord said with obvious relief. "Two green. *Moons*."

"Again."

"You said moons were good."

At Father Lygt's signal, one of the guards bent down to collect the stones. Opening the visitor's claw, he forced the stones inside. With a slap, he knocked the claw open and the blocks pitched out.

"Mox?" the Father asked.

"Six brown. Asteroids."

Father Lygt's head made a small gesture, his antennae barely moving. At this signal, the guards brought the Mound Lord to his feet.

"Six is the largest number," Father Lygt said. "Brown reflects trust. But asteroids? Asteroids are bad."

"How bad?" the Mound Lord asked.

"Show him."

When the guards had finished, Father Lygt said, "Notify the troops to prepare for travel. They'll need to maintain order in M'cchau until a new Mound Lord is chosen."

"What of the Comb?" Mox inquired. "What of your safety?"

"I have my guards. The Assassins will return shortly. It's enough." He looked down at Skirl. "Get rid of this. Share the carcass among different stewpots."

227

The body was carried off. Father Lygt picked up each of the starman's blocks and cupped them in his claw. "Mox, do you doubt my sanity?"

"No, Father." Mox squirmed his body to the floor. When he heard the starman's blocks being shaken, his chest began to pound.

The stones clinked onto the rough surface of the floor. "Four," Father said, "and blue. I so dislike it when the blocks are blue. What else do you see?"

Mox lifted up. To his horror, asteroids outnumbered every other shape outlined on the blocks.

Extending a curved nail, the Father turned the blocks over until engraved moons were the only form to be seen. "I'm as crazy as I choose to be," he said. "Tell the Reader I wish to see him."

* * *

Setting the Book on its pedestal, the Reader folded it open.

"Read for me," Father Lygt said.

Naturally, I'll read for him, the Reader thought. As far as the Father was concerned, it was his only purpose in life. Might he have greeted him politely? Perhaps asked how the Reader felt this day? Whether he'd slept well the night before?

The Father never did such things. The social niceties were beyond him.

"Why aren't you reading?" Father Lygt asked, breaking into the Reader's moment of introspection. "Is there a problem?"

"No, no."

"I've heard Readers can go blind." He peered into the other's eyes, as if searching for a clouded lens. "It's all those pages, all those words. Are you losing your sight?"

"My vision is fine," the Reader assured him. "Better than ever."

"Then why aren't you reading?"

The Reader cleared his throat. "Let it be known how a humble Bug became glorious," he began. "How he found his true self through the power of the Web and was born again as Father Lygt. Exalted above his peers. Invincible in wisdom, and cunning, and strength."

* * *

The story began long ago, during the Lost Days. This was the age when our lands were divided and each Bug fought the other for supremacy.

Seeking any advantage in their battles, the rich and powerful sought favor from the wizards. The wizards cast their spells and made their magicks, but the Fates shared their blessings with no one. A warlord tasting victory one day would taste his own blood the next. Septs were formed, but did not survive. Mounds were started, but lacked the opportunity to grow.

It was the blackest of times.

Then the seers sent word to every kingdom. There had been a double-hatching: Two birth mates, one male and one female, arriving in but a single sack. Their markings were identical. In every fashion save sex, they were two of the same creature.

229

Such an event had not been witnessed for nearly a thousand cycles. Such an event, the seers proclaimed, was a curse upon the world. The hatchlings had to be found and destroyed.

Hearing of the prophecy and fearful she, too, would be killed, the birth mother fled. Abandoned as harbingers of ill-fortune, the twined mates should have died. The searchers came upon their birthing place, but did not find them. To this day, it is not known how they survived, but survive they did.

Performing the lowliest of tasks, eating the meanest of food, they grew to maturity. In all of T'ing, they had only themselves for companionship. Joined in solitude and affliction, knowing they would be despised by any who knew of their true nature, they became as one. They shared each other's sorrow; they felt one another's joy. Each selected a name for the other, bestowing this weak honor as no one else had done for them.

The female became known as Plxr. The male became known as Lygt.

At the end of their fifteenth cycle, Plxr and Lygt were captured and put to work as slaves. Their first task was to tend to the krawlers. Endlessly scrubbing the reptiles with soap sand, they labored from earliest sun until well into the night. Hundreds of krawlers, tens of thousands of scales; few survived such difficult labor for long. It was work designed to stock the food pots.

* * *

"Enough of this," Father Lygt said. "You've told me these words too often. This whole section is depressing."

"It evokes a period of T'ing in which little else -"

"Start at their seventeenth cycle," Father Lygt insisted.

"But -"

"Their seventeenth cycle."

* * *

...such torment only strengthened them. Their hatred for their oppressors grew, feeding upon their thoughts like a great beast. Until, at last, the time came when they could endure these punishments no longer.

On the day of their seventeenth cycle, Plxr was alone in the stables. Her bucket was filled with a full measure of soap sand. Upon her claw, she wore a fresh stone pad as protection against the rough texture of a krawler's scales.

The Overseer entered the stable. He lowered his beak to her ear and said, not for the first time, "I desire you."

Plxr asked, "Why should I join with you?"

"Your work load would be lessened."

"I am not frightened to work."

"What would you have me give you?"

"Freedom. If not freedom, then payment."

"My mate counts every stick," the Overseer said miserably.

Plxr saw the heat rising within him, his sex protruding from its sheath. "Let me get to my chores. My workload will not be lessened this day."

"Why should your work load be lessened?" It was the querulous voice of Zex, the Overseer's mate. Walking over straw and dirt, she had entered the stalls in silence.

"Pay the slave no mind," the Overseer said. Zex saw his sex bulging from beyond its sheath. Her eyes narrowed and she grew angry.

Plxr faced them.

"Do you see? On her claw?" Zex asked. "She has taken a new pad when her last was barely worn."

The Overseer had watched Plxr's last pad fall into pieces. Still, he said, "She must be punished."

Zex lifted her club. The first blow landed squarely across the slave's chest, knocking her from her feet and spilling her bucket. From long habit, Plxr curled her body into a ball. She did not see the Overseer as he crept from the stables.

Zex beat upon Plxr until her arms grew weary. Absorbed in her task, she did not notice Lygt entering the stables.

Seeing his birth mate injured and helpless, Lygt launched himself upon the accursed Zex. His pincers slashed at her exposed neck. With a single cry, the Overseer's mate fell. Blood pulsed from the gash in her throat, washing over the stable floors.

The Overseer was the only one who heard Zex's call. Returning to the stables, he clubbed Lygt into unconsciousness.

"You will suffer," he promised him. "I shall make it so."

His thoughts were filled with fantasies of revenge when Plxr rose from behind him. Lifting her stone pad, she brought it down upon her oppressor. Fresh and new, the stone pad lasted a long time until, finally, it crumbled away.

So it came to pass that Plxr and Lygt fled from the township. Long would be the journey ahead, although they knew it not. Many would be their trials, although they little suspected as much. Harsh would –

* * *

"Skip ahead," Father Lygt interrupted.

"Past the plains?"

"Past the plains, past the desert. Past the mountains. Past everything."

The Reader flipped the pages. It was too bad. These passages were among the most descriptive in the Book. The flora! The fauna! It painted an image of an age that would never come again.

The Father didn't care. As far as he was concerned, the entire section should be condensed: *Despite countless obstacles, the twins survived for many cycles. They found their way into the mountains. Caught in an ice storm, they nearly died before being rescued by the Sktzers.*

Action and more action. It was all he ever wanted.

"At the Sktzer camp, then?" the Reader asked.

"Go on."

* * *

For the first time, Plxr and Lygt came to know acceptance. Mated to the Leader, Plxr gained stature within the sept. Lygt found honor as her brother and as a strong warrior. Welcomed as Sktzer born, their days passed in harmony. They would have lived in obscurity and died forgotten if not for the Web.

There was no beginning to the Web, or so the Sktzers claimed. It had always been in their possession. It was written that all became stronger in its presence but only one could join with it.

Whoever was strong enough to wear the Web was their Leader, for such bonding bestowed greatness. Joined in glory, the Web and its bondmate became as one. Death alone could tear them asunder.

Plxr's mate, Kring, wore the Web proudly. In the past, such an honor might have been warranted, for he had fought courageously. Over time, he had grown soft with age and complacency. Lacking courage, he brought an end to the Sktzer/Mentren Wars through the weakness of diplomacy. Rather than rise in protest, the Sktzers accepted this uncertain solution. They became lax. For the first time in fifty cycles, they were unprepared to defend their home should the Mentren decide to attack once more.

At Plxr's request, Kring allowed Lygt to hold the Web. At the moment of its touch, Lygt felt a power such as he had never known. Forgotten was the folly of those who had foretold his future, for he knew his destiny was not to be one of despair. With the Web in his claw, he saw all things clearly. If he were the Web's bondmate, T'ing would flourish. For this to happen, a sacrifice would have to be made.

Kring had to die.

The following evening, the Mentren leader, Bjrrl, agreed to sup with Kring and Plxr. In a show of good faith, Bjrrl came alone. He did not protest when he heard that Plxr's brother, Lygt, would join them at their table.

Lygt alone was suspicious of the wily Mentren. Bjrrl's pretense of embracing this period of peace did not fool him. He knew a foe could not become a friend and an enemy would never become an ally. In his vain desire to be a peacemaker, Kring insisted such truths be ignored. His failing endangered all Sktzers but only Lygt was wise enough to realize it.

Lygt could not let his sept remain blind to the enemy before them. With the Mentren leader on one side, and Kring on the other, he found his opportunity to prepare his brethren for the future. No matter his personal risk, he embraced this difficult challenge.

When Kring squatted to sup, Lygt artfully fed tainted morsels into the Sktzer's bowl. He knew the Leader would smell their rotted aroma and feed on them first. Kring dipped his claw into the bowl. Grasping two poisoned shreds of meat, he offered one to his mate before taking the second for himself.

Plxr raised the meat to her mouth. Lygt was tempted to cry out a warning but choked back the words, refusing to allow himself such an indulgence. If T'ing were to prosper, he would have to accept this deep, personal loss. He sat in silence, watching as both Plxr and Kring shared their meal.

It was Plxr who first reacted to the poison, grasping at her throat but unable to speak as fire tore through her. At last, she sensed the treachery that lay in the heart of the Mentren, Bjrrl, but she never

235

looked his way. Dying, her eyes remained fixed on her beloved brother, Lygt.

With his mate in agony, Kring pushed aside the table in front of him. His voice taken from him, knowing he was dying, Kring clutched for the dagger at his side. He pulled it from his sheath, intending to make short work of the villain at their table, but his strength withered. He crumpled at the Mentren's feet, his blade falling harmlessly from his claw.

Lygt picked up the dagger. Bjrrl came up from his haunches, shocked that Lygt knew of the duplicity in his heart. His confusion ended as the dagger's sharp edge found a path across his throat.

Casting its golden radiance into the room, the Web stretched its tendrils from the fallen Kring, seeking a new and better bondmate. Placing the prize upon one arm, Lygt threw himself upon the body of his birth mate.

"Oh, foul Mentren!" he wailed, and the Sktzers found him there, weeping.

Lygt told the others of the Mentren's plan to steal the Web and weaken their sept. Their Leader was gone, lost at the hands of the deceiver, Bjrrl. Lost as well was Plxr, Lygt's beloved sibling, who gave her life to save Lygt's own. Bjrrl had paid for his treachery, but nothing would ever lessen Lygt's pain.

* * *

"Enough," Father Lygt said curtly, cutting off the Reader's tale. "Why is this section of the story always the same?"

"Why?" The Reader tried to gather his thoughts. "These are the words as put down by the

236

Great Prophet. Written during the first times, a thousand cycles ago. I can't change the story. I have to read the exact same words every time."

"But I already know what happened. The Elders saw the Web on Lygt and embraced him as their Leader. The angry Sktzers swept down on the unsuspecting Mentren, slaughtering them. It's viewed as a great victory, Lygt is beloved by all, and he becomes ever more powerful. But how did Lygt go from cleaning krawler scales in his seventeenth cycle to becoming a world ruler in his twenty-fifth? What power did the Web give him?"

The Reader remained mute. He'd been through the Book several times, seeking an answer to the same question.

"Well?"

"I don't know, Father."

"Perhaps a new Reader could provide a different interpretation of the Book."

"He would have nothing new to share!"

Father Lygt appeared doubtful. "Turn the pages. You know the part I want."

* * *

His armies storming across the continent, Lygt conquered territory after territory. The disloyal and the disobedient were swept away. In time, every manner of Bug hailed Lygt as their ruler. Through the power of the Web, he became as progenitor of the species, the first to rule them all, and he took the name of Father.

Father Lygt.

As has always been, there were those who grew envious of their master. Poisoned by jealousy and greed, they sought to overthrow him. Always did he prevail, crushing his enemies as he forced submission and obedience upon the land.

And, yet, a day came when all was lost. A Sktzer, low-born and ambitious, corrupted an adviser to Father Lygt. Together, they conspired to drug the Father and steal the Web.

Awakening from his heavy slumber, Father Lygt discovered what had transpired. In righteous anger, he ordered all Sktzers be clipped, their wings taken in payment for the treacherous act visited upon him by one of their kind. Those who resisted were killed, their bodies given to the stewpots. A cowardly handful of Sktzers fled, scattering as needles in a high wind, banished forever from the kingdom of Lygt.

The Father called for his devoted followers to find the Web. His greatest hunters were sent forth. His most experienced trackers spread throughout the land. A great reward was offered. Following a long and strenuous search, the Father's treacherous adviser was found.

Wandering alone on a distant plain, the adviser made no effort to escape his pursuers. Madness had embraced him.

"The Cave of Doom," he sobbed. "The Cave of Doom."

The Web was gone forever, lost inside the Cave of Doom.

* * *

"End of story," said Father Lygt.

"Well, no," the Reader stated. "There are hundreds of pages left. The hunters bring the adviser back to the Comb -"

"Yes, yes. 'Stripped of shell and flesh, he died a thousand deaths.' His pain was well-earned."

The Reader kept his claw at the bottom of the page, marking his place. "Shall I continue?"

"No."

"The Book has other tales to share. There's a most amusing parable about a Twill and an empty stewpot."

"Is it a tale of a magical stewpot, allowing the Twill to live on, for a hundred cycles or more?" Father Lygt asked. "Or does the Twill die during its fortieth cycle?"

"It's not that kind of story."

"I thought not." Father Lygt shook his claw. Stones rattled from inside his grip. "Have you ever played with the starman's blocks, Reader?"

Before the Reader could respond, there was a knock at the door.

"It's Mox, Father," the servant's voice said. "The Assassins have returned."

"Yes?"

"They've found the Web."

Chapter Twenty-Two

I'm dead, Vykk thought. Flung haphazardly into a cart, a pincer bent here, a leg contorted there, he couldn't move, he couldn't breathe, because he was dead.

It was miserably uncomfortable, being dead.

"Shift your knee," said the body beneath him.

The comment destroyed the mood. Vykk shifted, taking his knee off Tskett's abdomen. *Now, I'm dead*, he thought. *More dead than before.*

"Your other knee," Tskett said.

It was hopeless. "You make it hard to be dead."

"Father's guards can fix that."

"Urk." Watching where he placed his knees, Vykk sprawled into position. It felt right this time.

"Absolutely, without a doubt, dead," he whispered to himself.

* * *

Lying beneath Vykk, surrounded by the body parts of his destroyed comrades, Tskett wondered why he'd gotten involved in such a foolhardy endeavor. No, he knew better. He knew exactly why he was riding in this cart.

Hhney.

After their retreat, they'd armed themselves before returning to their camp. The Assassins were gone. The torn bodies of Sktzers were everywhere. The mudhuts were ravaged, their food pots overturned and emptied, and the burgeoning Mound destroyed.

Hope, the weak beast living in Tskett's heart, fled. This hadn't been a battle; it had been a slaughter. Their rebel band was helpless before the Father's might.

"I have a plan," Hhney said.

This was no time for plans. It was time to flee, to count their losses and disappear. He'd abandoned all faith that justice would ever prevail. Why couldn't their Leader see this as well?

Instead, she said, "We still have the wagon and its krawler. We'll use them to retrieve the Web. Holding the Web, I can reunite the rebel tribes. Together, we can – we *will* - overthrow the Father!"

Such an impossible dream. They would never see the Tattered-rag again. Without it, Hhney's plan was useless.

Vykk volunteered to go with her. So did the female chund. The male chund, Dobbins, wanted to stay with the changer. For some reason, Hhney insisted he travel along. The chund protested until Hhney tired of it and threatened to remove his tongue.

Hhney expected Tskett to travel with her. Instead, he begged forgiveness. There was too much work to be done. A new living area to be secured, a shape-changer to be fed. There was no reason for him to go on a fool's errand.

But when the wagon rolled onto the road, he was somehow on it. His actions surprised no one.

Least of all, Tskett himself.

Now he was riding to his death, chasing the damnable Web. He wanted nothing more to do with it. In the instant he held it, he felt its power course through his body. He felt electrified; acutely alive in a way he'd never known before. Images flashed through his mind.

Brilliant, breathtaking images. Images of Hhney.

He shook the Web from his arm but its message lingered. He was bonded with Hhney. Forever. He was alive when he stood beside her, incomplete without her. He lived for her. He would fight and kill for her.

If needed, he would die for her. Would she die for him?

No, she would not.

The Elder had said that everyone carried a seed of greatness within themselves. The Web found the seed, causing it to flower. Modest gifts became potent. Potent gifts became extraordinary. Nations had been formed from less.

This was my gift? Tskett wondered. *An emotion? What value can be found in something as amorphous as... as love?*

A weakness multiplied did not become a strength.

"Better to have never known," he muttered.

"What?" Vykk asked from above him.

"Oh, be quiet."

* * *

Atop the courtyard wall, the guards studied the wagon advancing toward Father Lygt's Comb. A

242

small, brown Bug sat at the front of the wagon, controlling the krawler pulling it. Two chund, one male and one female, walked beside the cart. Each of the chund had a yoke on its shoulders with a tether attached to the side of the vehicle. Plodding along, each chund carried a food pot in its arms.

"What foul embarrassment is this?" the head gatekeeper said, studying the clipboard in his claws. "There are no wagons scheduled for today. There shouldn't be a wagon for another quarter-season!"

He marched down the stairs, waving for the gates to be opened. Let this sad mistake of an offering be brought to him for once; damned if he'd walk outside to inspect it.

Rolling past the sentries and between the courtyard's large doors, the wagon entered the inside yard. When the wagon's driver yanked at the stirrups in her claws, the krawler slowed to a stop.

The gatekeeper scowled. The wagon was rickety and cheaply made, its wood slats barely able to contain its contents. The wagon's driver, covered in dirt from her travels, knew it, too. Embarrassed by the quality of the goods she carried, she refused to meet his eyes.

The gatekeeper pushed his pole along the inside of the cart, prodding it among the loose body parts. "This is your tithing?"

"The proud offering of Mound Lord Srttz," came the driver's politic response.

"Of what region?"

"G'ggan."

"G'ggan is a poor land. Poorer than I recall." Located to the far north of the Comb, G'ggan was a small region with few resources. The wagons rolling in from its hills were seen infrequently and the tithing they carried had never been described favorably. Still, no Mound Lord had ever before dared to send so little.

"The Father will have record of what was sent," the gatekeeper cautioned.

The driver scratched herself, sending flecks of dried dirt into the air. "There are Sktzers. That should make the Father happy."

"Pieces of Sktzers. The arms and legs are chewed, the skulls have empty eye sockets. These are hardly the makings of a tithing."

"The Mound Lord has also sent food pots."

"Three small pots, likely half-empty. There are only two complete bodies." The gatekeeper knocked his pole against the head of the uppermost one. "Everything else is in pieces."

"The chund carry food pots as well," the driver said. Stirring out of her hunched-over position, she snapped a whip at the chund standing nearest the gatekeeper.

It was a male chund. "Ow!" he cried, touching the edge of one ear. Lowering his yoke hastily, he placed his food pot on the ground.

The gatekeeper took the pot's lid from its mouth. It contained a gritty goop he hadn't seen before. Dipping his claw into it, he stirred the liquid. No meat rose to the surface. The gatekeeper raised his claw to his mouth.

"Ah, a connoisseur," the driver remarked. "Not many like the taste of Blob."

Spitting, the gatekeeper wiped his claw along his leg. "Father Lygt won't want this!"

"Mound Lord Srttz feeds it to the chund."

244

The gatekeeper decided he would never, ever, eat chund again. He screwed the pot's lid on. "Anything else?"

"The live tithing." The driver gave a malevolent smirk toward the captives tied to her wagon.

"You used the chund to carry tithing," the gatekeeper said, "and they *are* tithing?"

"Not that they knew it."

The gatekeeper roared with laughter. With a jest this sweet, he could almost forgive the driver for carrying a container of remaindered Blob. "Go on, then. Dead tithing goes to the storehouse. Live tithing goes in the cages beyond it."

Shouldering the yoke again, the small male chund asked the female, "Is my ear bleeding?"

* * *

The storehouse guard opened the cage door and the chund climbed through the entrance.

"Too skinny, the both of them." He locked the cage door. "The meat will be stringy."

"The male is docile," the wagon's driver said. "He rarely moves. When the time comes, his meat will be laden with fat."

The guard nodded. The male did have a docile, almost relaxed, expression on his face. The female, however, was a different sort. Her mouth was pinched and her face was mean. She'd turn the stomach of any Bug who tried to eat her.

He felt a tap on his shoulder. "You're so strong," the driver cooed. "I could use some help unloading my wagon."

245

The guard recoiled. The wagon's driver was filthy. Even if she were in high heat, he wouldn't have touched her. "I'm not here to serve your needs. Unload it yourself."

The driver grunted unhappily. Wrestling with the krawler's harness, she brought the serpent around. She released the bit and the krawler curled itself into an unmoving mass.

"Move your beast," the guard said.

The driver ignored him. With dirty little clouds puffing from her feet, she shuffled a food pot from the cart and into the storehouse.

"The krawler can't stay here," the guard told her. "It's blocking the passage to the pens."

"The prisoners are in cages. They're not going anywhere."

"I need to watch them!"

Unmoved by the other's predicament, the driver lowered a second food pot to the ground. She dragged it away.

"I'll move it myself." The guard reached up for the animal's bit.

"Krawler bites."

The guard released the bit immediately. *So that's the way it's going to be, is it?* Until the wagon was empty, the cart and krawler would remain in place, blocking the view of the live tithing pens.

Setting aside his spear, the guard said, "Let me help you."

Together, they collected the bits and pieces of various Sktzers. In short order, only the two whole rebel bodies remained in the cart.

"They're too large," the guard complained. His mesosternum ached in anticipation of the burden ahead. "Why didn't you hack these up like you did the others?"

"Talk to the cutters. I just drive the wagon."

The guard rolled the top body over. There wasn't a mark on it. "Poisoned?"

The driver looked at him dumbly.

"The meat can't be used if it's tainted."

"Depends on who eats it."

The guard regarded the driver with new respect. "That's true, isn't it?" He tugged the body up by its shoulders. "Let's get this done then."

The two of them carried the body into the building. Inside, the storehouse held a cornucopia of riches, with rows of food pots stacked nearly to the ceiling on both the first and second levels of the building.

The first floor was devoted to dead tithing, sorted by species and body part, but harvest time had arrived. Soon, most of the dead tithing would be traded or sold to make room for the crops to come. Most of the food pots would have to go, too.

That meant there would be more lifting and carrying in the near future. Dropping the dead Sktzer to the floor, the guard said, "I hate lifting and carrying."

"Only one more."

The last Sktzer was even bigger than the first. Struggling under the tithing's weight, the guard and the driver dragged it from the cart.

"Why is it you're so much dirtier than your tithing?" asked the guard as they entered the storeroom. "By all rights, your offering should look as traveled as you are."

Lowering the Sktzer body to the storehouse floor, the driver caught her breath. "I rode up front. Dust."

A dust storm, maybe, the guard thought. "You're caked with mud. Your markings are covered with it."

"Who cares about the markings of a lowly wagon driver?"

From the guard's perspective, she couldn't have been more right. Still, as he surveyed the storage area, something about the situation felt wrong.

Then he had it.

"The last Sktzer," he said. "We left the body in the corner. Where is it?"

"Over here," a new voice said. The poisoned rebel stood at the storehouse door. He held the guard's spear in the crook of his arm.

"You're dead," the guard said.

"Not anymore," the Sktzer told him. He waggled the spear unhappily. "There's no respect for the dead. They get thrown around, poked, insulted. *Some* people hit them on the head."

"At least you were on top." To the guard's astonishment, the remaining dead Sktzer sat up. Removing the top of the Blob-fouled footpot, he wiped its contents over his bodyshell. The muck dried quickly, obscuring the rebel's markings.

Too late, the guard realized he should have run for safety. Before he could move, he felt the brush of the first Sktzer's claw, gripping him by the neck.

"Nobody really understands death," the Sktzer said, "until they've tried it themselves."

* * *

Rolling up his trouser leg, Dobbins said, "It's not that I don't like tattoos."

Aly could feel a headache building behind her right eye. She hated confinement. If it bothered her companion to be locked up, trapped in a cage while surrounded by other cages, he didn't show it.

He's probably used to being behind bars, she thought.

"A tattoo can be a beautiful thing," Dobbins continued. "It depends on the design." He picked at his calf until his fingers found a puckered fold. Pinching it tightly, he peeled it downward and a rubbery strip lifted away.

"Hurts when I do this," Dobbins confided. "Takes the hair right off." He unrolled the trouser leg, covering his denuded calf.

Aly's headache pounded more strongly.

Dobbins said, "I once saw a Lindelette with a gorgeous tattoo. It was the Cepheus constellation, done to scale. It ran right down the center of her two spines."

Holding the flesh-colored strip in his hands, he pressed at its center with both thumbs. The metal head of a pick lock squeezed to its surface.

Drawing her legs up, Aly rested her head on her knees. "Please quit talking."

"A tattoo should be a work of art, that's my point." Pulled free, the pick lock was little more than a stout wire, bent at an angle. Dobbins pressed the elastic strip again. "What you have on your shoulder is not art."

"You know how I value your opinion."

249

"There's no subtlety in it. Red-yellow-green-blue. It's all primary colors."

"It marks me as one of Hhney's sept. As a Sktzer born."

"That's another thing. The authorities, they're not exactly supporters of the rebel clans. You think they're going to be happy, seeing this triangular swirly thing on you?"

"The arms of the triangle represent wings," Aly told him. "Flight, freedom. The base is supposed to be the mesothorax. Spirit and strength."

Dobbins collected two more picks. Finished with the fleshy pink covering, he curled it in his fingers before letting it drop. "I don't remember asking if the tattoo had a meaning."

"I thought you'd like to know." Closing her eyes, she pushed the base of her palm against her right eyelid.

"I'll tell you what it means. Those kinds of markings mean trouble."

"That's not your concern, is it?"

"Oh, yes, it is."

"Really? Why?"

"It's my concern when it affects my mate."

Aly lifted her head. "Your what?"

Dobbins said, "Syr is quite pleased."

"Tell me you're joking."

"Coincidentally, the females on his world choose their partners, too. There's no official ceremony, so to speak. The couple makes a public pronouncement, just like you did at the Sktzer camp, and it's official."

"This isn't Syr's planet."

250

"The female usually chooses more than one mate, you understand. Three or four partners aren't uncommon on his world but you, being a Terran, well, a touch more modesty is understandable." He let a smile tease at the corners of his mouth. "Nobody expects a male changer to live very long, not in that environment. All of the women select more than one partner."

"I said what I had to say," Aly told him. "What I needed to say to save your lives."

Dobbins moved to the other side of the cage. Holding a pick between his thumb and forefinger, he slid it into the Lygt rod.

"Syr understands what happened. Why I spoke. Doesn't he?"

Selecting a different bit of wire, Dobbins reshaped it. He probed into the Lygt rod, sending yellow splinters of grass shedding from its once smooth surface.

"I'm not one of his kind," Aly said. 'He can't honestly think I'd mate with him."

Manipulating the pick, Dobbins said, "Oddly enough, the females on Fiorosov aren't very different from Terrans. Not physically, anyway. They're not strong, they can't change. There's the color thing, sure, but what does color matter?"

Tucking the wires into his upper pocket, he said, "Pleasure and food, that's what drives a shape-changer. They're open to anyone and anything, if they think the experience is going to be worth it."

"Syr must have a mate."

"He *had* a mate, sure. She wasn't happy when he went off-planet."

"But he'll be returning."

251

"Are you kidding? No one goes back."
Dobbins examined the roof of the cage. "Boost me
up."

"What is Syr thinking?"

"When we get out of here, you can ask him
yourself."

"I have the most terrible headache," Aly said.
"Pity."

"If I lift you, it'll only get worse. You can just
about reach the roof yourself."

"Just about."

Standing, she locked her hands together.
Dobbins put his foot inside the interlaced fingers and
she raised him up.

The cages latched where the roof met the wall.
The grasses had been stiffened and bent to intertwine
in such a manner that they were almost impossible to
separate. Dobbins' pick flashed in quick movements
above his head.

"Clever," he said. "If a prisoner pushes
against the wall, the pressure twists the grasses
together more tightly. Pull in on the bars and the other
walls prevent it. It's a great lock, it really is, but it
isn't perfect."

Aly knew he wanted her to ask him the natural
follow-up question. When she didn't, he casually
clipped her head with his foot.

"Tell me its weakness," she said.

"It was made to be opened."

Slivers of grass fell through the air. The pick
dodged in and out of the Lygt rod ever more furiously
yet Dobbins' fingers seemed to barely move.
Seemingly engrossed in his work, he cleared his
throat. "You think Syr's okay?"

It wouldn't do for him to appear worried about his friend, she thought. He had no such hesitation back at the rebels' camp. There, he'd been frantic when Syr collapsed into a coma.

"He'll be fine," she said, hoping she was right. Everything depended on the actions of the Sktzers who were caring for Syr. Almost everyone was afraid of a shape-changer, even the rebels.

But they're more afraid of Hhney and Tskett. If they believe their leader will survive this excursion, they'll honor her command to nurse Syr to health.

"Got it." Balanced on the lock pick was a single blade of grass. It stretched into the wall, the string disappearing into the corner of the cage. "At least, I hope I do."

He plucked at the blade. His wrist moved sharply and the line followed, growing taut. When it pulled free, the wall Aly was leaning against fell over.

She fell with it. Flailing his arms, Dobbins tumbled to the ground.

Aly rolled to her feet. The front wall had collapsed outward, affording her a clear line of sight into the storehouse. Vykk was in the doorway, wearing a guard's armband.

He nodded to her. Past him, their wagon waited at the entrance.

There hadn't been an outcry when their cage broke open. No guards came rushing across the room; the upper floor remained quiet. Hhney and Tskett had done their jobs well.

Aly helped Dobbins to his feet. "Let's get on with it."

"Every cage?"

"If you think you can."

253

Insulted, Dobbins said, "It's easier from the outside."

Shaken from their lethargy, the other inhabitants of the pen stared at them as if witnessing a miracle. The prisoners didn't speak. They were tithing and they knew it.

Lifting the hem of her robe, Aly slid a dagger from the sheath strapped to her thigh. "I'll do the talking."

* * *

There were twelve cages in the storehouse but only eight were occupied. Seven of the prisoners were Bugs of one type or another. While Dobbins worked on the Lygt rod closing each box, Aly chittered to each of them in their native tongue.

"We'll open your cage," she said to each, without any variation in tone or manner. "Wait behind the wagon at the entrance. When the wagon is pulled away, you can make your escape. If all of you go at the same time, you can rush the front gate. The guards can't capture you all. It's your only hope to avoid the stewpots."

Most of the Bugs nodded in understanding. When the fourth captive protested, preferring a more solitary escape, she closed with: "I have a knife, I'm in a bad mood, and I have a headache. You understand 'headache'?"

The Bug didn't answer.

"Or I can leave you here." She rubbed at the right side of her temple. "Your call."

It proved to be an effective argument.

The last cage held a Wamandu, a short creature with a densely-furred body and a pointed snout. Aly started to speak to him, but he only looked confused.

"Save me," the Wamandu said in Basic.

Playing with his lock pick, Dobbins said, "I'm working on it."

"You don't speak Bug! You speak Basic!"

"Yeah."

"You're a tourist!" The Wamandu clapped his paws together happily. "I'm a tourist!"

Tskett stamped up to them. Ignoring the prisoner, he scratched at the gunk covering his markings. "Aren't you done yet?"

"One last cage."

Vykk followed behind Tskett. "Aren't they done yet?"

"Almost," Dobbins said.

Hhney returned to the cart. Squatting in the driver's position, she watched as Dobbins worked.

The Wamandu pressed himself against the bars. "You won't believe the things Bugs say. The things they do. They were going to eat me!"

"Imagine that."

"This is my vacation," the creature said. "I only wanted a little fun."

Dobbins asked, not unkindly, "What kind of idiot would vacation on the Bugworld?"

Good point, Aly thought with a twinge.

"I was promised sinful pleasures," the Wamandu said. His black eyes narrowed. "Avoid drinks garnished with eyeballs and antennae."

"Finish your job, Terran," Tskett said, "or leave the furry chund to rot."

The Wamandu's mouth gaped open at this harsh command. Folding his pick into his palm, Dobbins plucked at a loose strand of Lygt rod. "Done."

The wall gave way. Aly told the Wamandu, "Wait behind the wagon at the entrance. When the wagon is pulled away, you can make your escape."

The Wamandu nodded.

Tskett raised his spear. "Now!"

Hhney snapped her whip and the krawler uncurled in alarm. It plunged ahead, jerking the wagon sideways and off its wheels. Tipped to one side, the cart scraped over the hard ground. Hhney tumbled from it, hidden behind the plume of dust spitting into the air.

The prisoners fled after the abandoned wagon, jostling among themselves to be at the head of the pack. As promised, the guards were stunned by this display of insurgency.

Belatedly, two of the sentries yanked at the massive levers controlling the front gates. Slowly, the courtyard doors began to close.

Aly, Dobbins and Tskett dashed for the front of the storehouse. Hhney picked herself up as they reached the opening.

"Are you all right, my Leader?" Tskett asked.

"For the moment," she said. "That may be about to change."

Gazing into the courtyard, Aly understood why Hhney sounded worried. Until this moment, everything had gone according to plan.

Not now. Now, the plan was falling apart.

They'd assumed the guards would abandon their posts to chase after the escaping Bugs, providing an open entry into the Comb. Instead, the guards remained at their stations as new sentinels appeared from behind them. Heavily armed, this second wave of sentries rushed after the prisoners.

"If we leave the storehouse, they'll see us," Vykk said.

Dobbins told him, "So we take a few minutes and come up with a new idea."

"Whether they see us or not, they'll be here next," Hhney said. "They'll check on the Father's riches."

"Let them," Tskett said. "When we die, they'll know they've had a fight."

"That's your new idea?" Dobbins asked. "Die?"

"Do you have a better one?"

"Fly away! Escape!"

"Only two of us have functioning wings," Hhney reminded him. "In these tight quarters, it doesn't matter, anyway. We'd never get over the courtyard walls."

The Wamandu's high-pitched voice called out to them, "Over here!"

He was at the storehouse's back wall, his claws hooked into the building's stony face. He pulled, his arms straining, and a section of wall followed, its hexagonal blocks rigidly aligned. "Aren't you coming?"

Behind the Wamandu was the mouth of a dark hole. Tiny lights flickered from inside the blackness.

"It's a passageway," Vykk said.

"I don't trust the furry tithing," Tskett said, in a low voice.

"Nor I," Hhney agreed.

The group waited uncertainly. Shrugging his tiny shoulders, the Wamandu trotted into the opening.

"Maybe it's a trap," Dobbins said. "I don't think so, but maybe. Still beats Tskett's plan."

Aly stared into the courtyard. "The guards are coming."

"Into the passageway," Hhney told the others. "Quickly!"

Chapter Twenty-Three

Tskett sealed the wall behind them. Turning to follow the others, he felt his leg bump against a small, furry body.

The Wamandu blinked up at the Bug. "You'd have left me to rot."

"Happily."

Ahead of them, the narrow corridor was dimly lit by widely-spaced lighting globes. Chittering voices surrounded them, muffled behind the earthen walls.

"What are they saying?" Dobbins asked.

"Nothing importantt," Aly explained. "Kitchen talk."

"Cooks and their helpers use this passage," the Wamandu said. "They come at night, collecting victims for the next day's meal." Pleased with himself, he added, "It's black when they enter the storehouse. They thought no one could see."

Vykk sniffed the air appreciatively. "Somewhere, a stewpot simmers with fresh meat."

"The next pot may boil with our flesh," Hhney reminded him.

The Wamandu's tiny brow furrowed. "You weren't captured and brought to the Comb. You came here on purpose. You have a scheme."

Tskett bent down. "The *scheme* doesn't include you."

"It does now."

"My Leader?"

"I helped you escape," the Wamandu said. "You'd have been captured except for me."

"He'll slow us down," Tskett argued. "He lacks speed, he doesn't have strength."

"I can see what others can't."

"We already carry one useless chund." Tskett's beak swiveled toward Dobbins. "We can't risk the weight of another."

"Leave me behind and I'll scream," the Wamandu said, unruffled. "You'd be surprised at how loudly I can scream."

"Then you'd best come with us," Hhney said.

"I thought so."

"In case," she added, "we need someone to scream."

The Wamandu's eyes widened. Hhney said, "Vykk, you go first."

Moving in single file, they started through the tunnel. Like the Comb it served, the corridor had a dirt floor and earthen walls. Despite its status as a servant's passage, it led them down a long pathway and numerous doors without a single encounter with another Bug. Finally, it split into a 'Y', with both forks wider than its stem.

Dobbins said, "There are more lighting globes to the left. It's brighter down there. Bright enough to see the walk is empty."

"But the leg to the right is more likely to take us under the Comb," Hhney said.

"It bends out of sight. It's darker, too, you can tell."

Vykk started toward the left leg.

"No," his Leader said, "not that way."

"Naturally not." Dobbins sounded morose.

"Do you feel it?" Hhney asked Aly. "The Web? It's calling to us."

"I don't feel anything."

Tskett said, "How can you not? To the right."

Hhney gave him a discomforting smile. "Let's go."

Following Vykk in the same ragged single file order, the party continued on with Tskett guarding the rear. He followed them with a heavy step, lost in thought.

"This passageway is forbidden." From inside the shadows, a stranger's voice called out to them in Basic.

Vykk stopped. A hunched-over Bug stepped inside the down-turned mouth of a doorway.

Hhney squeezed past her sentry. "Our apologies, Elder."

"Tramping up the aisle like a herd of goriks," the Bug said. "Stay in the passages with light, everyone knows that much. It's dangerous in the dark, very dangerous. "

"We're escorting prisoners to the Father," Hhney said, "We must have taken a wrong turn."

"To his food pots, you mean," the Bug said. "Be thankful I sleep lightly. The monster would have eaten you all."

Dobbins squinted, trying to see through the gloom. "Monster?"

"The most useless of monsters, playing with puzzles." A paralyzed leg dragging behind her, the Bug manuevered herself into the tunnel. "I should report you." She tilted her wizened head, examining Tskett and Hhney. "Why are you so dirty? Where is the female's spear?"

"I forgot it," Hhney said, as Tskett tried, "Lost."

Dobbins asked, with a bit more force, "What about the monster?"

"Guards are to be clean, weapons must be carried, armbands should be displayed with pride," the ancient Bug said. "Infractions, so many infractions."

"We beg forgiveness, Elder."

"Forgiveness can be had. For a price. Bring me a softbody, hairless and fat."

"Where would we find such a prize?"

"The same place you got these three," she said, pointing in the direction of Aly, Dobbins and the Wamandu. "I'll want it soon. I feed the chameleon at night." Returning to her blackened room, she slammed the door shut.

"A chameleon," Vykk said dully.

"I've never seen a chameleon," Aly said.

"I have," Dobbins said. "I'd rather not see another."

Taking Vykk's spear, Tskett went to the front of the group. "I'll lead. Quietly, now."

Cautiously, the others trailed behind him.

The hallway crooked inward, following in the direction of the Comb. Ahead of them, more of the sparse lighting globes were burnt out and black. Already dark in the tunnel, it grew even darker.

Tskett stopped. "Another doorway."

"A trap?" Hhney asked.

"Both, perhaps."

An opening was carved into the wall ahead of them. Through the empty space, there was a chamber hidden in shadow. Behind it, a faint circle of light

262

showed a second, larger opening. Only by going through the room could they continue down the tunnel.

"Let's go back," Dobbins said. "The other path."

"It won't lead us to the Web."

The Wamandu wrinkled his black nose, sniffing the air. "Can you smell it? The stink? This is the chameleon's den."

"Then where is the beast?" Vykk asked. "The floor, the walls, even the ceiling: They're all flat and true."

"A chameleon adapts its body to its surroundings," Dobbins said. "It can take the color and texture of anything."

"So?"

"It can't disguise its bulk. If its hiding in its chamber, we should be able to see some kind of bulge in there."

"It's here," the Wamandu said. "I smell it."

"When did you learn about chameleons?" Aly asked Dobbins.

"Syr changed into one once," he told her. "He was younger then, still working on his control. We lost the treasure, the Princess got eaten, nothing really worked out. But the change was an incredible sight."

"Syr ate a Princess?"

"She wasn't a nice Princess."

Hhney said, "If the Father has a chameleon, he'll want it contained. There's nothing barring this doorway. And the back doorway is bigger still."

"Which means the chameleon must be huge," Vykk said gloomily.

"It might lie in a pit," Aly said. "It could have torn a trench to hide inside."

"But where?"

Tskett eased inside the first opening. No new whisper of sound welcomed his entrance; there was no wrinkle of light to show a chameleon shifting in place. To all appearances, he was alone in the chamber.

The others pressed in with him. From behind them, they heard the old Bug's voice. "I told you not to come this way."

She waited in the passage, her dead leg bent behind her.

"We can explain," Hhney said.

"Too late now."

Reaching into a pocket in the wall, the Bug jerked down on a ring carved from bone. A latticework of Lygt rod dropped from the entry's arch, closing the opening behind them.

"So much meat," she said from behind the crisscrossed bars. "The chameleon will get fat."

Her leg dragging across the floor, the old Bug hobbled away.

"She closed the doorway behind us," Tskett said. "But the one at the other end of this room is still open."

Hhney said, "Then all we have to do is make it to the other side." In Y'togish, she told Aly, "Best if the Wamandu goes first."

In the same tongue, Aly answered, "He'll refuse."

"Convince him. If you can't, Tskett will pick him up and throw him into the chamber."

The Wamandu peeked at the group from around Dobbins' back. Aly said, "It's not my way, Leader."

"You owe him nothing."

She shook her head.

With an irritated grunt, Tskett swooped down, grabbing the Wamandu. He lofted the squealing creature from the floor and threw him through the air. The tourist hit the ground and lay there without moving.

A moment later, the Wamandu's curses filled the room. Sitting up, he pointed a small, sharp nail in Tskett's direction. "I don't like you!"

His cry echoed in the chamber. When nothing materialized to eat the newcomer, Dobbins said, "So where's the chameleon?"

"Maybe the chamber is empty," Vykk hazarded.

"The ancient Bug said not."

"But maybe it is." Vykk bolted ahead.

"Vykk!"

Within seconds, he'd crossed the space. Untouched, he leapt for the safety of the open exit.

The opening folded around him. Empty space flickered and buckled as the chameleon pulled itself inward. Tucked over the actual doorway, it had mimicked the appearance of a grand opening. With Vykk in its folds, the creature withdrew its claws from the walls supporting it and dropped to the floor.

The membrane between its forelegs and hind legs stretched over the Sktzer like a tent of skin, pushing him to the ground. Crouched over its victim, the creature lifted its triangular head from the cavity in its chest. "Stupid, stupid."

Scrambling to his feet, the Wamandu joined the others. He tugged at Dobbins' shirt. "While the chameleon feeds, we'll escape."

"Ordinarily, I'd agree," Dobbins acknowledged, "but not this time."

The chameleon let color flood into its body. "Easy prey." Sullenly, it batted at Vykk's beak.

"Think again, beast," Tskett said, brandishing his spear.

"Pointed sticks?"

"The best weapon for enclosed spaces," Tskett said.

Aly stepped to the front of the group. "We've come to hear your riddle."

The chameleon's eyes brightened. "The Crone told you. What did she say? Did she give you an answer?"

With the monster distracted, Vykk tried to slide out from under its hold. When he did, it caught at his leg and pulled him back.

"If she gave you an answer, it won't be right," the chameleon said. "I won't tell her, no matter how often she pleads." The last statement was made with great satisfaction.

"She told us nothing," Aly said. "Give us the riddle so that we may answer it and pass."

Her statement took the creature by surprise. "Let you pass? My exit is for Father's use only."

"What other reward would you offer? We've come to answer the riddle and gain safe passage."

"A game," the chameleon said. "Yes." Caged inside its room, it wiggled its tail with excitement. "I want to play this game. Are you ready?"

"No," the Wamandu said.

266

The chameleon said, "Listen to my puzzle, then. Listen for your lives:

> *It brings nothing when it comes*
> *But what was there, is more.*
> *It takes nothing when it leaves*
> *But what was more, is less.*
> *Some gain little*
> *But all gain the world."*

It let them consider its words. Pleased with itself, it thumped a heavy leg against the ground. "What is your guess?"

Trapped under one large foot, Vykk said, "Greed."

The chameleon's foot shifted, covering his mouth.

A reflective Hhney said, "I have an answer."

"So do I," said Aly. "It's the Web."

"Wrong!" the chameleon exploded. Lifting its foot from Vykk's head, it stamped its claws into the earth. "Wrong, wrong, wrong!"

A cackle of laughter came from outside the chamber. The old Bug appeared, her ancient frame visible through the Lygt rod.

"All these years," the Crone said. "I'd never have guessed."

The chameleon recoiled at the sight of her. Its muzzle flattened angrily.

"I'll tell everyone the secret of your riddle, beast. Everyone." With a throaty chuckle, she hobbled off.

The chameleon kicked Vykk away. Backing up, it blocked the exit. "There will be nothing left of

267

you," it promised the group. "Not shell nor bone nor flesh nor hair."

"We answered the riddle," Hhney said.

"Use your spear," the monster urged. "Test its point against my skin." An expression of concentration passed over its face and its scales shimmered. Their plate-like surface appeared to soften and melt until the chameleon resembled a breathing pile of dirt and twigs.

Tskett gripped his spear.

"You promised safe passage," Aly said.

"My riddle was stolen from me."

"The challenge was met."

"It was not!" the chameleon snapped. "*Greed* was the answer first given. That answer is wrong!"

Vykk steadied himself against the side wall. The Wamandu pointed at him. "The words came from that one's mouth. Take him."

"I'll take you all," said the chameleon.

"Try me first, beast." Tskett flared his wings, shielding the Leader.

"Flyer." The chameleon was momentarily nonplused.

"Sktzer."

"Sktzers are the enemies of Father Lygt," Hhney said soothingly. "We are all enemies of the Father."

"Sktzers built this Comb," the chameleon said. "Sktzers made my cage."

"It's the Father who put you here."

With hatred in its voice, the chameleon said, "The Crone is my keeper."

"She works for the Father," Aly said.

"You gave her my riddle!" The mound of dirt and twigs rose up, a paw swinging out from its midst. Sharp claws slashed at Tskett's spear, cleaving it. The blow threw the Bug from his feet, knocking him into Vykk.

They both fell to the ground.

"If you let us pass," Hhney said, "I'll give you a new riddle." She touched Aly's shoulder. "My sister taught me." She touched Aly's shoulder.

The chameleon kicked at the ground, disbelievingly. "A new riddle?"

"New. As good as your last."

"Both riddle and answer?"

"The answer when we return," Hhney promised. "If it's fair and true, you allow us passage again."

The monster studied her. "It will be too simple. The Crone will guess it."

"It takes wit to know this answer. Wit is beyond her."

"Too hard, then. It won't be fair. She'll mock me."

"No harder than your last," Hhney replied. "You'll know when you hear it. The Crone will know by your manner."

"How can I believe you?"

"I'll tell you the riddle."

And she did.

Chapter Twenty-Four

The District Manager called out, "Have you found anything?"

Straddling the limb of a sasga tree, Mel's main concern was retaining his balance. "Not yet."

"Go higher!"

Was he serious? The earth was already a dizzying distance below. If the DM would only leave, Mel could find himself a sturdy lower branch and squat contentedly for a very long while.

"I've got something," the DM said. "A clue."

Even from this distance, Mel saw the distinctive design and color of the object he was holding. "That's my nametag!"

The DM brought the item up to his eyes. "No, it isn't."

"It is. It's been on my chest for days now. You couldn't have missed it."

"Your name isn't 'Mel'."

"That's my new name," Mel said.

"Huh." The DM tore the nametag in half, dropping the pieces. "I like your old name."

"The Slavemaster -"

"- toils in his new owner's fields. Would you care to join him, Stynx?"

Feeling a familiar sadness settle upon him, Stynx said, "No."

"Higher."

Stynx reached for the next limb. How much more of this was he expected to tolerate? He wasn't a climber; his class of Bug was meant to stay on the surface. A Mentren should have been doing this job.

He didn't know what the DM hoped to get out of this expedition, anyway. They'd been to this site twice before, picking through rubble. The Assassins had destroyed nearly everything in their raid.

It wasn't as if the Sktzers might return, scattering fresh clues to their new location. They were gone. The female chund was gone with them.

The District Manager needed to accept the facts.

"Father expects the female," the DM had told him. "If he doesn't get her, who is he going to blame?"

Swaying in the tree, Stynx whispered, "He'll blame you. Yes, he will."

If the DM was replaced, Stynx could become Mel again. He could get a job at the chundhut in the southeast of town – *Mel's Travelrama*, did any business anywhere have a more glorious name? – and he'd find happiness at last.

Until that glorious moment arrived, the DM wasn't going to make things easy. Rather than face Father Lygt with bad news, he wasted their time hunting for the lost chund. Today, in desperation, he'd returned to the rebel camp. When a search of the grounds had proven fruitless, he'd sent Stynx up into the trees.

Stynx hated heights. But he hated the idea of being a slave even more.

His cousin, Jokynn, was the District Manager's favorite. If one of them was going to waste his time and his talents at the DM's command then, by all rights, Jokynn should have been here. But his cousin was missing. The last time Stynx saw him, he'd left with the DM to spy on the chund.

Jokynn had never returned.

It was worrisome. What happened to his cousin? Did the changer get him?

The shape-changer was reason enough to avoid the rebel camp.

The DM waited at the base of the tree. "You call that high?"

I do, Stynx thought.

Whenever a fresh burst of wind caused the needles to sway, his location seemed tremendously high. Releasing one clump of brush, he locked his claw onto a higher one. Gripping the trunk with his legs, he shimmied upward.

This far up, the branches of the tree weren't thick enough for someone of his weight. Most appeared barely able to support their needle clusters. If Stynx lost his hold on the tree trunk, he'd plummet to the ground.

When that happened, as he knew it would, he intended to land atop the District Manager.

Stynx poked his head through a matted layer of needles. This part of the tree had been stripped naked, possibly as a sentry's outlook. Providing an unobstructed view of the trail below, the forest opened up beneath it.

The trail was empty. Abandoned and beautiful, the land was the color of new copper. Forgetting his fear for the moment, he marveled at the sight.

From across the woods, a tree shook against the wind. The DM shouted, "Why are you sitting there?"

"I'm looking for clues!" *Maybe I will find a clue*, he thought. *Maybe I'll see a Sktzer.*

As unlikely as such a feat was, it no longer seemed impossible. From this vantage point, it felt as if he could see the entire world.

Another tree shook against the wind. Needles showered into the air before floating downward.

The rest of the forest was still. Stynx pulled himself still higher.

How can a current of air gust against a single tree without disturbing any of the others? What kind of wind blows hard enough to tear needles free, but so gently they drift to the ground?

Then he thought, *Uh-oh.*

When the next tree shivered, he happened to be watching it. The tree didn't move as if shaken by an air current; it jerked, as if it had been pushed. A second tree, standing across from it, jerked in the same fashion.

It was as if something was trying to squeeze its way between the trees. Something big, very, very big.

Something invisible.

The sound of breaking bark caused the DM to shade his eyes and stare into the woods. "What's out there?"

Clinging to his spot in the sky, Stynx didn't respond.

Another sharp, snapping sound echoed throughout the forest. A tree tilted up, its roots torn from the ground. A dull, thudding noise pounded against the earth itself. On the forest floor, fallen needles sagged inward, as if being squashed by some gigantic beast.

It can't be, Stynx thought.

Bark sprayed from the face of another tree as it moved abruptly to one side. The imprint of a huge foot squished into the dirt, burying needles.

Zneeth.

The DM stared into the nothingness in front of him. The footsteps became louder, growing closer. He leapt for the branch overhanging his head.

"Stynx!" he cried, straining to lift himself up.

Overhead, Stynx saw a thick cluster of needles. If he could pull himself through it, he'd be out of sight from anyone, or anything, below.

He spread the cluster apart. When he did, a beak sagged through the nest. A disembodied face looked back at him.

Not a face, no. A head.

His cousin's head. A small branch had pierced through the back of Jokynn's skull, pinning it to the tree.

"Yyaaaah!" In a spasm of fright, Stynx pushed away from the frowning skull. Losing his hold on the tree's trunk, he immediately reached out to save himself. Finding needles instead of branches, he fell into to space.

He plummeted through the brush.

Below him, the DM found his footing on the tree's lowest branch. He straightened as Stynx's body dropped on top of him.

The District Manager crashed to the forest floor. Winded, he lay on his side with his assistant's legs draped over his head. Pushing the limbs away, he clambered to his feet. "Get up, you stupid Bug."

There was no answer from Stynx.

"We have to go," the DM tried more urgently. Still, his companion refused to stir.

"Fair warning, then," he said with a smile. "Stay here. If there's trouble afoot, let it find you."

The DM considered the safest route of escape. *Through the camp, over the demolished Mound, and away from those fallen trees,* he decided when the Zneeth's trunk stabbed through his shell, killing him.

* * *

Letting the exo-skeleton topple to the ground, the Zneeth sniffed at the second Bug at his feet. It didn't move.

Eat it?

Why bother? The unconscious creature wasn't afraid. Even if it had been afraid, there was no fun in feeding without its Joy.

Nothing was good, nothing was right, without its Joy. After the Wicked One had taken it, the Zneeth wanted to die. Retreating to its lair, it hid in blackness. It didn't want to eat, didn't want to move.

All it wanted was to forget.

Emboldened by the Zneeth's apathy, the kildebeests dared to enter its den. Laughing, teasing, their mocking words filled the space around him. Moons crossed the sky and the kildebeests grew bolder still. Filled with bravado, they decided they were the new masters of the Cave of Doom.

One cold night, they attacked.

275

They came in a pack, their fangs biting against the steel of the Zneeth's scales. Stirred from its apathy, it rose before them. With the bellowed cry of a hundred voices, it trumpeted its anger. Ruler of this cavern for hundreds of cycles, it wasn't about to abdicate its kingdom to the likes of these.

Shrieking, the kildebeests ran for their lives. Chasing them, the Zneeth ripped apart their tunnels and destroyed their shelters. It caught and killed the oldest and slowest of its enemies as the rest of the pack raced for safety. When, in desperation, the kildebeests climbed from the cave, the Zneeth continued after them. It burst out of the ground and into the moonlight.

The Zneeth couldn't remember the last time it had been to the surface. In the open air, a vast nothingness whirled around it. There were no pathways to offer direction, no walls to provide comfort. Overwhelmed by the space around it, the Zneeth thought of retreating to its bed. With the kildebeests gone, it could have hidden below ground for the rest of its days.

Then it caught the vestigial scent of the defiler of its home. Alone in the center of this alien plain, cowering from the light in the sky, its spirit had awakened.

Inhaling mightily, it found a whisper, a hint, of the distant musk. Using it, the monster began to track its enemy. It followed the scent across the plain and through the jungle. Nearing the township, it grew wary. Under the cover of nightfall, it passed through its streets. Almost losing the trail at times, it found trace enough of the accursed thief to continue on.

At last, it arrived here.

The Zneeth prowled through the ruins. Yes, the Wicked One had been here. Her sign led just beyond the perimeter of the clearing. It stopped abruptly, almost as though she'd vanished.

But the Wicked One wasn't dead. Death always left a special kind of smell.

No matter. The Zneeth would find her. When it did, it would retrieve its only Joy.

Nothing was going to stand in its way.

Chapter Twenty-Five

Beyond the chameleon's chamber, the corridor widened. With Tskett in the lead, they marched up its slope. The upward path left no doubt they were rising.

"We made it," Aly said to Hhney. "We're inside the Comb."

"You're right, we are. How did you know?"

"The walls are a different color here. The color of ancient mud."

Vykk hurried to catch up to them. "When we return, the monster will want an answer for your riddle."

"I have an answer to give," Hhney said.

"It wasn't a trick?"

"No trick."

"Good." Vykk scratched at his chin. "Let it ponder its puzzle until we come back." Speeding up, he went ahead of the others.

"Slow down," demanded the Wamandu, his short legs pumping. "What's the hurry, anyway?"

"You never know what might be behind us," Dobbins told him.

"Hurrying, hurrying," the Wamandu complained. "Hurrying to our deaths."

He clutched at Dobbins' pants leg for reassurance.

The pathway stretched on without interruption. There were no new doorways entering into it, no adjoining tunnels crossing it. Its featureless walls ran on and on.

Suddenly, Vykk stopped. "Dead end."

A wall blocked the trail, lighting globes affixed to each of its sides. A white glow played over the colorful mosaic in front of them.

The wall's face was composed of tiled panels, each slightly larger than an adult human hand. The panels had been set in place without mortar to join them, leaving large black and empty lines to crisscross the tile's decorative design. The fragmented picture that resulted seemed to be an abstract depiction of some great creature.

Aly tapped a finger against a tile. "Another riddle."

"What kind of riddle?"

"It wasn't meant for chund, that's all I know."

Tskett said, "Above the tile."

Coarse-grained stone blocks ran in a framework along the mosaic. Lettering was chiseled into the blocks, with each segment divided by carved drawings of flying Bugs.

"It's Y'togish," Hhney said. "One of the early forms, first written when this world was young. Tskett, you've studied. Do you know what it says?"

"Some. The words are old, the carvings are primitive. The mosaic warns of danger." Tskett shrugged, his shoulders lifting his heavy shell. "The Elder could have told us more."

His gaze fell from the stones to the party around him. Finding the Wamandu, he smiled.

"Why are you smiling?" the Wamandu said. "I don't like it."

Tskett's smile grew larger.

"Bugs aren't supposed to smile. Bugs are *evil*."

Aly remained at the wall, her nose almost pressing against it. "It's a challenge. To pass through, we have to solve the wall's mystery. Otherwise -"

"What?" Dobbins asked.

"I can read some of this," Aly said. "The message promises a most pleasurable death…or a most deadly pleasure. But 'death' is definitely part of the warning."

"We could run away," the Wamandu said.

Hhney shook her head.

Dobbins ran his fingers over the panels in front of him. A few were firm and unyielding, but most rocked slightly at his touch. "I can open this."

"Can he?" Hhney asked Aly.

"It's a lock, a combination lock," Dobbins said. "As locks go, it's pretty basic."

To demonstrate, he pushed against the top of a tile. It cocked backward, bringing its base toward him.

"See? Now this stone is set. Each of these panels belong in a single position. If you move it in the proper direction, it takes hold. Once we've got them all in place, the wall opens."

The next panel swiveled under Dobbins' fingers, moving sideways before it snapped in place. "Want to try?"

Vykk stepped forward. "It would help if I knew which way this was supposed to turn."

He applied pressure to each corner of the panel and then to each side before the tile rolled over and locked. When it turned, an assembly of stone rods moved behind it. Briefly glimpsed, the elongated cylinders shifted in concert with one another.

"This takes too long," Vykk said. He pressed his head against the wall. "There's something inside this wall. It's moving."

Tskett listened, too. "Not moving. Pouring."

"Pouring is moving."

Dobbins' face tightened. He shoved Tskett aside.

"Watch yourself, chund!"

Dobbins reached for the top, upper left-hand tile – pressing here, pressing *here* – and the tile shifted and locked.

"What is it?" Aly asked.

Dobbins pressed the tile adjacent to the first. "When this tunnel was new, when this wall was first built, there had never been an off-world visitor. Hands were unknown to the architects of the Comb."

Press, *press*. The tile moved and held. He went to the next square. "They hadn't planned for fingers. Fingers are more sensitive than claws. They can feel the workings of a mechanism and they're dexterous enough to adjust for it. Let's hope so, anyway. It's our only chance."

"Our only chance?" the Wamandu said. "Chance at what?"

Press, *push*. The tile rolled over.

"This kind of lock works off a timer," Dobbins said. "It was probably activated when I turned the first tile. If we set the lock before the timer runs out, we win."

The Wamandu was about to speak when Vykk clopped him on the head. "Don't."

"I didn't say anything!"

"You were going to," Vykk told the furry thing. "I don't want to know what comes next. When we don't 'win' and the timer runs out, nothing good is going to happen. Maybe the roof will fall in or the tunnels will flood or the floor will crack apart and we will tumble through it and onto jagged spikes below. I don't want to know."

"What if it unleashes monsters?" the Wamandu asked.

Vykk clopped him again.

Tskett pressed his head to the wall. "There's water inside. A fluid of some sort, anyway."

"The timer isn't sophisticated, can't be when it's this old," Dobbins said. "Liquid was a favorite for the ancient traps. Something viscous, something designed not to evaporate. All it has to do is spill from one container to another, like an hourglass."

Aly joined him. Working together, they turned, swiveled and rolled every moving panel. When Aly shifted to the last square, Dobbins pushed his ear against the wall. "It's still pouring."

The last piece locked into place. As it did, a deep reverberation sounded from inside the wall. The two center panels, frozen side by side, jiggled at the sound.

The wall didn't move. The Wamandu retreated as Tskett and Vykk pressed against it.

"There has to be something else," Hhney said. "Some other key, some hidden device. Find it, Dobbins."

"It's a lock. I know locks, but -"

"Every lock has a weakness," Aly reminded him.

282

"Yeah, right." He put his hand against one of the center tiles. "Okay, it doesn't turn, it doesn't rotate, but it's not rigid. It's willing to move."

He pressed at the joint between the tiles. Both of the squares swung inward, forming a pocket as they opened.

"There's something in here. A pair of indentations." Dobbins eased his arm into the opening, stretching his hand out. "Can't do it. It was made for someone with claws. Someone able to reach into both holes at the same time."

"Vykk," Hhney said.

Tskett lifted his head from the fractured mosaic. "The fluid is almost gone. It's dripping."

"Quickly," the Leader said.

Spreading his claw, Vykk reached inside the hole. His arm pushed inward and a soft *thwick*! noise was heard inside the tunnel.

Noiselessly, the wall swung forward. Tskett looped an arm around Vykk, pulling his claw out of the pocket and bringing him back with the others as a passageway appeared in front of them. Past the threshold of stone blocks, the walkway was wide and well-lit.

Aly knelt at the edge of the opening. "The blocks framing this wall are thicker than the wall itself. Look at this: there are holes drilled all along the framework."

Evenly spaced, the holes dotted the edge of every stone. Dobbins frowned. "Game's not over yet. We can't move through here without passing these holes."

A milky drop fell through the opening, splashing onto one of the bottom blocks. When Aly traced its path, she saw a second drop forming at the base of an upper bore hole. "This isn't good."

To Dobbins, Tskett said, "Come here, softbody."

"Why?"

"I have something to show you."

"Maybe another time." Dobbins edged away from the Sktzer. The Wamandu watched them both, his eyes glittering.

Swooping downward, Tskett clutched the Wamandu by the nape of his neck. As the newest member of their party squealed, the rebel cocked his arms, ready to throw his wiggling victim through the threshold. Kicking out forcefully, the Wamandu knocked Tskett backward.

Falling from his grasp, the Wamandu dropped on top of the blocks. Instantly, spray jetted from the holes in the stones. White droplets of fluid coated his fur and filled his mouth when he tried to shout. Swinging his paws blindly, cursing loudly, he struggled to stand upright. The ground's wet surface betrayed him and his feet slid away. Crashing to the ground, he curled into a ball and waited for the rain to stop.

Tskett pulled Hhney into the corridor. Vykk grabbed at Aly, who tugged at Dobbins. They all stepped away from the brackish shower.

"You knew this would happen," Aly said.

"It went better than I expected," Tskett said. "I hoped to use the softbody to see if the trap remained lethal. If he stays atop the blocks, he'll drain the liquid."

"The symbols warned you."

"Sktzers carved the drawings on this wall. They're quite descriptive."

"A deadly pleasure," Aly remembered, "or a pleasured death."

"Words have power, too."

Dobbins asked, "What's in the liquid?"

"You'll see."

"You almost drowned me!" The Wamandu sat up. Around him, the hidden nozzles dripped wetly.

Under the corridor, scrabbling noises ran beneath their feet. The sound hurried past them, moving in the direction of the pathway ahead.

The Wamandu tried to get his footing. He slipped, backpedaling into the corridor before falling again.

"I hate you all," he said.

He rolled over, wiping at his fur. Facing the others, he didn't see the jointed foot reaching out from under a trap door in the floor.

Dobbins inhaled sharply.

"What's the matter?" the Wamandu demanded.

"Let him go," Hhney said. "It's too late to save him."

Hearing her words, the Wamandu spun around as an evil-looking invertebrate crawled out of the ground. It scuttled sideways, its erectile tail lifted up behind it.

"What is that?" Aly asked.

"Synge. An earth-dweller. It's poisonous."

Another jointed foot appeared under the trapdoor, keeping the lid from closing. Before it dropped, two more synge crawled through the opening.

285

Kicking his legs, the Wamandu pushed against the side of the corridor. "You – you stay away!"

Each synge was nearly his size. They moved slowly, their segmented bodies protected by a flexible hard shell and their tails curled into the air. Each tail ended in a ball. Growing out of the bottom of each ball were two needle-thin stingers.

It was the stingers that held the gaze of the frightened Wamandu. The nearest synge shook its tail rhythmically, the needles swishing from side to side. Unblinking, the Wamandu swayed with the movement.

"The Sweet Breeze has him," Tskett explained.

"That's what sprayed from the nozzles?" Aly asked. "A narcotic?"

"A 'deadly pleasure'. He's going into a dream state. The Sweet Breeze brings whatever you'd like to see. If the synge hadn't come for him, he'd starve to death and never care. He'd imagine he was supping at a banquet. The food would be the best he'd ever tasted."

The Wamandu reached out for the closest synge. "Wamandika," he said happily.

The synge's tail stabbed forward, its stinger jabbing the outstretched paw. The Wamandu pulled it back, looking at the tender pad in confusion.

Forgetting his injury, he staggered around. Stumbling, he faced Aly.

"*Wamandika*," he growled sensuously. He leered at her, his furry face transformed in its carnality.

Knees shaking, the Wamandu toppled over. The synge swarmed over him. Together, they tugged him through the trap door and into their tunnel. Under the flooring, the others could hear the body being dragged away.

"We have no more time to waste," Hhney said without emotion, "and he wasn't Sktzer."

She stepped over the stone blocks and the others followed. Skirting around the outline of the passage's trap door, they walked on.

"He was just a tourist," Dobbins said.

Chapter Twenty-Six

The corridor continued into the Comb. On occasion, faint voices were heard, speaking behind earthen walls, but there were no new doorways to be found. Dobbins listened for scrabbling noises beneath their feet.

"This way," Hhney said.

Dobbins told her, "I'll take lead."

When the pathway climbed, peaking like a small hill several yards away from them, he was the first to climb it. Reaching the crest, he extended an arm above his head. The ceiling of the Comb was so close his fingers swept only inches below its uneven surface.

Aly joined him. "What do you think?"

"Trouble ahead. What else is new?"

On the other side of the crest, the trail descended sharply. Tilted at a dangerous level, it dropped below a curved archway. The archway's opening gaped at them like a hungry mouth.

"Wish me luck," he said.

"Let's wait for the others."

"Why?" Dobbins asked. "Whoever crosses under the archway, well, I'm betting they've got an ugly surprise waiting for them. Hhney's made it pretty clear we won't be drawing straws to see who tries it first." He took a tentative step downward. "I'm not one of the sept."

"I'll go with you."

"You will?" He twisted toward her, putting one foot backward to maintain his balance. When he did, his foot went out from under him.

The downward pathway was greased.

Flailing, he grabbed for the hem of Aly's robe. He caught it, pulling at her. Losing her footing, she slammed into him and they both slid down the passage.

Riding over a coat of slime, Dobbins careened into a corridor wall. He dragged his hands against it, barely slowing his descent. Out of control, he spun back onto the center of the path.

Aly shot ahead of him. He caught a glimpse of her as she glided through the archway and out of sight. As she entered, a metal partition banged down behind her, sealing the corridor. Unable to stop himself, Dobbins banged into the barrier.

He shook his head, trying to clear his mind. At the top of the hill, Hhney was watching. The disappointment in her eyes was unmistakable.

He heard her say, "We've lost Aly. She's gone."

* * *

Hostage to the slick surface and her own momentum, Aly swept beneath the archway. When she did, a stone wall crashed down behind her. The surrounding light disappeared.

Abruptly, her slide ended. Her feet struck the gritty surface of a dirt floor, throwing her into the air. Somersaulting awkwardly, she crashed to a rough, jolting stop.

Bracing herself against one arm, she struggled to sit up.

What have I gotten myself into this time?

Within the surrounding gloom, there were slivers of illumination. Tiny cracks penetrated the walls, providing just enough visibility for her to get a sense of the chamber around her. Seeing – almost sensing - a black circle above her, she reached out for it.

At her touch, a lighting globe shimmered, casting a glow as it reawakened. The room around her was large and tall, stretching with empty space all the way to the top of the Comb.

Another trap.

She'd suspected as much but, even forewarned, she'd stumbled ahead. There was no use in blaming Dobbins for her predicament. He'd been prepared to go on without her.

She sniffed at the hem of her robe. Wet, it stunk of the Twill slime that had greased her ride. Pulling the robe away from her leg, she found the sheath still strapped to her thigh.

Aly unfastened its tie. Taking the knife in hand, she felt marginally more prepared for whatever nightmare roamed in this part of the Comb.

Indentations were carved into the wall in front of her. Two deep tunnels, with blackness behind them, led into this room. In the Cave of Doom, the kildebeests had used these same kinds of passages.

She returned to the sealed passageway, stopping at the coating of slime leading into the room. If she was a flyer, she could have carried herself over it. Without wings, she could go no further. She dismissed the tunnels at a glance before scrutinizing the cracks in the walls. None of the openings were very big.

A good blade can fix that, she thought.

Working on the largest crevice, she stepped onto a puddle of slime that had dripped from her robe. Her legs slid out from under her and her forehead slapped into the wall. A brilliant, blinding, flash of white light filled her vision. She fell to the ground, her fingers still clutching her knife.

She blinked up at the ceiling.

Not doing so good, transporter. You got a Plan B?

"Well, well," said a voice from within the chamber. "What have we here?"

Rising, Aly saw an Assassin entering the room. It regarded her with amusement.

From the tunnel closest to it, red legs emerged and a second kildebeest climbed from a tunnel. "What is it, Tink?"

"A softbody."

The kildebeest shuffled sideways. "It's covered with goo."

"Slime."

"It's all over the meat." The kildebeest couldn't have sounded more repelled. "It will taste of mucus."

"We don't have to eat it, Weege," Tink said. "We only have to kill it."

Keeping her knife concealed, Aly gathered her sodden robe around her. She smeared a wet sleeve across her face. Gelatinous ooze dripped down her forehead, nose and chin.

"You're disgusting," Weege said.

A third, fourth and fifth kildebeest appeared from the tunnels. Curious about the visitor, they made no effort to approach her. Instead, they lingered near the exit, as if to disassociate themselves from such a sloppy chund.

"The softbody made it this far," Tink said. "It must be determined. It survived the chameleon so it must be resourceful. It passed the locks; it must be smart. Why would it let itself be trapped here?"

"It must be food," a kildebeest said. The kildebeests laughed, with Tink chortling the loudest.

Abruptly, it was all too much for Aly. "Shut up!"

Their merriment dying away, the kildebeests viewed her with surprise.

"All you do is prattle. Endless, senseless prattle." She flexed her fingers before tightening them around the hilt of the knife. "I'm sick to death of it."

"Good choice of words," said the last kildebeest. It brought a burst of titters from the Assassins.

Tink strolled around to Aly's right side. "Weege?" he called.

Weege bobbed over to her left flank. It drew itself up short. "It has a blade."

Her secret discovered, Aly brought her knife hand in front of her body. She held it in battle position.

"It's not a big blade," Tink argued.

"It's pointed toward me."

"First to kill is first to eat."

"Who wants to eat this?" Weege tapped a leg nervously. "You kill it. You get goo all over your bulb."

292

Tink frowned. Concentrating, he said, "Together."

Aly felt her heart quicken.

Working in pairs, the kildebeests had been brutally effective in destroying the Sktzers. One would spring for a rebel's head while the other tore at its legs. Most of the Bugs died so quickly they never had the opportunity to use their pincers.

Not me, she thought. *I'm not going easily. If blood spills today, the kildebeests will lose their share.*

Tink feinted toward her, trying to draw the interest of her knife hand. When he did, Weege rushed ahead in a blur of crimson legs. With the wide-bodied kildebeest leaping into the air, Tink darted ahead. He held his fangs out and ready, seeking tender muscle and fragile organs.

Soaring, Weege swung his head in befuddlement as Aly disappeared beneath him. At the same time, Tink was almost upon her when he saw that she was braced for him. The tip of Aly's blade slashed at the charging kildebeest.

Kicking out his front legs, Tink managed to save himself. Spinning off sideways, he carried himself beyond the swing of his adversary's arm.

The laughter of the other kildebeests filled the chamber. Tink and Weege retreated to the far side of the room. Huddled together in unhappy discussion, they pointedly ignored the snickering around them.

The palm of Aly's right hand was moist with sweat. Transferring the knife to her other hand, she rubbed her wet palm against the dirt at her feet.

You're way past Plan B, she told herself. *How about Plan C? Plan D?*

293

Any options at all?

Hhney and the others had probably gone on without her. It was unlikely the Sktzers – or Dobbins - would waste their time exploring for a way into this chamber. This last trap had been sprung too near the center of the Comb. This time, alarms would have sounded throughout the hive. Father Lygt would be ready for them.

A realist, Hhney wouldn't wait for Father's guards to seal off their escape. Stealth and surprise had given them their only advantage against a superior foe. With the element of surprise lost, she'd have no choice but to retreat.

It wasn't an act of disloyalty. It was the only sane choice.

Syr wouldn't have left you, a stray thought taunted her.

You don't know that, she argued silently.

He'd never leave his mate.

"I'm not his mate!" she said out loud.

Dobbins and his nonsense. Why had she ever listened to him?

It wouldn't have mattered if Syr was here, anyway. A weakened changer couldn't help her now. She'd find herself fighting to save two lives instead of one and, at this moment, it seemed as if saving her own was going to be challenge enough.

Bending her legs, Aly centered herself. Tink and Weege were returning.

They trotted together, foregoing the silly chatter that seemed ingrained in their species. Their fellow Assassins more than made up for their silence, throwing out derisive comments as they passed. Tink

294

held his head high, above it all. Weege stuck out his tongue, refusing to respond.

Tink's purposeful manner indicated he wasn't going to let another attack fail. He wanted Aly to recognize his determination and be unnerved by it. Several feet in front of her, the two kildebeests stopped. They bumped their bodies together in a last conference. Then, at some unspoken cue, they attacked again.

Joined side-by-side, they came at her as if they were one creature. Driving boldly forward, they left her without any room to maneuver. She didn't have the leaping ability to go over them and they were too close to the ground for her to escape beneath them. Their combined width prevented her from dodging sideways. She couldn't step backward or she'd go down in the Twill slime.

The Twill slime. Of course!

She tightened her stomach as the kildebeests struck her at mid-body. She rocketed over the floor, splashing wetly as she glided over the goo-covered ground. The kildebeests' impetus carried them after her, sending them careening into the goo.

The monsters' legs splayed out from under them. Finding himself almost on top of Aly, Tink lunged at her. Avoiding his fangs, she wiped the robe's saturated sleeve across his face. Tink keened, the oily lubricant burning his eyes, and abandoned any plan to finish her. Kicking and crawling, he struggled for dry ground.

Aly felt something grab at her leg. Clutching at her with two legs of his own, Weege scooted through the slime until he was within reach of dry soil.

"Chund are such a bother." Weege checked to make certain the other kildebeests were watching his performance. He turned back to find Aly sitting up. Covered with dripping mucus, she slammed her fist into the side of her captor.

Staggered by the force of the blow, Weege released her.

"That hurts!" He snarled, pulling himself into the safety of the Assassins' chamber.

Tink watched him through bloodshot eyes. "Weege."

"Not now."

"There's a blade in you."

A line of blood curled along Weege's bulb. A thick black drop splashed at his feet.

Weege moved his head, trying to see the knife. "How far?"

"It's up to the handle."

A tremble coursed up Weege's legs. Gathered against the back wall, the other kildebeests stirred.

"You okay, Weege?" one called out.

"Yes."

"Cut," a kildebeest noted. "Looks deep."

More blood dripped from his bulb. "Not so deep," Weege assured the greedy faces around him. "It's a little blade."

Aly climbed out of the ooze. Shaking his head unhappily, Tink retreated into one of the tunnels. His red bulb tipped up as he disappeared inside it.

"Your friend has left," Aly told Weege.

"I don't need him to finish you."

"You don't have any choice, do you?" she said. "If you don't try, the others will think you're weak. There's no place in the Comb for a weak Assassin."

"You were lucky," Weege insisted, his voice too low to be heard by the rest of the pack. "Lucky to get past the guards. Lucky to defeat the chameleon and the synge."

"Lucky to stab you, too. Who knows? Maybe I'll get lucky again." Reaching for the floor, she filled her hand with slime.

Another kildebeest emerged from the rear tunnel. It wasn't Tink. Tink had apparently tired of this game.

Weege pushed out his tongue, rolling it against his upper lip.

"You can taste it, can't you?' Aly asked. "Blood, filling your mouth. Bleeding from the inside."

Weege viewed her unhappily. His bulb flattened as he readied himself to jump.

Breaking away from the others, the new kildebeest bounced over to them. "I know this softbody," she told Weege.

Weege huffed. His legs wobbled and he struggled to steady them.

"Don't kill her," the kildebeest said.

"Why not?"

"It's the Father's chund. The one the DM lost."

Weege squinted, as if trying to focus his eyes. "Puff?"

"When he lost her," Puff said with satisfaction, "the DM ran away."

"You're sure this is the one?"

"Father wants her badly."

297

Weege's legs let go and his bulb settled to the ground. "I should end her. She struck me!"

"It's a little blade," Puff said. Pulling it from the other's side, she dropped it. "Where's our reward if she's dead?"

Weege closed his eyes. "Since when can we hope for rewards?"

"Not from Father."

"Not?"

"No," Puff said. "When we brought back the Web, did we receive a reward? Not from Father."

In his huddled, lump-like state, Weege grew quiet. He listed to one side, losing his balance.

Puff chirruped at the group behind her and waited until they came to her side. They bounded forward happily, paying little attention to Aly. Most of them were focused Weege, hunger in their eyes.

"Tink saw you but he didn't *see* you," Puff said. "Tink thinks all chund look the same."

No chance to get my knife back, Aly admitted to herself. *Puff is practically stepping on it.*

One unarmed Terran against several kildebeests. With slime for a weapon.

She didn't like her odds. Maricela Salas Villalovos herself, widely recognized as the greatest living transporter in this or any other galaxy, wouldn't have liked these odds.

"I knew who you were at once," Puff said. "I recognized you because of your pointy little nose."

Now they're insulting me? "You're not going to kill me. Not if you want your reward."

"We could chew off your legs."

"I couldn't," a kildebeest in the back said. "She rubbed Twill slime all over her body."

298

Puff said, "Or we could make a deal."

"What's the deal?"

"Come with us and we'll offer safe escort. We won't hurt you."

"We won't even touch you," the kildebeest in the back said.

"You'll get something for delivering me safely?" On Puff's nod, Aly said. "What do I get?"

"We don't attack you. Father doesn't kill you. You get to live." She rubbed one leg against the other. "Longer, anyway."

Aly let the slime dribble from her hand. "Best offer I've had all day."

Chapter Twenty-Seven

Lifting its head from the hole, the ponger's long nose sniffed the air warily. The rich scent of new needles filled the forest. The ponger's rudimentary eyes scanned its surroundings, finding only the fuzzy images of familiar shapes. Briefly reassured, it pulled its plump body out of the ground. The ponger scurried under a nest of needles, its long tail dragging behind it.

Caution had come late in the ponger's life, and it didn't like it. Before, it had lived with little fear of predators. Food was plentiful. Nuts were always available; berries were to be had at half-cycle; and there was the pleasure of an occasional egg, stolen from a variety of woodland mothers. The ponger prospered. Its offspring flourished, riddling the ground with their barrens. In seasons past, a multitude of pongers could be found in these woods, frolicking beneath the trees.

No longer.

Recently, invaders had entered the forest. Dropping from the sky, they used clubs, stones and claws to attack the pongers. Within the first few days, dozens were killed. Skinned and boiled, the scent of their meat filled the air.

For every ponger taken, another still remained. The survivors turned to stealth to survive. Slinking from hole to hole, crawling among the fallen needles, they learned to avoid the invaders and skirt the site they'd cleared. Foraging was still possible when there was adequate cover.

The ponger waited quietly under its nest. There were so many new sounds to learn, so many different and dangerous smells to comprehend. Its nostrils twitched again, catching the sweet suggestion of a ripe tangleroot. This odor was familiar and teasingly close.

Running from cover, the ponger dove into another hole. It disappeared into its sanctuary, its heart pounding. Keenly alert for any possible threat, it listened.

The smell of tangleroot was stronger here. Scrabbling to the top of the cavity, the ponger used the hooked nails of its forefeet to hold itself upright against the slant of the burrow.

There it was. The blurred outline of a tangle plant was enticingly close, its swollen tubers exposed upon the ground. A new bud, brown and ripe, grew from its thickest stem.

The ponger's whiskers wiggled in anticipation. When it could stand it no longer, it darted from its hole.

The ponger bit into the plant as a Sktzer stepped out from behind a tree. With the smooth flick of a claw, she stabbed a sharpened pole through the ponger's body.

* * *

Watching from his hiding place, Atkyyn was pleased. "A big one, this time."

Diyss was a champion huntress. Of all the Sktzers, she was the best at providing meat for the

301

sept. Keeping her stick at the ready, she threw the ponger's lifeless body into a sack. When she bent to arrange the tangleroot into a more tempting position, Atkyyn made his move.

Sneaking around the tree, he reached into the bag. His claw found the prime ponger she'd caught and he slid it from the canvas sack.

A rustle of cloth betrayed him. Diyss whirled around. "Get away from there!"

Clutching the ponger, Atkyyn dropped the sack. "It isn't for me."

"Another one for the changer?" The Sktzer made no effort to disguise the disapproval in her voice.

"He's hungry."

"A changer is always hungry," she said. "Don't take it, Atkyyn!"

He ran, his bloody trophy pressed to his shell. Unable to fly, he scampered as quickly as he could toward the rebel camp.

His mudhut waited for him. One of the first shelters built in the camp, it had two spacious rooms but nothing else. Hastily constructed, the first strong rain would weaken its underpinnings; unless it was properly reinforced, a heavy snowfall would sink its roof. The other rebels didn't care. For now, it was suitable lodging for the sept's weakest member and the alien he tended.

Atkyyn had heard the murmurs of approval when Hhney picked him to care for Syr. "It's not like he's good for anything else," the newest sentry, Febrra, said, echoing the general consensus.

"Shape-changers grow stronger when they feed," his own brother muttered, not caring that

Atkyyn was beside him. "When he awakens, you can be his first meal!"

Atkyyn knew how the others felt. They'd labored for days to build their new encampment, but none of them wanted to spend a minute with Hhney's unwanted guest. The unstated, but understood, preference of the tribe was to kill the changer while he was vulnerable. When the Leader refused to consider the idea, they wondered who among them would be sacrificed in her mad desire to bring the humanoid back to health.

No one argued when she suggested Atkyyn's name. Not even Atkyyn.

He carried no status. Small and fragile, not particularly brave, he made a poor warrior. Born with a deformed wing, he offered no promise as a scout. He'd proven himself to be an unskilled liar, with no talent for deception. Even his own brother bemoaned his escape from the Assassins. He seemed to think Atkyyn's corpse would have bought time for a more worthwhile Sktzer to fly free.

It wasn't as if Arzyyn, his brother, was much better. He was as weak and undersized as his brother. But he could fly, he had a mate, and he'd made a life within their society.

Atkyyn didn't fit in with the others. Until now, he'd never been entrusted with a real job. But Hhney said she believed in him and, for the first time in his life, he wondered if it might be true.

She remained the Leader, even after her return from the slavers. Her wings were clipped yet she refused to show weakness. Unable to fly, she challenged those who doubted her. Somehow, when all odds were against it, she displayed the strength to remain in command.

Her indomitable spirit gave Atkyyn a sense of hope. When she spoke, he could almost see beyond the limitations of his own thin shell. So, yes, he'd feed the changer. The Leader asked him to do it as a service to the sept and he was honored to accept the duty. He'd do his best to make Syr healthy again.

Whatever it took. No matter what sacrifice needed to be made.

Ducking (regrettably little), Atkyyn entered the hut, hiding the ponger's carcass behind his back. Syr sat on his mat, rubbing a roughstone along the curl of a stave. He smiled at his visitor, his teeth visible in the shade.

He was growing stronger every day. Atkyyn could sense the power building inside of him.

I wonder if this is the day he decides to eat me, he thought.

* * *

"What's the absolute best meal you've ever eaten?"

"That's a hard one." Syr tapped the roughstone against the stave. "There are so many choices. But if I could have anything, I'd say 'ponger'."

It was a likely guess. Except for some berries and pieces of root, it was all he'd been given to eat for the last several days.

Grinning, Atkyyn showed him the body. Skinning the ponger and cutting away its tail, he gave it to the changer.

Syr bit into the meat. "Delicious."

He meant what he said. There were only good meals and better ones, with every food among his favorites. Each morsel helped smooth the outline of his ribs and added to his layers of fat. With the tiny rebel's help, he was eating regularly. He was feeling almost normal.

Atkyyn waited until the last small bone was crunched and swallowed. "I have something for you."

Syr cleaned the bits of meat from his lap. "The others begrudge the food you bring me. It's time I did my own hunting."

"This isn't food. This is better."

"Is Aly back?"

Atkyyn went out of the doorway, expecting Syr to follow him. Using the stave as his support, the changer stood up. He hadn't set foot outside the hut for days. He was ready to walk in the daylight again.

The Sktzer waited beside the towering tree sheltering the mudhut. Stepping to one side, he said, "I collected this for you."

It was a cart. Most of one, anyway. Sprinkled with needles, its floorboard was almost completely gone. Several of its timbers were cracked. Wooden dowels pinned the wagon together in ramshackle fashion and its shaky assembly rested atop a single axle. But the one axle appeared strong and, miraculously, its two wheels were true.

"It's beautiful," Syr said.

Atkyyn rubbed a claw along the cart's side. "It needed some repair."

"Where did you find it?"

"At the old camp. Do you remember when the scouts caught the District Manager spying on us?

When the sentries chased him, he drove his wagon into a tree. Most of the pieces were still there."

"The old camp is a long way away."

Atkyyn shrugged. "I gathered the pieces at night. I ran. I like to run."

"It's a wonderful gift. Even better than food."

"Will you use it to go after the others?"

The others. Dobbins and Aly had been gone for eight days. During that time, there had been no word from Hhney or anyone else.

"It's past time they returned," Syr said. "This cart will travel faster than I can walk. I'll find something to pull the wagon and I'll go."

"Not yet," Atkyyn warned. "You're not ready. You still need to feed."

"I'll forage along the way."

"I can get supplies enough for the both of us."

"It's better if you stay here."

Atkyyn crossed his upper arms. "I have to come. It's my job."

"What's your job?"

"You are."

The Bug held himself rigidly, as if ready for a fight. Syr rested his hand on his shoulder. "Ride with me, then."

Atkyyn brightened. "We'll need a beast. A krawler might work. A dalapoke is better, but the dealers are greedy. They'll want every stick in your pouch."

"The dealers can be as greedy as they like. I haven't anything to give them."

"Oh."

"Unless you -?"

Atkyyn shook his head.

"We'll think of something," Syr said.

* * *

The site below was perfect, its path narrowing to a bend beneath their two trees. Syr was hidden within the branches of the first tree; even knowing where he was, Atkyyn couldn't see him. The Sktzer hoped his camouflage was as good.

Yesterday, they remained in the trees until nightfall without a single cart approaching. Today was going to be different. Minutes ago, Atkyyn had heard a muttered curse from somewhere down the road. Now, he was greeted by the sound of wheels rolling over dirt and needles.

The wagon that appeared was a sorry vehicle. Rolling on rickety wheels, it wobbled alarmingly. Its occupants were every bit as ragged as their mode of transportation. There were three Bugs and a chund. The Bugs were encrusted with dirt and the chund looked unworthy of the poorest stewpot.

Despite his distance from them, Atkyyn imagined he could smell their ripe odor. Although their cart was hitched to a dalapoke (obviously stolen; almost certainly disease-infected), these characters appeared so disreputable that Atkyyn felt uneasy even spying on them.

It took an effort for him to imagine robbing them. It was much easier to imagine them robbing him.

Creaking uneasily, the vehicle lurched into the bend. Syr's tree shook and a lavender arm came out of the brush, signaling for the start of the assault.

Using his blade, Atkyyn chopped at the branch to his side. The limb gave way, falling in unison with Syr's, and their net dropped from the bottom of both trees. Cords of knotted vine fell onto the startled travelers.

The result couldn't have been more satisfying. The net enveloped its victims, its vines knocking the harness from the driver's claws. Without guidance, the dalapoke slowed to a stop. It waited in the middle of the pathway as its passengers struggled under the snare covering them.

Atkyyn spread his crippled wings and floated down to the prisoners. Touching to the ground, he kept his bodyshell parted and his wings spread wide. It was as commanding a figure as he could ever hope to present.

The motley bunch stopped in their efforts for freedom. They stared at him.

"Trespassers!" Atkyyn cried. "Defilers of the forest!"

His appearance was too much for the chund sitting at the back of the wagon. Lying onto his back, he let the netting drape over him.

"That's it," the chund said. "I quit."

Atkyyn gestured at the surrounding woods. "This land is under the protection of the rebels. This is Sktzer territory!"

"Who did you say you were?" the driver asked.

Atkyyn detected an amused quality to her voice. "My name is Atkyyn," he said sternly. "King of the Sktzers!"

The biggest of the captured Bugs clamped his pincer onto a cord. "When I get out of here, I'm going to kill you."

He sawed his pincer over the cord and it snapped. The big Bug smiled.

Pfffft! An arrow shot out of the branches, thunking into the side of the wagon. The Bug stopped straining against the net.

"Did you think I would travel alone?" Atkyyn asked. "I hold your life in my claws."

"Get me out of here, Atkyyn," the Bug said darkly.

"*King* Atkyyn," the small Bug reminded him.

Pfffft! A second arrow streaked through the sky. Shooting past the Bugs, it went through the netting and lodged in the floorboard of the cart. Its appearance brought the chund back into an upright position.

"Watch it!" the chund demanded.

The branches wiggled in response. Needles fell as the brush parted and Syr's face peered out at the group below. "Dobbins?"

"Syr?"

With a sinking feeling, Atkyyn took a closer look at the cart's driver. Faintly, he said, "My Leader."

Hidden behind her mask of grime, Hhney smiled at him. "King Atkyyn. Will you free me from your clever trap?"

Syr climbed from the tree. Setting aside his stave and quiver, he helped Atkyyn remove the netting.

"Tskett said he was going to kill me," Atkyyn told Hhney.

"He won't."

"Yes, I will." Once the net lifted, Tskett jumped from the footboard and stamped off into the forest. "I'm going to find camp."

"King of the Sktzers." Vykk snorted. Shouldering Atkyyn aside, he followed after Tskett.

Dobbins clasped Syr's hand. "You're looking fit."

Atkyyn knew the changer was fit; another week's feeding and he would be at full mettle. Despite his healthy appearance, his eyes turned glassy.

"Shape-changers have a keen sense of smell," Atkyyn reminded the others.

"Sorry," Dobbins said. "When we hijacked the wagon, it was full of offal. After awhile, you forget about the smell."

"You *do*?" Syr asked.

"Hhney and I were too heavy to be flown back to camp." Dobbins said. "It was too far to walk. This was our best option."

Syr said, "Where's Aly?"

Hhney said, "She was left behind."

"Alive?"

"I hope. She disappeared inside the Father's Comb."

"She's our mate."

"We had no choice."

Kneeling, Syr loosened the dalapoke's harness.

"She disappeared days ago," Dobbins told him.

"Aly isn't dead."

Collecting Syr's stave and arrows, Atkyyn brought them to the changer.

"The wagon barely made it here," Dobbins said. "It won't survive a return trip."

"I have another cart."

"Don't expect me to go with you. I'm exhausted."

The shape-changer shouldered the harness. Taking the dalapoke's reins, he urged the beast to follow him.

Atkyyn walked beside him.

"The Comb is nearly impenetrable," Dobbins called after them. "She fell into a trap, behind a huge wall of metal. Even if she's still there, even if she's somehow alive, there's no way around that wall."

"Through it?" Syr asked.

"Too thick."

"Would a tingle blaster be able to punch it?"

Dobbins paused. "No."

"I know where we can get a tingle blaster."

"I don't think so. No."

Leading the dalapoke, Syr went off of the pathway.

"Go with the changer," Hhney told Atkyyn. "Keep him fat."

Atkyyn managed a weak nod. So, after all this, it was time. His flesh would feed the changer.

He couldn't complain. It wasn't as if he deserved a better fate.

The Leader added, "I'll have the supplies made ready. Make certain he eats them. "

"I will!" Atkyyn chased after the shape-changer.

Dobbins reached Syr first. He told him, "It's a waste of time. He'll never let the tingler off the ship."

"You could find a way to get it."

"No, I couldn't. No one can. A tingle blaster is huge."

"You've always welcomed a challenge."

"It's in the hold of a starship," Dobbins said. "In a spaceport. Security is everywhere!"

Syr asked him, "Is it impossible?"

"I didn't say impossible," his friend responded. "But why?"

"You wouldn't have left me. The Sktzers wouldn't have left their Leader. How can we leave Aly?"

"This is different."

"She made a vow and we have to honor it." He added, "She would have come back for you."

Dobbins' entire body sagged. "Yeah," he said wearily, "she probably would." Reaching around Syr, he took the dalapoke's harness.

Atkyyn viewed the chund with new respect. "Can you really steal a tingle blaster?"

"Not a chance."

Syr said, "He'll find a way."

"Where will you find one?"

Dobbins seemed to shrink even smaller. He said, "Mulvaney's Scow."

312

Chapter Twenty-Eight

I have many faces but one name.
I have one name but many meanings.
I have been born,
I have died,
And still I live.
Those who named me,
Will never know me.
Who am I?

"What is this nonsense?" Father Lygt asked.

The chameleon didn't answer. It remained poised in front of the exit, a satisfied expression on its face.

Mox turned to the old Bug.

"It's the monster's riddle," the Crone said nervously.

"I know what it is," Father Lygt said. "Why does the chameleon say it? Why does he say it to me?"

"He gives the riddle to everyone."

"What does it mean?"

"Only the monster knows. It's his secret."

When the Crone spoke, her antennae danced in jerky motions, stabbing at the air in an anxious semaphore. Between words, her breath came in short, hard gasps. Her manner suggested that she was on the verge of panic.

It was all an act. Beautifully performed, Father Lygt acknowledged, if a bit familiar. He'd met with her twice before and believed she was on the verge of collapse on each occasion. He'd have believed it now, if not for the Web.

Despite her display, the Crone wasn't frightened by his presence. She knew to tremble before him, assuaging his ego and keeping her ruined body from the stewpots, but she could easily have avoided his arrival. Her curiosity brought her from her room.

Father Lygt could see, literally *see*, wisps of wonder rising around her. It colored the air like faint streaks of quizzical smoke, drifting above her head.

He couldn't sense anything from the chameleon. Perhaps the beast was too stupid to be read. Or it might be that a monster's emotions couldn't be understood by a Bug.

He almost appreciated his ignorance of the chameleon's motives. He didn't like these visions. Too often, they brought more questions than answers.

The Web remained wrapped around his arm as he stroked it. Controlling the Web was different than he'd imagined. Holding it, he hadn't become smarter or stronger, more cunning or clever. The Reader assured him all of these things would happen once the bondmate was destroyed.

Was it true? Not even the Reader could be trusted anymore. He'd grown vague of late, with more than a little smoke leaking from his own beak.

The mist came in different colors and different shapes. Most often, it appeared in the middle of a conversation, but there were those supplicants who continuously dribbled tendrils of color. Father Lygt had learned to recognize the vapors of deceit, fear and curiosity. For a select few Bugs, however, the smoke defied interpretation.

Was it supposed to mean something when there was more than one color of smoke escaping from a stranger's mouth? Did it matter when colors intertwined with one another?

How was he to know? Why didn't the Web tell him?

If there was more than one speaker before him, and if emotions ran high, the air filled with clouds of color. There were times his mind reeled under the insights he was offered.

Cycles without number, he thought. *The Web will bring them to me. Acceptance is the key.*

Rubbing at his eyes, he saw the Crone watching him with ill-concealed interest. "Is something the matter, ancient one?"

"Nothing, Father," she quaked, the air puffing greyly around her.

He focused on the chameleon. "What's the purpose of your word play?"

Its eyes shone with an inner light. "Those who can't answer my riddle are eaten. Those who can are allowed to pass."

"Allowed to pass?" Father Lygt wondered if he'd heard correctly. "You let them pass? Whose idea was that?"

The chameleon dropped his head. Mox said, "The Reader gave the chameleon his first riddle."

The Father frowned. "Tell me about the intruders."

"There were six of them," the Crone said.

315

The chameleon's stubbed tail slapped the ground, interrupting her. "Five."

"Six. Three Bugs and three chund. One of them was a little chund," she conceded. "I locked them in with the monster."

"And the monster -" Father Lygt wanted to make certain he understood this, "- let them go."

The chameleon flattened its head against its body. "They answered the riddle."

Father Lygt felt his antennae growing rigid with anger. In a low voice, Mox said, "It took a long time to find this beast, my Father. Longer, still, to grow it to its present size."

Yes, that much is true. Father Lygt's claw found the comfort of the Web. Forcing himself to remain calm, he said, "Six passed you. How many intruders came back through the passage?"

The Crone said, "Four. Three Bugs and a chund."

"One more question. An important question." The Assassins had told him about their raid on the Sktzer camp. Everything he'd heard suggested the Web's bondmate was there, a softbody among the rebels. She'd escaped the Assassins, either through the District Manager's bungling or through some supernatural protection offered by the Web. He'd expected her to try to retrieve the Web. He just hadn't expected it to be so soon. "Was the chund who survived a female?"

"Chund look alike, with their puffy faces and protruding ears," she said. The cloud of curiosity was so thick the hag's face almost disappeared. "The one who returned might have been female."

The chameleon nodded eagerly.

316

Father Lygt looked from the Crone's open face to the chameleon's guarded one. They hadn't a clue about the chund's sex.

He told Mox, "The synge took a victim."

"A Wamandu. I've seen its corpse, wrapped in a cocoon."

"The Assassins took at least one more."

"Only one," Mox said. "By the time I got to their den, the kildebeests had finished their slaughter. A few bones were left, nothing more."

Father Lygt watched his mouth as he spoke. There it was, a barely visible puff of vapor drooling downward from his beak. "They assured me their victim was male," Mox continued.

With each of Mox's words, the vapor darkened. Seemingly solid, it lay in coils across his servant's shell. Father Lygt regarded it with a repulsed fascination.

"Father?"

He shook himself. Making a pretense of rubbing his eyes again, he covered them. He willed the sight away and, thankfully, it worked. Mox's lickspittle face returned to normal.

"It doesn't matter," Father Lygt said. "It wasn't the bondmate. I'd have known if she died."

"The Assassins should have brought you the chund before feasting. I reprimanded them." Mox smiled unctuously, unaware that the gesture sent a new bubble of vapor squeezing from beneath his beak. "As you remember, I brought you the body of the one named Weege."

Father Lygt watched the bubble, tiny and rounded, and glistening with some unspoken emotion. It was the fourth or fifth time Mox had let one escape.

317

How to regard this particular phenomenon? Whatever it meant, he needed to figure it out soon.

As best as he could determine, the Web heightened his feelings of empathy. He'd always had some talent for sensing the feelings and motives of others. In the past, he frequently knew when Bugs were lying to him, even without any evidence to the contrary. Now, with the Web in his possession, his talent had multiplied. There were times when his body nearly shook from the force of the emotions carried by the creatures standing before him.

It was a learning process. Mox, in particular, remained a puzzlement. The colors in his vapor could change or disappear in mid-sentence. Was he to doubt the servant who remained at his side so faithfully, for so many cycles?

No, of course not. Mox had no reason to lie about the Assassins and too much to lose if caught in an untruth.
Everyone couldn't be untrustworthy, could they?

Father Lygtt said, "I remember the dead Assassin."

Mox said, "My dagger in its back."

"Quite impressive." Father Lygt focused on the chameleon. Hanging its head, the monster's scales were the color of the stones behind it. Unmoving and frightened, it joined with its environment so completely that it almost vanished into the landscape of its den. It was an amazing sight.

The beast stirred, about to slink away. The Father stepped on its tail. "No one is to pass through here without my permission."

"My riddle...?"

"Is no more. Kill whatever comes in here. Finish it, eat it. Don't play with it."

He lifted his foot and the chameleon tucked its tail into its body. Father Lygt gestured for Mox to pass in front of him, through the exit. Rather than follow, he stayed with the beast.

"Tell me, monster," he said, "what's the answer? Give me the solution to your riddle."

The chameleon risked a glance to the center of the room, where the Crone stood. She was listening intently. "Leave me my secret. None will pass."

"I want the answer."

"It isn't fair!" Wedging its body against a corner of the room, the chameleon watched him from beneath half-lowered eyelids. From the corner of its mouth, it whispered, "Father Lygt."

Creeping closer, the Crone put a withered claw on the chameleon's back. "Louder, my pet. I don't believe he heard you."

Wisps of gold streamed up from the Crone. Triumph, perhaps, tinted with no small amount of delight at the chameleon's misery.

The chameleon shot her a poisonous look. Turning its muzzle to the Father, it said, "Your name is my answer. Any who dared cross this chamber had first to speak your name."

With that, defeat settled on its shoulders. The old Bug remained hunched over him, an unpleasant expression on her face.

Father Lygt didn't need the Web to understand the parameters of their relationship. He said, "Feed the beast an extra portion tonight. It was a clever puzzle."

Clever enough for a monster, anyway, he thought. Mox remained in the outer passage. For the moment, no vapors drifted from his servant's beak. Grateful for this small reprieve, he swept from the room with his subordinate at his feet.

Once they'd gone, the Crone crept closer to her ward. "Your riddle is flawed," she gloated.

The chameleon shook off its downcast expression. "That wasn't the real answer. That wasn't even a good answer."

Extending its forelegs, it arched its back. Its bulk brushed against the Bug, pushing her out of his way. With a squawk, she fell over her own unbending leg.

Sitting in the dirt, she shrieked up at the chameleon. It paid no attention, gazing into the passage.

"Something is wrong with Father," it said. "Something is very wrong."

Chapter Twenty-Nine

Sixty-three years of age this very morning,
Tucker Mulvaney thought. *Happy birthday to me.*

The years had been kind to him. His body was
trim, his teeth remained his own, and he carried a full
head of hair. White hair, yes, but God-given. His
mind was sharp and his blue eyes functioned nearly
as well as the day he left the Academy. He'd
sacrificed his best hope of a private life to his career,
but he rarely regretted the loss.

He was the captain of a starship cruiser. It was
all he'd ever wanted to be.

It wasn't an easy job. Commanding a crew,
satisfying a contingent of passengers, and following
the Corporation's Code of Conduct was a daily battle.
Tucker Mulvaney understood his job and took pride
in doing it well. He could recite the Corporation
handbook, chapter and verse. Hell, he'd written a few
of the regulations himself.

It was a matter of discipline, that's what it
was. With discipline and careful planning, a man
could chart his future. Living by this creed had taken
him far but, somehow, all of his plans for the coming
years had gone askew. Without warning, he found
himself in the worse mess of his life.

What do I do now?

What he did at the moment was to reach
across the table and drop two dibblesticks into the
pot. He picked up his cards while the Bug bounced

the multi-colored ball. Seeing the two face cards stare back at him, Mulvaney knew he'd lost another hand.

Tossing his cards, he reached for his back pants pocket. While the others continued to play, his fingers found a well-worn notebook. Flipping it open at random, Mulvaney read: *'Before a man can truly believe in anything, he has to believe in himself.'*

He agreed with the sentiment but felt the words didn't have much bearing on his current situation. Somewhere in this notebook, he hoped to locate some fragment of wisdom that would point him in a new direction.

It hadn't happened yet. This morning, he'd found, *'There is no such thing as a free drink in a bawdyhut'* and *'The next honest Vengling you meet will be the first honest Vengling ever met'*.

Those sayings, too, were as true as the day he'd first written them but, again, weren't particularly helpful in this situation.

He tucked the book away. It was compact, with a red cover and blue-lined pages. This was his sixth one; the sixth volume, so to speak. The other five were back in his cabin on the ship, neatly banded together and available for his perusal whenever he needed.

Each of the books was filled with maxims and aphorisms, sayings that pleased his sensibilities or inspired him, however briefly. A very few sayings and life suggestions passed from book to book, a reflection of their value over time. These were the basic truths he obeyed and they became his spiritual rules. Mulvaney's Laws, he called them.

The Corporation had its own official stance on gambling. Because nautical law prohibited games of chance, so did the Corporation. But company law only applied to wagering done aboard ship. On shore leave, both passengers and crew had every right to a roll of the dice. Out of dress uniform, Mulvaney enjoyed a game of chance as much as the next man.

Perhaps a tad bit more.

Every notebook carried a warning or two about this most seductive sin: *'Bet whatever you'd like but never wager your integrity.'*

'When the chips are down, don't mistake a friendly face for the face of a friend.'

'It's easy to cheat a cheat. No one can cheat an honest man.'

He knew now that this last Law needed some revision. Either Mulvaney had experienced a terrible run of luck or it was quite possible to cheat an honest man.

'Don't play three-fingered narlap.' Now, *there* was a rule to put in the notebook.

"Take the ball, Captain?" The one-eyed Bug held it out to him. It was a gracious offer; it was within her rights to keep the deal. Accepting the ball, Mulvaney picked up the deck of cards. He began to shuffle.

Despite her display of generosity, he didn't trust the Bug. This uneasy feeling had nothing to do with the gaping socket in her face or her appearance of dissipation. It was just a gut reaction. Looking across the table, he realized he felt the same way about the other players as well.

Dropping the ball, Mulvaney passed the cards. Through some whim of fate, he found himself with a good hand. The bouncing ball destroyed it. Settling to the table, it favored the one suit the captain lacked.

323

He folded his cards, pushing them down to the table. One after another, the three Bugs threw their cards in, too. No one carried the needed suit. It was a wash.

His deal again. On the next round, he took the pot, as small as it was.

At last, a little luck.

He added the dibblesticks to his money pouch. Glancing up, he caught the pleased expressions on his opponents' faces. In their own private way, they were congratulating themselves on the hand as well.

He felt a knot in the pit of his stomach. *So that's the game, is it?*

The three of them weren't playing against one another; they were in a partnership against him. Stringing him along, letting him win just enough to keep him in the game. It had worked, too. To stay in the action, he'd borrowed from his retirement.

'Never bet more than you're willing to lose': Those words existed in one of his earliest notebooks. Mulvaney had ignored his own warning.

Conned like the greenest of rocket jockeys. Somehow tricked into thinking he could make some money, playing with professional gamblers on one of the worst possible planets in the worst possible galaxy.

Probably not the wisest of plans.

What little savings he had left were in the pouch at his waist. In a few days, a lifetime of careful accumulation had been reduced to two months' salary in dibblesticks and fractured gemstones.

Fool. Prevented from launching *TIAN'S GATE*, he let his restlessness carry him into the bawdyhuts. Combating worry and boredom, he'd risked everything he owned.

Too late now, he thought. He scraped his chair back.

"You're not leaving?" The question was asked with friendly concern but the black-faced Bug across from him appeared anything but friendly. "You can't take a pot and walk away. You've got to give us a chance to win some of it back."

The Bug had lifted from his squat, as if he might physically stop Mulvaney from leaving. He was large and wide-shelled, with the green and orange markings of some of the Mound guards.

"He doesn't work the Mound any longer," the one-eyed Bug confided, the night before. "They got him for excessive violence."

Excessive violence? On the Bugworld?

The trio of thieves waited for Mulvaney's response. They were a disreputable lot: the one-eyed Bug, the former guard, and a Mentren. The Mentren had the face of a toad but, then, that was typical for a Mentren. To expose the thick pads on his fingers and improve his feel for the narlap ball, he'd clipped back the crusty nails that distinguished his race. It seemed to have worked. Sleepy-eyed, he had collected more than his share of the winnings.

What was I thinking?

Even as a young man, writing in his first notebook, he'd known better. *'Don't judge a man by the words he uses. Judge him by the companions at his side.'*

These particular companions were ready to take offense if he left the bawdyhut. He brought his chair back to the table.

"Stretching my legs," Mulvaney said.

The big Bug picked up the deck. "You don't mind, I think I'll take the deal." His mouth twitched upward in a parody of a smile.

They weren't going to let him leave until he'd lost everything. Seeing him pocket his last winnings, they must have guessed at how little was left in his pouch.

You've got everything else, he thought. *What's left is mine. These few sticks, they belong to me.*

The problem was, he didn't have any idea on how to keep them.

He threw a dibblestick onto the table.

"Two," the one-eyed Bug reminded him. "We upped the ante, remember?"

Mulvaney tossed in a second stick.

The dealer reached for his own sackett. Not finding it, the big Bug felt at his side, then ran his claw across his back. "It's gone!"

"What's gone?" the Mentren asked.

The Bug searched the ground at his feet. "My sackett. My sackett and my carrybelt!" In a rage, he flipped the table over. It banged to the floor, bringing the bartender's head out of his quarters.

"Well, I don't have it," the one-eyed Bug said.

"Somebody does." The Bug rotated, considering each of the card players in turn. His eyes flicked past Mulvaney, focusing on the Mentren. "Never trust a climber."

"Funny, I've heard it said differently," the Mentren said. "Where I come from, we say you should never trust a moron." Rising off his haunches, he aggressively bumped his abdomen against the bigger Bug.

326

The one-eyed Bug pushed between them. "Use your head," she told the former guard. "Why would he rob you?"

"He's a Mentren. It's what they do."

The Mentren's wide mouth stretched even wider. "I'll take those words as a compliment."

Mulvaney remained keenly aware that the front door of the bawdyhut wasn't very far away. He could easily reach it within seconds. Stepping around the fallen table, he felt a claw lock around his arm.

"What's the hurry, Captain?" the one-eyed Bug asked.

Behind him, he heard a roar. "My belt!"

The big Bug's carrybelt lay on the ground behind the Mentren's feet. "Don't look at me," the Mentren said. "I didn't put it there."

"Why don't you tell me," the Bug growled, "where you didn't put my sackett?"

"I don't have your sackett!"

The Bug smacked his pincer against the Mentren's nose.

"I don't!"

Escaping from his room, the bartender hurried toward the table. The Bug smacked the Mentren again, harder, a ringing blow that caused the climber's legs to fold. He collapsed, falling to the ground and lying there.

"Trouble?" the bartender asked.

"Not anymore." The Bug loosened the drawstrings of the Mentren's money pouch, tying it onto his own carrybelt.

Waving for a slaver's attention, the bartender dragged the Mentren away. Mulvaney found himself being guided back to his chair.

"I need to return to my ship," he said, without much effort.

The guard set the table back in place. "Let's play a few hands first."

"Mind if I sit in?" asked a new voice.

The one-eyed Bug followed the sound. "I know you."

"I know you, too." The stranger grinned at the party.

Dobbins? Mulvaney twisted about, searching the room for the little man's inevitable companion.

There he was: the shape-changer. Syr shared an alcove with a small Bug. The changer had grown thick around the waist and chest. It wouldn't be long before he was fat again.

Syr watched the activity at the table. When the Captain locked eyes with him, he dipped his head in acknowledgement.

This is some terrible nightmare, Mulvaney thought.

He noticed the bulging purse at Dobbins' waist. It appeared to hold nearly as many dibblesticks as the big Bug's lost sackett.

The one-eyed Bug noticed his riches, too. "You ever play narlap?"

"I'm willing to learn," Dobbins said. "Let me find a seat."

With another Terran in the game, Mulvaney's luck began to change. His marginal cards caught the occasional winning bounce while his losers ended up costing him less. Slowly, he fed a few sticks into his pouch.

Thank the stars.

Not that the stars deserved any credit. He knew his luck hadn't changed.

The Bugs were letting him win.

The turnaround happened only when Dobbins joined the game. To make the game look honest and to encourage their newest player to open his purse strings, the Bugs were throwing the captain a few winners.

Poor Dobbins, he thought, but not without a sense of reprieve.

Hand after hand, nothing went the other man's way. No matter how he played his cards, he couldn't get a break. The ball consistently betrayed him. The captain had heard of Dobbins' prowess at the gaming tables but he was seeing, first hand, that the rumors weren't true. When Dobbins should have played conservatively, he bet with abandon. When he should have been bold, he folded. Baffled, he seemed to realize he was in over his head but couldn't quite fathom why.

Twice, the Bugs tried to give him a hand and Dobbins couldn't even manage their gifts. Throwing in his cards, he sent both pots to the captain. By Mulvaney's calculations, Dobbins had lost over half of what he'd brought to the table.

When the one-eyed Bug made a play for the rest of his riches, Mulvaney wasn't a part of the hand. He'd drawn face cards, costing him his ante, and he sat on the sidelines as the others played. The stake grew following two inconclusive bounces. When the bid came back to Dobbins, he emptied his pouch on the table.

"Bounce the ball," the human said.

"You're a stick short."

"I'm good for it."

"That's not how we play," the big Bug told him. "In narlap, you match the bet or you're out. Those are the rules, no exceptions." He put his claw over the pile of dibblesticks. "No refunds, either."

Patting his shirt pocket, Dobbins found a last gemstone. "Drop the ball."

The ball fell, the cards were counted - and, astoundingly, the softbody won. With one bet, Dobbins took back everything he'd lost and added a bit more.

Sitting beside him, the female Bug viewed the fallen cards through her remaining eye. Getting up from the table, she cinched her pouch closed.

"You're good," she told Dobbins. "As good as the Mentren. Probably better."

Ignoring the others, she left the bawdyhut.

"Chund-lucky," the remaining Bug said, mostly to himself. He pushed the ball across the table. "Your deal."

The Bug remained mesmerized by the purse at Dobbins' waist. Without a partner to help him cheat, he started losing more of his bets. While the thick bag held his attention, Mulvaney found himself collecting the largest share of the winnings. Dobbins won a little, lost a little, while Mulvaney's money pouch grew heavy.

Despite his newfound success, the captain rarely had control of the ball. The play swept around him, from the Bug to Dobbins and back again, and he was practically a spectator. It didn't jibe with his life philosophy - one of his Laws was, *'There is no such thing as fate. A man makes his own destiny'* - but he'd already decided to revise several of Mulvaney's

Laws. In fact, he could probably scratch out three-quarters of everything he'd written.

Life wasn't as ordered as he'd imagined it to be. Life was messy and illogical. How else to explain this sudden shift in his fortune?

Surreptitiously, he did a quick count of his holdings and relief washed over him. His retirement had returned to him; the better part of it, anyway.

With a few more hands, I'll be even and I can leave, Mulvaney thought. *The green-shelled Bug can stay and rob Dobbins, his bad luck. A man with his skills shouldn't have entered the game. I'll return to my ship and stay there until we receive clearance to launch.*

No more gambling. For him, it was a weakness. An addiction. He wondered if there might be a new saying there, something for one of his notebooks: *'It takes a strong man to acknowledge his weaknesses.'*

Yes, something along those lines.

He felt quietly proud of himself. He'd quit gambling forever. Not now, of course, not when he was winning. But soon.

Picking up the cards in front of him, he saw that Dobbins had dealt him a beauty. Six cards, no faces, and all of a different suit. No matter how the ball landed, he was covered. It was almost impossible to lose.

"Put something on the table, Captain." The big Bug was growing impatient. "Or are you out?"

Mulvaney extracted a handful of sticks. "My bet."

The Bug examined his cards. "I meet you," he said, adding in his own dibblesticks, "and I raise." He spilled open the Mentren's money pouch.

Dobbins tapped a finger against the back of his cards. He hesitated, tapped again, and waited while the captain matched the Bug's wager. Almost ready to drop his cards, he reconsidered.

At last, he said, "If had any sense, I'd let the two of you fight it out. But, sometimes," he gave them a brilliant smile, "you've got to take a chance."

He counted out the sticks to meet the wager. Pulling out a gemstone, he threw it down. "And I raise."

The Bug said, "You can't raise. That's all I've got."

"Match the bet or you're out."

"I don't have it!"

"How about you, Captain?" Dobbins asked.

The Bug reached across the table. Hooking his claws under the Terran's shirt collar, he dragged him over the center pile of riches. "You think you can cheat me, chund?"

A purple hand fell on the Bug's shoulder. "You should let him go."

The Bug froze, the shape-changer leaning over him. Syr said, "Release him."

"It's not right."

"These are the rules, you said so yourself. We all heard you."

The guard opened his claws. Straightening his shirt's collar, Dobbins sat down.

"If I had a gemstone left," the Bug said, "I'd get very drunk."

Dobbins dropped a nearly-flawless stone into his claw. Clasping it tightly, the Bug remained beside the table. He said, "I have to know, Captain. Are you in or out?"

Mulvaney had never seen such a pile of riches. To stay in, it was going to cost every stick he owned. He considered his cards. They were as good as he remembered.

Untying his pouch, he gave it to Dobbins to count. "I'm in."

"Bah," said the Bug. Throwing his own cards to the table, he left to find the bartender.

Face up, the Bug's cards spread across the table. Viewing them, Mulvaney felt a shock of revelation.

Six cards, no faces. All of a different suit. Nearly impossible to beat.

Sweeping the cards away, Dobbins slid them to the bottom of the deck. Picking up the narlap ball, he let it dance over his fingers.

It was then that Mulvaney understood what had just happened. Truly, his luck hadn't changed at all.

"Bounce the ball," he told Dobbins. "Be done with it."

Syr cleared his throat. "Captain, we need a favor."

The ball folded inside Dobbins' fingers.

"What kind of favor?"

"We need to borrow the tingle blaster."

"The tingler?"

Syr appeared to be serious. Dobbins, never completely serious, at least appeared sincere.

"Forget it," Mulvaney told them.

"You'll get it back."

"Drop the ball, Mr. Dobbins."

Instead, he set the orb on the table. "Let Syr explain."

"It's against every rule in the books. I'd lose my job. I'd go to jail."

"You've broken regulations before."

"Only in regards to the two of you," Mulvaney said. "Look where it got me."

"Get us aboard ship. We'll do the rest." Dobbins drummed his fingers on the table. "You could say you didn't know."

"It wouldn't matter." Mulvaney retrieved his empty money pouch, looping its strings around the belt on his waist. "A Captain is responsible for what happens on his ship. I'd be blamed, regardless."

"A life is at stake."

"I'm sorry."

"Are the rules more important than someone's life?" Syr asked.

"You have my answer, gentlemen," Mulvaney replied. "Our discussion is over. If you'll finish this game, I'll return to my ship. "

Reaching inside his shirt, Dobbins brought out a notebook. "You'll want this."

Mulvaney's hand went to his empty pocket.

"I particularly liked your section on courage," Dobbins said. "The part starting with, *'The measure of a man'* - now, how did that go?"

Mulvaney took his notebook. *" 'You'll find the measure of a man in his deeds, not his words'."*

It was on the notebook's front page. It was one of Mulvaney's Laws. He said, "I can't."

Dobbins rested his hands together. The ball remained beside the pile of dibblesticks and gemstones.

Feeling a decade older than his sixty-three years, Mulvaney snapped the notebook shut. "What was it you said earlier, Mr. Dobbins? You've got to take a chance?"

"It's my whole philosophy of life."

"I'll let you tell me your plan. The changer can tell me why this one life means so much to him. Both of you will explain how you'll prevent Father Lygt from getting his claws on my machine." Even as he spoke the words, Mulvaney couldn't believe what he was saying. "Now drop the damned ball!"

Dobbins knuckled it, giving the ball a spin. Bouncing, it twirled across the surface of the table. Slowly, it rolled to a stop in front of the captain.

It favored silver, the second highest color in Mulvaney's hand. There was only one possible combination of cards that could beat him. He watched as Dobbins spread out his cards.

Tucker Mulvaney was a winner.

"It's hard to beat a lucky man," Dobbins said. "I think I saw that in your notebook somewhere."

Syr pulled a chair to the table. He said, "Let's talk."

Chapter Thirty

"How much longer am I going to be here?" Aly asked.

"Eat," was Mox's only reply. Tilting a container under his beak, he drained it.

Aly left her bowl in her lap.

Mox drew a claw across his mouth, wiping it. "It does you no good to starve yourself."

In her travels as a transporter, Aly had gone for days without food. "I don't want this. Feed it to the kildebeest."

Stretched across the doorway, Puff wrinkled her nose. "I don't eat stew."

"I made this for you," Mox told Aly. "This isn't the gamy meat and clotted broth of past evenings. This meat is fresh. The sauce is new."

"I'm not hungry."

Mox's voice went flat. "Taste it."

His words held a menacing edge. *Interesting.* This wasn't the Mox who greeted her with pleasantries on their first meeting. This wasn't the fawning, ingratiating Bug who apologized for leaving an Assassin to guard her.

This was a different, deadlier Mox. He glowered at her.

"Father Lygt doesn't know I'm here, does he?" she asked.

"He –" Mox faltered, "– knows. Of course, he knows."

"You come to me at night, after your duties are finished. Never before then. Never with the Father."

"Father Lygt is busy. He hasn't any interest in a chund."

"That's not what your kildebeest says."

This more intriguing Mox, the one who acted almost dangerous, frowned down at Puff. "What did you tell her?"

"Nothing." Puff rose to her feet. "She tricked you, wanting to see how you'd react." The kildebeest snorted, amused.

Mox said again, "Eat the stew."

Aly dipped a fingertip into the bowl. The sauce was warm to the touch.

"It isn't poisoned," Mox said. "You've seen me eat it myself. Besides, there are other ways to be rid of you if that's what I wanted."

Puff nodded lazily.

Aly sipped at the sauce. Bland, it had an underlying bitterness to its flavor. Its aftertaste was acrid and unpleasant. She spit. "There's something in this."

"Yes," Mox agreed. "There is."

The aftertaste lingered. Aly spit again. Her lips and chin were numb.

"I had no choice. You weren't cooperating."

The bowl fell from her hand. Feeling dizzy and disoriented, she tried to stand. Instead, she crumpled to the floor.

She lay there, unmoving. *Paralyzed?*

Possibly. She couldn't move her arms or legs. She tried to speak, but her tongue refused to cooperate.

Puff padded over to Aly. Through her peripheral vision, she could see him staring down at her.

"That's that," the kildebeest said.

Mox lifted Aly up. Tilting her head, he slapped her face. Curiously, she felt the sting of his blow.

It was probably a good sign.

"Talk to me!" Mox demanded.

Love to, Aly thought.

Puff shifted uncomfortably. "They talk better before they're dead."

"I put a serum in her stew. I was told it would loosen the lips of softbodies."

Puff said, "Well, it certainly keeps them from lying."

"It wears off in time." Mox made a decision. "We'll take her to the Blue Room."

"The Blue Room?"

"I'm tired of the chund's evasions. There will be no more kindness, no more meals. No more drugs, either. It's time I tried something else."

"I don't like the Blue Room."

"Neither will she," Mox said. "But what's the good in having a torture chamber unless you use it?"

* * *

Lieutenant Shankhdhar turned as a great puff of air belched from beneath the *TIAN'S GATE.* Emerging through a cloud of dirt and dust motes, the spaceship's loading ramp extended to the ground below.

"Bring 'er down, boys," Captain Mulvaney said.

On command, the tingle blaster rolled down the cruiser's silver ramp. Shankhdhar's men followed after him as the machine settled onto the spaceport's floor.

What is Mulvaney doing now? Shankdhar wondered. *And where are the Bugs?*

Ah, there they were. Wearing the orange armbands of T'ing Security Officials, three of them approached the ship from the other end of the spaceport. Chattering to one another in Y'togish, they spat their words out so quickly Shankdhar barely understood them.

Even if he hadn't known the language, he'd have known the context: *What the hell is this?*

Mulvaney patted the side of the blaster as it came to a stop. Walking up to him, Shankdhar said, "What's going on?"

"How's the family, Gautam?"

"You don't have any authority on the ground. You know the regs."

"How's your daughter? She doing okay in the Academy?"

"You have my gratitude – and Amrita's – and you always will. This is something different. I need that sorry bucket of bolts back on the *GATE*."

"Not just yet." For a law-breaker, Mulvaney sounded remarkably relaxed. "I promise you, as soon as I can, I'll return the machine to the ship's hold."

"Until then?"

Mulvaney cocked his head.

Shankdhar said, "You can't, Tucker. Don't even think about it. Advanced technology doesn't leave the spaceport."

"Three or four days, at most."

"What if it's commandeered?"

"Won't happen," Mulvaney said. "There'll be a changer at the wheel. A fat changer."

"What if it breaks down?"

"No one on this planet has the knowledge or tools to repair it."

"You hope," Shankdhar said. "You're asking a lot, my friend. I could lose my commission."

"It's a twenty-year old digging machine. A piece of junk."

Shankdhar's officers waited for his response. Stone-faced, they remained alongside the tingle blaster.

"I don't have a choice," Mulvaney said. "I owe someone a favor. You understand favors."

I guess I do now, Shankdhar thought. *Funny how much a favor can end up costing you.*

Mulvaney said, "If you and your crew don't report this, it never happened. Your people only see what you tell them to see."

"Yeah," Shankdhar exhaled the word. "But what about the others?"

Taking the question as his cue, the shortest of the Bugs came forward. Casually adjusting the security band on his arm, he said, "This favor you're doing. Will it please the Father?"

"Not at all."

The short Bug brightened. "Tell your changer, safe journey."

Chapter Thirty-One

The Zneeth swiveled its head, listening.

Something was coming its way. A faraway sound rumbled with a different kind of noise than the Zneeth had ever heard. The strangeness of the mechanical whine seemed, somehow, threatening.

The Zneeth didn't like it. Visibility flickered about the monster as it lost its concentration. Alone on the road to the Comb, it had grown thinner, almost gaunt. Its scales had lost their luster, dulled to the color of dried blood. But its eyes, dark and sunken, remained as alive as ever. Wet with fever, they burned inside its forehead.

The rumbling sound grew louder and the Zneeth sought cover. The road offered no protection. Stretching beyond the township and through the forest, it led into the flat lands. There were few trees or shrubs to be found, and none in this immediate area. Those rare plants rooted to this arid soil were stunted, their limbs misshapen.

Down the road, a wall of dust grew. Inside the swirl of dirt, the whine rose and fell in response to the engine powering it. The Zneeth crouched beside the path and, with an effort, disappeared again.

Within minutes, the dust barrier was beside it. Leaves and twigs and dirt flew into the air as a tank-like vehicle trundled down the road. It was metal - the Zneeth remembered metal - and it was big. Bigger than the Zneeth. Heavily armored, it had a turret mounted to its top. From the turret, a wide-mouth tube projected. The tube carried neither teeth nor horns, but its foreign appearance was frightening.

At the vehicle's base, a skirt obscured the machine's wheels. Dust boiled from beneath it. Crouching, the Zneeth hid as it passed.

Once it was out of sight, the monster returned to the road. It had encountered machines many ages ago, in the days before they were banned from the Bugworld. Those were smaller machines, with less noise at their center. Some of those machines had been used against the Zneeth.

Machines were nasty things. The Zneeth suspected this machine was nasty, too.

The air smelled of oil and dirt. Once the foul odor faded, the Zneeth would find the creature's scent again. It had lost the trail once but not this time.

Not when it was so close.

* * *

With the Comb in view, Syr keyed the tingle blaster to reduce its speed. He'd learned to stay off the brakes whenever possible; they were worn past the point of safety. The vehicle had other problems as well. Its driving axle changed gears with an audible clang. Half of its instrument panel was dead and, worst of all, it no longer shifted into reverse. It was long overdue for a complete overhaul.

According to Mulvaney, the miners on Alcmene paid for the machine's transport in full knowledge of its condition. They were expecting to do some repairs. They only cared if the tingler itself still worked.

The miners aren't asking for much, Syr thought. *But expectations don't have to be too high when all you need to do is carve holes through rock.*

Preparing for an assault on Father Lygt's Comb, well, that was a different matter altogether. He asked, "Is everybody ready?"

Squatting in the chamber beneath him, Atkyyn clutched at the bag of food he'd brought. From the seat next to him, Dobbins said, "Nope."

"We're at the gates, changer." Hidden in the turret, Tskett sounded impatient. "There's no turning back."

Syr pushed a lever on the console, sliding it upward. Through the viewscreen, the turret rotated to face the courtyard.

He heard Tskett fitting his claws inside the tingler's oversized handles. When the Sktzer activated the cannons, the entire vehicle began to hum.

Sentries ran along the top of the courtyard wall. Leveling the tingler's mouth at the center point of the gateway's wooden doors, Tskett squeezed the cannon's triggers.

Hummm. The front of the tube trembled as sound vibrated along its length. Its mouthpiece spun within an inner sleeve, picking up speed with each revolution.

Hummmm. The tingler's pitch grew higher. As it did, the cannon's vibrating motion softened, smoothing into a gentle quiver. It locked in place, as if held by a giant's unseen hand.

Hummmmm. Through the eye of the monitor, the cannon's mouthpiece was a blur of motion. Buffeted by the tingler's invisible waves, the large

343

gates in front of the cannon creaked in protest, their doors bouncing against their crossbar. Splinters of wood flew from them, shooting off like tiny missiles.

The courtyard wall shook. A sentry staggered as the parapet danced beneath him. Before he could fall, a claw reached out and pulled him to safety inside a low tower.

Hummmmmmm. The gates squealed with an eerie, almost lifelike, shriek. Under the cannon's onslaught, fissures appeared in the wood. The cracks deepened and split, spreading in a star-burst that raced away from their source. Chunks of wood broke free as the doors bucked. The gates slammed against the crossbar holding them until the metal brace snapped, shattering with an explosive bang.

Suddenly, the cannon quit moving. The machine fell silent.

"We're in." Syr sent the blaster forward, bulling its way through the gates. As it rolled ahead, he heard the *tink!* of spear heads bouncing harmlessly against the machine's armor.

Sitting beside Dobbins, Hhney said, "Let's see the Father try to stop us now."

"Sentries are everywhere," Syr called to the others. With the blaster's two screens reserved for the machine's driver and gunner, only he and Tskett had a view of the path ahead.

"Run over them," Tskett shouted from overhead.

"He won't, you know," Dobbins said to Hhney. "He values life."

"You told me he ate a Princess," she pointed out.

"It was an entirely different situation."

344

"You said he ate a Lizard."

"*Part* of a Lizard. Not one of the vital parts."

"I value life, too," Tskett said. "My life. Run over our enemies!"

The tingle blaster ground ahead, the right half of the machine rising and falling noisily. Outside the vehicle, someone screamed.

"There are too many of them!" Syr said.

Again, the blaster rose and fell. This time, more cries accompanied the movement.

"Nicely done," Tskett said.

"Not on purpose."

"Effective nonetheless," the warrior told him. "Drive over a few more of the guards and the rest will run away."

It was true. Nearing the Comb's mouth, the entrance was open. Its patrol had fled its post, leaving an empty road for the invaders.

Flipping switches, Syr brought up the lights at the front of the vehicle. Hhney climbed into the space beside him. "Let's go."

* * *

Rolling into the blackness, the tingler's lamps lit the path before them.

Thump, *thump*.

The roadway was flat. The glow from the machine cut into the night surrounding them but failed to pierce the shadows hidden in the pockets and nooks of the curved wall.

Thump, *thump*.

345

Hhney climbed into the turret, her head appearing through the opening at Tskett's feet. "What's that noise?"

"An annoyance." Tskett remained in his squat. Through the screen, a determined sentry hung from the turret's lip. "We have a passenger. He keeps striking his claw against this machine."

"He irritates me." Hhney called, "Atkyyn, a spear!"

Moments later, Atkyyn clanked up the ladder with the weapon in his claw.

Tskett smiled thinly. "The one outside has become bothersome to our Leader. Take care of him."

"The one outside?" Atkyyn viewed the monitor.

Thump, *thump*.

"Your next challenge."

"Such courage," Atkyyn said. "A soldier in Lygt's army, has anyone had a more thankless task? Yet he risks his life."

"Without purpose. Without reward."

"He's fiercely dedicated to the Father. To his duty. I admire him."

"You admire thankless loyalty?" Tskett studied his crippled companion. "How is it, Atkyyn, you somehow manage to disappoint me more every day?"

Atkyyn remained on the ladder, waiting.

"Dedication to another creature has no value," Tskett said. "Dedication is for the weak."

Atkyyn refused to meet his eyes.

"You're useless." Tskett held out a claw. "It was too much to expect one like you to finish an

346

enemy. Give me the spear." He snatched the weapon away. "Want to see what dedication brings? Watch."

He touched a button and the turret's hatch *snkkt*'ed softly. Tskett jerked the lid up sharply, smashing its face against the sentry's beak. Tumbling from the tingle blaster, the soldier fell from sight as he dropped beneath the machine.

Standing in the hatch, Tskett said, "You see? You care about someone else, there's your reward." His statement ended as a brilliant light struck beside his head, causing the paint on the underside of the hatch to blister.

"Get down!" Atkyyn cried, lifting himself into the turret. Frozen, Tskett remained upright and exposed.

Atkyyn yanked at his legs before a second ray blackened the metal lid, lighting the cavern. The hatch slammed shut as both Bugs fell into the turret.

Tskett pushed the smaller Bug away. Through the viewscreen, a figure sprinted from one side of the chamber to the other. Running, he clutched a silver weapon in his claw.

"That's a spitzpistol," Tskett said.

"I saw it."

"The sentry has a pistol?" Sounding angry, Tskett said, "Don't think you saved me."

"No."

"You didn't," he said. "Someday, the time might come that Hhney will save me. Perhaps the changer will save me. Not you. Never you."

Atkyyn returned to the ship's ladder.

"Go," Tskett said. "Warn the others about the weapon."

Atkyyn found Dobbin and Hhney beside Syr at the driver's seat. Light flared against the viewscreen as the tingle blaster crept forward.

"Full splatter," Dobbins said. "Can he stop us?"

"The tingler is built for hazardous conditions," Syr said. "Spitzpistols were made to be used against shell and flesh, not metal."

Hhney said, "Father Lygt assured the Council the Comb was free of advanced technology. No sophisticated weaponry. No spitzpistols."

"Give me enough dibblesticks," Dobbins said, "and I could outfit your entire tribe."

Hhney studied him with interest. "Truly?"

"You just have to know where to ask."

"Do you know where?"

"Always," Dobbins said. "Maybe the guard did, too. Who's to say he didn't buy the pistol for himself?"

"Then who's to say there aren't others?" the Leader questioned. "Or someone with a weapon even more powerful?"

"Nothing on this planet can stop a tingle blaster," Dobbins reassured her.

"As long as it's going forward," Syr added.

In front of them, the guard raced up the corridor. When he'd distanced himself from the tingle blaster, he checked the charge on his weapon.

Hhney asked, "Can you speed this thing up?"

"How fast?"

"Let's catch him."

The guard steadied his arm to fire.

"Hold on," Syr said, punching a series of buttons. Clanging gears, the machine increased its speed.

The guard triggered his gun, its spray bursting one of the tingler's lamps. Adjusting the control on the spitzpistol, he acted unconcerned about the oncoming goliath. Spotlighted in its remaining light, he watched in cool contempt as they closed the space between them.

When the machine was almost upon him, the sentry stepped backward, fitting himself between a cleft in the walls. Protected by the earth around him, he let the long nose of the spitzpistol protrude into the corridor.

"Nice," Dobbins said.

"I've no use for such tricks." Stretching across the console, Hhney reached for the steering mechanism.

Syr grabbed at her wrist. "Don't!"

Tires throwing dirt into the air, the tingle blaster turned sharply. Spinning, it smashed into the cavern wall. Hhney, Dobbins and Atkyyn flew backward, crashing onto the vehicle's floor. Syr banged back against his chair before jerking forward, his head slamming into the viewscreen's monitor.

The tingle blaster's engine shuddered. A black cloud spewing from its undercarriage, it died.

In the turret, Tskett was cursing. "There's blood up here. It's all over my monitor."

Hhney got to her feet. "On the inside or the outside?"

"Outside."

"Good."

349

Dobbins returned to the driver's chair, checking on Syr.

"I'm fine," the changer said, a welt rising over one eye. "What's the matter with Atkyyn?"

The Bug lay where he'd fallen, his arm twisted behind him. When Dobbins shifted him, he moaned.

"Arm's broken, right above the primary claw," Dobbins said. "I'll get the medkit."

"We can't stay here," Hhney said. "The alarm's been sounded. Father's soldiers will be coming."

"We're lodged in the wall." Syr touched at the engine button, bringing the tingle blaster's motor back to life. "We can't back up."

"No?"

Syr demonstrated, stabbing at the controls. The gears ground against one another uselessly.

Hhney hesitated. "Take us forward."

"If this is a bearing wall…."

"It comes down on us. We have to try."

"Send the others out," Syr said. "I can do this by myself."

"We stay together." Hhney lifted the sleeve on Syr's tunic. Etched on his shoulder was a branching triangle, brightly drawn in primary colors.

"You, too?" Dobbins asked as the sleeve fell into place.

"I like it," Syr said.

"Where I come from, a tattoo is a thing of beauty. It means something."

"It means something here, too," Hhney said. "Syr, Tskett, are you ready?"

Syr nodded.

"Now," Tskett said, pulling the cannon's triggers and sending its mouthpiece in a spin. The air filled with dirt as a fresh hole bored into the packed earth. When the haze cleared, there was an opening into the adjoining passage.

An old Bug limped into sight. At the sight of the machine, she screeched and ran away, dragging a stiff leg behind her.

"That's the chameleon's keeper," Dobbins said.

"We walked this tunnel," Hhney remembered. "We're somewhere between the Crone and her monster. This path will take us to Aly."

The tingle blaster lurched forward, grinding over a lump in the surface.

"One less spitzpistol," Hhney said.

The chameleon's quarters stood in front of them. Through the viewscreen, the tingler's mouthpiece rocked into position and began spinning. Seconds later, a hole opened into the monster's quarters. The tingle blaster growled, crawling forward.

Inside its room, the chameleon dropped to the floor. Shrinking away from the invaders, its skin melted and reshaped, mimicking dirt and stone as it pressed onto the wall.

Raising the turret's hatch, Dobbins emerged through the lid. "Monster, give me your riddle!"

Cowering, the chameleon tucked its head against the cavity in its chest. Its yellow eyes hidden, it nearly disappeared inside its chamber.

"No riddle?" Dobbins said. "Then I challenge you to answer mine:

I have many faces but one name;
I have one name but many meanings.
I have been -"

The chameleon's long neck uncurled. "That's my riddle!"

"Answer it, then."

"*Chund* is the answer!"

From the rear corridor, a cackling laugh sounded. The Crone stepped from behind the tingle blaster, facing her ward.

"A grand riddle, monster," she said. "Mine forever, now!"

Chortling, she moved into the shadows of the passage. Aghast, the chameleon stared after her.

"Get in here," Tskett said, yanking at Dobbins shirt.

Dobbins resisted his pull. "You've solved the mystery," he called to the chameleon. "You may pass!"

* * *

The chameleon watched the machine trundle away.

"*You may pass!*" the chund had cried. Even in memory, the words stung. The Crone would have heard the sentence, echoing through the chamber. Soon, she would parrot the softbody's words, laughing in the chameleon's face.

His new riddle was lost. If he tried to use it on those seeking passage, the Crone would shout out its answer. She would tease him, ridicule him, mock him, every day until a new riddle came.

352

There was no one as wicked as the Crone. Not even Father Lygt.

"*You may pass!*"

The chameleon raised its head. With a sense of astonishment, it considered the room around it. The chund's words were true. The chameleon's cage had been breached, the side wall carved away. If it dared, it could escape.

Over the tingle blaster's receding rumble, the monster heard a familiar sound. The Crone came down the corridor, her dead foot scraping over the ground.

Rising up on its legs, the chameleon shook the dirt from its body. It wanted its liberty, oh, yes, it did. But there was something else it wanted, too.

It loped out of the chamber. At the sight of the monster, the Crone yelped in fright. She quickened her pace.

"Get back, beast!" she shrieked.

The chameleon went after her. In joy, its happiest colors flowed across its skin: Blue then green then white then gold.

"Back! Back!" the Crone cried. "No food for you! I'll let you starve!"

Despite her infirmities, she flew down the pathway. Her tiny room was in front of her, its entrance too small for the chameleon's body.

She almost made it.

Chapter Thirty-Two

"My Leader?" Atkyyn inquired.

"Not now," Hhney told him, a solemn expression on her face. Her attitude was as eloquent as words: *What a mess*. Although Dobbins was fairly certain she'd express the sentiment with more vehemence if she gave voice to her emotions.

Stuff happens, Dobbins thought. *Not always good stuff.*

Things definitely hadn't worked out as planned. The tingle blaster had gotten stuck again and, now, the windshield monitor was blown, leaving them without an eye to the outside world. But it was a hard world, no matter which world you were on, and sometimes things didn't fall your way.

Disaster looms. Defeat is near. Death beckons.

Still better than that weekend on Zesmonto.

Until now, things had progressed smoothly. After the initial confrontation, Father Lygt's soldiers had left them alone, apparently afraid to pursue them down the Comb's tunnels; after all, there were monsters in these passages. But the chameleon abandoned its home without presenting a challenge and the synge stayed hidden when the tingler reduced their tiled wall into shards. Activated by the vibration of the walls, the tubes of Sweet Breeze sprayed harmlessly into the air.

Having survived such challenges, who would have suspected that this last, small hill would stop them? It was the least of their obstacles. It was little more than a bump in the road.

Literally.

It presented one tiny problem: The Comb's ceiling wasn't much higher than the hill's peak. Man and Bug could stand there comfortably, but there wasn't room enough for a tingle blaster.

"I'll make room," Tskett promised.

Syr kicked the engine up to full power. The tingle blaster roared up the trail, its cannon poised to fire. Trying to time things perfectly, Tskett waited a fraction of a second too long. By the time he activated the guns, the tank was already topping the hill.

Several feet ahead of them, the tingler tore a hole in the Comb's ceiling. The ceiling received a second hole when the turret smashed through it.

Everything came to a bone-wrenching halt. Syr went into the windshield monitor for a second time, his shoulder striking it forcefully. The viewscreen cracked, blurred, and then went permanently black.

Blind and disabled, the tingle blaster remained wedged against the Comb's ceiling.

Dobbins doubted it would ever move again. "Mulvaney's going to blame me for this."

"Any luck?" Hhney called to Tskett.

"The tingler isn't working. Even if the turret could move, we're stuck."

"It wasn't like I was doing anything," Dobbins told a disinterested world. "I was a passenger. Passengers shouldn't get blamed when a machine breaks. Passengers just…sit."

355

"Sitting is your one talent," Tskett said, climbing down the ladder. "It's why you do it so well."

"There's something you need to know." Using his good claw, Atkyyn tugged at Hhney. His bandaged limb was grotesquely oversized on such a small Bug. Dobbins would have smiled if it weren't for their situation.

"Later."

Atkyyn swallowed. "I saw something as we came over the hill. You were probably watching the top of the viewing screen, with the ceiling so close, but I was looking at the bottom - and there it was." He paused, gathering his thoughts. "There it wasn't."

"I don't have time for this, Atkyyn."

When she rose from her squat, the smallest rebel was still there. He dropped his head but, Dobbins noted, Atkyyn remained in front of her.

"Tell me, then," Hhney said.

"The pathway is open."

"It's clear? You're sure?"

"After Aly was caught, they must have reset the trap," Dobbins said. "A big, yawning hole leading into the Assassins' den, just waiting for its next victim."

"Then we don't need the tingle blaster," Syr said.

"Not unless we want to get out of here again."

"We'll get out," the changer said. "After we find our mate." He walked to the rear emergency exit and kicked the door open.

Dobbins followed him. Atkyyn trailed behind them both, his nails clicking against the blaster's metal floor.

"Stay inside," Tskett told the small Sktzer. "Guard the tingle blaster."

"Me?"

"It's your job," Tskett said. "Your duty. Secure the ship." He closed the door forcefully, the interior locks *snicking* into place.

Hhney told her mate, "You let Atkyyn stay because he's injured."

"I don't want Father to get this machine." Tskett's cold eyes flicked over to Dobbins, as if to say, *Who else can I rely on? The chund?*

Syr said, "There's movement at the bottom of the hill."

* * *

When the changer turned in his direction, Tink scuttled into the darkness of the Assassins' den. *Something peculiar is happening. Something strange.*

Something bad.

Tink bounced nervously. He wished Flip was with him. Flip would know how to respond. Left alone in the den with no one to guide him, Tink had to decide for himself on what to do next.

All right, all right, I can do this, he thought.

He'd made his own decisions before. They'd been mostly bad decisions, he knew; decisions Puff usually caught and corrected before they became horrible decisions. But nothing too terrible had happened. He'd made his own decisions and nobody had died…except for Scrooch.

Yes, he admitted, the whole Scrooch incident was probably his fault. Well, at least he'd learned from it. Scrooch had learned a lesson, too, in his last

357

few seconds before ending up in a tligodon's belly, and the lesson was, don't believe anyone who tells you that tligodons aren't dangerous. Anything covered in barbs and rattles and fangs is usually dangerous.

With Scrooch no longer available, Tink would make an effort to do better this time.

First, he'd find Puff. He'd tell her about the strange rolling metal thing. (It looked so *funny* when it crashed into the roof.) He'd tell her about the Sktzers and the softbody. He would most definitely tell her about the shape-changer.

Unlike the time at the rebel camp, this was a healthy changer. Strange how similar they appeared, though.

This was important information. Enemies invading the Comb! This was such important information even Father might provide a reward.

But what if it's a very small reward? Tink worried. What if he told Puff and there was only reward enough for one kildebeest?

The figures on the hill were in action. Marching away from the strange metal thing, they were moving toward the slope leading into the kildebeests' chamber.

Better hurry, Tink thought.

* * *

"I don't suppose you feel like talking?" Mox asked.

No, she didn't. Aly's bleary-eyed glare made it quite obvious. The truth serum hadn't worked at all.

Pity.

358

Still, the drug's failure left open other exciting possibilities. The exploration of those possibilities was, in large part, the purpose behind the construction of the Blue Room. If the softbody had revealed all of her secrets, there wouldn't have been a need to use any of the Blue Room's toys.

And the Blue Room held so many toys.

Options surrounded him. There was the Pit of Endless Pain, the Clapper, the Twist and Shout, and the Box. Mox was particularly proud of the Box. With the chund in captivity, he'd made some expensive modifications to this prized possession.

What would he have done if she told him everything he wanted to know? He'd have no good reason to place her inside the Box. She would have found herself in there eventually, of course, but it wouldn't have been as amusing. Her suffering would have seemed almost pointless.

It helps to look on the bright side of things. Mox told her, "You're probably wondering where you are. You'd probably like to know what's going to happen next."

Nothing from the chund. At the least, she should have been frightened. Mox knew he would have been frightened, waking up to find his body imprisoned inside a large cube. The female, her head protruding from the opening in the top, appeared annoyed, at best. She gazed at him from the middle of the lacquered square, irritated but collected, and not visibly scared at all.

"As you wish." Mox closed his claw around the handle in front of him. He cranked it, one full revolution. Inside the Box, there came the sound of metal sliding across metal. "When I turn it again, you'll feel the needles."

Aly's eyes widened. "Don't."

Good, a response. "Are you ready to talk?"

"About what?"

"Please. Let's not play games." Holding the crank, he moved it another half-circle. He could almost envision the thousands of sharp points emerging from their pockets, stretching to touch the full length of his prisoner's body. Most of the needles would barely brush her skin. Only a few would draw blood.

Aly winced.

"Take this as a warning," Mox said. He should have expected problems with this one. She was a transporter and transporters understood pain. They'd been trained to deal with it. Even in agony, some of them managed to lie to their inquisitors.

He'd learned this lesson firsthand. It complicated matters. Anything less than the truth could undo him.

"I doubt you'll believe this," he told Aly, "but I want you to live."

Lying under a spike-covered table, Puff snickered.

Mox wasn't bothered by the scorn in Aly's eyes. Surrounded by instruments of torture, who could doubt death was near? Even the drain in the floor, ringed with the stain of blood, testified to the outcome of imprisonment here.

Had a prisoner ever left this room alive? He couldn't remember. It was too easy to kill them.

It was too much fun.

Which was exactly why he hadn't used the Blue Room until now. The transporter had to be kept alive. If the bondmate was killed, Father Lygt would absorb the full power of the Web. His strength would grow and his cycles would become without number. Mox would, forever, be nothing more than a servant.

He had far grander aspirations.

"When I first met you," he said, "I knew you'd hide the truth. You wanted the Web for yourself. You thought you could hide its secrets."

"I've answered your questions. Endlessly."

"That you did." Mox scratched a nail over the seam bisecting the top of the Box. "Every night, you told the same story. Your fabric of lies was so well-constructed, I couldn't move you past it. I had to find another approach."

"Truth serum!" Puff snorted, resting her head against her legs.

Mox pretended he hadn't heard her. The kildebeest was tired of watching the chund and her attitude was starting to reflect it. Puff wanted to take her reward and return to the Assassins' den.

She didn't know the promised reward, an assortment of gemstones, had already been spent. Altering the Box to fit an off-worlder had proven costly. Puff wouldn't care about unexpected expenses or the added cost involved in silencing the carpenters. The Assassins expected to be paid. They wanted to play with their pretty rocks.

It was a minor problem. It could be dealt with later.

"My new approach," Mox said, "is this. The Box."

"Needles," Aly said.

361

"There are needles, yes, but there's more. You've had some discomfort but only a handful of needles have tasted your body. When I reverse the crank, a hundred different ones will extend. There are new holes made with every revolution. It's never the same pain twice."

Aly wet her lips. "So you do intend to kill me."

"Not at all," Mox said. "The vital organs are protected. You'll feel it in the chest, the pelvis, the knees. Nothing will touch your lungs, your kidneys, your hearts."

"Hearts?" Puff asked.

"There's only a little blood loss, even when the needles go in deeper," Mox said. "Death never approaches but the pain holds you. You'll have agony without release."

"Unless I give you new answers."

"Unless you tell me the truth about the Web."

Puff came out from under the table. "Move the handle," she said. "I want to see if the needles miss her hearts."

"Not yet." To Aly, Mox said, "It's your decision. I won't do this unless you make me."

The line had a nice ring to it. It almost sounded sincere. Puff stayed at his side, a mocking grin on her face.

"What is it?" Mox asked.

"Chund don't have hearts," the kildebeest said. "They have one heart. A little, chewy one."

"There are different kinds of chund."

"This is Terran," Puff said. "I've had Terran." A wave of repressed laughter rippled her bulb. "Hearts," she tittered.

362

Feeling his temper flare, Mox fought down the emotion. "We'll discuss this privately."

"Did you test the Box?" Puff peeked up at the Bug's face. "You didn't."

"There wasn't time." Anger crept into his voice. This time, he let it be heard.

"I understand," Puff agreed. "It would take time to find another Terran to test. Harder, still, to find one -" giggling, she fell onto her side, "- with *hearts*!"

Her laughter filled the room. Swinging his foot as hard as he could, Mox kicked the Assassin. "Get up!"

A second kick caught Puff solidly on the bulb. Her good humor evaporated. With a snarl, she sprang to her feet.

"Do you think to bite me, kildebeest?" Mox challenged. "Be careful. Father Lygt is at the end of his cycles. There will be a new Father soon and I have a long memory."

Puff retracted her fangs. "You? The next Father?"

"Why not?"

Whatever her opinion, Puff didn't express it. Shaking her head, she remained silent.

Mox squeezed his pincers together angrily. Once he was Father, he'd have the Box altered again. Next time, he'd put Puff inside. Or, better yet, he'd tie her to the Clapper.

Such a thing had never been done. Everyone said it was impossible to fold a kildebeest.

But how many had really tried?

Focused on the Clapper, Mox saw a flash of light twinkle from the wall behind it. The momentary glitter, real or not, sent a jolt of panic through him. Earthen walls didn't produce a reflection. Such a sparkle came from a different source.

Spyhole.

If the adjoining room was lit, a careless watcher might have allowed a flash of light be seen. It would have happened in an instant, at the turn of a head or with an exchange of viewers.

Or it might not have happened at all.

He advanced slowly. Before his workers started revising the Box, Mox patched every peephole into the room. He'd done it purely as a precautionary measure. Father Lygt hadn't come to the Blue Room in two cycles and the guards avoided it out of fear. There was no reason to expect any surveillance on an unused torture chamber.

Every patch remained in place. Mox felt a surge of relief. Had he been caught at this stage of the game, everything would have been over. Father Lygt would have put *him* in the Clapper. While there was no novelty in bending a Bug's feet to meet his head, he'd have done it, anyway.

Dropping his eyes, Mox saw tiny mounds of dirt spilled onto the floor. He pushed a foot over the crumbling the piles. It was new dirt, predominantly brown in color but, spread out, showing traces of gray.

With a feeling of dread, he studied the wall again. *There*, at beak level: a series of holes, freshly bored for spying. Tilting his head just so, he could see a pin-sized point of light wink out from behind one of them.

"Uh-oh." Puff didn't sound happy.

Mox pressed his eye to one of the holes. The opposite room was vacant. Straightening, he saw Puff's spot under the table was empty.

Somehow, she'd crept out of the room.

Taking her action as his cue, Mox scurried around the Clapper. He was reaching for the door when it opened in front of him.

Father Lygt stood in the doorway. Behind him, three armed guards blocked the exit.

"My dear Mox," Father Lygt said. "I can't wait to hear your explanation for this."

The guards laughed.

Chapter Thirty-Three

Father Lygt stepped into the Blue Room, the guards following him.

"Father," Mox said, his voice strained, "I've found the bondmate."

Father Lygt watched the vapor, drooling from his mouth.

Mox said, "The kildebeests hid her. I found her in their chamber."

With every word, the vapor changed in color, gaining substance and appearing to grow more real. It crawled from his mouth, the very image of a headless beast from some unknown world.

The lies had begun.

"It was Puff –" Mox started.

Father Lygt gave his words no more attention. The Web had warned him of his servant's deceit and the Web had been right. He knew he should feel grateful. Perhaps he would be, later.

For now, he only felt tired. He hoped he'd find some rest when the bondmate died. Until then, the Web seemed less a blessing than a curse.

Its golden strands rewrapped themselves around his upper arm. Despite himself, Father Lygt caressed it. It felt warm and giving.

That's the problem, he thought. *It gives too much.*

The longer he held it, the more difficult it was to live his daily life. The revelations the Web offered were growing. Originally, he'd only been able to read Bugs. Later, a Txarrian and, then, a few other travelers. But, the previous night, an off-world trader had proven to be as depraved as any creature Father Lygt had ever met. Destroyed, even his meat seemed too tainted to be eaten. Father Lygt gagged, trying to swallow his stew.

Was starvation to be his final fate? Would he be forced to go from foodpot to foodpot, seeking the one pure soul that had been diced for an evening's repast?

How melodramatic of me, Father Lygt reflected without embarrassment.

His storeroom held enough stewpots to feed him for a hundred cycles. As long as he didn't meet the Bug he was eating, he'd be fine. He doubted he'd find a departed Bug's true nature floating in the broth of his evening's bowl.

Besides, there were still a few Bugs who escaped his gaze. The true nature of most chund remained hidden to him and almost every monster retained its secrets. But the Web's power was growing. The onslaught of images was growing, as well.

Father Lygt feared the visions that lay ahead of him. Was it any wonder he couldn't sleep? Hatred and duplicity surrounded him. He could rely on no one. At night, he'd taken to walking the tunnels of the Comb. He found peace only in solitude.

What would happen when, finally, he destroyed the Web's true bondmate? Would things improve?

Or get worse?

367

The bondmate. "What's the matter with the chund?" he asked.

It interrupted Mox in mid-falsehood. "Father?"

"What did you do to your captive?"

Aly's head was drooped forward, her forehead resting on the Box. Sweat puddled beneath her head. Her eyes were closed and her breathing was shallow.

Mox said, "It's a trick. She was fine, only minutes ago."

"Was that before or after you used the needles?"

"Before – after! Both."

"Take her out," Father Lygt told the guards.

Going to the torture device, a guard disengaged its lever. Its halves separating, the Box opened. A second guard loosened Aly's straps.

"I brought her here for questioning," Mox said. "I wasn't going to kill her."

"But you might have, don't you think? After all, the Box was never tested."

For once, Mox was speechless. His reaction was all Father Lygt could have hoped for.

Surprised, my deceitful toady? Oh, yes, I heard your conversation with the kildebeest. I know all about the Box as well.

I know about a lot of things.

The guard released the band from Aly's waist. Freed from her bindings, she fell into his arms. The guard juggled the body clumsily, trying to avoid the soft, naked flesh of the unconscious chund.

"Set her down," the Father said. "No, not on the spiked table. A safe place, out of the way. Stay with her."

Holding Aly, the guard's eyes darted about, seeking a safe place to rest his burden. Returning to the side of the Box, he gave up. Letting her body slump to the ground, he stood over her.

Father Lygt pushed Mox forward. "Put this one in her place," he told the remaining guards.

They each snapped a claw over one of the servant's pincers. Mox said, "Father?"

Smoke followed the word, coiling slowly around his neck. It created a fitting imagery. His servant said, "I beg of you, Father, don't do this. Don't leap to assumptions."

The guards drew the center tie over Mox's abdomen. "Straps are too short for his arms," one of the guards said.

"It's been altered," Mox said. "It won't work on our kind, anymore. I had some changes made. For your glory, Father. If you'll just let me explain!"

"Won't close, either," the guard complained. "The neck opening is too small."

"Give it a try."

Mox struggled against the band holding him. "It can't work!"

On Father Lygt's signal, the guards slammed the doors of the Box. Mox gurgled, his eyes bulging with the blow.

Father Lygt lifted Mox's head. "Let's try it again."

"Father!" The cry came from the outside corridor. "Father Lygt!"

It was the unmistakable sound of an Assassin's voice. Before Father Lygt could react, a red-bulbed kildebeest bounded through the doorway.

369

"A shape-changer, Father," the kildebeest said. Panting, he took a deep breath before he continued. "Two Sktzers and a changer!"

"Where?"

"There's a chund, too," the kildebeest added in the interest of accuracy.

If stupidity cast an aura, this one would offer the colors of a rainbow. "Is the shape-changer in the Comb?"

Before the reply could come, the guards yelled out. A second kildebeest rose from behind the Box. Using the newcomer's arrival as a diversion, she sprang past Father Lygt and fled through the door.

"Puff?" the first kildebeest said in surprise.

"Puff, is it? So that much is true." Turning to the remaining Assassin, Father Lygt said, "Now, you empty-headed thing, tell me where I'll find the shape-changer."

Flinching, the kildebeest said, "In the den."

As witless as the kildebeest was, it appeared to be telling the truth. A rescue party had come for the bondmate.

Father Lygt said, "I want one of you to check the Assassins' den. Which of you is fastest?"

"Durnn," said the first guard. The name rose from his beak in a honey-brown cloud of smoke.

"Me?" Durnn said. "I'm guarding the chund." Suddenly, he shot forward as if tied to an unseen rope. Stumbling, he fell into Father Lygt and dragged him to the ground.

The chund, awake and uninjured, rose over them. "This is mine," she said, grabbing at the Father's arm.

She tore the Web away. In that instant, he almost lost his mind.

He'd never felt such anguish. Screaming, he was only dimly aware the guards had frozen in position beside him. Paralyzed, they waited in the doorway.

They were letting the bondmate escape with the Web. His cycles would end. It was over. All over.

Over.

It was -

Father Lygt forced his head up from the floor. He clutched at Durnn, squeezing him so tightly the Bug cried out.

"Catch her," Father Lygt rasped to the guards. "Go!"

The two Bugs ran into the corridor. Keeping his hold on Durnn, Father Lygt climbed to his feet. He lifted the guard to his knees.

"It was an accident," Durnn said.

With a strike of his pincer, Father Lygt crushed the Bug's throat. Durnn fell, wheezing as he died.

Locking a claw onto the dead guard's spear, Father Lygt supported himself. Haltingly, he moved into the corridor. As weak as he was, he could feel the pull of the Web. It was drawing him closer.

It wasn't over yet.

* * *

Feeding sounds penetrated the mist fogging Mox's brain. He opened his eyes. Through a haze, he saw movement.

A kildebeest? Yes. It was devouring what was left of a guard.

"Tink?" Mox asked.

Tink ignored him. He popped the guard's antenna loose and slurped it down.

Mox kicked feebly at the walls around him. The Box wasn't secured but he didn't have the strength to force it open. "Help me."

Tink continued chewing on the antenna.

"I'll reward you," Mox said.

The kildebeest swallowed. "What reward?"

"Anything."

Lifting his long legs delicately, Tink picked his way over pieces of shell. "Father put you there. Father wants you there." He leapt to the doorway, giggling. "Mox in a Box."

"Don't go!"

"A shape-changer is coming. Sktzers, too." Tink glanced to his left, to the trail leading to the Assassins' den. "Empty-headed, maybe," he said, "but not dumb."

He bounded off to his right.

Chapter Thirty-Four

Moving through the gloom of the kildebeests' tunnel, Aly stepped on something. Under the pressure of her weight, it burst. A warm gush of liquid squirted up between her toes.

At that moment, she welcomed the darkness. There were things she'd rather not see.

Within this pervading murk, the Web offered enough of a glow that she could see the larger obstacles strewn before her. Picking her way to the side wall, she followed along its length. It narrowed as she walked, finally opening into a tunnel.

Stinks, she thought. *It's ripe with the smell of Assassins.*

Dropping to her knees, she crawled inside the opening. After all, what was it Father Lygt had said? "Tell me where I'll find the shape-changer."

And the kildebeest answered, "In the den."

Best hope it was the Assassins' den, she told herself, *because it's the only place you know to go.*

She knew the kildebeest might have meant some other place. The chameleon had its home; the synge had their secret dwelling. For all she knew, the Comb was riddled with dens.

Above her, Aly heard the movement of feet. A rounded shape briefly blocked the tunnel's exit before crossing to its opposite side. Slowing her crawl, she heard a voice. Someone was speaking from inside the outer room.

"I don't like threats and I don't give warnings," a male voice said in Basic, "but I think you ought to know, the shape-changer is getting hungry."

Dobbins. Aly never imagined she'd be so glad to hear his voice.

An Assassin replied, "Sounds like a threat to me."

"Sounds like a warning," said a second kildebeest.

"I'm getting hungry," a third said. "Hey!"

The kildebeest's exclamation came as Aly erupted from the tunnel. Sprinting past the startled Assassins, she ran for the clearing where her comrades stood. Syr caught her against his chest, stopping her before the momentum carried her into the outlying slime.

"You're alive!" Dobbins exclaimed.

"Alive," Tskett said, amazed, "and carrying the Web."

Syr kept her in his arms, pressed to his tunic.

"Okay, thanks," she said, coloring under his gaze. "I'm good."

She slipped from his hold. His tunic felt wet. Where she'd touched it, her fingers felt greasy.

Twill slime.

The others were streaked with it. Following her lead, they'd slid through the entry of the Assassins' den and been caught. The back of the den was sealed behind its metal wall.

"Does anyone have an idea on how to get out of here?" Aly asked.

"Ask the changer," Tskett said. "He was the one who insisted we come."

Syr smiled warmly.

"Or you could ask your other mate," Tskett continued. "He knows everything even when it's apparent he knows nothing. I'm certain he's made a hundred plans for escape."

Dobbins grinned.

The kildebeests waited at the opposite end of the room. One after another, they lowered their bulbs to the ground. Without a clear plan of attack, it appeared that they were willing to sit back and watch what happened next.

All except one.

Puff prowled through her pack. Walking over to a tunnel feeding into the chamber, she glanced back at Aly.

"You," she said, "are bad luck." With a jiggle of her bulb, she disappeared into the earthen shaft.

Hhney pressed a spear in Aly's hand. "We carried this for you. Syr told us we'd find you."

"You believed him?" Aly could tell she hadn't. "You came, anyway."

"For the Web," Tskett said.

Syr didn't come for the Web, Aly realized. *Neither did Dobbins.* She loosened the creature's strands from around her wrist.

Hhney said, "Keep it. It's best you hold it until we're back at camp."

"Back at camp?" A disembodied Bug's voice spoke to them. "You think you can escape from here?"

A guard rose out of the tunnel, strutting into the chamber. Aly recognized him as the senior guard she'd seen in the Blue Room. The junior guard crawled out after him. His confidence appeared more fragile.

"No one touches the female chund," the senior guard told the Assassins. "As for the others," his voice rose, delighted to give such an order, "kill them all!"

His stirring command echoed throughout the room. It died away with the kildebeests still on the ground, their legs tucked beneath them.

"Why do you lay there?" Confusion played over the senior guard's face. "Do your job!"

A much-scarred kildebeest asked, "Our job?"

"You're Assassins! You kill things!"

"Some things," said the much-scarred kildebeest.

"Most things," agreed another. "Not all things. Not *that* thing."

Syr remained with Aly, at the front of the group. Stained with slime, his tunic hugged his body, showing the rolls of flesh around his stomach. For the first time since she'd met him, he was fat.

"Strike now, before he changes," the senior guard urged the kildebeests. When that didn't work, he said forcefully, "You have your orders!"

"I've never killed a shape-changer." The scarred kildebeest flexed a foreleg casually. "Show me how it's done."

The senior guard sought his partner for support. The second guard refused to meet his eyes.

"We'll wait for the Father," the senior guard decided.

"Father Lygt is coming?" Hhney's face grew grim. "Syr. Are you ready?"

"When the time is right."

Aly knew what he meant. Trapped in the Assassins' den, outnumbered by kildebeests and the Father's guards, there wasn't any one change he could make that would save them all. If things went badly, he might not save any of them.

So why wouldn't he stop smiling?

Dobbins sidled up beside them. "A Belzian guffamer," he whispered to Syr. Before the changer could reply, he clapped a hand to his forehead. "A guffamer? What's the matter with me? A guffamer isn't powerful enough."

"It's a fine idea," Syr said soothingly. "I've never done one. Besides, they wouldn't expect a guffamer. That's important."

"It can't bore through a metal wall. It can't kill the Assassins."

"It's big, it has a frightening roar. It's strong, just not strong enough."

An image formed in Aly's mind's eye, as fresh as when she'd first seen it. "A starwolven," she said. "My third run, I was attacked by one. With its skin, no Assassin would dare touch it. It could eat through these mud walls in minutes."

"I've read about them. I've watched a holo."

Dobbins said, "It's not enough. Syr has to see one to change. Physically be there, view it. Has to be in its presence."

"There are rules for a shape-changer?"

"There are rules for everyone," Syr said.

"I hope you choose soon, changer," Tskett said. "We have a visitor."

Leaning on a spear, Father Lygt entered the den. He carried himself imperiously, expecting the kildebeests to leap to their feet and create a path for his progress. At the sight of him, they did. Stopping in the midst of his pets, he stared coldly at the intruders who had breached his home.

"Father Lygt," Hhney said. "Somehow, I thought you'd be bigger."

"Sktzer." Lowering his gaze, he caught sight of the one Assassin who dared to rest its bulb. "What's your name?" Father Lygt asked.

The unfortunate kildebeest scrambled upright. "Binger."

"Tell me, Binger," Father Lygt said. "What's happening here?"

"Happening?"

"These invaders, these defilers of our Comb. Why do they live? Why haven't you killed them?"

"Me?" Binger said in a squeak. "It wasn't my decision!"

"It was Puff," a soft voice suggested from inside the kildebeests' pack. A splotchily-colored kildebeest nodded at Binger with encouragement.

"Puff," Binger told Father Lygt. "Puff said to wait."

"And Tink," murmured the splotchy kildebeest.

Binger accepted the suggestion. "Tink, too."

"And Weege."

"And Weege," Binger agreed. He stopped short as sniggering sounds rose from the group around him. "No, no. Weege is dead!"

"You, too, Binger," Father Lygt said.

The Assassins acted immediately, the splotchy kildebeest attacking first as the luckless Binger fell beneath their fangs.

Father Lygt gestured for the senior guard to join him. He bent toward him, beak to ear, and the guard hurried for the nearest tunnel.

"Reinforcements," Aly told the others.

Father Lygt met her eyes. Raising his voice over the frenzied feeding, he said, "A useful lesson, yes? Death comes quickly to those who displease me."

"It wasn't your spear that slaughtered the kildebeest."

"Think again, chund. My guards are my left pincer; my soldiers are my right claw. Today, my Assassins are my knife. Tomorrow, one of my monsters will be my pistol. Here, in this Comb, every creature does as I command. My word is enough to strike you dead." He considered the group around her. "You hold the Web. Are you their leader?"

"I lead," Hhney said.

Finishing their meal, the kildebeests encircled their master.

Father Lygt asked Hhney, "Does the changer obey you?"

"We stand together."

He smiled without humor. "I don't need my Web to see your lie."

Aly's fingers played over the yellow fungus. *The Web calms me. It teased Hhney with the memory of flight. It heightened Dobbins' ability to steal. And, apparently, it helps Father Lygt see the truth.*

What else can it do?

"Your group was never meant to be on the same world," Father Lygt said, "much less stand shoulder-to-shoulder in battle. You'll betray one another when the first drop of blood falls."

"Try us," Aly said.

"Bondmate." His face hardened. "What do you see when I speak? Does smoke roll from my beak? Do my words turn into demons as you watch?"

He doesn't know, she thought. *He thinks I see what he could see.*

"You alone know I mean what I say. The others might not believe me but you do." To Hhney, he said, "My Assassins will be at your throats before the changer can save you. Stand together and, I promise, you'll die that way."

Dobbins whispered, "A bogwiler."

"It eats everything," Syr whispered back. "No one controls a bogwiler. Not even the bogwiler itself."

"Your one chance," Father Lygt said, "your only hope, is to return my Web. Leave the Web, leave the bondmate, and the rest of you can live."

"'Bondmate'," Hhney said. "That's the second time you've used that word."

"Father Lygt thinks I've bonded with the Web," Aly said. Her sessions with Mox were of some use, after all. "He believes my existence limits the power it gives him."

"It isn't true."

Father Lygt said, "My Reader tells me differently."

"The Reader is wrong," Hhney responded. "My sept's Elder shared the Web's history. If you've held it, you've had all it offers. It strengthens your natural gift. Hold it directly and your talent is realized. At its touch, you become its bondmate."

Seeing the strain in their enemy's face, Aly said, "He knows what it has done so far. He needs it to do more."

"Take the Web." On Hhney's pronouncement, Tskett nearly dropped his spear. "But not Aly. You can't have her."

A faint tremor shook the chamber walls.

"How foolish do you think I am?" Father Lygt asked, angrily. "I have the Book. I know the truth. By offering me half of what I need, you seek to rob me of my cycles."

The ground trembled again, more strongly. The kildebeests stiffened their legs.

"Father?" a kildebeest said.

"So be it," Father Lygt pronounced. "Let your lies follow you to the stewpots."

Dancing around him nervously, the kildebeests were deaf to his unspoken command. The innermost wall of the chamber quaked under the force of a violent blow. Dirt and twigs rained through the air as a second blow was struck.

"A gorgorrus," Dobbins whispered.

"Used it."

"A horned C.O.A.N."

Syr's face grew pale. "A C.O.A.N.?"

"You're right, you're right, forget it."

Thunder boomed inside the Comb and the entire cavern shook. Dust filled the air as a thousand dying voices cried from the adjoining chamber.

Rearing onto his back legs, the splotchy kildebeest shrieked, *"ZNEEEEEEEEEEETH!"*

"What's a Zneeth?" Dobbins asked.

* * *

381

The wall exploded inward, sending the kildebeests running in wild alarm. Chunks of hardened mud crashed down around them, killing both of Father Lygt's guards in a spray of blood and body parts.

Through a brown cloud, a giant shape entered the chamber. The Assassins in its path were slashed apart, their bulbs raked by unseen talons.

"What are you?" Father Lygt commanded the presence. "What are you, really? You're not a Zneeth. Not here, not in the Comb."

In reply, a ghostly form flickered for an instant, fading in and out of reality. Before it vanished, he caught sight of a dozen crazed eyes and a flapping tentacle.

"It isn't possible," Father Lygt said.

He tried to find an escape. The entrance was sealed by its metal wall. The closest tunnel was choked by the stampeding kildebeests and the second blocked by the great beast before him. On the opposite side of the room were the Sktzers and their changer.

Father Lygt held his spear in front of him. "What do you want?"

The Zneeth reappeared, its mad eyes studying him. It's wet, pink trunk whipped forward, shattering Father Lygt's beak and burying itself inside his head. Father Lygt tried to scream; found he couldn't; and the monster sucked him away.

* * *

The Father's body collapsed, the empty cores of his legs snapping as it dropped.

"Make your choice, changer!" Tskett cried.

The Zneeth was in front of them, its bones in vivid display beneath its scales. Lifting its trunk, it trumpeted in all of its dead voices.

So, Dobbins thought, *that's a Zneeth.*

The monster searched the creatures in front of it, finding Aly. It focused on her.

"What do you think?" Dobbins asked Syr.

"Isn't it beautiful?"

"Beautiful?"

"Yes," Syr said, sounding enraptured.

"Well?"

"Awfully big."

"You've done bigger. Once, anyway."

Syr nodded. Taking a deep breath, he held his hands over his face.

Cloaking itself in its invisibility, the Zneeth took a step toward Aly as its body wavered and disappeared. Cocking his arm, Tskett threw his spear. It flew to where the beast last stood and lodged itself in mid-air. The Zneeth grunted angrily. The spear wobbled and fell, batted away by a vanished tentacle. A tiny spot of color appeared in its place.

Dobbins ran toward Aly as Syr moaned. Rivulets of sweat ran through the changer's fingers. His shoulders heaved and a ridge of bone pushed up from the back of his tunic.

Its visibility flickering in and out, the Zneeth turned toward the Sktzers. Hhney dropped her spear when Tskett grasped her from behind, using his wings to carry her into the air.

They rose above their enemy.

"*ZNEEEEEEEEEETH!*" it screeched after them as they floated to the ceiling of the Comb.

Taking Aly's hand, Dobbins said, "When I start to run, you should run, too."

"From the Zneeth?"

"Or Syr. He's not always in control of his transformation."

Hunched over, the changer spasmed. New limbs pushed out from his body, shredding his tunic. His neck bent back in agony as his forehead bulged, knots throbbing under the skin. Then the skin broke and a white, unformed eye stared at the world around it.

The Zneeth lowered its head, abandoning the prey in the sky. His legs thudding against the ground, it moved toward Dobbins and Aly.

"Syr needs more time," Dobbins said, "The transformation is too big."

"I've got an idea." Aly pulled the Web from her arm. With a gasp, she staggered forward to set the moss upon the evolving changer.

Aly staggered back as Syr's mouth opened in a voiceless cry. A tube-like tongue uncoiled from between his widening lips, lapping at the air. Convulsions wracked his body and he crashed to the ground.

The wraith-like Zneeth stared at Syr, unmoving.

"Time to go," Dobbins said, putting his arm around Aly's waist. Weakly, she clung to him.

With the Web feeding him, Syr grew quickly. His arms became legs, his fingers became toes, and talons tore from the digits to grip the earth. His body swelled and stretched, assuming massive proportions as an encrustation of scales raced to cover it.

"I've never seen anything like this," Aly said.

"He's never changed this big, this fast."

"He's *huge*."

Syr swung his gigantic head around. His eyes stared down at them without any trace of recognition.

"Did you see?" Aly asked Dobbins. "The look in his eyes?"

In a blink, Syr vanished.

"Now!" Clutching Aly's hand, Dobbins raced toward the tunnels. Behind them, a voice called out, "My arm! The changer ate my arm!"

The Zneeth took a thundering step after Aly. Not seeing the Web, it bellowed in rage. Finding the golden glow hanging in mid-air at the other end of the chamber, it lifted its trunk and bleated in distress.

Syr's form flickered and held. Bigger than his adversary, he showed no fear of the Zneeth. His six powerful legs tensing, he jumped into the air.

The Zneeth fell as Syr rammed into him, carrying both monsters to the floor. Finding his feet first, the shape-changer leapt forward. He tore his claws over the Zneeth's dulled scales. Pieces of plate scattered, tearing lines of red where the talons struck.

Kicking at the ground, the Zneeth dodged its attacker. Syr struck again, knocking his opponent to the ground. For a brief few seconds, the Zneeth's underbelly was exposed. Syr's trunk shot out, seeking the vulnerable flesh, and the Zneeth's trunk slapped at it. Breathing heavily and dripping blood, it scrambled to its feet.

The Zneeth winked into invisibility, wavered, and was solid again. The flap in its throat opened, its

385

tentacle lashing at Syr's face. A second stinging blow sent Syr lurching across the cavern. His rear feet splashed into the Twill slime, sliding out from under him. With a cry, he lost his balance.

The Zneeth attacked.

It swarmed over the changer, slashing at his eyes. Swinging its dirty, ragged nails, the crazed creature forced Syr further into the goo. The Zneeth's trunk stabbed out, desperately trying to puncture the healthier animal's ungiving armor.

Roaring, Syr bucked his foe into the air. The Zneeth landed roughly. He quickly rolled away, barely avoiding the foreleg that tried to crush its ribs.

Struggling in the slime, Syr fought for his footing. The Zneeth darted toward him. Its tentacle snaked out and Syr turned his head, protecting his eyes. The tentacle grabbed at his leg, instead.

"The Web!" Aly cried.

The glowing fungus was snatched away. Wailing, Syr fell onto his side.

Slime splashed over his body as the Zneeth trumpeted in joy. Its form fading, the beast galloped from the chamber. Invisible, its pounding footsteps grew softer as it fled the Comb.

The changer writhed, his transformation devolving. Naked and markedly thinner, he curled into a ball.

Closing his eyes, he slept.

Epilogue: Ever After

'Sometimes you've got to take a chance.'
From the notebooks of Tucker Mulvaney

    Aly surveyed her cabin with a critical eye. Had the space been bigger and less austere, it might have qualified as a walk-in closet. Its bed, too big by far, nearly filled the room.

    Dobbins was right, she thought. *As space cruisers go, the TIAN'S GATE isn't much of a pleasure ship.*

    She could easily believe it had originally been launched as a mining ship. Everything about it had the hard, cold feel of an industrial vessel.

    Not that she was in any position to complain. The room was small but it was clean, adequately lit, and it had its own locking front door. The unpleasant smell lingering in the hallways failed to penetrate this tiny cubicle. She owed Captain Mulvaney a favor – and not a small one, either.

    The captain wasn't being altogether altruistic. The holdover on T'ing had resulted in a level of attrition among passengers and crew. Whether in slave pens or stewpots, they'd left seats to be filled. Since food supplies were adequate and accommodations were available, the captain had taken only a small risk in bringing her aboard.

"It's not exactly in keeping with regulations," he told her. "Life demands a certain level of flexibility, doesn't it?"

A knock at the cabin door brought her out of her reverie. "Yes?"

"Visitors, Miss," came an outside voice. The speaker had a Scottish accent. *Were Scots the only people they hired on this rig?* "A pair of Bugs, down at the Spaceport. Best hurry if you want to see them."

"When do we lift?" Aly pressed the release to open the door. The barrier slid for less than an inch before jamming. "I'm afraid it's stuck."

There wasn't a response. The crewman had given his message and left.

She shoved against the door. Making a *twoong!* noise, something snapped and it slid open. Leaving the room, she heard the door closing smoothly behind her.

She wondered if the door would open on her return. After all, a passenger riding on a C.O.D. basis wasn't likely to get a quick response to her complaints.

Well, if necessary, she'd sleep in the ship's lounge. The ship's metal floor would be a welcome change from the interior of a Box or the bottom of a cage.

Except for the security crews, the Spaceport was largely empty. The docking berths that might have been occupied by cargo vessel or passenger ships were vacant. The death of Father Lygt and the recent upheaval at the Comb had frightened off both traders and tourists while spurring a half-dozen vessels to launch ahead of schedule.

The *TIAN'S GATE* was one of only two ships in the hold. Even now, Aly wasn't certain the captain had permission to leave. She'd heard there wasn't any official resistance to the passenger liner going, and this seemed to be good enough for him.

Inside the Visitors' Center, two dusty, brown Bugs waited. Hhney and Tskett looked up as she entered.

"I didn't expect to see you," Aly said.

"Did you think we'd let you leave without saying goodbye?" Despite the mud obscuring her markings, Hhney was happy and relaxed. "I've got something to show you."

Tskett shielded the rebel leader from view. Hhney uncurled the wrapping covering her lower arm.

Aly gasped. "The Web!"

"Or a reasonable facsimile." The strands on this fungus were brighter, more golden, than those on the original. Secured around Hhney's arm, the creature sparkled in the light.

"It isn't alive," Tskett said. "It was woven from fiber and sprinkled with crushed gemstone."

"Atkyyn made it," Hhney said.

"Atkyyn?"

"He did okay," Tskett allowed.

Hhney folded the wrap over her arm. "The Web is a strong symbol. Using this copy, we'll unite Sktzers. The time is right. The rebel septs are ready to listen."

"After that?"

"We'll see. Not everyone is happy with Mox as the new Father. If a battle comes, he may not be able to rely on the Mound Lords' support. His guards

389

are disheartened and the Assassins have left. The Comb is vulnerable to attack."

"Father Lygt has never been weaker." Tskett dragged a claw around the base of his neck. "Can we go? The mud itches."

Aly said, "Have you heard from Syr? Or Dobbins?"

"They're fine," Hhney replied reassuringly. She touched the shoulder marked with Aly's tattoo. "Safe journey, my sister."

"My Leader." She bowed her head. Lifting her eyes, she saw Hhney and Tskett walking down the steps leading from the Spaceport. From the township, a cart would take them back to the forest.

They'd come a long way to say their farewells. Syr and Dobbins could have come with them, but they hadn't.

Aly felt irritated with herself. *Did you really think they'd come?*

Dobbins wasn't the kind for farewells. He'd undoubtedly found himself a new scam and needed the changer to back him up. She'd never meant anything to him…except that she seemed to matter to Syr.

Guess I was wrong about him, too, she thought.

She returned to the ship. It wasn't entirely fair to blame the little thief but she didn't care. "I'll blame who I want to blame," she said out loud.

She knew she wouldn't, though. A transporter needed to see things clearly, had to find the truth, in every situation. The truth was, she was at fault, too.

When Syr had come to her hut, the last night at the rebel camp, she'd let him share her bed.

No, she hadn't *let* him stay. She'd wanted him to stay.

When Dobbins appeared in her doorway later, she rebuffed him. He didn't act jealous, but was he? Did he honestly believe she'd stay in camp, lose her opportunity to escape the Bugworld, just because of some ridiculous story about mates and mating? Syr might believe in such nonsense but she didn't.

Dobbins doesn't, either. Does he?

Besides, she didn't have any desire for a mate. Not a muscular purple one, nor a short, Terran one. She didn't want – or need – anyone else in her life.

Although she'd almost changed her mind after the evening with Syr....

"Ms. Krebbs?" The ship's yeoman waited at the loading bay. "The captain is about to seal the hatch. If you're coming, you'd best do it now."

His voice was Scottish, of course. It had a musical lilt to it, quite unlike the heavy brogue she'd heard minutes ago. In comparison, the crewman standing outside her cabin, the one who told her about Hhney, sounded –

Wrong.

She knew the voice. She even knew the *accent*. "Dobernack Mulvaney."

"Ma'am?" the yeoman asked.

Boarding the ship, she went below deck. The hold was crowded with gamblers. Dice and cards and games of chance were everywhere. In one corner of the room, Captain Mulvaney sat at a makeshift bar, sipping at a drink.

Dobbins occupied the center table, a deck of cards in his hand. His pouch was open, a pile of dibble sticks and gemstones in front of it. She noticed

391

one of his shirt sleeves was rolled up. On his shoulder, a triangle tattoo was etched in primary colors.

Aly dragged a chair beside him. A hundred questions teased at her. After a moment's pause, she asked the one that kept coming to mind. "What is your first name, anyway?"

He said, "Syr's in our cabin."

"Of course. Wherever you go, he follows."

Dobbins shuffled the cards slowly. Playing their conversation in her head, Aly said, "What do you mean, 'our' cabin?"

"Ship's full."

"Not *my* cabin."

"Syr explained the situation to Mulvaney."

"We don't have a situation!"

His breather hissing, a Txarrian took the seat to her left. Almost instantaneously, a Wamandika climbed into the chair on her right. The Wamandika, missing patches of fur and smelling of smoke, tapped a claw against the table impatiently.

"It's a big bed," Dobbins said.

"You have to be kidding."

"Syr will stay on his half of the mattress," Dobbins said. "Me, I've always been a snuggler."

From the bar, Captain Mulvaney raised his glass in a toast to her.

"We are *not* mated," she said. "There was no ceremony, there's no certificate, nothing happened!"

"Nothing issss happening," the Txarrian complained. "Deal the cards."

"On Syr's planet -"

"This isn't Syr's world!" Aly stood up. "I have to talk to him. He'll understand."

Dobbins said, "Want to bet?"

Has there ever been a more aggravating man? Aly wondered. *As if I'd ever mate with someone like him!*

She was about to share her thought when she noticed he wasn't looking at her.

"Well?" he asked the other gamblers.

"Yessss," hissed the Txarrian. "I want to bet."

"Sticks or 'stones, I'm in," said the Wamandika.

Dobbins beamed at the players around him. Reaching for a well-worn, multi-colored ball, he asked, "Anybody here know how to play three-fingered narlap?"

-end-

About the Authors

"Renée Harrell" is the semi-pseudonym of Renée and Harrell Turner, a wife-and-husband writing team. Their first novel was written under a much more famous pseudonym and was published by Simon & Schuster, Inc.

Aly's Luck marks their third print publication with Hunting Monsters Press.

www.ingramcontent.com/pod-product-compliance
Lightning Source LLC
Chambersburg PA
CBHW031939260626
47157CB00016B/245